CURSES & KEYS

CURSES & GODS SERIES
BOOK ONE

STELLA BRIE

Cover Design: DESIGNSBY.*CED*

Page Edge Design: Painted Wings Publishing

Editing: Kaye Kemp Book Polishing

❀ Formatted with Vellum

AUTHOR'S NOTE

AUTHOR'S NOTE

This book is a Why Choose romance, which means the heroine does not have to choose between male interests. Welcome to Phaedra's story! Events, places, and history may have been changed for the purpose of this book.

Please take care of yourself and read at your own discretion. Recommended for 18+ due to mature content.

PLAYLIST

"PRETTY LIES" – WRITTEN BY WOLVES

"DANGEROUS GAME" – UNSECRET (FEAT. SAM TINEESZ)

"BAD LIAR" – IMAGINE DRAGONS

"UP DOWN" – BOY EPIC

"BREATHE" – FLEURIE

"BUTTERFLY ON MY SKIN" – BENT ARDI (ONLY ON YOUTUBE)

"BELLADONNA" – AVA MAX

"THIS LOVE" – NOVI

"SCARS" – BOY EPIC

PLAYLISTS FOR ALL MY BOOKS CAN BE FOUND ON YOUTUBE @AUTHORSTELLABRIE AND SPOTIFY STELLA BRIE AUTHOR

To all the fans who read my books. Thank you! You make me want to write the next story.

1

PHAEDRA

Hawkes House. It's been a long time. Not much has changed. The quintessential Regency-style London townhouse matches every neighbor in the row with its elegant white stucco façade and black wrought-iron ornamental fence. The epitome of refined luxury. A home for the wealthy. There is nothing to indicate the residence is anything but what it seems to be.

Sure, the impressive portico is a bit more ostentatious than its neighbor, but one could chalk that up to a pretentious ancestor. Held up by four fluted columns, the roof extends all the way to the street, a grand entrance designed to protect its visitors from the elements. Or, more likely, from the prying eyes of its neighbors, for those who visit Hawkes House are anything but ordinary.

Smoothing the long, pleated metallic-gold skirt of my

Grecian-inspired, one-strap dress until it falls elegantly around me, I step under the portico. Heels click in the quiet night air as I walk up to the imposing black front door. The golden knocker, a hawk, of course, is waiting to greet its visitors. I reach out and grasp the ring hanging stiffly from its beak, but instead of knocking, I pull down and twist it to one side. One golden wing slides to the right, revealing the true gatekeeper to the infamous Hawkes House—a smooth glass screen. Modern security surrounded by centuries of tradition. As I press my thumb, there is a faint click of the door unlocking. My cue to enter.

In the old days, the door would have been opened by a guard. With time came modernization and the implementation of biometric security. I sigh, wondering what new technology they will implement in another hundred years.

The foyer, light and bright with marble floors and lightly paneled walls, is familiar and welcoming. I stop and stare into the camera placed high in the corner and allow the facial recognition software to match me to my photo and the fake name I used when I joined so long ago.

Only members are allowed in Hawkes House. A little over a thousand years ago, Edzel Hawke, a shifter and one of the original members of the supernatural council, opened his house in Greece to high-ranking supernaturals of each race. Invitation-only, his "club" was designed to facilitate communication in a more conducive environment.

As the western world developed, he eventually moved it to the more central location of London. Membership is still invitation-only—you must belong to one of the six races: shifter, vampire, mage, Fae, demon, or Elven—to get an invitation, but the club has grown beyond the original Founding Members, and now includes the most powerful members of each race.

And although I belong to none of the six, I'm a member. I smirk. Sometimes, you need to think outside the box to get what you want, and I wanted entry to this house. A little black-mail and voilà, an invitation. Most of the members visit to socialize with the upper echelons of the supernatural society. I come to listen to their secrets.

Intel is so very hard to come by these days, especially the caliber of information murmured in these rooms. Because of its origins, Hawkes House is still the supernatural council's favorite place to meet. All kinds of secrets are whispered in these rooms. Who's in power, on their way out, climbing the proverbial ladder, and so forth. Boring political chatter for the most part, but occasionally, I strike gold and hear a nugget of truly useful information.

Entering the salon, I pause and glance around. The room is a clever rendition of an English gentleman's club with its dark wood paneling and trim, tufted brown leather club chairs and matching sofas, deep red Persian carpets, dim lighting, and walls filled with gold-framed art. I inhale deeply. The atmosphere smells like old money and magic. The conversations are barely audible, as if anything less restrained would be inappropriate, but unlike the clubs of old, there is no male-only gender requirement as evidenced by the elegant ladies scattered about the room.

Surprisingly, it's quite crowded tonight. Like me, several of the members are dressed formally, while others wear semi-formal or business attire. No one is dressed casually. After all, there is a reputation to uphold.

Magic stirs the air, lightly teasing my nose, but I ignore the delicious scents and head to the bar. The one thing you don't want to do in Hawkes House is act as if you don't belong. Subtlety is the name of the game. And staring at those in the room is not only rude, but it can be an invitation for them to look closer, and I doubt I'd hold up to their scrutiny. Thankfully, keeping secrets is normal in the supernatural world. You don't ask shifters about their animal or mages what magic they can wield. My secrets are my own.

Sliding onto a barstool, I artfully arrange the slit in my skirt to showcase my long legs and place my clutch on the mahogany bar top. A small smile flirts with my lips. I wonder if the fishing will be good tonight.

One of the green leather barstools two seats down from me slides backward. An elegantly clad arm signals the bartender in a smooth, barely noticeable movement as a man in an immaculate tuxedo seats himself. My interest flares as I study him. Blondish-brown hair clipped close, cleft chin set in a granite jaw, straight aristocratic nose, and high cheekbones. Tall, with broad shoulders and perfect posture. I raise an eyebrow. Impeccable genes.

Strong notes of amber, sandalwood, cinnamon, and vanilla tickle my nose. Mage… and a very powerful one too.

While all supernaturals have power, not all of them can wield magic, only mages, elves, demons, and Fae. Their magic is easily identified by its own unique scent. Elven magic smells like nature with its moss, sage, musk, and sweet hints of jasmine. Demon magic is full of earthier tones like tobacco, leather, and the smell of a roaring fire, and Fae magic is like a hot spring day, abundant with notes of wildflowers, citrus, and sweet honeysuckle.

Besides his magic, this mage also smells divinely expensive, but it's not as if they let just anyone into Hawkes House. Wealth is a minimal requirement nobody speaks about, but a necessary one.

He turns toward me, sweeping steel-blue eyes from my strappy gold heels to the dark hair styled in a low chignon at the base of my neck. A spark of interest appears in his eyes, but the buzz of his phone steals his attention away.

Pretending not to listen, I turn and lightly sweep the crowd behind me for anyone of interest. Hypnotic chocolate brown eyes meet mine, a question in their depths, but I give an almost imperceptible shake of my head. The corners of his mouth turn down, but after an elegant shrug of his shoulder, the vampire's attention quickly turns to another. When I hear the name of the museum I'm visiting later this evening, my attention shifts back to the mage next to me.

His crisp English voice is low but carries easily to my ears. "Dr. Samuels is unveiling Westgate's collection to society this evening at a gala. We have orders from the council to attend," he murmurs into the phone. "We all know our roles. Black tie attire. Low key. I'll meet you there in an hour."

My lips twitch. Guess we're attending the same gala.

Held at the Museum of History, the event is to honor the life of the vampire, Lord Nolan Westgate, and all his many achievements. Everyone who is anyone in the supernatural world will be there to pay homage to him. I silently snort. Most people couldn't care less about his death. He was a dangerous and formidable vampire, who held a sharp sword over the heads of many.

They do care about his legacy, though. During his life, Nolan amassed one of the largest collections of magical artifacts in the world, and everyone is salivating over it.

As one of the experts called in to review provenance and establish authenticity, I can confidently confirm it's full of powerful objects that should remain in a vault, but I'm not on the council, nor do I report to them. If they want to step in and bid on the items, it's for the benefit of all. It honestly doesn't matter to me. I've done my job. Plus, I've already taken the pieces I wanted and shipped them home.

I order a French 75 cocktail from the bartender, along with a cheeseboard. There are never good hors d'oeuvres at events, and as one of the guest experts, I doubt I'll have time to eat.

A flash of silver catches the corner of my eye, and I glance at the mage next to me. He's sliding a coin between his fingers, over and over, as he stares closely at me, then he switches to the stool next to mine.

"Tell me, do you always listen in on private conversations?" he asks in a crisp upper-class British accent, the lightness of his tone betrayed by his intense gaze.

Always. I lift an amused brow. "You're using your phone in public. Hard not to." I lean closer and tell him a bit of truth. "Sometimes it yields useful information." His eyes narrow, and my lips twitch. Time for a diversion. "I don't have…conversations…with men who are taken."

My eyes sweep from the ring on his finger to his broad shoulders and down his muscular body. Polished. Arrogant. He's not my usual type. I lick my lips. Then again, I don't like to limit myself. This man looks like he knows how to take care of a woman.

His eyes narrow, observing me intently, but then, with a shrug, his gaze softens. "Not married." He holds up his hand. "Signet ring."

A faint vibration plucks the air, and I grasp his hand. The thick gold ring is stamped with a distinctive crest—an eye, cross, pentagram, and crescent moon. It signifies his mage family. I run a light finger over its surface and feel a sharp prick of magic. It's definitely cursed. I could remove it, but it's dangerous to remove a curse when you don't know what it will do to the wearer.

His thumb caresses the back of my hand, causing goose-bumps to rise on my arm as I place his down on the bar. "Some illustrious mage family, I presume?"

He shrugs, but I can see the surprise and wariness in his eyes. "Something like that. I've never seen you here. How long have you been a member?" With a quick flip, he sets the coin down on the bar.

The details catch my attention.

"A few centuries, at least," I absentmindedly reply.

The bartender places my drink and food in front of me, but I ignore them and slide a nail under the rough, uneven edge of his coin and pick it up. The image of Athena wearing her Attic helmet is on one side, and—I flip it over—an owl on the other.

"Silver tetradrachm. Around 510 BCE. Coins widely known as 'the owls.'" I lightly trace the image. "Single pendant earring and necklace still visible. Her profile and helmet are clear. Mint condition. Very nice." I place it back on the bar.

His eyes narrow, and he tilts his head. "Impressive. Jamison de Vere." This time, he holds out his hand to shake mine.

"They were very popular in Ancient Greece. Minted for over four hundred years. There are quite a few of them out there, although not all of them are as nice as yours," I say with a strained laugh, a feeling of homesickness hitting me. "Phaedra." Deliberately leaving off my last name, my hand clasps his. Firm. Sexy. I like a man with a strong handshake.

Then his last name registers, and I barely stop my lip from curling. "Lord de Vere?" Now that would be an interesting but very dangerous connection.

He nods, watching me closely. "My esteemed father." There's little expression on his face, but the sneer is apparent in his clipped tone. I guess he's not a fan of his father either.

Jamison taps the coin. "Are you a collector?"

I don't push. After all, I'm the last person who would share family secrets. Instead, I focus on answering his question. "Supernaturals live a long time. I collect knowledge."

His response is a wide smile, but the watchful look in his eyes tells me he's trying to figure out who or, more importantly, what I am. Unable to smell magic on me, he's not sure if I'm a vampire, shifter, or supernatural hybrid.

Mages don't age like humans, but they do age. I study him for a second. He appears to be in his mid-to-late twenties, which means he's probably closer to three hundred years old.

"If you know most of the members, I'm guessing you come here often?"

His food arrives, temporarily distracting him. "Too often." He carefully arranges the glass of water and silverware until it meets his specific spatial requirements.

I can't help but raise my eyebrows. Everything in a precise order. The man is meticulous. Pays attention to the details. Certainly not a bad thing in a lover, but dangerous in any other capacity. A thrill runs up my spine.

Exhilarated by the unexpected edge to this night, I prop my chin on my hand and take a sip of my drink. "So, tell me, de Vere, what do you do?" I deliberately use his last name to remind myself of his dangerous father and to see his response.

"Jamison," he stiffly corrects me, confirming my suspicions. "I work for the council." His answer is short, but his gaze is speculative, probably wondering where I'm going with this conversation.

The apple doesn't fall far from the tree, even if there's discord between the two.

I wrinkle my nose. "What a shame. I was hoping to have some fun." With a deliberate pout, I turn away and slather some goat cheese on a cracker, then take a bite. My eyes flick to his, and I wink.

He clears his throat. "Hmm. Unfortunately, I'm leaving shortly to attend an important event. If you give me your number, I'd love to take you to dinner tomorrow." There's a seductive quality to his voice that was absent a minute ago.

I silently snort, certain his sudden interest has less to do with my appeal and more to do with figuring me out. He would be a truly relentless adversary.

An important event.

I stifle the laugh choking my throat. Unable to resist the urge to play, I finish my food and take the last sip of my drink before setting it down. Leaning into him, I trace a nail over the shell of his ear, watching as a slight shudder runs through him.

"I'd love to go to dinner." *And anything else you might have in mind.*

My fingers caress the back of his neck while I whisper my number in his ear. I inhale deeply, taking in all the delicious smells of magic, man, and power, then brush my lips across his cheek.

Steel-blue eyes darken with desire, but it's the spark of determination in them I find most thrilling. "I look forward to our next encounter." His tone is husky and full of promise.

Standing, I nod my thanks to the bartender. He'll close out the tab and put it on my account. "Me too." *Sooner than you know.* "Have a good evening, Jamison."

2

JAMISON

Her luscious body brushes mine when she leaves, taking the delectable scent of jasmine and vanilla with her. Initially, the smell made me think she was Elven, but when I probed, I could detect no magic. And while she's certainly captivating, her bright blue eyes didn't have the compelling nature of a vampire. Something is off. My brain ticks over the possibilities as I turn to watch her walk away. Graceful. Stunning. Her olive skin and raven hair the perfect foil for her gold dress. She draws every eye in the library as she passes by. Shifter maybe? Or hybrid? The lack of magic and answers is driving me crazy.

After entering her number in my phone, I send her a quick text.

Jamison: Dinner, tomorrow? Nine?

> Phaedra: Checking to see if this is my number?
> *wink emoji* Tomorrow at nine works for me.
> Text me the address.

> Jamison: I'll pick you up.

> Phaedra: I'm staying at The Hari. Will meet you
> in the lobby. Don't be late.

A satisfied smile stretches across my face at the tidbit she just dropped. She doesn't live here. The Hari is an upscale boutique hotel in Knightsbridge, favored by the supernatural and, coincidentally, not far from my condo.

She intrigues me. I thought I knew every member of Hawkes House, especially the women, most of whom would sell their soul to get into my family's good graces, even if it meant dating me. Phaedra didn't recognize me at all, and while she could be better at hiding her reaction than most, I doubt it. The tightening around her eyes when she heard my surname tells me she isn't a fan of my infamous father. Another point in her favor.

With a nod toward Rutherford, the bartender, I head out twenty minutes later, my mind already switching to tonight's mission. It's imperative we tag the most powerful pieces of Nolan's collection and mark them for the council to bid on at the auction. Several of the items are too dangerous for one person to own.

The painting of Dorian Gray, for example. A talented demon became so obsessed with Oscar Wilde's story, he created his own version of the painting. In exchange for someone's soul, he paints their likeness into the canvas. The image grows old while the benefactor remains young, until the demon comes to collect his payment.

For centuries, the demon has struck deals with humans, mages, and shifters—the only races not immortal. Humans, with their short life spans, rarely turn down the offer, but demons don't prize those deals quite as high as one struck with a supernatural because our souls contain power.

Mages and shifters have very long lifespans, aging a year for every two to three decades, but compared to the immortality of the other supernatural races, it's a blip in time, and it makes them greedy for more. Immortality is a powerful lure.

Nolan discovered the painting a few centuries ago, and it's been a part of his collection ever since. As a vampire, he had no need to make the deal himself, but stated he felt it too dangerous to be loose in the world. Or at least, that's what he told the council. We suspect he used it to make his own bargains with the demons, but Nolan was always too wily for us to catch him in the act.

I slide into the backseat of the black SUV waiting at the curb.

Vampires are immortal. It takes a lot to kill one. Despite the old wives' tales, a stake through the heart is not enough. They must be incinerated with fire born of magic. I guess someone finally had enough of Nolan and his reign. They were either extremely powerful or exceedingly clever to have accomplished it. Likely both. Of course, the council assigned a team to investigate his death, but I doubt we'll keep them on the mission for long.

Tonight is supposed to be a celebration of Nolan and his many accomplishments. One of the first vampires to cross the portal to this world of humans, he was instrumental in establishing a society for his brethren and leading them to a position of power in the supernatural community. Nolan held the vampire seat on the council, but his reign was tyrannical and bloody. Very few will miss him.

There are two reasons the upper echelon will attend tonight's gala: to view Nolan's extensive magical collection, and to jockey for votes in a bid for the vampire seat on the council. Everyone who is anyone will be in attendance. The crème de la crème of supernatural society and, more importantly, members of the supernatural council.

Avoiding the line of vehicles dropping off passengers to the red carpet, I direct my driver to the rear entrance. There's no need to announce my presence. The de Vere family will be well represented by my father. His assistant always makes sure the press is there to herald his arrival.

As I get out, I toss orders over my shoulder. "Take the rest of the night off. I'll find another ride home." When the driver nods, I slide out and stride toward the door.

With a flick of my hand, the cuff of my shirt slides up to reveal my security credentials, a magical tattoo, to the guards. It's invisible until it's invoked and can only be seen by other supernaturals. The council has so many teams, we needed a secure way to identify them. Once the team chooses their mark, a spell is used to tattoo it onto the skin. Our team chose the gryphon to represent us.

Upon seeing the mark, the guards snap to attention and open the door.

"The rest of your team is already inside, sir," says the guard on the right.

"Thank you," I reply, stepping into the brightly lit hallway, which I follow around to the stairs, then up to the second floor.

Events are held in the massive, round, three-story lobby that greets visitors on arrival. A circular staircase winds up to each floor, providing access to each wing of its treasures. When I slip through the side door, it's still early and most of the guests have yet to arrive. Catering staff rush to and from the kitchen, setting up the individual stations with food and drink. Museum staff are on the small stage, positioning the podium beside an impressively large painting of Nolan.

The air moves beside me, and my magic instantly flares, settling a second later when it recognizes the vampire standing next to me.

"Status," I murmur.

Mathias replies in an equally low tone, "Letz' list is accurate. Thirty-seven pieces, including the painting of Dorian Gray, register at the power level identified as a threat by the council. My initial estimate of their worth is one-point-two billion pounds, but given the power of seven of them, I would reserve at least another five hundred million."

Mathias is a financial wizard. Regardless of the market or currency, his knowledge is unparalleled. It doesn't matter if it's bought, sold, traded, or stolen, he knows their value. These thirty-seven auction items probably took him half hour at the most, and his prediction will be spot on.

I quickly text the info to my father and receive a reply instantly. "He'll need an itemized report with your threat assessment of each piece, along with a suggested bid."

Mathias dips his head. "Of course. I'll also include pictures. He can expect the report an hour after the event. I want to make sure they don't unveil any surprises." He pauses for a second. "The locket isn't here."

My hand drops. "Everything from Nolan's houses and storage rooms were sent to the museum. Did you check everywhere?" I turn to face him.

He's casually leaning against the railing, but his relaxed stance doesn't fool me. The second he heard about Nolan's death; he's been thinking of nothing but the locket with his daughter's picture in it.

"Don't worry. If we have to tear this museum apart, we'll find it."

His fingers curl tightly around the balustrade. "We have to find it before they name Nolan's successor. If not, the ownership will transfer to the new vampire councilmember and will be out of our reach." Obsidian eyes stare unblinking at the people entering the event. "They brought in three experts to assess the authenticity of each piece. Maybe one of them will remember the locket."

I check my phone. "Yes, a Dr. Galanis, a renown expert in ancient languages and civilizations; a Dr. Kline, professor of ancient Near East, from Yale University; and our own expert on ancient supernatural artifacts, Letz, although most of the world thinks of him as Dr. Samuels, archaeologist, from the British Museum." I scan the room below us. "There's Letz. Ask him for the info."

Mathias disappears and reappears a second later next to Letz. I study the dark-haired vampire stiffly leaning over the smaller man. He hates revealing anything of importance to others, but it can't be helped. There are thousands of pieces in the collection, and searching for something as small as a locket could take forever.

Whenever a vampire found himself in this world, Nolan would take them under his wing and help them find their way, but always for a price. Vampires could offer him a hundred years of service if they had nothing of value. Mathias offered his locket, thinking it would be returned once he paid him back, but out of sheer spite, Nolan refused, and it's been in his possession ever since. My fists clench at the thought. Good thing the bastard is dead.

"Gatlin, report," I murmur, knowing he'll hear me through the earpiece.

"De Vere is here," he drawls in his gruff voice, referring to my father. "Security is the tightest I've ever seen. Not only do we have several teams from the council, but everyone's brought their own bodyguards to the party as well. I'm ordering our people to cover the councilmembers and the collection. The rest can fend for themselves."

"Any sign of Hawthorne?" I ask, bringing up the blueprints of the museum on my phone. Letz just told Mathias the rest of the collection was being held in storage room B3. He couldn't recall the locket, but Mathias is welcome to search for it. After a quick scan, I locate the large room in the back corner of the B wing.

"Negative," Gatlin replies. "He's in the greenhouse."

I pinch the bridge of my nose. Nolan's collection didn't just include inanimate objects, but various plants too. Some of which do not belong in this world. Hawthorne's assignment was to identify anything potentially dangerous. If he's still in there, it's either worse than we expected or he's down a rabbit hole.

"Check on Hawthorne. Mathias will be leaving the floor for a bit," I inform Gatlin, just as the vampire appears next to me. Using two fingers, I zoom in on the room to show him its location. "I sent you a map to the storage room. Go. We've got this covered. If you don't find it, we'll help you look after the event ends."

Relief fills his dark eyes, and he clasps my shoulder in response. "Thank you."

After Mathias leaves, I sweep the floor and instantly zero in on my father. Although he's almost eight hundred years old, he appears to be a human in his mid-forties. Handsome, charming, and one of the elite. This evening he's escorting the elegant Lady Catherine Carrington, a favorite of his. Moderately powerful mage, she knows when to be silent and supportive and let him shine. I pass over her to the individuals standing with them. I recognize Letz, but the other man is a stranger. He steps back to let my father greet the other guest, and I tense when a vision in gold steps forward.

Phaedra. She must have known the whole time she was sitting at the bar that we would both be at this event. She extends her hand, but after a brief shake, she pulls it back to her side. A line appears between my father's brow, but my lips turn up in satisfaction. She's definitely not a fan.

With a graceful dip of her head, she excuses herself from the group. I leave my perch and walk down the circular stairway to the first floor. Focused on following her, I don't see my father move to intercept me until it's too late.

"Jamison," he calls out, his tone full of autocratic authority.

Gnashing my teeth, I turn to face him. "Father."

Eyes narrow in anger, but the tone of his voice never changes. "I expected you to come greet me the moment I arrived, but no matter. Come. Meet the experts in charge of authenticating the collection."

Pasting a pleasant smile on my face, I put one hand in my pocket and stroll over to the group. "Letz—excuse me... Dr. Samuels."

With my other hand outstretched, I shake his hand. Although he appears to be in his late sixties, Letz is one of the oldest mages alive. A verifiable genius, he's served as the council's expert sentry for years, keeping magical artifacts out of the hands of humans. He's also been a mentor and friend, treating me better than my own father over the years. I have nothing but the greatest respect for him.

Letz eyes me with a smile on his lips. "Good to see you." He turns to the man next to him. "Jamison heads our council's security forces, but I've known him since he was a boy. Smart as a whip."

The other man turns to me, and I'm surprised by the smell of smoke and tobacco. Demon. "The younger generations know so much more than us. I guess that's the benefit of technology and the ease of finding massive amounts of information with just the tap of a finger. I know my sons are smarter than me." He chuckles. "Dr. Doran Kline. Nice to meet you, Jamison."

I flash a smile and shake his hand. "It's nice to meet you. We absolutely have it easier." My hand waves at the walls around us. "What do you think of the collection?"

A dark expression comes over his face. "Too powerful for one person. Although I know many who will try to bid on the entire collection, including several of my brethren."

The smell of jasmine and vanilla drifts closer, and I turn to face the woman coming up behind me. Not wanting my father to know we've met, I introduce myself, hoping she'll take the hint. "Jamison de Vere."

A mischievous look enters her bright blue eyes, but after flicking a glance at the rest of the group, she holds out her hand. "Dr. Phaedra Galanis." Her hand clasps mine, and she leans forward to place a kiss on each cheek. "It's a pleasure to meet you, Jamison."

"Dr. Galanis," my father stiffly interjects, a note of anger in his voice likely because she didn't greet him the same way.

Stifling a laugh, I tuck her hand in my arm. "Dr. Galanis. You must be the other expert Dr. Samuels called in for this collection. Ancient languages and civilizations. Correct?"

She leans in closer. "Yes, that's right. Although, I have to confess, my love for Ancient Greece knows no bounds." Her eyes twinkle when she looks into mine, reminding me of the ease with which she identified my coin.

"Would you care for a drink?" I ask her huskily. Her dress wraps itself around my leg, responding to my magic, but I don't dare call attention to it. With a subtle twirl of my finger, I unravel the fabric before anyone can see it.

My father's hand comes down on my arm. "Aren't you on duty?" He turns toward Phaedra, his eyes full of interest. "I'd be happy to get you a drink."

Phaedra's lips curl into a smile as she raises an elegant hand. A nearby waiter immediately comes over and hands her a glass of champagne, which she presents to us. "There are plenty of men to cater to my needs. Please. Enjoy yourselves. It was nice meeting all of you." She slips away into the crowded room, disappearing in a blink.

My father grunts with displeasure, and I watch Catherine run a soothing hand down his arm. She really is perfect for him.

I glance at her and almost take a step back. Her eyes are completely blank. No emotion, almost like she's been spelled.

Disturbed, I turn to my father, but he's already moving on to the next important person in the room. Taking advantage of his distraction, I head upstairs to view the crowd, and perhaps watch the beautiful enigma who calls herself Dr. Phaedra Galanis.

3

PHAEDRA

Eyes follow me around the room. Am I important or a plus one? Is it worth cultivating an introduction? A few know *of* me and my expertise but most can only speculate. Well, except for Jamison, of course. The sharp awareness I feel between my shoulder blades is him. No matter where I go, his eyes follow. His interest in me is both a delight and a complication. Between us, there's the heat of attraction, a large dose of curiosity, and a well-bred suspicion of anything unknown. Although part of me relishes the danger he represents.

Working on this project was a risk, but a necessary one. Too many pieces needed to be evaluated in person. When Letz called asking me to be one of the three experts, I jumped at the opportunity.

I pass several mages standing in front of the Dorian Gray painting whispering to each other, and my lips curve in a satisfied smile. That's one object that won't be used to capture souls in the future. It still hums with power, but anyone who tries to use it will get a nasty little surprise. My lips curve into a particularly satisfied smile, happy with the solution I devised for that piece.

Technically, it's my *job* to protect humans by eliminating threats from cursed or magical objects, but sometimes I'm surprised by how much I enjoy it.

When supernatural races from other worlds first stepped through the portals into this one, the gods feared the corruption and downfall of humans. They fought viciously, eliminating many who dared cross over, but supernaturals continued to pour into the human realm, overwhelming in numbers, until the only option for peace was a treaty. So, the gods offered them sanctuary in exchange for secrecy.

In response, the supernaturals formed a council and promised the gods they wouldn't reveal themselves to the humans, and for the most part, they do everything in their power to enforce those rules. If a member goes rogue, they deal with them harshly. If a powerful collection comes up for auction, they bid on the most dangerous pieces. Whatever it takes to maintain the peace, they do it, albeit sometimes reluctantly. After all, not all supernaturals feel they should have to hide from humans.

But the loophole of discovery remains. If humans are exposed to magic or supernaturals in a way that can't be covered up, the council will not stop the evolution of their existence. The gods reluctantly agreed but created a backup plan of their own—me. The council isn't aware I exist. Over the last three thousand years, I've hunted down the most dangerous objects while keeping an eye on them. From a distance, of course. A task that gets more difficult by the day.

Normally, I operate in an incognito manner, but with such an extensive and high-profile collection, I couldn't sneak in and steal the pieces. I thought about waiting until they went to their new homes, but the sheer number of items made it impossible. Instead, I had to expose myself to get access to the collection.

The risky plan worked, and I was able to carefully remove the danger from several of the worst pieces. While the artifacts still exude power, their harmful intent has been altered. As for the rest, large crates filled with a mix of powerful and powerless artifacts, are on their way to various locations throughout the world, including my home in North Carolina.

My eyes flick to Jamison, who's watching me stroll around the gallery. I'm sure the gods would tell me to brush off his interest and disappear, but after carefully following their orders for thousands of years, I'm feeling a little rebellious. Besides, a man like him is worth a little punishment. It's not as if the gods will kill me.

I lean against the balustrade and deliberately meet his stare with one of my own. Heat rises, and I lick my lips in anticipation of our date. My eyes slide from his head to his toes. Most would only care about his power or the prestige of his name and rank. I don't care about either. It's the heat and determination in his eyes I find intriguing, and of course, the challenge I'll face as he tries to extract my secrets. I smile in anticipation. It adds such a delicious edge to the attraction simmering between us.

Suddenly, his eyes widen, and he swivels around quickly. Hand to his ear, he hurries off, making me wonder where the fire is. I let my gaze drift lightly across the crowd. There are more than a few tense faces, but nothing out of the ordinary for this kind of crowd. I'm actually amazed they can be civil to each other for an entire evening.

I make my way down to the main hall for the dedication ceremony. Several security men sprint toward me. My heart speeds up for a second, wondering if I'm their target, but I remind myself I haven't stolen anything this evening, and slide to the left to let them pass. Something is happening, though.

The second my foot touches the first floor, Letz grabs my arm and whirls me around to go back up the stairs. "Someone attacked security in storage room B3, where we put all of the smaller pieces. Unfortunately, they escaped. The room is secure, but they're going to need our assistance to identify if anything is missing. Since you were in charge of inventory for that room, I'll need you to come with me," he tells me in a rush, whisking me down the hall to the other wing of the building where the room is located.

My mind immediately starts racing, trying to figure out what they could have possibly taken, especially since I removed anything of concern yesterday.

"Should I get the catalog?" I ask, playing the role I've assigned myself—that of an expert only interested in cataloging the collection and sharing key historical pieces with the world. Which I am, but I'm also here to ensure the most dangerous pieces are neutralized or removed from the collection. When he nods, I tell him I'll meet him at the room and head toward the office I was assigned to use during my stay. I grab the latest version of the catalog and make my way to the scene.

When I get there, the room is in shambles, and Jamison is barking orders left and right to the security team. I look around for Letz and find him staring down at his feet, so I make my way over to him. It's only when I get closer that I see the large bloody boot prints on the marble floor and quickly step to the side.

"Whose blood?" I ask Letz quietly.

He shakes his head. "That's not the important question here." Holding out his hand, he murmurs an incantation, and the prints begin to glow white. "As I thought." His finger traces the outline of the pattern. "Tactical gear. Have you ever known a supernatural to wear it?"

This just got a hell of a lot more complicated. "Humans? Are you sure?"

"The spell I used is designed to identify race," he says thoughtfully. "Humans render white." Letz walks carefully around the space, twisting and turning to follow the prints, until he can get an accurate picture of the scene. "It was one hell of a fight, but they were well prepared."

Perplexed, I scan the bloody floor. "How can you tell?"

He tilts his head. "Because it only took five humans to severely wound one of our oldest vampires."

Jamison hears his comment, and his head snaps toward us. "Are you sure?" His eyes sweep to me, and the amount of anger in their depths causes me to take a step back. He stalks over to us. "Show me."

While Letz is pointing out the pattern of the fight, I carefully walk around with my senses out. The few remaining items of power haven't been touched. Instead, the boxes of smaller items piled with jewelry, coins, and various trinkets, have been tipped over one by one. I slip my hand into one of the small upright boxes and lift up a handful of gold coins. "Well, they're not your run-of-the-mill thieves."

"They were searching for something specific. Small," Jamison says grimly. "Could you have missed a powerful piece in the collection?"

Letz looks at me for the answer. "Dr. Galanis completed the inventory of this room. Did you find anything of note?"

I pretend to think about it. There are only a few people who had access to this room in the last few days. Someone saw something of power and relayed that information to another, which means this is an inside job.

"There could have been, but I didn't examine every piece." Only the most dangerous ones. "I can check the catalog. We might want to question Dr. Kline's assistant, Sia, and a few of the museum staff who had access to the room to see if they noticed anything suspicious."

Jamison raises his finger, and another mage comes running

over so he can give them orders. "I want to question everyone who had access to this room." His eyes dart to me. "Including you, Dr. Galanis."

I smile. "Of course." I hand him the catalog. "Here's the final inventory report, the assessment of each piece, and a corresponding picture." I frown. "What was security doing in here?" When he looks at me blankly, I raise an eyebrow. "The vampire. It's odd he was in here, don't you think?"

Jamison's jaw tightens. "I can vouch for him. He had my and Letz' permission to search for a family heirloom. It was last seen in here."

Relief washes over me. They don't suspect anything. "Can you describe it?"

He thrusts a hand through his hair and picks up his phone. Seconds later, he reads off a description of the locket to me. "Gold locket, on a thick matching chain, with tanzite embedded in the cover. It opens to reveal the image of a dark-haired little girl."

A beautiful piece. I walk over to a box in the corner of the room, on the third shelf, and sift through it until I find the necklace. "Here. Maybe this will help your man recover." I hold it up by the neck and watch it swing back and forth, then hand it over to Jamison. When he takes it, I motion to the catalog in his other hand. "I need to make a notation on the catalog to mark its absence. Everything needs to be documented." I want him to see how serious I am about documentation, because I need him to look past me to find another suspect.

He hands it over. "Can you tell if anything is missing?"

I walk over to a nearby clipboard and grab the pen lying on top. "It's hard to tell. Most of the items in here are small. It took us weeks to organize them into boxes and another three weeks to inventory all of it." I pause and motion to the messy pile of items on the floor.

His mouth curves down. "So, you think it will be weeks before you know?"

I shake my head while I note the removal of the necklace. "It will take someone weeks to go through it all, but it won't be me. I'm only here for a couple more days."

He looks at Letz, who confirms my statement. "For her services, Duke University will receive an endowment of several of the pieces. Same for Dr. Kline and Yale. Both could only assist for a short time."

Jamison stiffens. "I see. Dr. Galanis, if you'll step over here. I'd like to get an official statement." He motions to the corner, and I follow him over.

Steel-blue eyes study me intently until the air is thick with tension. If I were anyone else, I'd probably crack under the scrutiny. "Tell me everyone who had access to this room and their purpose for being in here."

"Everyone had a different reason for being in here. Dr. Kline's assistant was to identify Ancient East items. Given my expertise in ancient civilizations, I tend to focus on the artifacts and tools used in everyday life. The smaller items. Dr. Samuels tasked me with examining the items in this room to determine authenticity and value. A collective inventory was created…"

"What do you mean, collective inventory?" he interrupts.

"Items in this room will be loaned or endowed to museums and universities for further study or display. In fact, some of the pieces have already left. The remaining items in here will either be loaned out based on request, or they will return to the vault held by the newly elected vampire councilmember, whoever that might be. The inventory in your hand is a complete list of everything, but not all the items are still here."

Realization dawns, and he runs a hand down his face. With the pieces scattered around the world, it would take a massive team to track and catalog every item, and even if something went missing, it would be almost impossible to determine if it was stolen or simply lost in the overall shuffle. It's the perfect scenario for a thief.

"We need to look at this from a different angle."

Exactly. I give him an apologetic smile. "Is there anything else I can do to help?"

He narrows his eyes at me. "Not at this time. I have your number, and I'll give you a call if I have any more questions." A rueful smile crosses his face. "I'm afraid this means our date is canceled, though."

If I didn't know better, I would think it was fate, but I stopped believing in that propaganda a long time ago. I sigh, full of disappointment. I haven't been this intrigued by a man in a long time. "Too bad. I was looking forward to it. I'll be in London for two more days if you have any additional questions." I hand him the catalog.

His thumb swipes across my hand as he takes the document. "This isn't goodbye," he curtly informs me, then turns on his heel and strides over to the group of security men who just arrived, leaving me standing there with a bemused smile on my face.

4

JAMISON

Official council headquarters are housed in a large manor outside of London in Surrey, but when warranted, the council uses Hawkes House for urgent meetings. Like today. This situation certainly qualifies. Each of the six races has a seat on the council. Although Nolan's death means the vampire seat is empty right now. Tonight, the remaining members sit around the U-shaped table waiting for me to give my official report on the attack at the museum.

"The footage revealed something interesting. Five humans entered the building. Based on their point of entry and path through the building, that room was their only target. Upon entering, they were surprised by one of our security team, Mathias Blackwell, who was checking the contents for additional items of interest. They incapacitated him, searched the room, and left without taking anything with them," I inform them. "They were searching for something specific but didn't find it."

Verilin, the Fae councilmember, leans forward. "Someone on the inside fed them intel." She looks at me for confirmation.

I nod curtly. "We don't have a suspect identified yet, but that is our assumption." I deliberately let my gaze touch on each one of them, silently conveying my concern. "This group is well-prepared and well-funded. Not only were they wearing state-of-the-art tactical gear, which enabled them to brush off the strength of a vampire, but they also had a new handheld mass spectrometer with them. Based on the video footage and their commentary, it detects magic." When I reveal the last bit of information, they all straighten in their seats.

Over the years, we've seen more and more items capable of detecting magic, but none has proven to be a threat. Most of the time, they spit out blurry images or spikes in temperature or other irrelevant pieces of data. Nothing that gives humans concrete evidence of our existence. If this scientific tool detects magic, it means it's quite capable of identifying each one of us. In a dark alley or a crowded restaurant, we could be exposed. Or it could be used to search the world for items of power to use against us.

"What are you doing to capture these men?" my father, mage councilmember, asks imperiously.

"We investigated all those who had access to the building and, in particular, that room. Everyone checked out," I reluctantly admit. "CCTV footage allowed us to track the humans to a garage, but they switched vehicles, and we lost them," I inform him, much to his impatience and displeasure. "Right now, we're tracking every vehicle that left the garage that night and questioning the owners."

Humans are tougher to find than supernaturals. They can hide in plain sight.

He scoffs and turns to his fellow councilmembers. "The

auction will be held a week from now. I propose we continue with our original plan to acquire those items of power. It's clear those pieces aren't the target." When they nod in agreement, he continues, "I'm less concerned with what they wanted to steal. We need to find this group. Well-funded, organized humans are a threat to our continued co-existence. This has the highest priority. Agreed?"

My jaw locks in disagreement. All teams will be pulled off their duties and placed on this task. Sounds great in theory, but in reality, it would be a logistical nightmare. "If we pull everyone off their duties, the group will vanish. I propose we take a quieter approach. My team will continue to investigate and track down the drivers, but everyone else will be pulled off the case. I want this group to think we've deemed the situation a low priority, and hopefully, give them the confidence to make their next move. Anyone this prepared must have an agenda."

My father's lips compress in fury, a silent refusal of my idea.

The current leader of the council itself, as well as the designated councilmember for all shifters, a dragon named Daegan, thoughtfully nods his head. "The emphasis of putting all the teams on this one case will send a message of concern to the supernatural community. It's the last thing we need right now. Too many are already aware one of us was attacked by humans. Emotions are high." He motions to me. "I agree with Jamison's proposal. We need to handle this quietly. The details of this case will only be discussed here in this room, where we can control the spread of information. We'll reconvene each week for an update. All those in favor, say aye."

All but my father give their agreement, and they hurry out, leaving via a secret tunnel only available to them.

I'm sure I'll get an earful later, but for now, I turn on my heel and leave. Exiting the hidden room, I pass through a secret hallway, then another door, and come out into the main salon, where the rest of my team is waiting, including Mathias. Vampires heal quickly when given a pint or two of pure blood.

I sit down, and Mathias slides a glass of scotch in front of me. "Thanks." With a quick flick of my wrist, I down the small amount and signal for another. "They agreed to our proposal, but they want blood. We need to find the traitor." My mind ticks over the options at our disposal.

Gatlin shifts restlessly in the small chair, his big body pushing the boundaries of its construction. "A trap. But with what bait?"

Mathias slides a photo over to me. "A key." The grainy photo is a man holding an instrument over a pile of metal objects. Confused, I raise an eyebrow. With a slight smirk, he whips out another photo from the folder in his hand. "I magnified it and cleaned up the image, but it's almost impossible to see with your eyes. Even I missed it the first couple of times. The only time they used the spectrometer is to scan keys."

I stare at the man kneeling close to the floor, but it's still hard for me to make out the objects in the image. They resemble a small dark pile to me, but vampire eyesight is keener than most, except for Gatlin's, whose shifter vision rivals his.

Gatlin picks up the photo and narrows his eyes. "These are old keys, too. The ones used to open an ornate lock." He shifts his body slightly to the left and hands the photo to Hawthorne. "They're looking for a key. One they didn't find. It must be pretty damn important to risk stealing it in the middle of an event with the highest level of security I've seen in at least a hundred years."

"Phaedra," I say, then clear my throat when Hawthorne flashes me a confused glance. "Dr. Galanis mentioned shipments being sent to other universities and museums. Most of them are historical artifacts, not powerful objects, but somebody could have slipped a key into one." I pull up the catalog on my phone, and tap find, then enter "key" into the search. Seven instances found. I tap the right arrow, and the document automatically finds the first mention. "A box of objects, including keys, was sent to be displayed at the Met in New York City in their Asian art galleries. Dr. Kline's assistant, Sia, signed off on the contents."

I tap the arrow again. "Yale, via Dr. Kline, will receive a box of items as well that includes keys. Dr. Galanis and Duke University will too. One set of keys went back to the vampire's vault. The Louvre received several from the early Renaissance period." My eyebrows go up. "The Vatican received a pair of keys with Knights Templar symbols etched on them." I wonder what secrets those unlock. "And finally, the National Archaeological Museum in Greece received quite a few keys from various periods, including Ancient Greece."

Gatlin frowns. "There was a break-in last night at that same museum in Greece. The news is reporting it as a prank because nothing was taken." His blue eyes meet mine. "My guess is we can take it off the list. Or at least put it on the bottom."

Damn it.

"Italy's next door. I wonder if they'll hit the Vatican next?" Throwing my drink back, I pick up my phone and raise an eyebrow toward Gatlin. "We need to get to the Vatican. Can you make it happen?"

His full brows lower, and he instantly picks up his phone to bark orders at someone on the other end.

Gatlin, Hawthorne, and Mathias are all on my heels as we make our way out of Hawkes House. "Tell them to find the shipment from the British Museum and secure it in a safe place. We're on our way."

Gatlin relays the information to the person on the phone.

I look over at Mathias, who moves the phone away from his mouth to tell me, "Jet's at the airport, flight plan filed."

Gatlin grunts. "Good thing I restocked it after our last mission."

The SUV waiting outside drops us off at a private airstrip outside London. When we land two and a half hours later, the gendarmerie, a shifter named Nico, is there to greet us. "You're too late. They hit us early this morning. In and out. Nothing was taken." He shakes his head. "We didn't even know until we received your call and looked at the security footage. Whoever this group is, they're good, and their tech is extremely advanced. We'll be upgrading our systems after this incident." A hard look of determination rests on his face.

I'm sure he got raked over the coals for this one. I pat him on the back. "We'll let you know what we find out. Thanks, Nico."

We file back onto the plane. "They're at least a day ahead of us and moving fast. My guess is they've already hit Paris. Mathias, can you check with your contacts there?" I pause, remembering what Nico had mentioned. "Have them check the security footage first. We're after ghosts."

5

PHAEDRA

Aisles filled with crate after crate go on forever in the massive warehouse, but I'm not deterred. This isn't my first visit here. I pull up an app on my phone. A small, blinking white dot shows my location, and a solid red dot indicates the crate's location. It's to my left and up a couple of rows. I step forward, and the white dot moves accordingly.

A good fifteen minutes later, I reach my destination. Now comes the hard part. The locator only gives a general location. I have to physically find the exact crate. My eyes skip over the ones different from mine and settle on the remaining three. Not too many, but they're on the second, fourth, and fifth shelves. I search for a nearby ladder, but don't see one, which means I'm doing this the hard way.

Gripping the first shelf, I pull myself up until my toes are resting on the edge of the second shelf and shine the light on the top. An unfamiliar address shines back. Not mine. I look up.

The next crate is over five feet and up on the fourth shelf. I slide to the right and climb. When I get closer, I see it's not mine either and barely suppress the groan at the edge of my tongue. The one on the top shelf is mine.

I contemplate the location and decide to go up before I go left. If I'm correct, it should put me right beside the panel I need to access. It's not until I'm stretching for the next shelf that I realize it's a foot higher than the previous ones. I shine the light on the crates next to me, but there's nothing to step on. If I try to use the crates themselves, I might accidentally kick one off. I dart a glance at the floor far below. That would be disastrous.

After taking a deep breath, I slip the light into my pocket, squat down, and spring up. My fingers miss the top of the shelf but find the holes along the side of the metal lip. Dangling by the literal tips of my fingers, I swing lightly back and forth. Damn it. There's very little room to maneuver and nothing to push off of to get higher.

Options. My eyes dart to the crates next to me. I might be high enough now to lift my foot on top of one and use it for leverage. It's risky, though. I glance to my left and see the support for the shelving unit. Better. I can shimmy my way up the pole to the top.

Ten sweaty and agonizing minutes later, I reach the corner. Immediately wrapping my legs around the pole, I peel my fingers away from the sharp metal holes and throw my arms around it. Stable now, I take a precious minute to massage my fingers and get the blood flowing in them again.

After wiping the sweat away, I carefully use my arms and legs to climb the pole to the top shelf. Thankfully, this shelf is wider than the others, and I'm able to walk along the edge by placing one foot in front of the other. I get to the crate, and the Duke University address label makes me quietly sigh in relief.

With deft movements, I pull off my knapsack and get to work opening the outside panel. Using a manual screwdriver sucks, but anything else would be heard. I carefully unscrew and pull off the outer side panel, putting it on top of the crate. Then I take out a large magnet. Placing it against the wood, I slide it up and to the left. I do this three more times to unlock the secret secondary panel, then remove it, too.

Customs uses imaging and x-ray machines to examine the contents. The only way to get it through was to build a hidden compartment in the crate that was solid and impervious to their scans. It only works for small items, because the dimensions need to be the same on all sides of the crate, so it doesn't arouse suspicion.

I carefully pull out the five items hidden in the crate and put them in my knapsack, then grab the five items of equal weight I brought with me and put them into the crate's hidden compartment. The gross weight needs to stay the same between entry and exit. Reversing the entire process, I board up the crate and secure it.

While I could have brought these home on my private jet, I didn't want to risk it. Transporting them in a crate directly from the museum allows me to easily add the items to the university's shipment without anyone being the wiser.

The slight squeak of a boot against the floor alerts me. I look down and see a dark figure moving down the aisle. Frozen, I watch as they stride toward me. My lips compress. Something's wrong. No flashlight or uniform. Whoever this person is... they're not a guard or customs officer. Another thief? Then, I see the faint green glow around their eyes. Night goggles. Thankfully, the fabric of my full-body suit is designed to match the temperature of my environment at all times, rendering me completely invisible to infrared technology—a sweet little invention I picked up that's come in handy so many times.

They're moving quickly. I slip the knapsack on and start walking along the top shelf in the opposite direction. There's a skylight at the rear of the building. It's farther away from where I entered, but it offers roof access.

I peer over the edge and see the person has stopped close to where I was earlier. My heart rate kicks up. Coincidence? Maybe. But I don't like coincidences. I pick up the pace and get to the skylight. Scaling the nearest crate until I'm on top, I look down the row and see the figure reach the top shelf and my crate. Definitely not a coincidence. Curbing my curiosity, I reach up, grab the edge of the skylight, and slowly lift myself off the crate and onto the roof.

Feeling a sense of urgency, I jump to my feet and run across the roof until I reach the rope I left coiled earlier. With a quick flick of my wrist, I send the rope down the side of the building and follow its smooth descent to the ground. Once I land, I press a button on my belt, and the rope cuts away from the hook at the top and falls silently to my feet.

My fingers deftly pluck it up from the ground and coil it back into a loop to hang on my belt while I listen intently for the slightest of sounds. My eyes dart from one corner of the alley to the other. I'm alone. Sliding the black nylon knapsack from my back to my chest, I press against the shadowed walls of the warehouse and make my way to the bike I left tucked behind the dumpster. Matte black paint renders it almost invisible. I roll it into the alleyway.

After taking one last look around to see if I have any unwanted company, from either the person inside or nearby customs officers, I slide on the helmet, take a deep breath, and start the engine. Even with the exhaust modifications I made to the bike, the rumbling of the engine is noticeable in the night air. It can't be helped. When you need speed and maneuvering, there's nothing like the Kawasaki Ninja H2R. Not wanting to attract attention, I keep the speed at a steady throttle as I leave the alley and enter the parking lot.

Movement on my right catches my peripheral, and I swing

my head around to watch the figure on the roof raise his arms in a silent signal to someone on the ground.

That's my cue.

With the slightest of touches, the motorcycle picks up speed. I dart into a line of stacked containers and carefully make my way through the maze I mapped out earlier in case I needed a less exposed escape. Blood rushes through my veins, making my heart pound. Colorful boxes surround me, hiding me from view, but that doesn't mean much. Depending on their technology, they might have eyes on me right now.

Hearing a noise to my right, I stop the bike and listen. There it is again. A low whistle. Definitely not customs officers. Doors slam shut. They're in a vehicle. Not wanting to be trapped in the sea of cargo, I rev the engine and shoot out from the next opening onto the main road.

"Call gate," I state clearly and concisely into the Bluetooth intercom built into my helmet. The guard at the gate picks up on the first ring.

"I've got company. Not official. Open the gate. Do not interfere." I hang up. The last thing I need is a human getting killed trying to help me, especially not a guard looking to make an extra buck.

I glance back and see a large SUV swing out behind me, the rev of their engine roaring through the night air. Apparently, they're not too worried about getting caught, which means they have power of some sort. Unwilling to get into a fight unless absolutely necessary, I map the streets of Newark in my head, trying to figure out if I can outrun them and get to my destination or if I need to figure out a different escape plan.

Bright lights shine on me, almost blinding in their intensity, and I squint into the dark. Wind rushes past my helmet. These guys aren't playing around. I kick up the throttle as I hit Port Street, flying past the guard at the open gate. Minutes later, I'm zooming past the New Jersey State Police station, a blur to any cameras, but there is no way to disguise the sound of the screaming bike. Troopers immediately race to their vehicles just in time to see the SUV behind me fly by too. Sirens and lights flip on, and cars peel out of the lot. It's a full-on chase.

I watch in the right rearview mirror as a cruiser pulls up behind the SUV, lights flashing. Another takes the outside lane to follow me. Subtly shifting on the bike to get into a more comfortable position, I push it to 200 mph. The state trooper drops back a little but not much. I weave in and out of cars, hoping to lose my trail of followers, then spot two semi-trucks in the right lane. The perfect opportunity to hide. I slide into the middle lane in front of a car, then move over one more. With the car on my left, I'm now covered on all sides. The state trooper flies past. It won't take him long to figure out I'm not in front of him, but that's okay, because I see my exit. At the last second, I slide right and take the ramp for the Newark Liberty International Airport.

Sirens sound in the night, but there are no blue lights shining in my rearview mirror. Relieved, I make my way to the short-term parking lot where I've stored a black pickup and trailer. As a precaution, I fixed the cameras in the garage before I left, so I don't worry about someone finding the footage of me rolling the bike into the trailer. All they will see is me entering the garage. With a roll of my shoulders, I slide into the front seat, lean my head back, and heave a sigh of relief.

That was close. And puzzling. I still don't know why they chased me. Not wanting magical objects to be sent to Duke University, I always intercept them at customs. Different ports each time. I pack and label the contents. If there are ten items on the manifest, there are ten items in the crate. Nobody is aware of the additional items hidden in a false side. So why were they there?

I picture the figure on the roof. Definitely a man. Did he target me out of gut instinct? Or did something tip his hand?

I'm certain it wasn't the shipment itself. There wasn't enough time for him to get inside and get to the roof in such a short time. What was it? Five minutes? Or maybe they didn't need to if they had cameras set up. Again, why? How?

A crying baby jolts me out of my thoughts. Plenty of time to think about these things on the road. I quickly reach into the back and grab a change of clothes, along with a wig and hat. A young man drove this vehicle into the airport a couple of hours ago, and the same one will drive it out. I throw on my fake glasses and head out.

I switch vehicles in Washington D.C. Hitched to an older green truck, I pull the wrap off the trailer to change its appearance from solid black to white with a logo on it. While I haven't seen anyone suspicious in the last few hours, caution has been carved into my bones over the last three thousand years. After all, nobody likes a thief, regardless of good intentions.

Hours later, I pull into an abandoned strip mall parking lot in a small town in the middle of nowhere, park the vehicle, then wipe it down. Once I've changed back into my jumpsuit, I put on my helmet and leave the keys in the ignition. Hopefully someone needs a truck. In less than a minute, I'm throwing my leg over the bike and heading to the vault hidden under an old farmhouse out in the country.

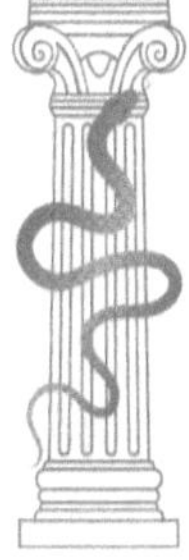  

6

PHAEDRA

Crickets chirp in the warm, humid North Carolina night air as I come to a stop on the gravel drive in front of the large farmhouse. It's had many facades over the years, but I like this one the most. Like a white sentinel standing guard over the surrounding land, it's reminiscent of a time gone by. Two stories tall, the austere wooden farmhouse is softened by the massive wraparound porch surrounding it. Filled with rockers and swings that are just begging visitors to sit and stay a while, it's the perfect place to catch a breeze on a spring day or cozy up on a crisp fall evening. Tonight, every-thing is silent and still.

Finally able to slip off the helmet, I peel the jumpsuit from my head and shoulders, then comb my fingers through the sweat-drenched hair sticking to my head. Without a cool breeze, there's little relief, but at least the sweating slows.

There's work to be done before I can wash off all the dirt and grime from the night.

I roll the bike to the back of the garage, where a hidden wall opens with my thumbprint, leading to a secret room. Roughly ten by ten, it's large enough for the bike and the tool cabinet in the corner. In another life, this was the tack room in the barn, but those days are long gone. I converted the barn to a garage once the modern world caught up with me but left this spot relatively untouched. Brown slats cover the walls, an indication of its true age, but the modern vent in the corner keeps it free of dust and debris. Given how frequently I use this bike in my nocturnal activities, I need it in good working condition and stored away from prying eyes.

I rub an appreciative hand over the seat, then drop a cover over it. While I love horses, I don't miss using them as my main mode of transportation.

Walking over to the cabinet, I place the helmet and gloves inside, then close it. A quick twist of the latch on the side and the cabinet swings away from the wall, allowing me to step into the main area of the garage. It closes softly after me, leaving a seamless expanse of wall behind.

Five bays sit side-by-side, but only two vehicles are in the space right now. The black Mercedes-Benz GLE Coupe is my main vehicle, and the old, beat-up Range Rover gets me around the farm. While the garage feels a little over the top, it needed to be big in order to hide the basement below.

I walk over to the opposite end of the garage and slide another cabinet to the side. A light pops on, illuminating the stairs I need to take to get to the bottom. Once down the steps, I lean in close to let the security system scan my eye while I also give it a token of my blood. With a hiss, the sealed steel door slowly opens, allowing me to step inside the vault.

Bright lights shine across every available surface. Unlike newer vaults made with slabs, this one is made of solid steel-reinforced concrete with 20-inch-thick walls that are nearly impenetrable. A large rectangular table sits in the center of the room with trinkets scattered across its surface. Small and innocuous-looking, they're actually some of the most lethal items in this vault. Most of them are either cursed or spelled with dark magic, which I haven't figured out how to nullify yet.

The rest of the interior is filled with museum-quality glass cabinets displaying objects from various periods in history. Most of them don't have a home because they were either excavated or stolen, so they stay here with me. Except for the large vessel in the corner. That one is mine. A secret from the gods themselves. One that could get me killed.

I slip the knapsack off and pull out the five items I took from the crate. Stolen from Nolan's collection, the items are worth more than a pretty penny. Most of them will cost you your life.

I hold the first one up to the light. Any woman would love to wear this piece. Delicate white gold branches link together to form a bracelet, and a delicate chain wraps around the wrist and across the back of the hand, forming a small loop, which is designed to slip on your finger. Such a pretty trap. Once on, the Elven bracelet binds you to the gift giver. Forever. I sigh and toss it into a pile of small trinkets.

A rough shard of pottery is the next piece. I recognized it as soon as I saw it. Carefully carrying it over to the ugly brown vase in the corner, I hold the piece up against the edges until I find the place where it matches. Crazy Glue seals it in place. Before it was shattered, the vase was roughly twenty inches tall, pink with gold inlay, and had an ornate lid on top. Once the magic was released, the vase lost its luster, turning the color it is today.

For the past three thousand years, I've searched for the pieces, but I'm only about three-fourths of the way to the top. Sometimes I wonder if I'll find them all. But I refuse to give up. I can't. I owe it to my sister.

The gods gave the vase to my father to hide in the caverns beneath our palace. Unfortunately, from the moment I saw it, I was drawn to it. It was mesmerizing. Shadows moved inside. I had to know what was in it. Stupid, stupid girl. Sometimes I wish I could go back and shake some sense into that spoiled princess. Because of it, I lost the one person I loved more than any other.

Guilt fills me, tearing at the seams of my heart, and I press a hand against my chest to hold it all in. Every time I find a piece of the vase, all the emotions come rushing back, but the guilt is the worst. It's a vicious monster, ripping me up inside. All I can do is stuff the memories down deep until the pain stops. After one last stroke across its surface, I lock it all up and return to the table.

The next piece is a thick gold arm cuff with a tile design on its surface. In an intricate pattern of white, bright teal, and orange, a mountain sits against the backdrop of a sunset. This pattern was exclusive to Pompeii before the eruption of Mount Vesuvius, and the curse placed on it reflects its heritage. Whoever puts this on their arm instantly turns to ash. Such a shame, but the piece should be salvageable. Once I remove the curse, the cuff can be shipped to the National Archaeological Museum in Naples to be showcased amongst the rest of the Pompeii collection.

I set it aside to work on it when I return. Next, I pick up a hammered gold ring with a dome on the top. Popping open the latch, I tap my finger on the tip of the golden sundial hidden inside. This clever little beauty steals time. How much? I'm not sure. But even a minute is too much. I toss it on the pile.

The last piece is a pendant. Britain. circa 1540. There might have been a chain or a strand of pearls attached at some point, but it's long gone. I turn the pendant from side to side. It's a stunning piece. Two hammered gold squares linked together, one on top of the other. Each square has a jewel set into its center, one an aquamarine and the other a topaz. Below the squares hangs a third stone, a large teardrop sapphire. Around the flat edges of each square is an inscription. I pull over the magnifying glass and read the words. *Ubi Amor Ibi Dolor. Where there's love, there's pain.* This is a woman's pendant, typically worn close to the hollow of the neck. I can't quite tell what the curse does yet, but its aura is dark, tinged with red. Nasty little piece. For now, it goes into the pile I've designated as urgent.

Exhausted from the long night, I glance at the monitors near the door and see nothing but empty fields and dirt roads. All by myself. The years weigh on me tonight. Maybe I'll stay here for a few hours. I hang up the knapsack and secure the vault. Once upstairs, I lock the garage and head to the house.

My hand caresses the smooth railing as I walk up the wide front steps, peace settling over me with each step. Sometimes I wish I still lived here, but the world is too small for comfort. I used to pass the house down from myself to myself each generation, or from one alias of mine to the next, but it's now owned by a corporation. Hidden behind multiple shell companies, of course. I own the parent company, but a subsidiary, P&P Inc., owns this house. While I visit often, it's too dangerous to live here full time. If others tracked me here, they could find the cursed treasures I hide from the rest of the world.

Still, I can't help but inhale deeply when I enter, filling my soul with the smells. In three thousand years, it's the only place I've called home. Prior to this house, I lived in many places, all of them nice, but there are only two places I've considered home. The palace I grew up in and this one. And I've owned this one for the longest... over three hundred years.

Exhaling, I savor the peaceful feeling, knowing it's temporary. Change is coming. Humans attacking supernaturals isn't new, but I've never seen one physically win a fight with a vampire. Whoever they are... they're well-funded, intelligent, and resourceful—a dangerous combination.

7

PHAEDRA

Refreshed after my stay on the farm, I head to the condo I'm leasing in Durham. Off West Main Street, the mid-rise building sits in the perfect downtown location, close enough to walk to campus if I wish. I ease my car into its reserved parking spot and take the elevator to the top.

Unlike the farmhouse, everything here is sleek and modern, with high-end finishes and all the latest appliances. There isn't an ounce of warmth in the cold, sterile place except for the bank of windows in the corner that allows sunlight to flood the space. Airy and modern. Livable, but not home. It's the perfect ruse for my life here.

I toss my keys into a wooden bowl on the entry table and hang up my purse. My stomach grumbles loudly. Walking over to the refrigerator, I open it and stare at the empty shelves. School starts tomorrow. I slam it shut and tap on my phone to order groceries.

While I wait for my order to arrive, I grab my laptop and pull up the cameras I hacked into the other day. The port is busy this morning. Shipments arriving and leaving all over the place. Once I find the camera for the warehouse, I bring it up and start rewinding the video footage. There. That's me running across the roof. I note the time and switch to a second camera. The second camera shows the inside of the warehouse. I rewind the footage an additional twenty minutes and see myself moving away from my crate to the skylight.

Behind me, a shadow quickly scales the shelving in the warehouse until it reaches my crate. It's too dark to get much detail, but the person's bulk and height make me think it's a male. Plus, there is something about the way he moves. Confident and sure-footed. Military training, maybe.

From a third camera, I see myself reaching the skylight and disappearing up to the roof.

I switch back to camera two and watch him probe around the crate. Instead of opening it, he waves a green light back and forth over the outside of the crate, then stares down at the device in his hand. That's it. He puts the item in his hand away and walks around the crate. *What's he doing?*

His head suddenly jerks up, and he takes off running across the top shelf, following the same path I'd used minutes earlier, until he reaches the skylight and disappears. I switch back to the first camera and catch him on the roof a minute later, peering over the side of the building. He must have heard the motorcycle. Moving to the front of the building, he waves his hands a few times in a series of practiced maneuvers, obviously communicating with someone on the ground. I watch as he leaves the roof but lose him in the shadows of the building.

I rewind the footage of him inside the warehouse to watch it several more times. He's clearly running the green light over the crate. Not once does he open the crate. Is he scanning for a specific type of metal? The pieces inside are mainly made of gold and silver, not rare minerals, but maybe he's searching for something unusual. Some of the supernaturals brought materials from home when they came through the portal. Compounds not known to this world.

Groceries arrive, and I spend several minutes putting those away, then fix an easy butter, parmesan, and veggie pasta for dinner. I take it out to the patio, along with a glass of wine, and watch as the sun turns the sky into shades of pink and gold. Tonight is the last time it will set after eight p.m. this year. I watch every second. Soon, my favorite season will be gone.

Once it's dark, I pick up my phone and glance at the tracker app. My crate is on a truck bound for Durham and scheduled for delivery tomorrow.

DESIGNED in a collection of Revival styles, the Allen Building's majestic façade reflects the Classical Studies program it offers inside its hallowed halls. Built in the thirties, Duke University's West Campus, including this building, was designed to represent a romanticist interpretation of the historic medieval universities in England. It was meant to be a symbol of Duke's status and credibility to the rest of the world, and almost a hundred years later, it stands firm with all the hallmarks of prestige.

Unwilling to walk in the sweltering heat this morning, I swing the car into my assigned parking spot a few minutes early. The staff meeting starts promptly at nine a.m. Usually, I wouldn't be expected to join, but the department chair asked me to give a brief update on the pieces coming from the collection. I glance at my watch. I need to tell security the crate is arriving today before the meeting. They don't like surprises. My heels click rapidly on the tiles as I rush to their office at the other end of the building. Hurrying around the corner and through the door, I slam into someone who's standing a few feet inside. Thankfully, their strong grip catches me before I fall.

Horrified, I glance up and find the most captivating sea-green eyes staring down at me. "Sorry. I'm in a rush and didn't look. Are you okay?"

A half-smile graces his lips as he flicks his eyes down. "No harm done."

My eyes linger on his masculine features in appreciation, then widen when they get to the pointed ears. Elven. Humans can't see them, but I do. Undoubtedly why he is so beautiful with his strong nose, firm lips, and high cheekbones. Symmetrically perfect.

What is he doing here? My phone pings, and I jerk out of his hold.

"Damn, I'm going to be late," I lament, shaking my head. "Tony." I pop my head around the man standing in front of me to focus on the burly guy seated behind the counter. "I've got a crate coming this afternoon. Could you please call me when it arrives?"

Tony writes it down on the pad beside him, nodding in agreement. "Sure thing, Dr. Galanis."

I glance up at the elf and wish I had more time. "Again, I'm sorry." Stepping away from him, I turn toward the door. From the corner of my eye, I spot a messenger bag on a chair. Does he work here? I swivel to get one last look at him and nearly clip my nose on the doorframe. *Idiot.* He's going to think I'm a complete klutz.

Minutes later, I walk into the conference room. Of course, I'm the last person to walk in and take a seat. All eyes turn toward me when I enter, and I hear a long-suffering sigh from the department head.

"Sorry I'm late." My apology is out of respect, but it's all she'll get from me. As a visiting professor, my only job is to provide the university with artifacts from my travels. I'm not here to teach classes or interfere in the day-to-day operations.

Dr. Florence Berne shuffles the papers in front of her, but the door opens before she can get a word out. We all turn to see who it is. Personally, I'm curious to see the person who would dare interrupt Dr. Berne's staff meeting. Besides me, of course.

Dr. Berne giggles, and my mouth drops open in shock, but when the elf I ran into earlier steps into the room, I completely understand. Tall, serious green eyes, tanned complexion, and tousled hair the color of mahogany—dark brown with the slightest hint of russet. Fit, too. I subtly wipe the invisible drool from my mouth.

"Dr. Wylde," she practically purrs. "Welcome to Duke University and to the Classical Studies program." She motions to the chair beside her, and he strides over and sits down, all eyes following his every move. Whispers fill the room, but one glare from Florence silences them all. "Everyone, this is Dr. Hawthorne Wylde. He'll be visiting us for a few weeks. An expert in ancient botany, his seminars will be offered to any of our graduate students who wish to expand their knowledge of the historical evolution of plants and their importance in ancient civilizations. Please introduce yourself after the meeting."

After beaming a wide smile at him, she continues with the agenda. I tune her out and focus on the man sitting beside her. As if he can feel my eyes on him, he flicks his gaze toward me. An intense look of concentration comes over him, and I realize he's trying to use his magic on me. Like mages, the Elven wield elemental magic, but they also have an empathic-like ability to sense emotions in others, especially humans.

His power snakes around me, searching for a door, but finds nothing. His attention shifts to the people around me, as if he's testing his magic on them, and his shoulders relax in relief.

Green eyes immediately move back to me; they narrow when he, again, gets nothing.

Unable to resist, I wink at him, and his eyes widen. When I hear Florence say my name, I tune back into the meeting, ignoring the perfect specimen at the end of the table. It's a good thing I do, because Florence is touting the work I did this summer on Nolan's collection in London. While she doesn't know anything about vampires or magical objects, she's a renowned expert in archaeology, and I consulted with her on several items.

"It's an incredible collection. Thank you, Dr. Berne, for your assistance in identifying several of the pieces," I state firmly, giving her the credit she deserves before continuing. "I managed to secure a few pieces for the university. They should be arriving later today. I'll send an email to the staff with a list of the items, the provenance of each piece, and a picture, in case you want to integrate them into your curriculum."

Several professors nod enthusiastically. Dr. Wylde eyes me with a speculative gleam, but I see his fingers moving across his phone. He'd better not let Florence catch him. His good looks won't save him from her blistering lecture on the use of cell phones during staff meetings. I should know.

Florence finishes with her usual spiel about making this the best year for students and ends the meeting. I ignore the queue of people moving toward Dr. Wylde and quickly head out the door.

8

<u>PHAEDRA</u>

Everyone gathers around the crate in anticipation. While the university often receives pieces on loan from a museum, it's rare to obtain objects that have been hidden in a private collection for years. I've given the privilege of opening the crate to the graduate students with the caveat that they must take a guess at the provenance and history of each piece.

Blake, a tall, dark-haired young man from Ireland, lifts the heavy crowbar and pops open the lid. With gloves on, he reaches in and pulls out the first piece and whistles. "Cool. It's a mace-ax. Egyptian." He holds up a magnifying glass to the flat edge of the ax portion. "14th century BCE."

My lips curve upward. "How did you come to your conclusion?"

He flips the mace-ax around and holds it up for everyone to

see. "Tiny symbols are etched in the flat part of the blade here." He points to a specific area. "A reed, a wave of water, a falcon, an ankh, and a series of staffs. King Tut's name in hieroglyphics." Everyone shuffles closer to study the weapon.

Someone steps up beside me, and the scent of amber, sandalwood, cinnamon, and vanilla fills the space around me, but it's the scent of powerful magic accompanying it that makes me turn my head. It's him. Jamison de Vere. And he's looking utterly divine in a three-piece navy-blue pin-striped suit that makes his steel-blue eyes appear even darker. I inhale sharply. My memory didn't do him justice. For a second, all I can do is stare at him and think about how incredibly powerful and good-looking he is.

"Jamison?" I murmur.

His firm lips briefly curve in greeting, and my brain finally starts working again, wondering why he's here and not in London running his investigation. My stomach churns. I doubt he came all this way for a date.

"Dr. Galanis?" a young student named Alisha calls out.

I immediately turn my attention back to the scene in front of me. "Yes, Alisha?"

She holds up a blue stone ring. "Roman. Man's ring. 1st century CE. Woman's face carved on the side."

"Very good. Do you know the stone?" I ask her.

"Lapis lazuli?" she guesses.

I shake my head and glance around the room. My eyes stop briefly on Dr. Wylde, who's staring at me from across the room. "Anyone else?"

"Sapphire?" a graduate student named Reese guesses.

"Correct."

As each piece is brought out, I feel Jamison's tension beside me increasing until his magic is all but crackling against my skin. A sliver of disappointment slides over me. He's definitely here for the artifacts in the crate, but why? There isn't anything magical in there.

It takes an hour to empty the crate and detail each piece. When it's over, I encourage the graduate students to make placards for the items. Everything will be placed in the university's small glass museum for the students to study.

Jamison leans in close and murmurs in my ear, "Do you have a moment?" He lifts a hand toward the back of the classroom.

"Mm, I wish you were here for something more exciting than work," I murmur, watching his eyebrows slam together in confusion. *Stop flirting with him, Phaedra. He's dangerous.* Sometimes I hate the voice of reason. "Never mind. Yes, I have time." I walk to the corner, his hand lightly pressed against my back.

"The thieves are searching for a key. We've been chasing shipments across the globe in the hope of finding it before they do, but we haven't had any success," he reveals in frustration. He pulls out his phone. "In the catalog, it states a shipment of keys being sent to you and this university, but there were none in the crate."

My brows draw together. "A key? What kind?" When he merely stares at me, I shake my head in exasperation, then pull the manifest out of my pocket. "This is the manifest. As you just saw, the students opened the crate a few minutes ago. Everything on this list matches the items in the list."

His timing is impeccable. Too impeccable. He knew they would be opening the crate today, and he wanted to be here to see the contents for himself. Disappointed, I hand him the paper.

He takes the list and compares it to the catalog on his phone. "The only difference is the set of keys." Setting them both on the table, he points out the difference. "Why would it be on the list if it wasn't in the crate?"

Before I can say anything, he answers his own question.

"Either someone added the keys and stole them at customs the night before last, or it's a deliberate attempt to get us to follow a false trail." He compresses his lips together.

That's very specific and extremely concerning. How did he know what happened at customs? "Why would you think they had been stolen at customs? The box was sealed when it arrived here today... the same seal I placed on it in London. The university has one specifically for customs." I pull out my phone and tap on photos. "See. I took these in London. You can see the museum floor beneath the crate."

He lays my phone on the table and swipes through the images. "Somebody was at customs. I know that for a fact, because our team gave chase. Unfortunately, we didn't catch them, so we can't know for sure if they stole anything."

The black SUV. Also, the man in the warehouse? Maybe. *Damn, that's concerning.* But I don't have time to think about it. Nor do I want to tip him off.

"Sounds exciting." I bet few get the best of Jamison de Vere, head of council security. "You're right. Someone changed the catalog. I didn't add the keys to the catalog, nor did I add them to the shipment, and then steal them. But somebody did." I bite the inside of my cheek while I think for a minute. "I only gave academic faculty access to the catalog. Myself, Dr. Kline, Dr. Samuels, and their two assistants. But if this human organization is resourceful, they could have easily hacked into the system."

"Your shipment is the only inaccurate one so far," he informs me with a speculative gleam in his eyes. "It's even more interesting when you factor in your responsibility for the accuracy of the catalog."

I cock my head to the side and stare into his blue eyes. If I weren't a thief, I would be offended. But technically, I am, so I'll let most of his statement slide. "If I were trying to set someone up, I'd look for the most obvious person. Wouldn't you?" Time to end this fishing expedition before he picks up on something I don't want him to know.

Picking up my phone, I move closer to him. In my two-inch heels, we're almost the same height, which must put him around six feet. "It was wonderful to see you, Jamison." He stiffens when I lean forward, but I simply place a kiss on his right cheek, then his left.

His fingers slide around my wrist. "Have dinner with me."

Don't tempt me. One of the most interesting men I've met in a while, and I have to turn him down. I laugh. "It would be an interrogation, not a date."

I leave him standing there with a look of speculation on his face and return to the students. As I review their placards, I see him stalk from the room, magic bristling and face set in stone.

Once the pieces are in the museum, I head to my office to contemplate Jamison's information. My fingers twitch with the need to delve into this deeper. There are a few places I have access to that Jamison doesn't, and I want to dive into this mess from the inside.

As I turn to leave for the day, I notice the white, handmade clay dish on the edge of my desk has been moved. It's only a centimeter off, but it's been sitting on my desk for two years in the exact same spot. The dust around the base shows a distinct line. Someone has been in here. I set my bag down, place it back in position, and walk around my desk. Opening drawers, I systematically go through the contents. Everything is here. If I hadn't seen the dish, I would never have guessed someone had gone through my things.

Jamison is thorough, I muse.

With a shake of my head, I head home. The only thing of value in my office is the white trinket dish. It's the first magical object I found and removed a curse from... and it's a constant reminder of my real life behind the cover of this temporary facade.

I walk out to my car. As I get in, I see Dr. Wylde striding over to a sleek black luxury car. Not once does he look my way, but I watch his long legs eat up the distance. Two tantalizing supernatural men in one day. I doubt it's a coincidence. Did Jamison send him to spy on me or someone else? Possibly the same person who added those keys to the catalog? I knew accepting Dr. Samuels' invitation was a risk, but I didn't expect it to put me on the council's watchlist. I'm also having a hard time believing humans are behind it all.

When I get home, I pull out my laptop and enter my credentials into the London Museum's faculty portal. Thankfully, I've only been gone a week, and the IT department hasn't cut off my access. Once in, I'm scrolling through all the different versions of the catalog. Every day, we would pick up the previous day's version and create a new one. A way to maintain the integrity of the catalog.

I scroll to the section where the catalog lists the items being sent to my university. The last change was the day before it shipped. The keys were added to the list, and the change…was made by…me. I stare at the entry, trying to figure out how they did it. Either someone used my computer, or they hacked into it. Hacking feels unlikely, given the small change.

It takes about half an hour, but I go back through every document and version to review all the changes "I" made and find several false notes. Most were minor. Changed, then changed back. Maybe they were testing the system or checking to see if I'd notice. On the same day "I" added keys to my shipment, "I" also added a set to Kline's, as well as a Ming vase.

This was clearly an inside job. I rarely saw Dr. Kline or Dr. Samuels. Both were interested in the larger pieces, particularly items with supernatural origins. Samuels' assistant, Conor, a young mage from Scotland, did his tasks as quickly as possible so he could get out of work early and meet his friends at the pub. Sia, a demon and Kline's assistant, had the most access to my computer. Quiet. Studious. She said little but worked hard. It wouldn't be the first time an archaeology student had taken something to sell, but she doesn't really fit the profile. It's usually the brash know-it-alls who take the chance, but maybe the lure of the black market and a huge financial payout trumped her integrity.

As I told Jamison, it's likely I'm being used as a diversion to whatever is really happening, although I'm curious why someone would be after this one item. There were few magical keys in the artifacts, and I didn't sense any with real power. Biting my lip, I exit the program.

When I get back to the homepage, I see the announcement I missed the first time. The auction is being held tomorrow. I wonder if Jamison and his team will be there to secure it?

Speaking of delicious men, I leave the museum's site, open a search engine, type "Dr. Hawthorne Wylde," and hit enter.

The only images of him online are recent pictures, but that's to be expected. The council employs a huge tech team whose sole job is to remove outdated information about supernaturals. It wouldn't be good if a photo from 1910 surfaced with Hawthorne's face. Although it's happened more than they might wish.

Media says he's an eligible bachelor from London. There's a picture of him squatting beside a bench in the park with his face in a bush. I laugh. He really does love plants. I delve a little deeper. A PhD from the University of Manchester in Plant Science. And a second PhD from the University of Galway in AgriBiosciences. There's a serious brain in that sexy man. *Mm, I love smart.*

There's not much else here. I wonder when he came through the portal. If it was a long time ago, he's probably had many aliases and a slew of degrees. When you're immortal, you have to do something to occupy yourself.

I look around the sterile condo. Should I get a plant? It might help soften up the space. The idea makes me snort. I doubt Dr. Hawthorne Wylde is going to be interested in a fern. Maybe something exotic, but I don't know the first thing about plants, nor am I the nurturing type. I nix the idea and head to bed.

9

JAMISON

S he dismissed me. Infuriating woman. What is she hiding? Her lies are like honey, sweet and thick, and every time I speak to her, I hear them echoing in my head. I can't help it. It's one of my most enraging traits, or so the women I've dated have told me. I smile grimly. When you grow up with a father like mine, you learn to separate fact from fiction. Truth from lies.

When Hawthorne texted me earlier to let me know he was in place at the university, he also confirmed the crate was arriving in the afternoon and said he would be there for the opening. I was completely comfortable with that play. After all, he's been working for the security council a long time, and his elemental Elven powers are similar to mine in strength. It's not as if sensing a magical key is advanced magic.

Yet, I still found myself in the car and on the way to the university. I tried to convince myself it was due to my obsessive need to control the situation, but I simply couldn't stop myself. The urge to see if the spark between myself and Dr. Phaedra Galanis was real…was too hard to ignore.

The moment I stepped into the classroom and saw her standing there, raven hair cascading down her back, I knew. Alluring. Sexy. Complicated. My magic hums around her. Everything about her is a challenge, and there is nothing I love more. At first, I thought to observe from the door and slip out, but the urge to be next to her overrode my common sense. Moving closer, her unique scent surrounded me, and I knew I couldn't leave without speaking to her.

But the best part … she knew who I was without turning her head, and when she finally looked at me, I saw the reaction in the depths of her eyes, and it was real. Need. Desire. Probably one of the few honest things about her is her attraction to me. Everything else is hidden behind the sweet lies that spill from those full pink lips.

Hawthorne's eyes danced between the two of us the entire time, and I practically ground my teeth to the nub thinking about the explanation I was going to have to give him later. I refuse to lie to my team. While my job requires me to withhold information, I only lie if it's absolutely necessary and never to them.

The four of us are a tight-knit group. As a team, we've been together for the last two hundred years. Gatlin and I met first. We served on several missions together, and when I was appointed to lead the security division, he formally requested a transfer to my team. I'm lucky to have him. He's a brilliant tactician and the most loyal of friends. Plus, his protective nature means he takes care of all of us.

Hawthorne had zero experience with security. I was working a case and needed to identify the obscure poison used to kill an elf. He was the expert brought in to help. Not only did he figure out the plant used to create the poison, but he also helped identify the suspect. Bloody brilliant. He fit seamlessly with us, so I offered him a position. The work intrigued him, and he joined my team shortly after.

I was walking home from one of my father's dinner parties when I met Mathias. He was in an alley fighting off ten of Nolan's most feared vampire guards. He'd already taken out three of them, but I couldn't let him have all the fun. After finishing off the rest, we quickly became friends, but it took another year for me to convince him to join the team.

Parking the car, I take the elevator to the condo we're leasing on the same floor as hers. When I walk in, Mathias has a computer and a bank of monitors set up in the living room. Every inch of her condo has been bugged, except for the bathroom, of course. He flips through each angle to show me while I fill him in on the afternoon.

Hawthorne's background was a perfect fit for the university. A few phone calls, and he was eagerly invited to be a visiting professor. Not only will he be close to her during the day, but he'll also live here in her building, along with Mathias.

Never seen and rarely heard, Mathias will monitor her movements via his computer. Our fourth member, Gatlin, is currently securing a position at the gym she frequents. Since I'm the only one she's met, it made sense for the others to go undercover.

"I'm heading to Connecticut tonight to set up the surveillance team on Dr. Kline and his assistant, Sia. They received their shipment yesterday. I'll ask to check the contents against the listing in the catalog," I inform him. "So far, only the contents of Phaedra's container don't match. She suggested it was a setup. It's one of the few times she sounded as if she was telling the truth, but one truth doesn't make her innocent."

Mathias arches a dark brow. "You seem a little agitated. It's unlike you." His eyes wander to the locket hanging from the corner of one of the monitors. It's the same one Phaedra found for him in the storage room at the museum. "There were a lot of valuable pieces in that room. The key is purposeful and potentially magical. We need to look for a bigger picture."

"We're flying in the dark, I know. All we can do is chase the leads we have in front of us."

"The auction is tomorrow," Mathias reminds me, his hands busy on the keyboard. "Phoenix and Medusa are in London and will manage security for it."

The two teams I picked for the auction are a good mix of elegant style and lethality. My father, along with the rest of the council, likes security to blend into the background, especially for prestigious events. Naturally, I prefer the council's safety over image.

"She's home," Mathias says softly, pointing to the screen. Dark eyes slide to mine with a mocking glint in them. "She's not your usual type."

I scoff, but I'm unable to turn away. The stunning woman on the screen has my full attention. "What type? The only women I date are the ones my father forces me to escort from one event to the other. This is a temporary attraction. She's a suspect. Anything between us would be foolish." I need to keep my distance.

"By the way, I managed to set up a couple of cameras in her office. They should be available to you." While Mathias confirms access, I watch her sit down at a small desk and open her laptop. "Can you get a better angle?"

Mathias switches cameras, but the glare from the sun on her screen prevents us from seeing what is on it. With a tap, he tries another angle, but it's too far to the side. He returns to the first camera.

About twenty minutes later, the sun shifts enough for us to see her screen. Mathias, with his sharp vampire eyesight, chuckles when he sees what's on it. One click of his mouse, and the camera zooms in closer for me to see.

She's researching Hawthorne. "Do you think she's suspicious of him?"

Mathias' dark chuckle has me looking at him. "I think she's interested in him."

I say nothing. Is she really attracted to Hawthorne? Aristocratic supernaturals in London consider him a highly sought after bachelor, although reclusive. And Phaedra's exactly his type. Smart. Interesting. His field of study is similar to hers. They probably speak in the same obscure academic terms.

My jaw tightens as I clench my teeth. Wonder what she'll think when she realizes they're neighbors? It's too late to move him. The university has him at this address.

"Find Gatlin and me a place to live that's close enough for all of us to meet regularly." If she sees our entire team coming out of this condo, she'll get suspicious. "I'm going to Yale to check the contents and make sure the surveillance team is in place, then on to London to secure the items from the auction and report to the council. I'll return in a few days."

My eyes slide to the woman sitting at the table, staring into the computer with a smile on her face. She definitely finds Hawthorne interesting.

"See what you can dig up on Dr. Galanis. It's rare someone goes unnoticed in our society, especially someone as beautiful and accomplished as her. Something is making my gut churn," I order Mathias.

He tilts his head at the screen, eyes sparking with interest. "Few can truly hide in this modern world. I'll get right on it."

I scowl at the look of intrigue on his face and head out the door. Time to go to work.

CONNECTICUT IS A BLOODY SHITSHOW. Sia, Kline's assistant, was found dead beside the crate an hour before I arrived. Based on the footage, she was killed by humans. Contents are strewn everywhere. Apparently, she surprised the thief, and he wasn't alone. Like the attack on Mathias, the group of five humans was well-armed and prepared to fight a demon. Cameras show they didn't take anything. Sia was killed for nothing.

Dr. Kline glares at me in fury but answers all of my questions. He's adamant Sia didn't know anything about a magical key, or she would have told him. In the demon world, he's her superior, and she has little ability to act without his permission.

Doran Kline thrusts a hand through his hair. "Don't look at me like that. It's fucking archaic, I know, but demons aren't known for their democracy. Satan's a bit of a dictator, if you haven't heard." He slams his fist on a nearby table. "Damn it. Sia didn't deserve to die. She sure as hell didn't deserve to die at the hands of humans." His lip curls as he says the last word. "Satan is going to push more demons through the portal in retaliation, which is the last thing any of us needs."

His eyes sweep the room. "Did they take anything?"

I hand him the catalog with no explanation. "You tell me."

Kline walks around the small room, ticking off each of the items in the catalog. He bends down and traces over the shattered pieces of a vase. "This was a six hundred-year-old Ming vase. It was to be the prize of our collection. Worth an estimated twenty-one million." His eyes turn red. "Whatever they're after, it's not money." He returns the catalog to me.

"The catalog lists a set of keys, but we didn't sign off on any keys. I'm not sure why they would be on there. Regardless, if they were in the crate, they're not here now," he informs me, his eyes still on the broken vase. "When can I get a team in here to salvage the contents?"

"Our forensics team will be done by tomorrow," I assure him. "Where should we send Sia's body?"

He shrugs. "It will be ash by the end of the day. Demons return to our creator, one way or another. There's no escaping the devil, Jamison." A wicked smile spreads across his face. "If there's nothing else, I need to leave and pick up my children."

Mostly truths, but there's also a hint of nervousness. "You're good to go. If you think of anything that could help us, give me a call."

He takes one last look at Sia and the vase, then heads out the door.

I call over Cian, head of the surveillance team who will be stationed here. "I want to know everything about him." The blue lines of the vase are bright in the dim room. "Pay close attention to his finances."

I could repair the vase, but I don't. Some things aren't meant to live forever. As a mage, I probably understand that more than most supernaturals. Our life span is typically shorter than the other races but not always. Sia's sightless eyes stare at me from the floor. She deserved better.

10

———————

PHAEDRA

L ibraries are magical places full of knowledge, adventure, and people, and one of my favorite places to spend time. Even with all the years I've lived, there is always something new to learn. It's also a great place to search for information behind a wall of anonymity.

Desks are hidden around the library, but I leave those to the students. Instead, I head to the one on the left that provides me a clear view of anyone approaching. Some universities offer a dedicated nexus linking journals, websites, chat groups, and other sources for students of that department. We offer one to our Classical Studies students. Every student has access to the most in-depth information in their field of study, allowing them to easily research topics without spending an inordinate amount of time searching for it or weeding through irrelevant topics.

Clicking on a specific chat group, I enter and post a message.

> *CursedGreek: Seeking information on a key; original*
> *origin unknown; source: vampire collection. Willing*
> *to pay.*

I scroll through the most recent posts, but I don't see anything that mentions a key. Leaving the chat, I open a second window to search for information on Egyptian weaponry. The mace-ax in the museum is the first Egyptian piece I've collected for this university. I wonder if there are other items I could bring back from Egypt.

Engrossed in reading about the khopesh, it takes me a second to realize someone is standing next to me, but the subtle earthy smell of sage, moss, and musk slowly pierces my intense concentration. I look up to find Hawthorne Wylde standing next to me with his eyes on my screen.

"I came over to ask you about collaborating on a seminar," he inserts smoothly. Pointing to the screen, he continues, "A combined lecture that will get them thinking about ancient civilizations and the tools and weapons crafted from the same materials. Like copper, then bronze, and later, iron."

Passion sparks as his gaze returns to me. *For the topic, not me,* I remind myself, clearing my throat. "Yes. Sounds great. When would you like to get together and discuss the details?"

"How about now? Unless you have a class?"

"I don't teach classes here. Only procure items for the museum," I reply with a smile.

He walks off to grab his messenger bag and the chair he was using. While he's gone, I click to the chat window and close it. When he returns, I scoot over to share the small single desk with him, and he crams in beside me.

Hawthorne turns his head and asks, "Is this okay?" Green eyes search mine intently.

"Yes," I tell him, conscious of his big body next to mine. Warmth spreads from him to me, making me want to curl closer, like a cat seeking the sun.

We spend the next hour planning the lecture. Deciding it would be best to supply our students with a list of approved materials, we research and argue about the best ones to include in the discussion. It's exhilarating to speak to someone with more knowledge of ancient civilizations than me.

At one point, he leans over to point to something on the screen, and his body curves around mine, making the small space shrink. The air becomes charged with tension, and I have to repeatedly remind myself we're in a library. But instead of dampening my interest, my mind wanders to the dark stacks located in the back, hidden from the rest of the world, and I silently groan at the images flooding my brain.

We finally finish laying out the details, and he leans back to scan the notebook in front of him. Breathing a little easier, I take a moment to contemplate the man beside me. Elven men are genetically gorgeous and inherently sexy, but the way this man thinks, his brain, is the ultimate aphrodisiac. He's exactly my type.

"Would you like to grab lunch?" I ask as nonchalantly as possible. Or search for an obscure book in the back. Find a deserted room. Go back to my office.

He stops making notes. "Sorry. I can't." He flips the notebook closed. "Taking this position was sort of a last-minute decision for me, and I haven't prepared for my first seminar. I'm working on it over lunch."

Disappointment hits me, but I brush it off. "Completely understand. Maybe another time." I don't care if he is a spy. It's not as if I have to share my secrets with him.

He nods. "Thanks for working with me on this. I'll type up the notes." After grabbing his stuff, he glances at the monitor, then back at me. "Are you going to be at your office later? I could drop it by."

I nod and give him my hours. "Thanks, Hawthorne. I'm looking forward to working on this with you."

"Me too." He flashes me a wide smile and strides off.

Tempted to lean over and watch him walk away, I restrain myself. Once I'm sure he's left the library, I drop my head in my hands and groan. The man is smart and passionate, and I could sit beside him for hours. I almost wish he were an ogre. How am I going to keep my guard up around him?

By doing what I always do... getting back to my real job. I lift my head and open up the chat screen from earlier.

AncientFangs: Key went up for sale a week ago. LINK. Seller took the post down a couple of days later. Original ask MMs.

Nothing truly disappears from the web. After paying for the information, I click on the link, which takes me to the original seller's post. An image of an ancient-looking key pops up on the screen. I study it, but it's not familiar, so I turn to the archived post.

User9738432: Platinum key with Hephaestus' symbol on bow. Non-magical. Serious collectors only. 20M GBP

Non-magical. Then why is everyone after it? Is this a money play? My eyes dart back to the image, and I zoom in on the bow, the portion of the key a person holds in their hands, and see the metal stamp Hephaestus often used to sign his pieces. A simplified version of the hammer and anvil. I frown. Anyone could have stamped this onto the piece.

Given the attack at the museum, and Jamison's subsequent search, the piece must somehow be connected to Westgate's collection, and if it was in the vampire's possession, it could be thousands of years old. Westgate was ancient and reported to be one of the first vampires to cross the portal. Objects with a symbol of the gods are rare, but they do exist. If it's been authenticated, it would be worth the twenty-million-pound price tag.

I flick back to the post. The seller's use of "non-magical" tells me they're supernatural. A human wouldn't make that distinction.

Beyond curious, I decide to send the anonymous user a note.

CursedGreek: @User 9738432 If the key is authentic,
I'm interested. DM me if still available.

I close the chat and head to the sandwich place on campus, then back to the library. Someone's using my favorite desk, so I drop into another. I'll only be here a minute. Entering the chat room, I check for messages, but there's no reply. Disappointed, I log out and decide to head to the gym early to blow off some steam.

Cara stops me the minute I walk in. As the gym's owner and resident fitness guru, she spends most of her time here and is one of the few supernaturals I speak to on a regular basis. "Guess what? You're never going to believe it. A new supe moved to town, and he's a trainer. Here. In my gym. What are the odds?" She drags me around the corner to the weight room. "There. See him?"

I scan the faces around me. Most of them I recognize as regulars. "Where?"

She smirks. "Keep looking. You won't miss him. Believe me."

Shaking my head, I stretch up on tiptoe to see the back of the room. "Holy... Huge" The man is freaking big and muscular. Stacked in all the best ways. "What is he?" I keep my voice low, so he doesn't hear us.

She licks her lips. "Shifter of some kind."

One of the men working out in front of me moves, giving me a clear view. At least six feet, seven inches tall, he's definitely massive, but surprisingly, it's not the first thing you notice about him. "He looks like a golden god. Or a Nemean lion." Big, powerful, with acres of golden skin and a full head of white-blond hair.

She hums. "He does, doesn't he?" As a panther shifter herself, she's practically purring at the idea.

I continue to watch him train the woman next to him, showing her how each piece of equipment works and how to do the reps. She's not even looking at the weights. "He's not the only new supe in town. There are two more."

Cara jerks me around to face her. "Seriously?" Folding her arms across her chest, she motions for me to continue.

Unable to be completely honest, I keep it light, telling her I met Jamison in London, and he showed up at the university today. Then I tell her about the new Elven professor who's joined the staff for the semester.

Eyes as wide as saucers, she slaps me on the arm. "I'm so jelly. Two lovely, unbreakable men. Sounds like you already have dibs on those two, so I'll take this one for myself. Come, I'll introduce you."

I chuckle and shake my head. "He's busy. I'm just going to grab a run on the treadmill, then hit the wall. It's been a while, and I need the practice."

She heaves a huge sigh but pushes me toward the cardio area.

After completing a five-mile run, I make my way over to the climbing wall on the other side of the gym. This is my favorite activity. It's the best thing I've found that mimics scaling a wall or building in real life. Skills every thief needs. I visually trace the climbing holds I want to conquer today.

Exchanging my sneakers for climbing shoes, I step into the harness. After hooking everything up, I chalk my hands and nod to the trainer on duty to let him know I'm starting the climb. He gives me a thumbs up, then turns back to watch the beginners on the wall next to me. I've been here so many times, he's used to me.

Taking the most difficult route possible, I traverse my way up the wall, pushing myself to take the farthest hold instead of the nearest. As I get closer to the top, I arch my neck to find the ceiling. There. It will require a big leap to get there, but it's the best move. Arms straining, I look down to position my feet, and see Cara's new supe standing below, watching someone on the wall to my right.

Golden eyes swing to me briefly, then with a frown, move back to the woman he's training. I roll my shoulders and refocus on the ceiling. Twisting my body, I spring forward, but instead of landing the jump, my fingertips graze the hold, and I find myself falling. "Damn it!" Thankfully, I'm far enough from the main portion of the wall to let myself fall directly to the mats below.

An *oomph* escapes me when I hit a wall of muscle instead of the floor. A subtle smell teases my senses. Juniper, maybe. Confused, I look up. Fierce gold eyes stare down at me, almost glowing in their intensity.

I might be immortal, but that only means I can't die. In the meantime, I can bruise or break bones. Feeling the hit, I lie in his arms for a second.

"Are you okay?" a gruff voice asks. Body tense and closed off, his energy reflects his gruff tone.

"Yep, just catching my breath," I reply, easing out of his bulging biceps to stand beside him. "Err, thanks. The mat would have broken my fall."

His brows lower as if he's offended.

"Cara says you're her new trainer. I'm Phaedra. You'll see me here a lot. Hopefully, you won't see me falling much." I laugh. I've fallen in this place far too many times to count.

"Gatlin. Try not to kill yourself on my watch," he spits out, then walks—or rather, prowls—away. His stride and smooth gait suggest he's light on his feet. Maybe he's a cat shifter like Cara. He certainly snarls like one. A literal ball of sunshine. Cara will love his grumpiness.

With a groan, I force myself up and add more chalk to my hands. I'm determined to nail this move despite grumpy's warning.

11

MATHIAS

Tucked into an alley off of Main Street, the Trick Unicorn Pub is Gatlin's pick tonight. Brick walls, black booths, a wooden bar with an astounding array of beers on tap, and pictures of Ireland's green hills on the walls. Lively, but surprisingly, it's not too packed tonight. I slide into a booth at the back and order one of the beers on tap. It's not as if I'm going to drink it, but we're in a human bar, and it would seem odd not to at least order something.

Gatlin settles into the chair in front of me, lips curled into a snarl, then signals for a beer. Since that's his usual countenance, I don't take it personally. The server comes by and drops off his drink, foam dripping down the sides of the glass. I immediately slide a napkin across the table. His eyes flick to mine, but after spending the last two hundred years on the same team, he knows I can't abide a mess and wipes off the glass.

Hawthorne slides into the chair beside me. Once he places his order, I bring them up to date on the latest. "Cameras are installed in her condo. Jamison checked them before he left for Connecticut."

I lean in a bit closer. "Dr. Kline's assistant, Sia, is dead. Humans. We're not entirely sure if their target was the mysterious 'key,' but they're definitely part of the same group that attacked me at the museum. Same tactical gear." Anger flares at the thought of the humans who attacked me, killing another supernatural, but I tamp it down. No one needs to see death tonight. "Basilisk is investigating both her and Kline's recent activity. They'll report up to us."

Basilisk is one of our top security teams, and they take their job seriously. If there's something to find, they'll ferret it out.

Hawthorne and Gatlin grab a menu while I continue. "Jamison is now in London, overseeing the auction. Once the pieces are in the council's vault, he'll head back here. In the meantime, we're splitting our residences." I slide a piece of paper and a set of keys across the table to Gatlin. "That's the address of the apartment you'll share with Jamison."

If anything, his scowl deepens. "I don't like it when we split up. Less secure."

Gatlin's expertise is security. He's a natural-born leader, an expert battle strategist, and, with his size, he easily inspires both confidence and fear.

"Phaedra's met three members of our team. It would look suspicious if we all lived together," I remind him. "Besides, there's only a small population of supernaturals in the area, and we don't want to call attention to ourselves."

He raises an imperious eyebrow. "I understand the why, but I don't have to like it."

Our server comes by and takes their order. When she looks at me, I shake my head. "I've already eaten, thank you." I might have to pretend to drink this beer, but I refuse to order food I won't eat.

After she leaves, another thing pops into my head. "There was quite a bit of chatter on the boards today. Someone is looking for information on a key," I say softly, giving them a pointed stare. "I tried to follow the IP address, but it went into a public network, and I lost it. I'll continue to monitor the situation."

Hawthorne leans back in his chair, and the server sets down his order. "Thank you." He flashes her a smile that makes her pause.

Before she can return his smile or, heaven forbid, start flirting, I take off my glasses and compel her to leave. "You're too busy to talk, and when you walk away, you'll forget him."

Instead of getting irritated, Hawthorne nods his appreciation.

A vague smile appears in her glassy eyes, and she slides an unsure glance down at the dish in her hands.

Gatlin huffs and takes his food from her, then glares at me. "Next time, wait until I have my food." Gold eyes narrow, and he tilts his head. "How did you know I met Phaedra? I didn't think we had cameras at the gym yet."

"The gym has plenty of cameras," I coolly inform him. "I simply tapped into them. Good catch, by the way."

His scowl deepens.

An alert pops up on my phone and I tap on it to open the app. The cameras I installed show Phaedra walking in the door of her condo. When she's safe inside, I close the app and turn my attention back to them.

After taking a few bites, Hawthorne sets down his fork. "Jamison didn't need to be at the university today. I had it covered." There's a troubled expression on his face.

I can only guess at the answer. "You'll have to ask him to explain. He did drop by the apartment before he left, but he didn't say anything about it. He was distracted. By her. His reaction to her feels more personal than a simple introduction at the event. I don't know if he's met her before or if it's something else, but he's acting out of character."

Hawthorne frowns and stirs the food around on his plate. "I see." He darts a glance at Gatlin. "What did you think of her?"

Gatlin lifts a meaty shoulder. "Attractive. Unique scent. Friends with the panther who owns the gym, but I can't tell if Phaedra's a shifter or not. She didn't smell like one." He grimaces as if the bare-bones description annoys him, which it probably does. He doesn't like anomalies. "Maybe she's been around humans too long, but she doesn't exhibit the mannerisms of a supernatural. She fell off the indoor rock wall tonight from a pretty good height. While she recovered pretty quickly, she acted like the fall was normal for her. It was…odd."

Hawthorne nods in agreement, then turns to me and chuckles. "You're the only one she hasn't met. Any first impressions."

Olive skin, raven-hair, and bright blue eyes spring to mind. "Nothing worth noting." Although she did find the locket with my daughter's picture in it. She's an enigma, but purely from a professional perspective. There's no need to get personal.

After paying the check, we say goodbye to Gatlin. "Tell me if the apartment lacks anything, and I'll take care of it."

With a gruff agreement, he heads in the opposite direction from us.

When we step out of the elevator, Hawthorne glances at her door. "Is she home?"

Having checked my phone periodically throughout the night, I nod. "She's already asleep."

HAWTHORNE HEADS out the next morning for the university, and I watch Phaedra leave five minutes later. With London hours ahead of us, the auction finished early this morning. Jamison sent a text to let me know it went well, and he'll likely return in two days. After I send him an update, I sit down with a warm cup of O-positive and start the methodical process of searching the chat boards for updates while I simultaneously run a background search on our woman of mystery.

Once we knew it was a key, I created a program to continuously search for mentions of keys in black market chat rooms. If someone wants to sell something valuable, this is where the deal gets done. I hit the jackpot and found the original post pretty quickly, but it was already inactive by the time I saw it. I kept the program running just in case something new popped up.

And it did. Yesterday, a user named CursedGreek started asking about a key. In response to their request, I sent them the link to the archived post. When they sent me payment for the information, I knew they were serious, and I've been trying to trace them ever since.

The software pings, and I see CursedGreek is online, but they're gone seconds later. I wait for them to join again, but after thirty minutes of no activity, I reset the software to autopilot and work on finalizing the transfer of auction funds from the council to a holding account.

They still haven't named the new vampire leader, but only because they're fighting it out. Literally to the death. The last thing a new leader wants to do is leave a potential usurper alive. As one of the most powerful vampires, I should care about the election, but they destroyed my loyalty years ago, and now they can all burn in hell together.

The phone rings. Hawthorne.

"We were supposed to meet after class to work on a project, but she canceled. Did she return to the condo?" Hawthorne asks when I answer.

I hear the sounds of students calling out to each other in the background. "Hold on." With a click, I bring up the monitors in her condo, then the garage. "She's not here. Let me conference in Gatlin."

"Gatlin," he answers in a bored tone.

"It's me and Hawthorne," I inform him. "Have you seen Phaedra?"

He pauses, and I hear him say something to someone in the background. "Sorry, had to move away from prying ears. She's not at the gym."

"Is her friend there? The shifter?" I ask impatiently.

"Unfortunately," he replies with an irritated sigh.

I remind myself to ask him about that comment later. "Hawthorne, when did she text you?"

"A little after noon," he replies. "I'm heading to the condo." His breathing increases as he hurries down the loud hall.

"Let me see if I can track her phone," I tell them, navigating to the site. "Cell towers report her last known location as...the university. Are you sure she isn't there?"

Hawthorne stops. "Yes, I used a spell. I've checked her office, the loading dock, library, teacher lounges, classrooms. Basically, the whole damn building. My magic says she isn't here. I wouldn't have called you without checking." Irritation bleeds into his usually calm voice.

"Let's regroup here. See you in ten." Hanging up, I bring up the campus CCTV system and pinpoint the six cameras associated with the entrances and exits around campus. Then I start methodically rewinding them to noon so I can watch all the vehicles leaving between twelve and one o'clock. The first two cameras yield nothing. On the third, I spot her black Mercedes leaving at five past two. She's definitely not on campus.

The door opens, and Hawthorne and Gatlin walk in. "Did you find her?"

I swivel around in my chair. "She left campus. East Entrance.

Five minutes after she texted you. Unfortunately, she took the highway, and I lost her." I look at Hawthorne. "Didn't you put a tracker on her car?"

He holds up his phone to show me the dot blinking on the map. "I did. It's still in the parking lot."

"She removed it," I insert, suspicion rising at her evasion tactics. "I'll call Jamison."

12

―――

PHAEDRA

ser9738432 sent me a message early this morning with several complex archaeology questions to past finds. Knowing there was a reason, I sent the anonymous user an in-depth reply to each one. Way beyond what could be found by a decent Google search. At noon, I received a meeting time and location, plus instructions for sending the money to an escrow account until the deal is done. I transferred the money, sent Hawthorne a text to cancel our regroup, and jumped into my car.

When I turned the ignition, a special app on my vehicle touchscreen lit up with a message and a dot. Furious, I got out, slid under my car, and yanked off the tracker. After a quick look around, I left it in the center of my parking spot. Probably Jamison, but out of caution, I decide to take the back way to the airstrip.

Owned by a paranoid demon who jokingly calls himself Maverick, the private airstrip outside Raleigh allows me to come and go without having to fly commercial or use a portal. I call to let him know I'm going to be leaving on my private jet in half an hour and to let the pilot know we're headed to London.

Thankfully, I keep the plane stocked with everything I could possibly need, from weapons to surveillance equipment to the crack technology I use to break into today's sophisticated security systems. I quickly pull the car into the hangar and cover it with a tarp.

I wait outside the small jet while Charlie checks it over. Maverick introduced us a few years ago, and we've flown together ever since. Charlie, real name unknown, is a pilot and mage, which comes in handy. After performing the usual maintenance checks, he then runs a spell to check for trackers and other nasty surprises. I snort. Come to think of it, we all might be paranoid. He jerks his chin in my direction, and I board the plane.

Once on, I buckle in and open my laptop to start viewing the arca around tonight's mcct. It's a derelict warehouse called The Millennium Mills. Abandoned for over forty years, it sits quietly on the edge of the Royal Victoria Docks in East London. In its heyday, it was once the largest center for flour milling in London. Today, the area is undergoing revitalization. Fortunately, they haven't touched the warehouse yet.

I scroll through the images online to get a feel for the place. Mostly concrete and broken windows, the main building stands roughly ten stories tall with a couple of additional abandoned buildings nearby. Eerie and grey, the outside is full of overgrown weeds, the perfect setting for a zombie apocalypse. I chuckle. Or a secret meeting to sell a stolen archaeological piece.

I get to work. With the blueprints pulled up on one monitor, I create a replica and overlay it onto the actual building. I note several places where I can set traps without bringing the building down on top of me, memorize all the exits, and estimate the proximity to the water from every angle in case I need to use it as an exit.

Once everything is plotted, I call a contact in London to request specific ammunition and detonation devices. Mercer sends me an invoice for the entire amount. Non-refundable. We've been doing business together for four hundred years, but she still insists on full payment. I pay it and tell her to stop worrying so much. While she doesn't know who I am, I'm sure she's pieced a few things together over the years, especially when I request something unique from her. She always delivers but demands payment upfront to mitigate any risks.

I wish I knew her real name. Everyone refers to her as Mercer or The Merchant. She's part of a larger underground group called Harlequin. We've met a couple of times when I've picked up my order, but she's overly cautious in giving out any personal information. Not that I blame her, but it would be nice to have more friends instead of acquaintances.

Finally, I pack. Climbing gear, electronic devices, handheld weapons, magical potions, and my bulletproof suit that has fabric to render me invisible to infrared technology along with a few other surprises. I stop and look around, but there's nothing left to pack or do. I drop into the seat to grab a catnap. It's going to be a long night.

HEFTING the duffle over my shoulder, I begin the long trek up to the roof. Dark and cold, the stairway in the center of the building was the least exposed. I move quickly, floor by floor, until I reach the top, then prop open the door. Keeping my body low, I cross from one side to the other to set up the ropes and stash weapons in several key places, then add a few cameras to give me visuals.

I'm tempted to peek over the side and scan the surrounding area but fight the urge. It only gives away my position, and I need every advantage I can get. Leaving the door propped open, I head down, then over to an interior staircase to lay one of the traps. I do the same with the one on the other side. Forcing everyone to the center evens the playing field. Shutting the roof door, I add a tiny laser tripwire to alert me if it's opened.

Downstairs, I slip out a window and crawl through the weeds to the overgrown bushes near the front door and set up another tripwire. Sticking low to the ground, I slide around to the back of the building and do the same. Of course, they could come through one of the many nonexistent windows, but larger groups will likely use one of the entrances.

I return to the building, make my way to the designated meeting spot, and wait. An hour later, the cameras pick up a shadow moving along the side of the building. Small in stature. No weapons that I can see, but that means nothing. Supernaturals have their own built-in arsenals.

A small green sphere moves from the shadow to the building. It floats along until it comes to a stop in front of me. It scans my body, changing from green to purple. I mentally flinch, unsure what that means, but I don't like it. After a moment, the sphere disappears, and a shadow stands in its place. Nice trick.

"Forgive the intrusion, but I had to know you weren't one of the humans who have been trying to get their hands on this key," he says in a shockingly familiar voice. "I never expected the buyer to be you, Phaedra."

Is this a trap? Frantic, I move toward the door, my head on a swivel, ears straining for the slightest of sounds, trying to find the men he brought with him. Magic wraps around me, but I shrug it off.

"Wait, I beg you," Dr. Samuels pleads behind me. "It's just me, Letz. I came alone. Please hear me out."

I stop but don't turn around.

"Me and my...colleagues have been tracking you for centuries. We know of the work you've done to remove curses and dark magic from artifacts," he reveals in a rush. "You could say we're your biggest fans."

That's not good. All these years I thought I'd hidden myself well. I bite my lip and slowly turn to face him. "What are you talking about?"

He conjures another ball and floats it up to the ceiling. The glow sheds a little light into the room, showing me Dr. Letz Samuels isn't even wearing a disguise. "That's better."

After a sigh, he continues his story. "Over the years, we narrowed it down to a handful of people. You were at the top of the list, but until we could prove it, we had no way of knowing for sure. We needed something big to lure you out in the open. Nolan's collection gave us that opportunity. The work you did to remove the threats was incredible. We were very impressed."

Damn, he does know who I am, or at least what I do, but I refuse to admit to anything. He's an old, powerful mage. Who knows what magic he can wield.

"What do you think you know about me?" I draw the weapon at my side, along with a potion. I may not be able to cast magic, but I can wield it.

He eyes the vial in my hand. "There's no need for violence, I assure you." When I keep the items raised, he gives me a gentle smile, then continues. "I first stumbled across your work about a thousand years ago. A young mage, interested in the world's artifacts, I went to work for the Catholic Church." He chuckles. "I know. A mage working for a human religious organization. It was a leap of faith on my part. They, of course, thought I was human. It sounds bizarre, but back then, they were the only legitimate game in town. They had amassed the largest collection of relics, art, and other historical pieces, and I wanted access to it."

His eyes shine with memories from that time. "Most of the apprentices were human, except for me and two others. As we sifted through the items, we could sense the magic in them, and not all of it was good. So we started working together to remove the spells designed to hurt humans or supernaturals."

Astonished, I slide my weapons back into their holders.

He exhales loudly. "Thank you. Now, where was I? Oh yes. When we finished cataloging the collection for the church, the three of us formed a pact to continue our work on any future pieces. We recruited more members, and a thousand years later, we now have sixty dedicated supernaturals who do everything in their power to follow in your footsteps."

His words hit me like a sledgehammer, and for a second, I forget to breathe. For three thousand years, I've felt alone. Trudging through life, doing the job I chose to do, with just a kernel of hope to fuel me. Invisible to the world. No family or friends to give life meaning. Only a singular, never-ending, and unappreciated purpose.

His words... I swallow hard. I feel *seen*. Valued. I should be concerned the gods will find out that I've been exposed, but if Letz' group has been operating this long, they know how to keep a secret, including mine.

My voice is barely a whisper when I ask the question burning in my mind. "Why me?"

"Because of you," he says simply. "One night, a stone figurine was stolen from the Vatican. We'd been working on the piece for weeks, trying one spell after another to remove the curse on it, but nothing worked. Disturbed about the theft, we worried about the intent behind the person who had stolen it, but two days later, it reappeared...without the curse. This happened several times. Intrigued, we started tracking the thefts. Sometimes the items were returned, sometimes they weren't, but if they were, the curse or spell would be broken."

I remember the small clay figure, and the pieces that followed.

He rubs his chin. "We wanted to know who you were, but except for the thefts, all roads led to dead ends. Before we knew it, you became an obsession. When we left the church, we continued to track every incident, but we were always a step or two behind. Meeting you was a pipe dream. We thought it would never happen, but then Westgate died, and the collection gave us an incredible opportunity. Once I confirmed it was you, I planned on asking you to visit our society after the auction, but then I messed everything up."

Reeling from his story, I don't know what to do or say. I love the fact that there are others out there doing the same job, but completely revealing myself to sixty supernaturals who can tell the council of my existence is not an option.

His mouth compresses in anger. "The key was in a box along with a blue panel. It was part of Westgate's collection. The two items intrigued me. Based on my research, they were found in Greece in 300 BCE, in the Temple of Hephaestus, along with several other relics. To my relief, neither piece was magical, but given their provenance and age, their value was immense." He looks at me as if he expects me to understand, and I do. This is about money.

"Our group's resources have been depleted over the years. I thought selling the items could solve our problems," he admits with a heavy sigh. "The panel sold, but something happened during the sale that made me realize the group who broke into the museum and the one who bought the panel were the same. I panicked. Didn't know what to do. When another buyer appeared, I jumped at the chance to get rid of the key too. But that was before I knew it was you. For some reason, this key has stirred up a lot of trouble, and I don't want you in the middle of whatever this is. You're too valuable."

Why do the humans want it so badly? "Let me see the key."

When he holds out his hand, the key appears, and he reluctantly hands it over. "There's something mesmerizing about it. Not magical. I don't know what it is, but it's hard for me to put it down."

The key lies flat in the palm of my gloved hand, looking exactly like the image on the chat board post. "I'm not getting anything from it," I admit to him. Although that could be due to the glove, but I won't remove it here. "No magic." I turn to him. "I don't usually buy non-magical items, but I'm curious as to why they want it so badly. And why they're willing to set me up for its theft."

Understanding and relief fill his face as he holds out his hand to take it back.

I shake my head. "The key in exchange for the money and your silence. You tell no one about me. Don't worry. I'll figure out a place to hide it from the humans." Whatever this is, he's clearly in over his head.

For a second, he hesitates but then takes a step back. "I don't suppose you'll consider visiting me and our little secret society? It would mean the world to us."

I say nothing in return, silently tucking the key into a small pocket on the inside of my suit, and pulling out my phone to release the money to him.

He chuckles at my silence, but the laughter fades quickly. He puts a finger up to his mouth. With a flick of his wrist, he sends several orbs flying from the room.

I look down at my now-buzzing phone. Two alerts. Nobody on the roof, but there are two large groups entering the building. One at the front and one at the back. I type in a code to release the funds.

"They must have been watching you. Go. The funds are in your possession."

He shakes his head. "Come with me. There's so much I have to share with you."

"It's better if we split up," I tell him. When he refuses to budge, I blow out a frustrated breath and grab his arm. "Let's go. We can argue about it later. They're closing in on us. Head to the middle stairway. The roof is our best escape option." I shove him in that direction and pull my weapons.

Two men come around the corner, and I immediately shoot both of them in the head. Silencers muffle the sound of the hits. I turn to follow Letz and see a ball of electricity headed straight toward me. At the last second, it swings around me, and as I turn, it hits a third man. He goes down, body jerking with magic.

I raise an eyebrow. "Nice shot."

Letz turns and rushes toward the stairway. I follow. Floor by floor, we fight our way up. I holster one gun in order to fling potions. Four men dissolve into a puddle of skin and goo. Letz uses his magic to string up two more like puppets and dance them over a balcony. More men fill the stairs below us.

"Faster," I yell.

He nods and starts flinging magic right and left. I toss potions with one hand and shoot anything that moves with the other. Letz bursts through the door at the top, and I follow, but instead of the safety I expected, we land in the middle of a war zone. Men in camouflage are fighting men in black fatigues. Bullets and magic are flying everywhere.

Slamming the door shut, I point to the knob. "Can you remove it?"

He waves a hand toward the knob, and it melts into the door. "What now?"

A bullet whizzes by my ear. "Take cover!" I point to the metal shed behind him. Wind whips my hair, and I look up to see a dragon flying by. There are several other beasts flying in the air beside him.

Letz conjures a shield and wraps it around us. Bullets and magic bounce off it, giving us a temporary respite. "What now?"

"We need to find a way out of here," I tell him. "I don't know either of these groups, and I don't like being in the middle of them."

"I can open up a portal," he offers.

A chill races down my spine. I'm not ready to extend that much trust. "No. You go. I'll meet you at the museum tomorrow morning." When he shakes his head, I sigh. "I promise I'll be there."

He thinks about it for a second, then reluctantly agrees. "Fine. I'll help you escape, then leave."

I glance around to find the weapons I stashed, but there are too many soldiers around them. I point to the black nylon coiled on the ground. "If you can get me to the edge of the roof where that rope is, I'll get to safety."

With his nod, we slowly stand and move toward the side of the building, weaving in and out of the men and creatures around us, Letz' shield taking the brunt of the hits.

Two men appear behind us, wearing face masks that obscure their features.

"Friends of yours?" I shout, turning around to cover our back. I raise the gun in my hand.

Letz shakes his head. "Not mine." With enemies at our back, he starts moving faster. He suddenly jerks to a halt.

The two guys behind us start shouting, but with all the noise, I can't hear what they're saying. They start to run forward but stop when I raise the gun higher. Turning my head, I glance over my shoulder. Standing in front of Letz is one of the biggest and ugliest guys I've ever seen. Muscles stacked on muscles and a face hardened by life. Lips curl in a sneer as he raises his weapon toward Letz.

Protected by Letz' shield, the gun doesn't concern me, but the glowing knife held in his other hand is another story. I've never seen anything like it, and I have all the latest gadgets.

Letz holds his palms up, releasing a stream of magic. The man stumbles back a couple of feet but remains standing. Changing tactics, Letz conjures a huge fireball, then motions for me to go around him. I slide past, my gaze darting between this new threat and the two men behind us as I grab the rope and throw it over the side of the roof.

Before I can move to protect Letz, the giant thrusts the magical knife straight through his shield and into his chest.

Someone roars. I scream and immediately swing my gun in his direction and put three bullets in his brain and body. A microsecond later, Letz' ball of fire incinerates him.

"Letz!" I drop to my knees beside the mage, my hands scrambling for the healing potion on my belt.

Pain lines his face. "Stop. The spell on the knife... It's too late," he informs me, blood trickling out of his mouth. "Come closer."

I open my mouth to protest, but I know death when I see it. With a slow nod, I take his hand in mine and put my ear close to his mouth. He whispers many things, then slides a small key into my hand. "Go there. See it all first. Then decide. Promise me."

Tears slip from the corners of my eyes, but I refuse to let go of him. "I promise." It's the least I can do for him.

Someone drops down beside me and places a glowing palm on Letz' chest. "Damn it, Letz."

I freeze. I'd know that voice anywhere. Jamison. From the corner of my eye, I see the black fatigues covering his body. That must be the standard uniform for the council's army. Sweat rolls down the back of my neck, but even with the suit covering my face, I don't dare turn my head toward him.

A whistle pierces the air, and Jamison jerks his head up. "The whole building is going to blow. We need to get out of here!" Grabbing my arm, he stands and signals to the rest of his men across the roof, and they disappear.

I look down and see Letz staring sightlessly into the night sky. A loud rumble fills the air, traveling from the outer edges of the building to the center, and the concrete beneath my feet shakes violently. Taking advantage of the moment, I jerk my arm from Jamison's grip and leap over the lip of the roof to grab the rope. A bullet strikes my shoulder just as I grab it, causing me to slam into the building. Pain radiates across my body. The rope slips through one hand, causing me to fall several feet, but I snatch it with my other hand and slow my descent.

Right before I reach the bottom, I look up and see two huge fireballs flying toward me, but they swerve at the last minute. Unnerved, I follow their path and watch as they hit the two men on the ground below me. For the second time today, a mage protected me.

My feet land hard in the packed dirt, now full of ash, blood, and guts, and I tilt my head back. Jamison steps through a portal just as the roof explodes behind him. *Damn it, Jamison, that was close.* I take off running toward the water and dive in.

13

<u>PHAEDRA</u>

My shoulder is almost healed by the time I land in North Carolina nine hours later. I slip into the car and make my way to the farm. Numb from last night's events, I grab a shower then sit and swing on the porch with my head on my knees, thinking about Letz and everything he told me, letting the peace of the house and the sounds of the night soothe me. A light breeze drifts across my heated skin.

For three thousand years, I've been alone, doing this job for the gods. Sometimes I've felt like a ghost. Here but not here. Time sliding by like sand in an hourglass. No permanent relationships. It's lonely, but the alternative, serving Hades in the Underworld, was a much worse option. The only thing keeping me sane is a tether to the real world and the humans in it, living their best lives. It reminds me I was once human like them. What I am now is what my own actions made me. This existence is my doing. I chose this path because I believe it will eventually lead me to my sister. I try to remember that on the hard days like today.

I look down. The large key, still in its velvet bag, lies on the table beside me. I've yet to study it. The second smaller key, the one Letz gave me right before he died, lies next to the bag.

I don't know what to do with everything he told me. His dying words were full of pride and caution. He made me promise to visit his group's headquarters, see for myself the work they've done. Help them continue it.

But his most urgent words were rushed and hard to hear, warning me not to trust the council. They were divided and no longer interested in serving the people.

The last two words he uttered were an apology.

I drop my head back and sigh. Letz and I worked together for two months, establishing a camaraderie and professional respect for each other, but I realize now our secrets prevented us from really knowing each other. And as I learned last night, he was a truly remarkable supernatural. Most supernaturals don't think the way he does. They couldn't care less if humans were hurt by magic or if the council took over this world.

I gave him my word to visit, but honestly, I'm reluctant to open that door. While I haven't spoken to the gods in at least two hundred years, they're quick to reveal themselves if I veer off their chosen path. Technically, a visit won't break the rules, but if more supernaturals find out about me and share that info with the council, it would be the end of my usefulness, and I refuse to let that happen. I've got too much at stake.

Maybe I should wait. Let things cool down. Immortality gives me an abundance of time, and Letz' group is full of supernaturals who have been doing this for years. I doubt his death will make them stop, especially since they now have the necessary funds. Still, a tinge of guilt hits me, knowing he wanted me to visit sooner rather than later.

The sun rises on the horizon, and the sky lightens. Dawn.

My eyes drift to the table beside me. The damn key is calling to me. Snatching up the bag, I pull it open and tip it over, letting it fall into my palm. The second the cold metal touches my skin, a white light encompasses my vision, and the key begins to burn like fire. I try to drop it but can't. It's welded to my hand.

Images appear in my head, scenes from my past fly by in a whirl as if they're reminding me of who I am and the path I chose. Pain and sorrow flow through me as I watch the scenes unfold. Before my emotions can bury me, new images appear. Unfamiliar objects shining brightly. Blue panels with gold scenes etched on their surface. I tilt my head but can't quite see the details except for one. Gods standing in a circle. The panels fade. A lock appears, then this key. Everything goes dark, and the key stops glowing, but the burning sensation remains, and when I scan my left palm, I see Hephaestus' symbol branded into my skin. A deep-seated fear rises at the sight of it.

I hold the key up to the light to get a closer look. The reason it doesn't register as magical is because the gods don't use magic. They have powers from a source I don't even understand. This key with Hephaestus' symbol—an anvil and hammer —is real…and now it's branded into my palm. He obviously created this for me, but why? Is it another punishment? What are the gods up to? Am I not doing enough?

Before I lose the details, I jump up and run inside to grab a pen and paper. I sketch out the panels and the way they connect. It's definitely a box. He must want me to find it. But why and where? Letz said the key was found at Hephaestus' temple in Greece. Are the other pieces buried there too? What will happen when the box is assembled?

Sharp pain pricks my palm, and I peer down at the brand just in time to see the symbol fade into my skin. I wait for it to reappear, but nothing happens. Was it temporary?

My alarm goes off, startling me, and I tap the phone. I've got an early morning meeting with Dr. Berne to discuss an expedition to Egypt. While there, I can use the campus network to do a search for this key and the panels.

Hurrying to dress, I drop both keys off at the vault, then drive to work. I rush into my office to pick up my notes on possible Egyptian digs that could lead to pieces for the university.

A knock on the door startles me, and I look up to find Hawthorne standing in the doorway. "Hey, sorry I missed you the other day. Do you have time to meet about our project later?" While his smile stretches across his face, there isn't an ounce of amusement or kindness in his blank eyes.

Surely he isn't upset because I had to cancel. "I'm sorry I couldn't meet, but something came up. Yes, today works for me. How about one o'clock? In the library."

He nods. "I'll see you there." Without another word, he's gone.

I frown. Maybe he really is upset with me. The only supernatural I spend time with these days is Cara, and that's mostly at the gym. She's pretty easy to read, though. Her shifter nature is closer to human than she cares to admit.

With a sigh, I head to my meeting. Sticking to the Egyptian theme, I show Dr. Berne a map of all the historical sites found and the ones yet to be found. We have a lively debate about whether the land under the sea holds the treasures archaeologists are seeking and whether it would be beneficial for me to join their expedition. Reluctant to commit to one project, I promise to get back to her after I've done more research.

My stomach growls as the meeting ends, and I head to a bakery in town to grab a sausage and egg bagel, a special treat, and a coffee. The true nectar of the gods. Scrolling through my phone while I eat, an alert pops up, telling me the council is giving a press conference in ten minutes.

I rush through the rest of my breakfast, then head back to the university. Not wanting to use my computer, I slip into the library. A few clicks later, and I'm on the council's site. Protected by a magical password, only supernaturals can access it.

Jamison's father stands at a podium. "Dr. Letz Samuels was a respected member of our community, a friend to this council, and a powerful mage. We all mourn his passing." He looks at the other councilmembers, who nod back at him. "I, personally, mourn the loss of a great man and trusted friend."

I roll my eyes at his statement.

"Unfortunately, we have to inform you of the circumstances surrounding his death. We debated whether to bring you this news, but we believe transparency is necessary to ensure your safety. Letz was working with council security to uncover a theft from the museum. There was a skirmish two nights ago, and he was killed by humans. This was not a random attack. They purposely targeted him," he reveals, outrage in his voice.

Are they covering up Letz' theft because he was a high-ranking mage? Or do they not care?

"Letz isn't their first victim, either. They attacked one of our security men at the museum earlier this month and killed a young demon named Sia when she surprised them during a burglary." He pauses to let the crowd express their outrage.

Sia. I hadn't realized they'd also killed her. An image of the studious young demon flashes in my mind. Dark hair, small build, she wouldn't have hurt a fly. Killing her proves this group will go to any lengths, but for what? The key? Could they possibly suspect it's real? De Vere starts talking, and I shift my focus back to him.

Holding up a regal hand, he reins in the chaos erupting around him. "This new group is resourceful, connected, and powerful. They have the means to detect magic and, apparently, strike against it. We're doing everything possible to find out who they are and eliminate the threat they pose to us and our way of life."

While I don't like the man, I can appreciate his tactics. With their ability to detect and nullify magic, these humans present a huge threat to supernaturals. Exposure is the least of it. Elimination is likely their end goal.

The crowd roars in his favor. In the background, I see two councilmembers clapping, but the other three are stoic. A divided council. Probably the only thing unifying them is the pact they made with the gods. Eliminating the human group will prevent the world from finding out supernaturals exist and keep magic contained. It's a harsh reality, but in order to live together, here in this world, we all had to make pacts with the gods.

Photographs flash up on the screen behind him. Most of them are men dressed in familiar camouflage, but it's the single solitary figure covered head to toe in a black bodysuit that makes me want to bang my head on the table. *Shit.* That's me. The gods aren't going to be happy about my appearance on a council press conference or the reward they're offering for any information on me. Thankfully, I'm completely in disguise.

I'll have to lie low for a while. Easy enough to stay here and do my university job or go on the Egyptian expedition. Better yet, I could lie low at the farmhouse. Catch up on the objects in the vault that need curses removed and give several of those to the university to maintain my cover. Plus, it would give me time to research the key. Figure out what the gods want from me. It's not as if they'll suddenly appear and tell me. They believe in making me work for the answers.

My alarm goes off, and I hurriedly click out of the screen and delete the history. I bring up a website about Dr. Kathleen Martínez' search for Cleopatra's tomb. It's truly a fascinating story. My gut says she'll find it. Right now, though, this is just a cover in case anyone snoops on my browsing.

I run out of the library and head to my office to grab my things. As I fumble to get the key in the lock, I realize it's already unlocked. Cautiously, I enter the room. It's empty. I did lock it, right? I remember grabbing my things earlier, but I don't remember if I stopped and actually locked the door. I grab my lecture notes, then step outside and lock the door. I jiggle it twice to be sure. Then I practically jog back to the library.

SUN GLINTS off Hawthorne's dark brown hair, bringing out the natural red highlights. Broad shoulders block the sun from hitting the book in front of him. Several female students sit nearby, gawking at him, but he doesn't glance in their direction.

I set my peace offering on his book, then sit beside him.

He looks at the white bag suspiciously. "What is this?"

"Open it."

Flicking a glance at me, he plucks the bag off his book and slowly eases it open.

I laugh. "It won't bite you."

He stares down into the bag, then reaches in and grabs the cupcake. Holding it up, he raises an eyebrow. "Why are you giving me food?"

"It's not food," I snort. "It's a double chocolate mocha cupcake from the best bakery in town... It's also a peace offering."

He stares at me, as if trying to decide whether I'm sincere or not.

"Take a bite," I urge him. The air is filled with the sweet scent of chocolate intermingled with his earthy smell. All of which smells delicious.

A small smile replaces the stoic expression. With a discreet flick of his wrist, two forks appear in his hand. "Share it with me?"

Smart man. "Only if you take the first bite. I'm dying to see the expression on your face."

He purses his lips but gives in to my request. The moment he puts the bite in his mouth, his sea-green eyes light up. Not a word passes his lips until he swallows. "This is hands down the best cupcake I've ever eaten. It's pure bliss. You're forgiven."

I watch his tongue slide across his lips to catch the lingering frosting and almost groan at the thought of how delicious he must taste. With a shake of my head, I lean in close and whisper, "There might be a teensy bit of magic in the recipe. A Fae owns the bakery." I snatch up a fork and take a bite. Flavor explodes in my mouth. *Mmm.*

A knowing look passes between us. "I'll need the address of this miraculous place."

I shake my head. "Sorry, I can't. Sworn to secrecy. Besides, this is my secret weapon. You never know when I'll need to bribe you or ask for forgiveness."

A shutter comes down over his eyes, the laughter fading away as if it never existed. He studies me for a second. "Or you could just be honest with me."

When I say nothing, he shakes his head and takes another bite. "Maybe one day." He finishes his half, then motions to the notebook in front of him. "Let's work out the final details for this project. I'd like to work on the outline for the lecture this afternoon."

This is exactly why none of my relationships has ever worked out. Who wants to date someone who can't tell them the truth? Who always hides things from them? I can't reveal myself to anybody, but especially not to a supe. It's so tiring. Maybe I can tell them some of my secrets. Not about my pact with the gods, but perhaps I can share things about me. My abilities. I need to think about it.

I paste a smile on my face and open my notebook. It takes us about an hour to finalize the details. Once we're finished, I pack everything up and make an excuse to leave. For now, it's probably best to keep things strictly professional between us. I lick my lips, catching the lingering taste of chocolate on them, and feel kind of sad I won't taste his lips on mine.

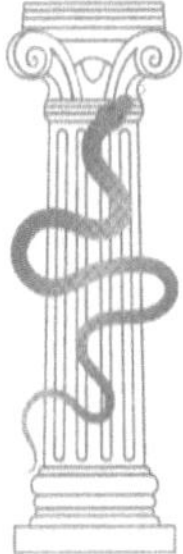

14

<u>JAMISON</u>

Everything I just told the council was half-truths. Maybe even an outright lie or two. I admitted to them that Mathias hacked into the black-market website to get the address of the abandoned warehouse where the sale was happening. True. I did not tell them that the disappearance of Phaedra Galanis prompted us to take this action. Omission.

I told them we sent Dr. Letz Samuels to purchase the key because we needed a credible buyer. I did not tell them that he was the seller. Why? Because he protected her. He could have easily conjured a portal to leave the premises, but he stayed and fought beside her. He shielded her. Hell, he died for her. That means something. What, I don't know.

All of these years, he's been an honorable man, the kind of supernatural who puts the true greater good before himself. I couldn't let his presence at the warehouse tarnish his stellar reputation. I lied.

103

Besides, there was enough truth for the council to see. Body cams on our suits revealed to the council how bloody and brutal the fight was, and it showed the horrific sight of a human stabbing straight through a mage's shield and killing him. Shock rendered them speechless, the same way it did me when I saw it in person. What is this weapon that can nullify our magic?

The video footage showed an anonymous figure in a black bodysuit dropping to Letz' side and listening to his last words. I wasn't close enough to hear. Thankfully, none of my body cams were close enough to catch Letz' last words either.

When they saw me drop to my knees beside Letz, they drilled me for information on the stranger next to me—race, magic, scents, auras—any clues that would lead them to this person, but I told them the suit blocked everything. Most of the information I gave them, such as height and build, they could see for themselves via the footage. I didn't tell them about the scent of jasmine and vanilla or the thought that crossed my mind.

Besides, if Phaedra was the buyer, she had done nothing wrong. Buying or selling an archaeological piece on the black market is against human law, not ours. Technically, neither Letz nor Phaedra did anything wrong. But then, why conceal it? More importantly, why is a group of humans willing to kill for it?

We brought several human soldiers back to the compound for interrogation, but they couldn't tell us anything. Literally could not say a word. Several opened their mouths to spill the secrets in their eyes, but nothing came out. We could only deduce they were under a mage's secrecy spell. It's the only answer that makes sense.

Humans having the ability to detect or nullify our magic always seemed like a tremendous leap forward to me. Impossible unless someone with magic helped them develop that technology.

I've always held my loyalty to the highest standards, but I just chucked it out the window and lied to the council. Not for her or Letz.

In order to take a large force to the warehouse, I had to first get the council's permission. There should have been minimal risk. Even if the humans knew about the transaction, they wouldn't have brought the number of soldiers they did. Their force rivaled ours. Men died under my watch.

Someone leaked our information to them, which means we have a traitor at the highest level. Five councilmembers knew the details. Add in the magic the humans are using...and the answer is obvious.

Before I leave the council meeting, I study each of their faces. Ancient and powerful, the leaders of our races; their stoic expressions tell me nothing, but one of them is responsible. I feel it in my gut. My father raises an arrogant eyebrow when my gaze drifts to him. All of them are capable, especially him. With a dip of my head, I drop my report on the table and promise to keep them updated.

Instead of taking the jet like I should, I open a portal to North Carolina. My vision blurs, and the world shifts on its axis, the effects of using magic to traverse the globe. I reach out to a nearby wall to steady myself. Portals are extremely efficient, but it takes a toll to go so far with one step. Thankfully, it doesn't last long. My magic begins to rebuild, giving me back my strength along with it, and I'm able to continue to the condo.

The moment I walk in, I see them waiting for me. My team. They deserve the truth. With a sigh, I grab a beer and take off my suit jacket.

"We have a traitor," I begin, telling them about the council meeting and the report I submitted. They need to know what I've put on the line.

Gatlin's face hardens. "I wondered about that myself. It

should have been a skirmish, not an all-out battle." Hands on his hips, he stares steadily at me. "You know your father could be the traitor. He's always been vocal about the need for supernaturals to own their place in this world."

I rub a hand down my face. "Yes. He's at the top of my list." It's true. In his eyes, we should be leading the world, not hiding from an inferior race. There are very few lines he wouldn't cross to protect what is his. "Is she back?"

Mathias nods. "She's at the university. Hawthorne met with her about an hour ago." Dark eyes shift to the male standing next to him.

"Do you really think Letz' mysterious friend was Phaedra?" Hawthorne asks, a troubled expression on his face. When I nod, he crosses his arms over his chest. "What is it with you and her? And don't tell me it's nothing. I dismissed your appearance at the university. Thought it was just your need to control everything, but I hear how you say her name. Then you go and lie to the council. You knew it was her on that roof."

"I met her at Hawkes House the night of the museum event," I reluctantly confide. "You're right. There's something intriguing about her. Half of me wants to know what she's hiding, but the other half doesn't give a damn. I know she's a suspect. Believe me. It's driving me crazy."

"Do you think she's involved with the humans?" he asks, a note of concern in his voice.

"No, but I don't have any proof. Call it a gut feeling. She's mixed up in this, but I haven't figured out how or why yet," I admit to him, watching the tension ease from his shoulders. "You like her, don't you?"

"She has a passion for history that rivals mine. I could talk to her for hours," he says with a puzzled expression on his face, as if he can't figure out why that makes her so attractive. I want to chuckle but don't. Despite being one of the most eligible bachelors in London, he finds most women boring, but apparently, not Phaedra.

"We need to concentrate on finding this group," Mathias interjects, with an impatient glare at us both.

When did Mathias take on my role? I sigh. He's right. "You're right. This group is meeting somewhere. Communicating with each other. Training together. I want to know where. Tap into all your resources and see what you can find. I'll quietly start investigating the council's activities. See if there have been any significant changes in their lives."

Since my father is the most likely candidate, I'll begin with him.

Gatlin jerks his chin and picks up his phone to start calling his contacts.

For the next few hours, I use a backdoor to access my father's calendar, then I double-check his attendance at those events. Most of the time, his demand for publicity proves his whereabouts, but there are a series of private meetings that I can't confirm. As his son, I know most of the afternoon meetings are code for a rendezvous with one of his lady friends. There doesn't seem to be anything out of the ordinary.

I throw down the pen I'm using and stretch. "I've got nothing so far."

Mathias shakes his head. "The council's finances are steady. With the exception of the auction, there have been no large deposits or withdrawals. Not even in their personal accounts."

I glance at Gatlin.

Gatlin slowly nods as he puts down his phone. "There's been a huge uptick in activity at a training camp in Greece. One of our counterparts said he reported it a few months ago, but when I requested the report, he couldn't find it. I checked with the records department. They have no record of it either."

I raise an eyebrow. "We should get a team over there to at least check it out. No contact. Surveillance only."

Gatlin agrees and places the call.

Hawthorne has been diving into Dr. Kline. "Kline's in trouble. Owes a serious amount of money to a bad group of supes. Word on the street is he reneged on payment," Hawthorne says, then looks up from his notes. "Have you heard from Basilisk?"

"No, and that's odd. Usually, they're on top of things, and this is something they should have found relatively quickly," I reply with a frown. Picking up the phone, I call the team lead.

"Cian," he answers.

"Jamison here. Do you have an update on Kline?"

He's silent for a second, then a loud curse fills the line. "I knew you didn't make the call. Should have listened to my gut." I hear rustling in the background. "Sorry. Had to get out of earshot. We were pulled from the investigation two days ago. Told we weren't providing security for a demon with a gambling addiction."

"Who pulled you?" I ask, furious that an order was given without my knowledge.

"Order came in via encrypted text. Official channel. No name attached," he replies in a gruff voice. "I thought it odd. You never use that channel. I did text you, but when I didn't hear back, I assumed you were out of touch, so I followed the order."

"I see," I say nonchalantly, although the implications of what he's saying is causing magic to spark from my fingertips. "You did the right thing. I was on a mission. The council must have decided on a different course. Would you mind sending me your report?"

"Will do," he replies quickly. "Call if you need anything." The tone of his voice tells me he knows something's up and is willing to help if there's trouble.

"Thanks, Cian. Appreciate it," I say, hanging up. The second I hear the dial tone, I pulse magic through the phone, instantly frying it. Then I motion to the others to give me their phones and do the same to each of them. "Mathias, can you get us new ones, please? Something a little more secure."

He immediately turns around and orders us new encrypted phones from his contact. Someone he knows isn't affiliated with the council. "He'll courier them over in an hour."

After taking a few deep breaths to calm down, I tell them what Cian said. "I never got his text, which means someone is monitoring us and interfering in our communications. Damn it!" I flick my fingers at the nearest chair, sending it flying across the room.

Mathias suddenly blurs out of the room, shouting for us to follow. Phaedra's in trouble.

15

<u>PHAEDRA</u>

Dreams hold me hostage. The past blurring into the present. I see my sister on that terrible day, see the vase shattering, and hear her scream as I grip her hands, trying to hold her to this world, but I fail, and she slips away. Letz appears, handing me a key, whispering words I don't understand before he falls dead to the floor. Screaming for them both, I sit up…and realize it's just a nightmare. Sweat coats my skin. Trembling, I sweep the hair out of my eyes and look around for the second time. I'm alone. Always alone. I need water.

When I step into the main living area, someone grabs me from behind. I stomp down hard on a black leather boot. Bone cracks, and a guttural scream escapes, but it's immediately silenced. Hands slacken, and a heavy body pushes into me from behind. I jerk away and swivel around to face my attacker.

Blood is flowing from the man's neck. He's trying to stop it, but can't, and falls to the floor, dying. Stunned, I look from him to the man next to him, holding a wicked knife. He killed his teammate before the scream could escape into the night. Brutal. I take a step back. He moves forward. My eyes dart from his face to the knife. It's similar to the one that killed Letz, but this one isn't glowing.

He tilts his head to the side and holds the knife out. It remains dark. A light bulb goes off. Somehow, it detects magic.

I chuckle. "I don't have magic, asshole."

Grabbing a kitchen towel, I flick it hard into his face, and as he rears back, I flick my wrist again, wrapping the towel around the knife, and yank. Surprisingly, he manages to hold on to it, but at least I've neutralized the sharp threat for a second. Before he can unravel it, I pull him forward and knee him hard in the groin.

He grunts, but it's not near the reaction I was expecting. What did Letz say at the museum? Five of them took on a vampire, which means their suits must be fortified somehow. *Damn it.* I swing him around and throw him into the far wall. He crashes into the plaster and falls still. I may not have magic, but I'm not exactly human either.

Laughter fills the silent room behind me. I turn until I can see the kitchen. Three more guys, dressed in matching camo, armed to the teeth, stand there laughing.

"Who decided the party was at my house?" I ask, stalling while I try to decide whether to go after the gun taped under the kitchen island or the one in my bedroom.

"It's only fair since you crashed our party last week," the man in the middle drawls.

I study him, wondering if he's the leader of this little band. He looks hard, like a career soldier, with his constantly shifting eyes and finger on the trigger. He nods to the men by his side, who immediately start tossing kitchen drawers to the ground.

How did he know it was me? I wonder.

Bedroom it is. I pivot, hoping to get there before he does. My fingertips are grazing the knob of the nightstand when a jolt of electricity catches me in the back, and I fall to the floor writhing, muscles and teeth clenched, trying to catch a breath.

The one I've dubbed the leader stands over me grinning with a taser in his hand. "That's the easy setting. Now, all we want is the key and panel. If you tell me where they are, I'll kill you quickly." He tilts his head, waiting for me to answer.

I thought the humans bought the panel, so why is he asking me about it? "Letz sold the panel. I sold the key. Made a few million too," I spit out when I can talk again. A little truth will help sell the lie. "How about an exchange? Buyer's name and you let me go. What do you say?" I pull myself up against the side of the bed within reach of the nightstand.

In answer, he jabs the taser into my forehead. "Guess you'll be going with us then. Stand up."

I slide my feet under my body, then launch upward, throwing my entire body at him. He stumbles backward but doesn't go down. *Damn, he's strong for a human.* I use the angle to slam my elbow into his temple. With a roar, he shakes his head and shoves me off, then pulls a familiar-looking knife.

"You might not be magical," he says, waving around the knife. "But you'll still bleed when I cut you." He jabs forward, and I stumble back.

I dart a glance around and spot a book on my nightstand. Snatching it up, I block his next hit, then slam the book into his face. He parries and thrusts again. The knife slides across my ribs, and I leap up and clock him in the eye with a superman cross. The bones around the outside of his eye cave in and blood seeps from a vicious tear in the corner.

He yells for help, and the other two soldiers rush into the room. "Hold this bitch down." Hand over his eye, he sways back and forth.

With him slightly incapacitated, I swivel around to deal with the two men moving in to surround me and see a third in the doorway, plaster coating his uniform, knife in hand.

"Three against one really isn't fair," I admonish them. "Let's even the odds, shall we?"

A beautiful strand of pearls comes to mind. Fifteenth century. Used by the Earl of Salisbury to choke his mistress. I place my hands on the guy nearest to me. He lurches backward, coughing and wheezing, then starts clawing at his throat. Red creeps up, covering his face. He motions frantically for his friend to help him.

Darkness starts dragging me under.

His partner closes in and jerks me away from his friend. "Stop whatever you're doing!" His eyes dart from me to the other guy, watching in horror as something invisible chokes him. "Do something! The Heimlich! Or whatever!" he screams at the other soldier.

I sway. When I remove a curse, it leaves the object and temporarily becomes mine to use. How? I'm not really sure. I rarely use them as a defense tactic because they take a lot of energy. My eyes drift to the nightstand, but it's too far away. The only weapons nearby are theirs. Letting my knees weaken, I wait until he grabs me with both hands, then pull his gun out of its holster. He immediately grabs it, wrestling for control, but I've got a firm grip. My finger caresses the trigger, but before I can shoot, I'm forced to let go to grab the meaty hand squeezing my throat.

The leader yanks me back and slams me against the wall. Hand clenched tightly, he dangles me above the floor. I kick out, but his suit is too fortified for me to make a dent. He squeezes, tighter and tighter. My throat closes, cutting off all the air.

He glances back at his men. "Did you find anything out there?" When they both say no, he motions to the room we're in. "Toss this one. I have a feeling she's telling me the truth, but we need to be sure." As they move to follow orders, he leans in and drags the knife across my cheek. "I really hope we find what we're looking for so I can gut you."

Well, damn, that's going to hurt.

I open my mouth, but his grip is too tight. He eases back, allowing me to suck in huge gulps of air. When I've filled my lungs, I give a raspy chuckle.

"It wouldn't be the first time I've died. Won't be the last. But when you die, I'll make sure to send your body to the demons. There's nothing they like more than human flesh," I promise him. It's true. Bonus, it takes care of loose ends.

Enraged, his face turns purple, and he slams my head against the wall several times, making me wish I'd saved the curse for him. My strength is rapidly declining, so I hold off on using another or striking back. Finally, he stops.

"Did that old mage tell you where to find the panel?" he roars in my face.

Another man appears in the doorway. Tall and dark, but this one isn't wearing a uniform like the other two. He blurs, and I blink. Vampire. Where did he come from? The big guy I threw into the wall earlier disappears in a blur.

His friend shouts and follows them out of the room.

The leader jerks me off the wall. Using my body as a shield, he holds the knife to my throat while he marches us into the living room.

"Let her go," a furious, familiar voice orders from across the room.

I look up. Jamison wears a thunderous expression on his face, and his hands swirl in a pattern, magic forming between them. Next to him is Hawthorne, whose hands are also raised in attack. Behind the two of them…is Gatlin, the shifter from the gym. I glance at the vampire fighting the other two soldiers. Another lightbulb moment. This must be Jamison's team. Wonderful.

"Catch," Jamison spits out.

Catch what? Seconds later, mage magic, biting and cold, rips me from the soldier's grip and flings me toward Hawthorne, where his Elven magic, soothing and earthy, wraps around me like a cloak.

Cradled in his arms, I turn to watch Jamison conjure magical spears to pin the man to the wall. A stream of magic wraps around the knife, taking it from him. The guy swears loudly, then looks at me, but the words he intends to say never leave his mouth. When it's obvious he can't speak, Jamison uses his magic to shove the knife into his heart.

Brutal. I smile in satisfaction.

Gatlin heaves a sigh and brushes past us. "Mathias, stop playing with them." He grabs one of the soldier's heads in his large hands and twists hard, dropping him to the floor, his neck broken.

"Efficient," I murmur, impressed by his method.

Hawthorne sets me on the island, and I see anger in the clenched line of his jaw. Strong fingers grip my chin and pull my head higher. Magic cascades down my neck, healing the torn muscles and bruising instantly. "I would have healed." I don't tell him that the sheer amount of magic in the room is helping me heal considerably faster than I would have on my own. Whether it's a curse or not, my body absorbs magic. But I can only manipulate curses not magic itself.

He studies me, searching for answers, but I can't give him what he seeks.

Mathias whips out a long, thin blade and slices the throat of the man in front of him. I raise an eyebrow, and my focus turns to the fourth member of this team. The epitome of a vampire. Everything about him is mesmerizing and dark. Eyes filled with shadows and framed with glasses. Styled hair, a pure, silky black. High cheekbones and a square-cut jaw. Rich brown skin. Tall and lean but with broad shoulders thrown back in perfect posture. Stunning.

Jamison bends down to go through the pockets of the soldiers on the floor.

"There's another one in the bedroom," I inform him, my voice clear again thanks to Hawthorne.

Gatlin disappears into the bedroom and reappears moments later, the dead soldier thrown over his shoulder. His gaze is speculative. "This one died from strangulation, but I didn't see a weapon nearby." Tossing him into the pile, he raises a sharp eyebrow at me.

Silence is my answer.

Mathias walks by to grab the man in the kitchen. "This one's throat is cut."

I point to the big guy on the floor with his neck broken. "He killed him."

Once they've pulled anything of interest from their pockets, Jamison uses mage fire to burn the bodies to ash, then Hawthorne's clean wind sweeps them out the patio door. Now that they're taken care of, all four turn toward me.

I clear my throat. "Thanks. I wasn't sure I'd make it out of this battle without dying at least once."

Nobody smiles at my statement. Tough crowd.

I hop off the island and walk over to the vampire. "Hello, handsome. I'm Phaedra. You are?" Supernaturals are known for their good looks, but the four of them together are a potent sight.

Obsidian eyes dart to Jamison, then return to me. He dips his head in acknowledgement. "Mathias." His hand clasps mine briefly, and he frowns.

A man of few words.

"Hmm. Well, this is awkward. What happens now?" I glance at Jamison when I ask the question. "Obviously, this is your team. And given how fast you came to my rescue tonight, I assume I've been under surveillance?" When in doubt, play possum.

Jamison stalks forward, his eyes tracing over my body. "You're lucky we did. This group has killed more supes in the last few weeks than humans have killed in the last fifty years. The fact that you're alive tells me they didn't get what they were looking for." He pauses for me to say something, but I simply lift a shoulder. "A key, perhaps?"

I remain silent, not really wanting to lie to him.

"We can always search the footage," he taunts me.

"He lied to the council for you," Hawthorne interjects, a look of disapproval on his face. "The least you could do is answer his questions."

Jamison scowls at Hawthorne. "I told you I had other reasons."

Shock renders me speechless. Jamison lives to serve the council. "What did you lie about?"

"Seeing you on the roof." Gatlin jumps into the conversation. "He knew it was you. The only reason we didn't kill you was because of Letz. He protected you. Saved you. Jamison respected Letz more than his own father. If he gave his life for you, he thought you were worth it."

I flick my gaze back to Jamison. "You knew it was me?" He nods. "And you didn't tell the council? What about the images at the press conference?"

"Body cams," he replies gruffly. "I didn't lie to the council for *you*. Or at least, it's not the only reason." He glares at Hawthorne and Gatlin. "As far as I'm concerned, you didn't break our laws. Neither did Letz. It's not a crime to sell or buy a human artifact. But somebody high up is working with these humans, which means we have a traitor. Until I know who it is, I'm *withholding some* information from the council." His blue eyes assess me for a second. "Did these goons say anything to you?"

I didn't break any laws by buying the key. Stealing from the collection is probably a crime against the vampires, but no one really cares about those items. "They're searching for the key and a panel."

Jamison straightens when I say panel. "What kind of panel?"

I shrug. "Letz didn't give me a panel." It's not as if I can tell Jamison that Hephaestus sent me a vision.

He pulls out his phone and taps on it. "No, but there was one listed in the catalog." Flipping it around, he shows me the screen. "It says a panel was sent to Dr. Kline, but when we got there, he denied knowing anything about it."

I scan the image. Blue with gold. Certainly looks like one of the panels in my vision. Sia's death must have caused Letz to panic. "Letz said there was a panel found with the key, but he sold it. To the humans."

Jamison's brows crash down. "The same group? Then why are they here asking you about it?"

"That's what I was wondering."

16

JAMISON

"Pack a bag. You're going with us to see Kline," I order her, then turn my attention to Mathias. "Can you see if the phones have been delivered?"

I can feel her staring at me, arms crossed over her chest, trying to decide if she's going to argue or do what I told her.

"One condition," she snaps back. "Tell me how you knew it was me."

I clench my jaw, not wanting to tell her, but I can see she won't budge until I do. "Your scent is…unique." I inwardly snort at the bland description of a scent that has burrowed into my skin and captured my senses. Returning her stare, I wait for her to say something.

She slides the computer off the counter, places it in the backpack, and hands it to me. "I'll need to take this." With her head held high, she returns to the bedroom and slams the door.

With her gone, my voice hardens with fury. "They sent five

119

men after her tonight. They'll send more when the first crew doesn't return. She stays in our sight at all times. Understood?"

Gatlin narrows his eyes. "We could take her to a safe house. One of ours, not the council-sanctioned ones."

Hawthorne holds up a finger. "First, I doubt she would go. Second, we need her. If we work together, we might find out what's truly going on. If humans believe the key is important, supes will too."

We can't stop our investigation, and I refuse to leave her unprotected. "You're right. We'll go to Kline's, and based on what we find, we'll make a decision on how to proceed from there."

They all nod in agreement. While we wait for her, I take a few minutes to place a quick spell on the condo to alert me to any unwanted visitors. It's obvious the enemy easily bypassed the mechanical ones tonight.

The door behind me opens, and I turn around. Phaedra's standing in the doorway, her body encased in a black knit long-sleeve shirt and a pair of dark leather pants molded to her every curve. All woman, she's one hell of a distraction. My body tightens. She tosses her raven hair over her shoulder and gives me an irritated look, and it only makes me want her more.

Ahem. I take her bag and motion for her to follow Gatlin. "Right, let's go."

Gatlin walks down the hall and opens the door to the condo we're using, and I hear her curse. I'm tempted to smile but manage to hold back.

"We don't have much furniture," I tell her as she enters the room and sees the single dining room table and Mathias' desk. "But we'll be leaving in five."

She pulls out her phone. When she sees the expression on my face, she holds up a hand to stop me. "It's encrypted. Military-grade."

A blur swipes it from her hand, and she sighs.

Mathias holds it up. "She's good. Plus, our phones are compatible. Same encryption software so we can send secure texts and messages." He hands it back to her, and she rolls her eyes at him. He ignores her response and turns to the rest of us. "Here. Don't set these down anywhere or hand them to anyone."

The second the phone hits my palm, I call Basilisk. "It's Jamison. You don't happen to have the original footage from Kline's burglary, do you? Can you send it to me?" After he agrees, I hang up and look at Gatlin. "Transportation. We need to get there without using council resources. Do you have anyone who can assist us?"

Gatlin turns to Phaedra. "Are there any private airstrips nearby?"

"Yes, there are a few," she replies cautiously. "What size plane?"

"Light jet," Gatlin answers. "Phenom 300."

She whistles. "Only two of them can accommodate a ten-seater."

He picks up the phone. "Gatlin here. We need to borrow your plane." There's silence as he listens to the person on the phone. "Got it. Thanks." He hangs up and looks at me. "Maverick has a plane on a private airstrip not far from here. He'll even supply a pilot."

Phaedra snickers, but when I turn toward her, she simply lifts a shoulder.

Something's amused her, but I don't have time to delve into it. "Sounds good. Grab your bags." I take mine from Mathias and pick up Phaedra's. We've worked with the demon on a few occasions. He's expensive, but worth it. Plus, he keeps his mouth shut. As usual, Gatlin takes lead.

She grabs her backpack and follows me out the door with Hawthorne and Mathias in the rear. It doesn't take us long to get to the garage, then the plane. We pull up at a nearby hangar and wait for Maverick to show up with the pilot.

"Well, well, well. This is an unexpected surprise," Maverick says as he materializes in front of us, another man at his side. He eyes the four of us, then moves his gaze to Phaedra. "Charlie's your pilot. Let him check the plane before you board. You can never be too careful."

Charlie's eyes are fixed on Phaedra.

I step forward. "Is there a problem?"

Charlie raises an arrogant brow but leaves without saying anything in return.

I glance at Gatlin, and he makes the sign for "stand down."

Uneasy, I step back. Amusement flashes across Maverick's face. The atmosphere is tense as we all stand there together. Finally, a signal comes from Charlie, and Maverick motions for us to board the plane.

"Have a safe flight. I'll see you in two days." The demon's words almost sound like a warning.

Gatlin nods, then turns and ushers us up the steps. "They know each other." Keeping his voice low, he subtly points to Phaedra. "Both Maverick's and Charlie's eyes widened when they saw her with us."

"Is that why he warned us?" I ask, wondering if Phaedra owes something to the demon. "Do you think she's in trouble?"

He snorts. "Not likely. They're friends. The warning was for us."

For someone who seems to lead such a solitary existence, she certainly has interesting friends. The kind you don't want to double-cross. "Thanks."

When I get on board, I see Charlie leaning over her. She immediately waves him off. He leaves, but glares at us on his way to the cockpit.

"Everything okay?" I ask her, irritated by their closeness.

"Fine," she replies with an innocent look I don't buy for a second. "All set?"

"Someday, you'll decide to share something with me," I tell

her as I grab the seat next to her. "Are you sure you're up for this?"

Her laugh is sultry and unexpected. "For the flight or us?" For a second, she appears startled, as if she didn't expect those words to come out of her mouth.

I inhale sharply and search her blue eyes. *Both*, I think, but say nothing. The jet takes off a moment later.

Basilisk sends the footage through a few minutes after we hit cruising altitude. "Unedited version" is the title of the file. The video is different from the one I viewed previously. This one shows Sia opening the door, greeting a group of human men, and handing them a case. Unfortunately, the angle of the camera prevents us from seeing what's in it. One of the men takes the case out the door, while the others stay and ransack the place. When they pick up the Ming vase, Sia rushes to stop them, but they quickly turn on her. After she's dead, they smash the vase and leave.

"Bastards," Phaedra snarls. A few tears slip down her cheeks. "Sia wouldn't have hurt anyone, and they knew it. They were looking for an excuse."

"I'm sorry. They're definitely targeting supes," I inform her. "But I'm confused by this video. This proves that humans bought the panel. Do you think the traitor double-crossed them?"

"The group tonight knew I was the one with Letz," she tells me. "You recognized me by smell. How did they know me? I haven't figured that one out yet." Her gaze is distant as she thinks about the possible options.

"Maybe they know you too?" I murmur, hating the fact that she's their target.

She bites her lip, but shrugs. "Maybe."

"Kline seemed particularly upset that the Ming vase was shattered. Couldn't he have repaired it?" I decide to change the subject to something safer.

A tiny frown settles between her brows. "He could, but it's considerably less valuable to supernatural collectors if it's been repaired with magic," she informs me. "Do you think he was going to sell it?"

Hawthorne hears her question and leans over. "He owes money to the wrong people. I'd say it was his plan all along."

She thinks about it for a minute, then gives a troubled sigh. "Anything's possible."

Half an hour later, we land at a private airstrip close to Yale University and take the waiting SUV to Kline's house. The large blue Federal-style home sits on a traditional tree-lined street, looking like a piece of Americana. When he opens the door, I see the gun in his hand and immediately step in front of Phaedra.

Throwing up a light shield, I hold up my empty hands. "We're here to ask you a few questions. Can we come in?" Magic swirls in and out of my fingers, letting Kline know I'm prepared to defend us.

He blows out an irritated breath but allows us to enter.

Gatlin is the last to step inside and plants himself by the door.

"What's this all about?" Kline snarls, blood-red eyes darting to each of us. He stops when he sees Phaedra. "Dr. Galanis?" He finally lowers the gun.

"Hi, Doran," Phaedra says softly. "I'm sorry to hear about Sia. She was a lovely demon."

At the mention of Sia, Kline sets the gun on the hall table and falls into the chair beside it. "She died trying to save that stupid vase. It's all my fault. If only they'd taken the panel and left."

She kneels down in front of him and takes his hands in hers. Not comfortable with her so close to the gun, I step forward, but Mathias grabs my arm.

"Who gave you the panel?" she asks, keeping her voice in the same low tone.

Clever. Let him think we don't know about the deal.

"Letz added it to my container. He asked me to keep it until he could find a buyer for it. A couple of days later, he called and gave me a date and time. At first, I didn't want to do it, but he offered me the Ming vase. He knew I needed the money," Kline tells her.

She tilts her head. "Why do you need money?"

"You know my wife was human, right?" When she nods, he continues. "She was sick. Terminal illness. I took her to all the best specialists, trying to save her. It cost a fortune. The demon community banished me when I married a human, so I had to borrow money from some really bad people. In the end, the doctors couldn't save her," he explains in a shattered voice. "I didn't know what to do. Letz offered a solution. The Ming vase would have covered the debt and the accrued interest they keep piling on top."

He looks around the foyer at all of us. "Without the vase, I have no way to pay them back. My sons just lost their mother. Now, they're going to lose their father, too."

Phaedra squeezes his hand. "Here's what I'll do. Tell us everything you can about the panel, and I'll pay your debt. Okay?"

Astonished, he stares at her as if he can't believe what she's saying. "You would do that for me? Why?"

"Because you're a good man, Doran, and your kids deserve to grow up with their father. One mistake shouldn't change your future," she says, a sad expression crossing her face. "Now, what do you know?"

He reaches for the side table, and my magic whips out and grabs his wrist.

Phaedra swivels her head around in disbelief and shoots me a furious look, then turns back to Doran. "He doesn't like guns."

Kline waves a hand. "It isn't even loaded. I was getting paper from the drawer."

I almost snort. Not loaded. Some of my tension eases.

Phaedra pulls open the drawer and grabs a pencil and paper. She hands them to Kline, then takes the gun so he can use the table's surface. As he starts sketching, she places the gun behind her back and signals to us. Mathias smoothly steps over and takes it from her.

He holds up the picture he just drew. "Found with a key at The Temple of Hephaestus in 300 BCE. It's made of blue sapphire with a gold relief carved into its surface. Depiction of the Greek gods standing in a circle. Gold accents highlight the sun and other objects like Hephaestus' hammer."

Face white, she takes the sketch from him and stares down at it. "Thanks, Doran. Make the call, and I'll pay your debt on our way out."

While Kline makes the arrangements, the four of us crowd around Phaedra. "Do you know what it is?"

She shakes her head. "No, but when I held the key, I got a vision. It showed me several different panels. One looked exactly like this one."

A vision. It's the first time she's shared something important with me, and I can't help but feel grateful for that little kernel of trust. But why is she the one getting the vision?

"One group has the panel. One doesn't. Neither has the key. It's our only leverage," I remind her. "Where's the key?"

Her face goes blank. "It's safe."

Mathias takes the sketch from her. "Where do we start looking?" He passes it to Hawthorne.

"Archaeology network, old tombs, the original dig, and artifact finds from digs at similar sites," Hawthorne informs him, and she nods in agreement. He passes the paper to me.

Phaedra bites her cheek for a second, then says quietly. "I think Letz told me where to start."

Kline walks over before I can ask her to elaborate and hands over a piece of paper. "They don't want to meet, especially not with a security team from the council. This is their account number. Make the payment tonight, and they'll recall the marker." His voice breaks as he hands her the paper. "If you ever need anything, please call. I'm in your debt."

She squeezes his hand. "Thank you. Go hug your kids."

17

PHAEDRA

The money transfer goes through immediately, and we head back to the airport. Gatlin boards the plane first, and when he deems it safe, the rest of us join him. I settle in and study the image Kline drew. Six gods are depicted on the panel. Hephaestus with his hammer. Athena, easily recognizable in her helmet, with her spear in her right hand. To her left, Ares, his shield half-raised toward Hephaestus. Those two never did get along. Then, Apollo, laurel crown on his head and bow in hand, stands next to Artemis, his sister, with her own bow and arrow. Last but not least, Demeter. Gratitude overwhelms me as I trace a finger over the last god. The one who advocated for me so long ago. Why does the panel only show these six and not the twelve Olympians? Maybe one of the other panels shows the rest of them? Some of the details in the vision are hazy.

Hawthorne leans over my shoulder. "There's something in the middle."

The low timbre of his voice sends a shiver down my spine, but I force myself to focus on the sketch. "Show me."

He points to the way Athena's head is tilted, and Apollo's eyes are downcast. "It looks like they're staring down at something."

Flipping it around, I stare at it from a different angle. "I'm not sure. Maybe?" My eyes drift up to meet his, and I find myself staring into his green eyes.

He raises an eyebrow. "Where do you think we should start first?"

His use of "we" sounds better than it should. It's on the tip of my tongue to tell him about Letz and his society, but too many years of caution hold me back. "Besides the place Letz told me about, we should look up the original dig. See exactly where the archaeologist discovered the items."

He leans in closer, inhaling deeply. "At first, I thought you might be a siren. Or a succubus. But you don't smell of fire and tobacco, just the sweet, luscious scents of jasmine and vanilla. I've never smelled the combination on anyone else. What are you?"

The low, husky tone of his voice sends shivers down my spine. Jamison was telling the truth. I wonder if I smell different to everyone or just them. Nobody has ever commented on it.

Part of me is tempted to lean forward and kiss his firm lips, but the other half is amused at his attempt to seduce the answer out of me. I lean in until our lips are almost touching.

"Does that work on most women?" The husky tone of my voice conveys my interest in him. I don't mind the seduction. Just the reason behind it.

Half-lidded, he stares down at me. "Most women want to share everything about themselves." He holds up two fingers a half-inch apart. "You share little. I'm left to guess. Something I don't like to do."

Another thing we have in common. "I'm a woman. Isn't that enough?"

He chuckles. "A very smart, intriguing woman with too many secrets."

I blush at the blatant interest in his gaze, but I avoid replying by picking up the sketch again. "You know what's weird? I don't remember hearing about this discovery, and I can recall almost all of the Greek expeditions."

Brows furrow as he thinks about it. "Neither do I. And I was alive back then."

So was I. "When did you cross over?" I ask him, thinking of all the things we have in common.

"Three thousand years ago," he replies softly. "I was one of the first here. Not by choice, either. We didn't know the portals existed back then. One day, I was walking in Langit, the Elven world, enjoying the view of my land, then suddenly, I was here. I tried to step back through, but it was a one-way ticket. No matter what I did, I couldn't return."

There's a depth of sadness in his eyes that I've seen many times over the years. Crippling guilt seizes me. This is why I never tell anyone the truth.

"Did you leave someone...special behind?" I ask, breath held.

His voice lowers. "My family, but thankfully, not a mate."

I lay my hand on his. "I'm so sorry." More than he'll ever know.

His thumb rubs across the top of my hand. "Thank you."

Charlie's voice comes on the speaker. "We're landing in fifteen minutes. Seatbelts on. I don't want to be responsible for injuring the council's most illustrious security team."

I have to fight the urge to smile at Charlie's snarky comment. He's never been one to pull punches. Jamison and his team bristle at the remark, but they buckle up even when they don't need to do so.

Tuning out their discussion about where we're staying tonight, I slip my phone out and send a quick text. I need to get the small key Letz handed to me right before he died, but I sure as hell don't want to take them to the farmhouse. Unfortunately, my only other option is Maverick, who hates to lend his car to anyone. This is going to cost me.

After we land, I turn off my phone, murmur something about the restroom, and head to the back of the hangar. Gatlin's suspicious gaze follows, but I ignore him. Making excuses will only make him more wary.

As Maverick walks past me, he slips a key into my hand. "When you're done, just tell it to go home." Glee lights up his face at the chance to distract Jamison and his team. Trouble stirs his demon blood.

I walk out the back and stop dead in my tracks. Maverick didn't give me his car. He gave me Charlie's Lightning LS-218 electric motorcycle. The fastest on the market. What was he thinking? It might be quieter than a gas-powered engine, but it still roars.

Shit!

I look around, but there's no other vehicle out here. It's this one or I try to sneak away later. Cursing the devilish demon, I swing a leather leg over the bike and grab the helmet. A quick prayer and I turn the key. Not a peep. I lay my hand on the engine. Small vibrations assure me it's on. Charlie must have used magic to kill the noise.

With a grin, I lean down, release the brake, and the damn thing shoots off like a rocket. Unlike a gas motorcycle, there is no gradual increase in speed. Within two seconds, I'm at 60 mph. Ten seconds, I'm at 200. This is fantastic. I know what I'm buying myself for my birthday this year.

18

JAMISON

T know she's gone the moment she crosses the protective shield I set up around the hangar. Designed to keep our enemies at bay, my magic does nothing to stop her from leaving. Furious she put herself at risk again, I flick a glance at Mathias, who immediately moves to follow her.

He's stopped before he can get ten feet.

"She had something to take care of," Maverick informs us with a smile on his smug face. I look from his glowing red eyes to the faint black vapor surrounding us.

Blood boiling, my magic responds by swelling and pressing against his defenses. Sweat beads on his face. I flash a grim smile. He didn't expect this kind of power from me, but he should have. After all, mages pass their magic to their heirs, and the de Veres have been wielding it for centuries.

Charlie comes running out of the plane, eyes darting wildly

132

from side to side, his own magic sparking. He takes a defensive stance next to Maverick, who responds with a wink.

"It's fine. They're upset because Phaedra left," he explains in an amused voice.

Gritting my teeth, I spit out. "I'm not upset. I'm bloody pissed. Humans attacked her at home earlier tonight. Now, because of you, she's in danger again. Whether you like it or not, we're leaving. Remove the barrier."

Hawthorne and Gatlin move in closer.

Maverick's brows crash together. "She failed to mention that bit of juicy news. Still, Phaedra's been around a hell of a long time. She'll be fine. And if she needs any assistance, Charlie's bike is practically a weapon with all the spells he's put on it."

Curses spew from Charlie's mouth, and Maverick winces as he turns to face him. "I was going to tell you. I swear."

Charlie glares at him, then stalks off. "Clearly, you've got this under control."

Maverick sighs and looks at the clock. "She should be at her destination by now." The barely visible wall around us dissipates.

"Let's go," I order the team, heading toward the SUV. "She couldn't have gone too far."

"Some unsolicited advice I'm sure you'll ignore," Maverick calls out behind me. "She's been on her own for longer than you've been alive. Don't demand her trust; earn it."

The black Maserati next to us roars to life and flies out of the hangar with Charlie at the wheel. He flips Maverick the bird as the car shoots into the night.

"Fuck!" Maverick roars behind us.

If I weren't so pissed off myself, I'd smile. "Mathias, can you track her?" I get into the passenger seat.

After sliding in the back next to Hawthorne, he fiddles with his phone for a second, then shakes his head. "No, she turned off her phone."

Gatlin slides into the driver's seat. "Where to?"

"Your place," I tell him, thoughts swirling. "She won't go back to the condo. Can you check the cameras in her office and the gym?"

Mathias looks down at his phone. "I've gotten no alerts from her office." He taps and slides his finger across the phone. "She's not at the gym. Or her friend Cara's."

I hadn't realized Mathias had bugged Cara's place. Damn, he's thorough. "We've missed something." My phone rings, and I see her name. "It's her."

Hawthorne reaches around and takes my phone. "You're too angry to be civil." He hands it to Mathias. "Talk to her."

When I hear him give her Gatlin's address, I realize she's coming back to us, and it's as if a switch flips inside me. I swing from fury to relief, then back to fury. Magic sparks between my hands. Silence reigns in the vehicle, but their concern is obvious.

Besides Gatlin's surliness, the rest of us are not prone to emotional outbursts. It's why we work so well together. Cool-headed logic rules our group. But ever since I saw her on that roof with bullets flying, I've been on edge, filled with the need to wage war against our enemies. Knowing she willingly left our protection pushes me to the precipice.

What did Maverick say? Earn her trust. I don't expect Phaedra to trust us. Or to inform me of her every move. Hell, I've been half expecting her to bolt all night. So why am I so furious?

I take a deep breath and think about it. Because I don't allow anyone to threaten my team. They mean everything to me. A bond that supersedes anything else. Somehow…she's slid under my armor, become one of us. Her role undefined but there, nonetheless. The thought startles me, and some of my anger settles.

We get back to Gatlin's place, and I hop out of the vehicle. "I'm going to wait for her out here."

Gatlin grunts in disagreement but slams the door and leaves. Mathias follows him without saying a word.

Hawthorne stops beside me. "Try to remember she's not a member of our team and someone you can order around. If you do, she'll leave. For good. Phaedra's independent, and as Maverick pointed out, she's been around a long time. Be honest with her." He opens his mouth to say something else but closes it after a second.

I've noticed him watching her, trying to figure her out. Most of the time, he avoids women, except when necessary. Yet, he seeks her out. When she talks, he listens. Intently. None of us trusts anyone outside of our circle, but the fact that he just spoke up on her behalf is a huge indication of which way he's leaning.

He tilts his head to the side and gives me one last warning, then leaves me standing there alone.

Hawthorne is wrong. I don't want to order her like she's a member of the team. I want her to join us. Willingly. On mutual terms. But he's right too. She has to make that decision for herself.

19

PHAEDRA

Charlie's motorcycle cuts my commute time in half. At the farmhouse, I'm in and out in less than five, and ready to head back when I realize I don't know where I'm going. While the helmet has Bluetooth, I don't dare call Jamison from it. Who knows what kind of tracking Charlie installed on it.

Sighing, I stop the bike, pull off the helmet, and pick up my lovely encrypted phone and dial. Instead of Jamison's crisp British accent, a deliciously smooth voice answers. "Mathias."

I pull the phone away from my ear. Nope, I dialed Jamison. He must be more pissed than I thought. I'm tempted to hang up and do this on my own. Seconds go by while I sit and mull over my options. I breathe in and out a few times. Finally, I grit my teeth and ask for the address.

"Good choice," Mathias says coolly, then relays the information before hanging up.

I wipe a hand across my brow. That was a hell of a lot harder than I expected. Over the years, I've made some ironclad rules about working with others. My network supplies what I need, and I pay them for it. Clean. Easy. Limited interaction. I might wish for friends, but it's safer on my own. Lonely, but at least I'm not endangering anyone else.

This…Jamison…thing is already messy and full of everything that can go wrong. Not to mention the attraction between Hawthorne and me. All these years spent by myself, I've never felt the urge to change my ways for anyone or put my identity at risk. With them, I find myself wanting to show them who I am, share my secrets, and it's terrifying. How do I keep some distance between us?

For a second more, I contemplate disappearing. There are plenty of places to hide in the world, although they're shrinking by the decade. My hands tighten on the handles, as if rebelling against the thought, and I blow out a breath. Putting the helmet back on, I take off.

The brick industrial building is on the same street as my gym. Lights shine dimly in the early morning light. I swing a leg off the bike. "Go home." It leaves instantly. I smirk. That's a handy little spell.

When I turn around, Jamison's standing there with a blank expression on his face. Oddly enough, I don't sense any anger, and my own irritation fades. When he didn't answer the phone, it pissed me off. I knew he would be angry I left his protection, but I didn't expect him not to answer. Although I probably would have ignored his call had he done the same. Irrational, but there you go.

Throwing caution to the wind, I decide to tell him the truth. "I couldn't take you with me, and I wasn't sure you'd let me go alone."

He thrusts his hands in his pockets. "I hated that you left my protection…and I didn't think you were coming back."

The quiet words sting, but he's not wrong. Every mile back to town, I thought about turning around and going home. "It's easier on my own. Not just for me, but for you and your team too. Doing this together, it's bound to be…"

"Complicated," he says, completing the sentence. "I know. I prefer order. Things packed neatly in boxes and tied with a bow. But from the moment we met, my life hasn't conformed to my normal rules. You don't fit in any box. Instead, you're an enticing enigma who makes me question things I've known my whole life." He frowns, as if he finds the thought upsetting. "Maybe it would be best if we part ways."

The words slam into me, and my heart literally stops in my chest, making me forget to breathe. I stare down at my feet instead of at him and force myself to look at this objectively. He's right. I inhale sharply. Seriously. What am I doing? Jamison works for the fucking council. The absolute worst choice for someone who needs to stay off their radar. And if they knew he was working with a representative of the gods, he would lose everything.

"I agree," I reply in a near whisper, lifting my head to stare at him. I wait for him to say something, but when he doesn't, I know it's for the best.

Numb, I walk away. My feet carry me mindlessly down the block, but when I reach the corner, I stop, unsure of where I should go. The condo isn't safe. The farmhouse is too far away. That only leaves the gym. I peer down the street and see the familiar sign shining like a beacon.

I lift a foot, then put it down. I glance at the curb. There's nothing stopping me from stepping off. Yet, I stand here completely frozen. Bright streaks light up the sky. Sunrise. A new day. The sun's rays hit me, and I raise my face, expecting to feel their warmth. Instead, all I feel is him watching me. The same prickling awareness I feel whenever I'm around him. Why is he still here? I turn around.

Fists clenched, he stands in the middle of the sidewalk, staring at me. His aristocratic good looks are carved in stone, but his fierce blue eyes are full of storm and magic.

As if they're on autopilot, my feet start moving and not once do they falter. Step after step, I walk until I'm standing directly in front of him, searching his face.

"Do you really want me to go?"

A muscle tics in his jaw. "It's not up to me." The words are dragged out of him, as if he hates the very flavor of them.

Ahh. He's giving me a choice. And the decision is easier to make than I expect it to be. It comes down to one overriding thought. "I want to stay." As I say the words, the enormity of this moment hits, and it scares the hell out of me. I'm choosing not to be alone. I'm choosing not to do this on my own. I'm choosing to stay with them. Whatever that means.

He takes a deep breath and steps closer. "I want you to stay." Gravel coats his voice as if he has a hard time saying them too.

Panic flares. "This doesn't mean I'll share all my secrets," I warn him. "And I make no promises for the future." Two statements that sound simple but have caused havoc in all my relationships.

He tilts his head to the side and gives me a long look of consideration. "Understood, but if you can't tell me the truth, don't lie." His eyes narrow. "And don't betray us or the gods themselves won't be able to save you."

Not exactly true, but the promise in his eyes tells me he would be a ruthless enemy.

"As to the other..." He shrugs. "Not all of us are immortal. Let the future take care of itself." As a mage, he must feel the press of time compared to the others, but he shrugs it off as if it has no bearing on the way he lives his life.

I can live with those rules. Raising up on my toes, I place my lips against his in a sensuous, but brief kiss. "Deal." His breath mingles with mine, and I hover there, waiting for his next move.

His eyes darken, and his hand lifts and slides around the back of my neck. Head tilting, his lips claim mine, deepening the kiss, eliminating the spaces between us and taking control until I'm surrounded by him. This is the kiss I've been waiting for all my lonely life. A statement of intent with a tinge of possessiveness.

From the moment we met, I've been attracted to this man and the danger he represents, but I never thought he would be more than a passing fling until now. This kiss pulls at the emotions I keep hidden from the world. The wants and needs I tell myself I can't have and certainly don't deserve. I pull away and lean back, needing to see what's in his eyes.

Blue eyes stare down at me, the earlier storm of anger and resistance replaced with desire and acceptance. I wonder if he sees the same in my eyes.

Satisfaction crosses his face, but all he does is motion to the building. "Let's find the others. We have a lot of planning to do."

When I move forward, his hand is at my back, reassuring and steady. Opening the door to a small apartment, we find the rest of his team waiting for us. Hawthorne's standing by the balcony door, staring out at the city. Mathias is on the computer, but I see his hands pause, telling me he's aware of our every move. Gatlin slows his pacing.

All of them turn to face us, their gazes locked on us. A spark flares in Hawthorne's eyes. Gatlin's mouth is a flat line of anger. Mathias' expression is completely blank.

I stiffen, unsure if I'm the cause.

After a second, Gatlin's fury spills over. "They sent a second team to her condo. Trashed it. As far as we can tell, they didn't find anything." Fists clenched, he stands there waiting to take on the world.

I shrug. I knew they'd come for their comrades. Instead of getting upset, I reach out and pat Gatlin on the arm. "Of course, they didn't. I wouldn't leave anything of value in there. It's a place to sleep."

Jamison frowns. "That's odd. I set up a magical alert, but it never pinged me."

Gatlin goes rigid. "That is fucking odd."

"Only another mage could dismantle my spell," Jamison spits out, his own anger rising at the thought. "Who, though? One of my father's lackeys?"

"It doesn't matter," I tell them. "Their attention will soon turn from the condo to us."

All four of them turn to me, and I hold up the small key. "Letz gave me two keys that night. The ancient key I bought from him and this one."

"What does it unlock?" Jamison asks, looking closer at it. "Is it a house key?"

Mathias holds out his hand. "May I?"

"So formal," I murmur, teasing him a little. "Here."

Lightly running his thumb over the dips and valleys, I can practically see the wheels turning in his brain. "It's thinner than a house key. Safety deposit box?"

"Correct," I reply. He holds the key out, and I take it. "Ever hear of C. Hoare?"

Only Jamison nods. "C. Hoare & Co is one of the oldest private banks in England."

"You got it. I've banked with them myself in the past. Very discreet," I confirm. "Letz passed along the key and box number. He also gave me a password. Further instructions are in the box."

This is where it gets a bit tricky. I want to share the parts of me that I can without revealing the full truth. "Letz belonged to a society of supernaturals whose sole purpose was to find cursed objects and remove the danger from them. To protect both supes and humans." I bite the inside of my cheek for a second, wondering how to tell them. "I've been doing similar work for a long time. Apparently, they've been searching for me. To join them, I think. He made me promise to find them because they have the answers to some of our questions." I watch their reaction.

Hawthorne's face fills with interest. "A secret society that neutralizes dangerous artifacts?" When I nod, he lifts a shoulder. "I've never heard a whisper. How long have they been around?"

"It started with Letz and two others about a thousand years ago," I inform him, telling them the same story Letz told me, but without my part in it.

"And how long have you been doing this same work?" Hawthorne asks, a speculative look in his eyes.

"A lot longer," I reply, but hold up a hand when he opens his mouth. "My age is not something I share with anyone." It might be too easy to connect the dots, especially for someone with his knowledge of history.

He chuckles, but if anything, the interest in his eyes flares brighter. "So, are we going to London?"

Gatlin's expression becomes fierce. "Does that mean I have to call Maverick again?"

Jamison snorts. "Hell no. There's no need to hide our actions from the council. We're returning to London to file our weekly report." He turns to me. "With a secret passenger, of course."

20

Mathias slides into the seat beside me on the plane. Incredibly handsome and impeccably dressed in a black button-down shirt and pressed slacks, he exudes sophistication. If it weren't for his glasses, I'd be a bit intimidated by his demeanor, but the latter lends him an almost nerdy vibe. A divine smell wraps around me, and I subtly inhale. Vampires have no magic and, therefore, no scent, but whatever cologne he's wearing is seductive.

He's the quietest of the group, and I can't help but wonder if he resents me being here. Not that he has said much to me. The only times I've been around him are in my condo when he slit the throat of my intruder without an ounce of remorse or when he's lost to the computer he commands with such speed.

Which is the real Mathias? The ruthless adversary or sophisticated tech genius? By all standards, he's unusual for a vampire. Most of the ones I've met seem kind of cold. He radiates a quiet confidence that comes across in his loyalty and dedication to the team.

He sets his laptop on the table in front of us. "Do you want to see footage of the last break-in at your condo? I must warn you. Their search caused a lot of damage." His dark eyes flicker with concern.

I couldn't care less about the damage, but I do want to get to know Mathias a little better, so I nod. He presses play, and I watch them destroy the beautiful condo. "There's nothing of value in there, but I hate that they've done so much damage."

"Do you recognize any of the faces?" he asks, tapping on one face in particular. "How about this guy?" When I shake my head, he flashes a dangerous smile. "He was one of my attackers at the museum. At the time, the cameras couldn't get a clear enough shot of their faces, but I remember him. Pretty soon, I'll have all his information."

The cold satisfaction in his voice makes my toes curl. A predator stalking his prey. "Let me know if you need help." My words seem to surprise him, and his gaze drifts from the computer to me. The corner of his mouth lifts.

"Who's the girl in the locket?" I ask softly.

For a brief moment, he stiffens, but then he reaches into his pocket and pulls it out to show me her picture. "My daughter. She's still in Kallias. The vampire world," he explains with an anguished expression on his face. "Our king asked for volunteers to enter the portal, find out what's on the other side, and report back to him. I never thought I wouldn't be able to return." One elegant finger strokes softly across his daughter's face.

There have been so many stories like his. Guilt tightens my throat, but I force myself to continue. "I'm sorry to hear about your daughter. How old is she?"

He smiles. "She was around three hundred years old when the painting in the locket was completed. A little over two thousand years old now. Vampires in my world don't become adults until they're at least five hundred."

Wow. The girl in the locket with her dark curls and deep blue eyes appears to be around ten years old in the picture. "What's her name?"

His dark eyes study me before he replies. "Calla."

"That's a beautiful name," I tell him, wanting to know more but afraid he'll be able to read the guilt on my face. Still, I press on. "Tell me about her."

His eyes light up. "You really want to hear?"

I can see how badly he wants to talk about her. "I do."

He shifts his attention from the video to me. "She got her mother's blue eyes. It's unusual for a vampire to have anything but brown eyes, so when she was born, I knew she was special. Her laughter was my favorite sound in the world. And her favorite thing to do was ride her beloved Shigari, Safro." I frown, and he elaborates. "They're similar to the horses in this world, but they're much, much faster."

"Vampire fast?" I ask, exhilarated by the thought.

A gleam of satisfaction shines in his eyes. "Exactly. She was fearless and mischievous. Always pushing boundaries. Doing stuff I'd forbidden her to do." He lifts a shoulder and flashes a smile. "I could never stay mad at her, though."

"And her mother? Was she your…wife? Mate?"

His smile dims. "She was a friend. Her name was Sybil. Calla was a happy accident for us both. Unfortunately, she passed when Calla was around a hundred."

His leaving left his daughter an orphan. I take a deep breath and clear my throat. "I'm sorry." Those are the only words I have for him.

He falls silent, lost in the memories of the past. A second later, his dark eyes meet mine. "Sorry. I miss my daughter so much. I can't help but wonder what she's like now."

Guilt pierces my heart at his anguish, and I lay my hand on

his. "I understand. My sister... she...disappeared when I was a teenager. I think about her every day. It's hard to live without them, isn't it?" It's been a long time since I spoke to anyone about my sister.

Not wanting him to ask any questions I can't answer, I quickly steer the conversation in a different direction. "How did the locket get into Westgate's collection?" It seems odd that he would give such a treasured item to that psycho.

Black eyes darken with fury. "Westgate, self-appointed leader of the vampires, didn't offer his help for free. A vampire could exchange something of value or a hundred years of service. Only then would he help us acclimatize to this world. I refused to give him my life, so I parted with the only thing I valued in this world."

"A hundred years of service," I state, keeping my voice neutral and my envy tamped down. Sometimes I wish my sentence had a limit. But with all this time, I still haven't found a way to save my sister, so it doesn't really matter how many years go by.

Mathias closes the locket with a snap. "It infuriated me. In our world, he had no power, but because he was one of the first here, and exceedingly ruthless, he climbed his way to the top. Ruled over our entire race as if he were our king." He snarls, and the hair on my arm stands up.

This is the first glimpse I've seen of the turmoil beneath his calm exterior.

He stops when he notices my reaction. "Sorry, I didn't mean to scare you." He briefly closes his eyes to gain his equilibrium. When he opens them, they're studiously blank. "Did you want to watch any more of the video?"

I'm the one who should be saying sorry. Instead, I shake my head. "No, I think—" Leaning closer, I see something strange in the paused video. I point to the patio door. "What is that?"

He blinks and turns to face the laptop. "What?"

"Can you rewind? Then, forward frame by frame," I ask, sure I saw something reflected in the glass. I lean in. There. "Stop."

He taps a few buttons to magnify the image. Light bounces off the glass, and for a second, it shines on the person standing in front of it. "Can you make it clearer?"

Fingers dance as he tries to clean it up. "It's a mage spell. It makes the cameras skip and obscure their image." He finally stops. "That's the best one we'll get."

Wavy lines blur most of the image. "There." I point to the pair of brown shoes reflected in the patio door. "He must have forgotten to obscure his feet."

Mathias captures the image and saves it. "Those aren't the boots of a soldier, which means he's someone higher. They really want that key. Are you sure it's in a safe place?"

"The safest place I know," I tell him. In fact, when I grabbed the key to the safe deposit box, I moved the other one to a more secure location. While the vault walls appear to be seamless, there are a few surprises built into them.

"Thank you for asking about my daughter," he says with a warm smile. "I love talking about her."

He pauses and looks from me to Jamison and back. "All four of us know what it's like to be alone in this world. Unable or unwilling to ask for more. To reach out to another. Jamison made us into a team, trusting we would find our way, and we did." He closes the laptop. "Sometimes the fates place us exactly where we're supposed to be."

After delivering his message, he leaves me sitting there, thinking about him and our conversation. Do I dare find what I want in this life, or will the gods continue to punish me? In all these years, not once did I ask them for more.

Eventually, I drift off to sleep, only waking as we begin our descent into London. "Where are we staying?" I ask Gatlin, who's sitting across the aisle, studying me.

Big arms stretch high above his head. "My place. Lord de

Vere has Jamison's house under constant guard. Mathias lives like a vagabond, rarely settling in one location for long. The press regularly follows Hawthorne." Folding his massive arms across his chest, he stares steadily at me.

"Why is the press so interested in Hawthorne?" I ask.

His scowl disappears, and he gives me a strange look. "He's royalty." When my eyebrows rise, he elaborates further. "Brother to the Elven king. Most supes know this."

The weight of his scrutiny is intense. I'll have to watch what I say around him. "I see. Guess I'm not up-to-date on who's who."

"It shouldn't matter here, but Hawthorne says the Elves like to cling to the old world," he explains. "They see him as a symbol of prestige."

Poor Hawthorne. I shudder thinking of all those eyes on him, watching his every move. Royalty isn't all it's cracked up to be.

Without thinking, I stare at Gatlin, wondering what type of shifter he is. He screams predator, and because of his size and golden eyes, I immediately think of a lion, but he isn't the least bit friendly. Cara's family is full of cats, and they all want to rub up against me. I can't imagine Gatlin wanting to do something so playful.

Although with his body, a woman would probably give a lot to rub up against him. I lick my suddenly dry lips. "What did you think of Cara?" I force myself to ask. He gives me a lazy shrug. "She's incredibly cool. Has a huge family that's wonderful. Smart. Owns the gym. Fantastic friend."

He stiffens. "I only joined the gym to keep an eye on you, not to flirt with your friend." His gaze turns dismissive. "We'll be landing soon." With those words, he gets up and moves to the back of the plane.

A minute later, Jamison joins me. "When we land, we're splitting up. You'll go with Gatlin and Mathias. Hawthorne is going to run a few errands. I'm going to make my report to the council."

"What are you going to tell them?" I ask tentatively.

The silver coin I saw the first night appears in his hand. "I'm going to tell them about the panel, but I'm not going to reveal the image Kline gave us. I'll tell them about your place getting ransacked, but explain you were gone when it happened. Maybe you can send a message to your department head telling her you need time off?"

"I have a flexible arrangement with the university," I inform him. "As long as the university continues to receive artifacts and endowments, I can come and go."

He slides the coin in and out of his fingers. "Gatlin has a lead on a training camp in Greece. I doubt it's our enemies' camp, but it doesn't hurt to have a team check it out. Plus, it will assure the council that we're investigating every lead."

"You're worried," I say, watching his hands. "Why?"

"The council will try to label you as their prime suspect, and I'm not sure I can stop them. Right now, they need to divert the public's attention away from the human group. A single person is less of a threat, and your anonymity will likely play against you," he explains, a deep line between his brows.

Sliding my hand over his, I carefully pluck the coin from his fingers. "We all have our roles to play. You lead the council's security forces, and if you don't do your job, they'll become suspicious of you. Label you a traitor." I carefully slide the coin into his palm and place mine over the top of his. "We both knew this wouldn't be easy. You'll find a way to protect us all."

His jaw firms as he stares down at our hands. "You're from there, aren't you? Ancient Greece."

"I lived there," I reluctantly admit, giving him as much information as I can without lying. With the tip of my finger, I circle the ring he's wearing. This is the first time I've seen it on him since the night we met. "Do you know your ring is cursed?"

A mocking smile twists his face. "Yes. Several of my ancestors gifted me with their magic instead of my father. So, he had this ring made to suppress mine. It took me a while to figure out why I felt so powerful whenever I took it off and muted the rest of the time. I only wear it around him."

Appalled, I stare at him. "That's diabolical. Do you want me to remove the curse?"

He chuckles. "One day. Only because I actually like the ring." He plays lightly with my fingers. "I appreciate the offer, but I can deal with my father."

I wink at him. "So can I." It would be a pleasure, too. Let him see how it feels to have a curse laid against him.

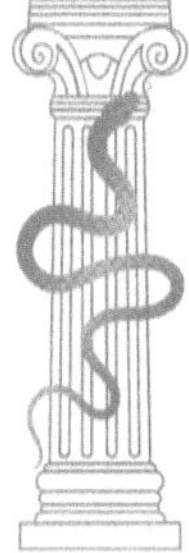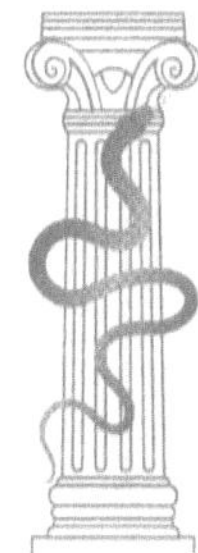

21

PHAEDRA

Hawthorne and Jamison leave the jet together. After a quick perimeter sweep, Gatlin pulls the second SUV close to the plane for me to hop in. It takes thirty minutes to reach his home in the heart of London. I'm not sure what I expected, but it isn't the industrial-looking brick building sitting in front of us. With its massive windows encased in a startlingly cobalt blue color, Gatlin's home stands out from its mundane neighbors.

My surprise must be apparent because when I catch Gatlin's gaze in the rearview mirror, there's the slightest hint of satisfaction in his eyes. When I wink at him, his expression immediately slides into its usual scowl.

Intrigued by the exterior, I hop out of the vehicle and follow him into his home. The brown brick extends to the interior walls, but the bright blue casing is gone.

From the light wood floors to the white beams in the ceiling, the bright and airy interior has been completely renovated. Patio doors at one end of the long living room lead out to an extensive balcony. From beyond the railing, I see a small courtyard.

I turn toward the other end of the room and gasp. The large windows I saw on the exterior frame the living room from floor to ceiling, extending the view from the inside to the outside. Light pours through their wide openings, drenching the room in the warmth of the sun and bringing an open and peaceful feeling to the space.

I slowly walk around the room, admiring how the tan and white furnishings continue the airy theme. White wooden bookshelves stand tall against the brick and are full of worn books, framed pictures, and small mementos. I lean in to study a snapshot of a younger Gatlin standing in front of a pyramid in Egypt with a broad smile on his face. The carefree expression looks good on him, better than his usual permanent scowl.

Feeling a presence behind me, I swivel around. "You should smile more often."

Gatlin is leaning silently against the wall watching me. He shakes his head. "That was a long time ago."

That's too bad. "Your home is stunning. Did you design everything?"

He snorts. "Hardly. It used to be a warehouse. A famous artist in the seventies converted it."

I wait for him to say something more, but he only stares steadily at me. Is he trying to figure me out or waiting for me to steal something?

Mathias glances up from the laptop where he's buried his head since we arrived. "Sorry, Phaedra. I should have asked sooner. Would you like something to eat or drink?"

My lips part in surprise at the sound of my name on his lips. Maybe he's right, and I should reach out more. Our conversation earlier has eased things between us. I wink at him. "Thank you. That would be lovely. What a gracious host you are."

Gatlin glares at Mathias and pushes past me to head to what I presume is the kitchen.

Mathias chuckles. "It's taken me a few decades, but I swear he has manners."

"Ha. Ha," Gatlin snarls at Mathias as he returns with a glass of ice water. "I hope this is okay. I'll order some groceries and get you something better."

I take the glass and smile. "Water is perfect, thanks." After taking several sips, I find a coaster and set the drink down. "I'd love a tour." His home has been the biggest surprise with its reflection of warmth and spaciousness. The polar opposite of the intense man across from me. I want to see more.

Gatlin gathers his hair and puts it into a bun, making him look much more relaxed. "Living room. Dining." He waves his hand from one end of the room to the other. "The kitchen is this way."

I laugh at his brusque demeanor but then realize I would probably be the same if he came to the farmhouse. It's my sanctuary. What would I do if I suddenly had a visitor?

"I'm sorry you had to bring me here," I offer as we step into the kitchen. "I expected you to live in a bachelor pad, not this wonderful home. It took me by surprise. But I get it. It's your sanctuary. I'll try not to disturb you too much."

Surprise crosses his face. "It's fine. I'll get used to you." He stops. "Sorry. I mean..." He blows out a huge breath. "I'm not used to anyone but the four of us."

I don't know what to say. I like being around them, but I don't want to cause any trouble. Maybe I should call Mercer and ask for a room somewhere. Thinking about it, I lean against the counter and look around at the kitchen.

White cabinets and walls continue the aesthetic from the living room, but with the butcher block counters and a slightly distressed medium-toned island, there is an overall cozy feeling to it.

The deep, rich countertops are full of nicks and scratches. I run my hand over the grooves. "You cook?"

"I do," he confirms. "Ready to continue?"

Mathias walks in with a troubled expression on his face and stops between the two of us. "Jamison needs me to bring our surveillance footage to the council's headquarters. They claim it's to see the faces of our enemy, but I suspect they want to confirm you didn't use any magic during the attack." His dark gaze falls on me.

They're trying to figure out which supernatural race I belong to. "But I kind of did." When he looks confused, I motion to the laptop in his hand. "Can you bring up the attack?"

He sets it down on the coffee table and pulls up the video. "Is there a certain part?"

"I assume you had cameras in my bedroom?" I ask. I can't help the irritated glare that crosses my face when I think about him watching, but I shove it down and take a seat beside him on the couch.

His blank expression says nothing, but I can see the glint in his eyes. "Yes."

His fingers move rapidly on the keyboard. "This is the camera you want."

I peer at the screen and see myself sleeping peacefully. I squirm a little but continue watching. Suddenly, I go from sleeping to sitting up in the blink of an eye.

"Did you hear them enter?" Gatlin asks gruffly.

"Bad dreams," I reply, a blush creeping across my cheeks.

"I've got plenty of those," Gatlin mutters in return.

A warm fuzzy feeling wraps around me at his attempt to make me feel less embarrassed. I reach over and hit fast forward until I see me dash back into the bedroom with the soldier following, my sudden halt, my back arching, and then me dropping to the ground. Thank the goddess, there is no sound.

Gatlin presses stop. "What the fuck?"

"Taser," I tell him, brushing his finger off the keyboard. I press fast forward again, but Gatlin stops it and presses play to watch the fight.

He hums when I snatch the book up from the nightstand to defend myself against the knife, which turns into a grunt when I clock the guy with my superman cross. "Nice move."

Rolling my eyes, I point to the screen. "It's coming up." The video plays for the next few minutes, showing the three other soldiers entering, and then it leads into me touching the soldier and him choking to death. I stop the video. "There."

Before Gatlin can reach out again, Mathias pushes his hand away and takes over. He rewinds the scene and plays it again and again. "I don't get it. I don't see any magic. Did you poison him?"

I look from Mathias' obsidian eyes to Gatlin's golden ones. "No, I used a curse on him." Sucking in my bottom lip, I wait for them to catch up.

Gatlin whistles, but Mathias tilts his head, a puzzled expression in his eyes. "I don't sense magic in you. How did you curse him?"

"Technically, it's not my magic. When I remove a curse from an object, I sort of absorb it and it temporarily becomes mine to use," I explain, watching his expression.

"Temporarily?" he asks sharply.

"I can only use it once," I hesitantly tell him.

I've never told anyone about what I can do. I'm not sure if the gods know. They're obviously aware of my ability to change or remove a curse from an object, because they gave me those powers but not this one. This evolved over time.

Mathias asks where this curse came from, and I tell him about the fifteenth-century strand of pearls. His eyes widen, but he suddenly becomes angry. "Why did you only use this ability once during the attack? Why not hit them with more curses?"

Feeling vulnerable, I lift a shoulder. "My access to them is sort of…limited." I'd rather he think my power is inconsistent than tell him it weakens me to use it. "Which is why I developed one hell of a right cross." I wink at Gatlin, but he's back to scowling at me.

Rolling my eyes, I point to the screen. "What do you think the council will do when they see this?" My brow puckers. The last thing I need is for them to change my status from suspect to threat.

Mathias stares at me. "Anything unknown becomes a threat. If they can't identify or control you, they'll try to eliminate you."

Gatlin curses and starts pacing around the room. "Fix it."

Mathias throws him a fierce glare. "I plan to. Give me a second." His fingers tap lightly on the keyboard as he thinks about the situation. "I might have something that could work." His fingers fly across the board, faster than I can comprehend, until they're nothing but a blur. He slides through his files, opening the ones he wants, extracting and copying, then he closes them. This continues for at least thirty minutes.

Gatlin continues to silently pace, his gaze flicking between me and Mathias.

Mathias stops and holds up a finger. Gatlin moves behind us to watch. I lean forward, eager to see what he did.

Mathias presses play, and I watch the entire thing again.

My brow furrows. "I don't see anything different."

"Look closer," he tells me.

This time, I watch it frame by frame. There. "I touch his neck?"

"Actually, your ring touches his neck," he says with a slow smile. When neither Gatlin nor I says anything, he heaves a sigh. "Your ring, full of poison, touches his neck."

Ohhh. I play it again. This time, I can see the flash of gold on the dark screen. Clever. "Where did you get the footage?"

"We have tons of surveillance from various jobs," he reveals. "I simply spliced a few seconds from one video and pasted it into this one." He plays it one more time, examining each frame, then with a nod, he snaps the lid shut. "This will work."

I hope so, or this is going to get ugly pretty fast. "So, what's next?"

Mathias stands. "I'll take this to the council and show them that you didn't use magic. Right now, they suspect you're a shifter or hybrid." He stares at me. "That was what we put in our first reports. Anyway, they only see those who can wield magic as a threat. If they think you don't have any, they'll dismiss you."

"Thank you," I tell him, placing my hand on his arm. "It means a lot that you would protect me."

He looks down at my hand with an unreadable expression. "Jamison vouched for you. If the council thinks you're a threat, they might start to wonder why he covered for you and whether his loyalty to them has changed."

His matter-of-fact explanation sends chills down my spine and drives the point home. Whether we like it or not, we're all tied together now.

22

<u>PHAEDRA</u>

J ust when I think I'm getting comfortable with my choice to stay, the doubts start to pile up again. I shove my hand in my pocket and finger the gold key inside. It would be so easy to slip away and do this on my own. Safer for everyone else too.

Gatlin steps up beside me. "Still want a tour?" His gruff voice is softer than usual, and when I look up at him, there's a warmth to his golden eyes that wasn't there previously.

I hesitantly nod. "Sure."

He stares at me for a second, then grasps my hand in his. "There's not much more." His muttered sentence makes me wonder if he's talking to me or reassuring himself.

I stifle the laugh rising inside me.

At the top of the stairs, he waves a hand. "Three guest bedrooms with en suites."

I pull my hand from his and wander from one to the other.

Each one is beautifully appointed and almost identical to the others. Four bedrooms. A lot of space for one person. When I return to the hallway, I notice the double doors at the end of the hall and glance at Gatlin with a raised eyebrow. He gives me a curt nod, but there's tension in his shoulders that makes me pause.

"I'm good," I inform him, ignoring the doors and walking over to him.

He stares into my eyes for a second, then walks over and flings the doors open. "It's a room. That's it." Standing at the threshold, he waits for me to join him.

I slowly walk past him and into the room. Unlike the rest of the home, this room is full of dark earthy colors and masculine tones. The deep brown paint drenching the walls and ceiling lends a dramatic appearance to the room that is only lightened by the sky outside the large floor to ceiling windows.

Heavy velvet drapes hang on each side as if waiting to shut out the world. Dark tufted leather chairs surround a massive fireplace, and overstuffed bookcases line the wall beside it. Unlike the neat shelves in the living room, these ones have books shoved into every nook and cranny.

I drift over to study their spines. *Flight in the Modern Age. Myths and Legends. Auto Repair. War Strategies.* There are a lot of books on war tactics and weapons, but that's the only consistent theme. Most of the topics vary across the large collection. Worn spines tell me they've all been read, some several times.

My gaze finds his, trying to see past the gruff exterior to the layers underneath, but his expression remains blank as if he's unwilling to let me in. Instead of deterring me, though, it makes me more curious.

Knowing it isn't what he wants, I move past him to the rest of the room. The massive four-poster bed on the far wall catches my eye. Pillows and blankets are piled high in its center, and large velvet drapes are tied haphazardly to each post. It resembles a luxurious nest. I silently groan as the image of him lounging in that bed pops into my head. The man obviously likes his creature comforts.

Slamming doors intrude on my naughty thoughts.

He rushes past me to the window and looks out, then swears loudly. "We've got company." Hurrying to the bookcase, he trips a hidden lever, and it silently swings open, revealing a small room full of weapons.

Curious, I walk over to the window. Familiar men in camoflauge are pouring from several SUVs. "How the hell did they find us?"

Instead of answering, he slams a cartridge into a 9mm pistol. "Do you have a preference?" He waves a hand toward the wall of guns in front of him.

I quickly scan the choices. "I'll take the Glocks. Think they're around back too?" While he prepares our weapons, I run to one of the guest bedrooms to check and find men pouring into the small yard. I return to him.

Taking the guns and extra cartridges from him, I slide the ammunition in my back pockets and grip a Glock in each hand. "We're surrounded. Tell me there's another way out of here."

He grunts. "Several. Do you have the key?" When I nod, he motions with his hand. "Follow me." The sound of glass shattering below us makes his jaw clench in fury. "They're going to fucking pay for that." Stalking off, he strides to the staircase and peers down the stairs.

Smoke rises from the flash bombs. Holding my breath, I move to take a position on the other side, but he stops me and jerks his head toward the second set of stairs behind us. I shake my head. His jaw tightens, but before he can say anything, he raises his arm and shoots the man coming up the stairs. A barrage of fire is returned, and we both duck down behind the wall.

I point back and forth between him and me, silently telling

him we're in this together. He glares at me in return, but I refuse to leave without him. The gunfire continues for another minute, and his scowl gets darker and darker. He knows we have to leave. His gaze flicks to mine, and he gives me a curt nod.

I mimic walking up the stairs with my fingers, and he jerks his head. The gunfire ceases for a second, and he crawls to the bottom step, then points up. Staying out of sight, I slide over to him.

He mouths "roof," and I nod and take the stairs halfway up. Once I'm in the middle, I turn and raise my guns to provide him with cover as he follows me. We continue to frog leap each other until we reach the door at the top.

Instead of reaching for the knob, he taps on the keypad next to the doorframe. The sound of metal gates closing surprises me. Gunfire erupts, but it's the ding of bullets ricocheting off metal that carries up the stairs.

"This should trap them in the house for a few minutes."

I wince. "I'm sorry. I can see how much you love this place."

His eyes glow golden in the dark. "It's a house. It can be rebuilt." He punches in a code, and the door opens. "Go. I'm right behind you."

A bullet hits the doorframe above his head. A ferocious expression crosses his face, and he swiftly turns and kills the shooter. He takes a step down, but I grab onto his arm.

"We're both going, or we're both staying," I remind him, knowing he's dying to take this battle to them.

Knowing they likely heard me, he swears and shoves me through the door, but he follows close behind and slams it shut.

Hands on his hips, he glares at me. "I was only going to send a message."

Too busy scouring for the exit, I roll my eyes. "How the hell are we going to get off this roof? Is there a secret tunnel? A rope nearby?"

Bullets hit the door behind him, and I flinch, but he doesn't turn around. "It's bulletproof." He looks up at the sky. "You're a good flyer, right?"

My eyes dart from one corner of the large roof to the other. "I don't see a helicopter. Or a hang glider. And I sure as hell don't have wings." Shouting comes from the ground below us. "We don't have much time."

"Good thing I've got wings," he informs me with an arrogant smirk, handing me his phone. "It's been a long time since I carried anyone else, but all you have to do is hang on and carry my phone. Can you do that?"

I stare at him and realize I never did figure out his animal. Dread fills me. "What kind of shifter are you?"

Broad shoulders straighten with pride. "Gryphon. Big one." A bullet pings off the lip of the roof. "You ready?"

Fuck, fuck, fuck. I thought gryphons were extinct? Why didn't I ask him sooner? "Wait." I pace back and forth. "If I fall, promise me you'll pick up my body." Or what's left of it.

I cringe. It's not like I'll die forever, but damn, falling would totally suck. The landing would be the worst part, but it would be over in an instant, right? Poof. Dead. While I'm contemplating the worst-case scenario, he begins changing.

Talons appear first, razor sharp with huge claws that could shred me in seconds. My eyes widen, then I look up and see golden eyes staring menacingly down at me. Mesmerized, I find myself staring back even as I internally scream at myself to look away. For the first time in ages, fear makes me freeze.

When his back half begins to change, I tear my gaze from his and watch him half shift into the paws and body of a lion. He finishes, and I study the point where his body changes from lion to eagle. It's almost seamless. Brown feathers meet brown fur over a cluster of massive muscles.

"Am I supposed to climb up?" The tremor in my voice tells him how I feel about this idea.

A shrill sound emits from his beak, and he extends a wing toward me.

In three thousand years, I thought I'd seen and done it all. A hysterical laugh escapes as I flip the safeties on and shove the guns into my waistband. I guess not. Aware of the urgency, I grab onto the feathered appendage and crawl up to his neck, then straddle him. "I'm on." My voice is barely a whisper.

Bullets pierce the air around me. Some of the shots go wide, making me wonder if they're even aiming at us. Muffled sounds follow. His body shudders as it takes a few hits. He launches into the air like a rocket, high in the sky with me clinging to him in sheer terror. Pausing for a second, we peer down at the small army surrounding his house. There must be thirty men outside. Plus, however many inside.

They really want this fucking key.

He banks sharply, and I bury my face in his neck. The spicy scents of myrrh and juniper fill my senses, reminding me of the Middle East. Shifters have scents, but they vary based on their origin or the type of animal inside them. In human form, the juniper comes across but not the myrrh. Interesting.

Gripping his stiff feathers tightly, I wait until he levels off before I open them again and see all of London spread out below us. *Shit!* Supernaturals aren't supposed to show themselves to humans. How are we going to hide this?

A few minutes later, he sets us down in a nearby park. Not one person looks over at us. Puzzled, I slide carefully down his wing and peer at their faces. They return my gaze, but every time one of them tries to look in his direction, their gazes skip and move on.

He silently changes form while I keep watch. As he finishes, he groans and falls to one knee.

I swivel around and see holes and blood all over his golden body. He turns his backside toward me, and even as I hurry toward him, I can't help but admire every hard line and hollow stamped into his golden skin. A part of me wishes he would turn around so I could see the other half of his magnificent body.

Clearing my throat, I gesture to the wound on the back of his thigh. "Do we need to find a doctor?"

Pain strains his deep voice. "If you can find me some clothes, I'll work on healing myself." Reaching back, he grips his thigh, and I watch as the muscles contract to get rid of the bullet. He pushes it out through the entry hole, and it closes a few seconds later.

He throws me a sharp glance. "Clothes?" He pauses. "My phone too."

"Right. I'll be back. In a second. With clothes," I stammer like an idiot after handing him his phone. Pivoting, I shake my head to clear the vision of him in all his glory.

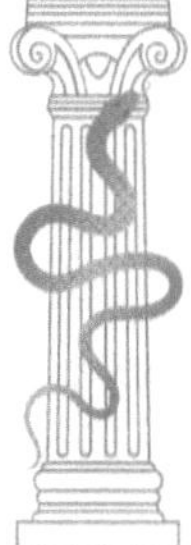

23

GATLIN

Sluggish from the toll of healing, I rest my back against the trunk of a tree while I wait for her to return. "Too fucking close. I barely got us out of there. They had a small army with them. Has to be a council member. Nobody else knows where we live."

He knows I'm pissed, but I don't tell him it was worth it. It's been ages since I've flown with a rider, sharing the skies and wind with someone else. In the old days, gryphons had riders assigned to them, and I miss it.

Jamison softly curses on the other end, bringing my attention back to the call. "Can't talk right now. Location?"

Phaedra strides into view, hair mussed from the ride, with a white plastic bag in her hand. Her long legs eat up the sidewalk as her head swivels to find me. "Hyde Park."

"Seven," Jamison murmurs into the phone. "Keep her safe." He hangs up.

Her blue eyes are dark with worry as she strides up to me. "Here." She thrusts the bag into my hands as well as one of the guns she's still carrying. For a brief second, her worried eyes scan my naked body, but when she realizes I'm okay, she mutters something and turns her back to me.

I smirk. Shifters don't have much modesty. Although if she'd stared longer, my reaction would have been hard to conceal. Reaching into the bag, I pull out a XXXL white t-shirt with a bright red double-decker bus on it, a pair of loose cotton pants, and canvas shoes. I wince. "Guess the park wasn't the best landing place."

She laughs and tucks a piece of hair behind her delicate ear. "Sorry. No military shops nearby. You'll look like a tourist, which isn't a bad thing." She stops talking when a couple strolls by staring at me with wide eyes. "When you're in your other form, they don't see you, do they? I thought it was odd when nobody started screaming bloody hell at the sight of a giant gryphon landing in the park."

"Gryphons were created by the Magi in ancient Persia," I explain to her while I dress. "We served at their command. They gifted us with invisibility so we could carry out our duties. It's only viable in our shifter form, though."

"Wow. Ancient Persia. No wonder you're cranky and bossy," she murmurs with a sort of reverence. "So, you didn't come through a portal like other shifters?"

"I was here long before most humans," I gruffly admit. The years weigh on me heavily. Never thought I'd be alive this long. "You can turn around."

She swivels to face me, and her face scrunches up as she tries to hold her laughter in. Sputtering, she nods several times, then manages to get a few words out. "That is one massive bus." Laughter bursts out of her as she stares at my broad chest.

Huffing in irritation, I wait for her to find control. When she continues to laugh, I can't help but roll my eyes at her amusement. Taking her hand in mine, I head toward the park exit, stopping only to purchase a flat cap to shove on my head. It won't hide my hair but will help shield my face from the cameras.

"Did you know your gryphon smells like juniper and myrrh?" She muses with a side glance toward me. "In human form, though, I can only detect the juniper."

I tear my gaze from the map on my phone to give her an incredulous look, barely resisting the urge to sniff myself. "What does that have to do with anything?"

She lifts a shoulder, but her cheeks flush. "Nothing. Never mind." Her gaze sweeps past me to the sidewalk in front of us. "I turned off my phone. You should too."

Keeping her hand in mine, I veer north toward "seven"—the seventh safe house on our private list. It's about twenty minutes away, but I haven't been there and need to doublecheck the GPS. "I don't know exactly where we're going, and I can't conjure a portal."

After a few minutes, she tugs me to a stop. "I need water and a burner."

Suspicious, I shake my head. "We need to keep going."

Her right eyebrow rises. Jerking her hand from mine, she backs up a few steps. "Fine. I'll meet you at the bank in two days."

Furious, I step into her space. "You've got a whole fucking army after you. There's no way in hell you're going anywhere without me." I lightly tap her chest with my finger. "You're not dying on my watch. Got it?"

She brushes my finger away and pivots away from me. "Don't be so melodramatic. The leak is on your side. Nobody knows my contacts or safe houses. Besides…you're not exactly inconspicuous. I'm sure every camera in the city has picked you up. It's only a matter of time before they swoop in and grab us."

My jaw locks for a second, then I scoff. "I'm sure we're both on their radar. You think you can disappear without them noticing?" In disbelief, I watch as she keeps walking. Striding up beside her, I grab her elbow.

She raises her narrowed gaze to mine. "Yes. All I need is a phone."

I thought my place was damn near impenetrable. Maybe she's right. I'm burned. With only the two weapons, we need to find somewhere that isn't known to anyone who works for the council, including our group.

"Fine," I grudgingly concede as I motion to the convenience store behind her. "They have burners."

She pats my arm. "I knew you'd see reason." With a jaunty smile, she heads into the store while I stand there gritting my teeth.

Most females would be hysterical with everything that's been thrown at them. She acts like it's an everyday occurrence. Not that I'm complaining. It's just…unusual.

A minute later, she returns with a couple of waters and a burner. I gulp down my water in seconds. Healing burns a lot of calories and makes me incredibly dehydrated. "Where did you get the money?"

She pats her pocket. "I learned a long time ago to carry an untraceable credit card, some cash, and anything valuable on my body, not in a bag. It's saved me more times than I can count."

She holds up a finger and moves closer to the building, then dials the phone. "SOS. Corner of…" Her eyes swivel to me, and she raises an eyebrow.

"Oxford and Duke," I supply with a smirk. Maybe I'm useful after all.

She repeats my words and hangs up a second later. "One minute."

I snort, not believing anyone will be here in a minute. We

can't use portals in the middle of London where a human might see it.

"You'd better be right. We're sitting ducks, standing here on a busy street. And I'm a walking billboard for London's double-deckers." With a grimace, I glance down at my clothes.

Uneasy with waiting, I subtly move to shield her from the passersby, but she quickly shoves at my back with her small hand.

"Move, or we'll miss it, and I'm dreading it enough as it is. I don't want to have to wait for the next one," she practically snarls at me. "Not to mention, she'll double her already outrageous fee."

Surprised, I shift to the side in curiosity. Her eyes are darting from one corner to the other. Suddenly, the phone in her hand buzzes, and she moves onto the sidewalk.

"There," she motions with her head. "Follow in my exact footsteps. Do not deviate."

Irritated at her orders, I bite the snarl at the tip of my tongue and do what she says. With complete confidence, she strides toward the street. Cars and buses are whizzing by at top speed. A few bicycles careen around the corner. I reach out to grab her and pull her back to safety, but between one second and the next, she disappears. Astonished, I stop and scan the area.

A trembling hand appears in front of me and grabs my shirt, yanking me toward the street. It's only then that I realize it's a portal. As I pass through, I stare at the barely seen wavering edge. Remarkable. There's little to separate it from the real world. If she hadn't guided me, I would have missed it. I've never seen one so transparent.

When we step through, we're in another part of London. Shoreditch. Almost thirty minutes from where we entered. From there, she pulls me through another nearly transparent portal, but instead of a street this time, we step into a bustling office of some sort. Marble floors grace the entryway. A receptionist sits behind a large mahogany desk, greeting visitors. Blank walls give no indication as to where we are. The portal closes behind us. Unease skates down my spine. I don't like it.

"Stay here," she murmurs to me. "I mean it. They're not your friends." With those words, she strides off toward one of the hallways. "I'll be back in two minutes."

My fists clench. I don't have the faintest clue where I am, but if she doesn't come back in exactly two minutes, I'll tear this place apart to get to her. I'm responsible for her safety, and I'll be damned if I let anyone prevent me from doing my job. The receptionist at the desk eyes me with a dark look, as if he knows exactly who I am and what I'm thinking and he's relishing the idea of putting me in my place. I meet his gaze with a clear warning.

He raises a cool eyebrow, and I take a step forward, but before I can say something, Phaedra emerges from the back.

"Next time," he promises, and a snarl rips from my throat.

Phaedra cocks a hip and rolls her eyes. "Stand down. A fight between a dragon and a gryphon would be a hell of a match, but not today. I don't have time for this bullshit."

Dragon, huh? No wonder he wouldn't back down. A worthy opponent indeed. A fleeting expression of respect crosses his face.

Phaedra pivots and heads toward the entrance, where another portal opens. This one is much more visible, and familiar, than the previous two. "Let's go."

She disappears, and I hurry to catch up with her. This is getting tiring, and my patience is wearing thin. It's almost like she's protecting me. *Damn it.*

This time, we land in the lobby of a hotel. Wait. The rich chocolate brown walls, gold accents, and white marble floors are unmistakable. "Is this The Hari?"

She smiles. "They keep a suite of rooms for those who need

extra privacy. I like to stay here when I come to town." She gets on the elevator. "Coming?"

With a frown, I cross my arms, refusing to step into the box. "Hotels have cameras everywhere. They'll find us in minutes." I smirk. "Plus, if you're a regular…" I leave the statement hanging.

She snorts. "I'm not in London often, so I doubt they'll detect a pattern. Besides, it's the safest place in the city." When I give her a skeptical glance, she continues. "This is a special wing with private entrances, advanced tech, and a myriad of protection spells. Nasty ones. Trust me." At the sight of my raised eyebrow or maybe it's the expression on my face, her lips compress. "Fine. Don't trust me. Your choice. Quite frankly, I'm tired. I need a shower, and this is where I'm staying."

I get into the elevator. "You'd better be right."

24

PHAEDRA

This is killing him. Face set, arms crossed, he stands stiffly just inside the door as if death is waiting to greet him instead of a luxurious suite in the poshest of hotels. I stifle the laugh in my throat. Honestly, he's done better than I expected. From what I gather, he takes his security role very seriously, and giving up control to a…suspicious… Ahem… unknown supernatural who hasn't proven her loyalty is pure torture.

The doors open to reveal an elegant foyer and sitting room. In creams and deep browns, the room exudes a quiet luxury that makes me want to sink into the plump sofa with a sigh. Every piece of furniture is designed with a sophisticated eye. There's nothing traditional or stuffy about this hotel. The bank of windows, flanked by thick curtains, allows copious amounts of sunlight into the room. Sumptuous fabrics and wood floors give hints of warmth and coziness.

I take a step forward, but his arm stops me.

"Let me at least make sure it's secure," he growls, drawing the weapon I gave him earlier.

I motion for him to proceed and lean against the elevator door to keep it open. Roughly thirty seconds later, he returns and gives me a curt nod.

"All clear," he informs me, watching as I walk into the room, letting the elevator doors close behind me.

"Thanks for checking," I tell him, meaning it. He's right. I should always check. The tension eases a bit from his shoulders.

On the small table in the sitting room are a bottle of wine, some chocolates, and a familiar cream and gold envelope. I pull out the card. "Our concierge's name is Sheraton. The room is soundproof. Make any calls you want but use the burner. The hotel phone is only for the concierge. I'm going to grab a shower."

His golden eyes flick to me, and he mumbles something about taking the first watch.

Leaving him to explore the security of the suite by himself, I head into the bathroom and shut the door. My eyes close, and I slump against the door. I hate taking portals. If it had just been me, I would have found a disguise that worked and slipped through the labyrinth of London's city streets until I made it to one of Mercer's safe houses and disappeared, but that wasn't possible when toting around a beast of a man with flowing white-blond locks. A flat cap can't conceal that gorgeous hair.

Pushing away from the door, I strip down and step into the white marble tiled shower. Water set to nuclear, I lavish the most extravagant body wash across my body and let the heat and water work their magic. Soon, steam rises along with notes of bluebell and wild strawberry. I close my eyes, inhaling and exhaling until the tension in my shoulders eases. Then I wash and condition my hair until it's as soft and sweet smelling as the rest of me.

Once out, I slip into the monogrammed robe and comb out my hair, then smooth on the body lotion. Now that I'm relaxed, all I can think about is getting something to eat. I walk into the living room.

He swivels around the second I enter the room. For a big guy, he moves quickly.

"I'm going to order some food. Do you want anything?" I ask him, picking up the hotel phone.

His eyes scan me from head to toe. "Steak—rare, potatoes. Please," he gruffly replies.

I push the single button on the phone.

"Concierge, how may I be of assistance?" asks the smooth voice on the other end.

"Hello, Sheraton, I'd like to order the steak, rare, with potatoes, a BLT on toasted sourdough, and several bottles of water," I tell him. He confirms the order, then I add on one last request. "Can you also send up a selection of menswear, including shoes? Larger sizes, please. And clothes for myself too. My sizes are on file. Thank you." I hang up.

He grimaces. "What? You don't like my style? The double-decker buses are all the rage."

My lips twitch. "Could be worse. You could have been traversing London naked." The image of his buff golden body, stalking through the streets, slips into my mind. "Although I'm not sure anyone but you would have minded."

He smirks. "Wouldn't bother me." Then he lifts a shoulder. "Although I wish I'd strapped on some more weapons before I left."

"Mmm, I do feel naked when I'm not carrying," I admit with a smirk. His golden eyes flare the tiniest bit. "Quite frankly, you barely flinched when I dragged you into an unknown portal."

The corners of his eyes tighten. "Next time, warn me." He crosses his arms. "What was that place? How did I not know about it? I've lived in London for centuries."

"I'm not surprised. They don't cater to the council or its representatives. Harlequin's part of the underground," I inform him. "They offer a myriad of services to supes in need… Provided they can pay the price, of course. Mercer, a friend of sorts, runs one of their divisions."

Harlequin vets potential clients for years before they give them access to their headquarters to make sure they aren't associated with the council. Very few clients have seen the location we stopped at today. I've only been there a handful of times. Mercer was not happy I'd brought Gatlin there, but I didn't really have a choice. The elevator chimes, and I move toward it.

Gatlin tosses me a vicious scowl.

"Go for it," I tell him with a shake of my head as he stalks over, gun in hand. I should give him a break. He's been pushed out of his usual comfort zone today. Plus, he did watch the enemy destroy his house.

The elevator doors slide open, and the concierge's wide smile fades the second he sees the massive male standing in front of him. "Good afternoon. I'm Sheraton, the concierge. I've brought up your request. Where would you like me to place the food and clothes?"

"You can place the tray here," I tell him, motioning to the small table by the window where the bottle of wine sits. "Clothes in the bedroom."

Gatlin sniffs the air, then stiffens. "Wolf?"

A tiny bit of arrogance crosses the man's face, and he lifts his chin. "Yes. The Sharma pack owns the hotel." He pushes the cart past Gatlin and grabs the tray of food. After placing the dishes and cutlery on the table, he rolls the rack of clothes and shoes into the bedroom. "Will that be all?"

"Yes, thank you, Sheraton," I say with a smile. When the doors close, I stalk over and glare up at him. "If you want to be rude and grumpy, go do it somewhere else. The Hari is one of my favorite places to stay in London, and I won't have your suspicious nature ruining it for me. Got it?"

He gives me an incredulous look, then glances down at the finger jabbed into his chest. "My job is protecting this team, and I'll do whatever I damn well think is best for your safety." His eyes lock on mine. Reaching up, he takes my finger from his chest and captures it in his warm hand.

My eyes narrow, but I refuse to give him any satisfaction by jerking my hand from his. As the battle of wills continues, his body heat stretches across the space between us, making me flush.

"Didn't anyone ever teach you not to poke the bear?" he practically snarls.

I snort. "Didn't anyone teach you not to get between a woman and her food?" When he continues to hold me close, I flick a stiletto out of my other sleeve and press it to his neck. My heart races as the tension builds between us. "We can become quite bloodthirsty when we're hangry."

He blinks in surprise, then a wide smile appears. "I was beginning to worry you had zero self-preservation. Nice little blade you got there." Golden eyes begin to glow. "I don't think you realize how tough a gryphon's skin can be."

The skin beneath the stiletto hardens until it's almost impenetrable. I move the blade to somewhere more vulnerable and much further south and stare up at him, a challenge in my eyes. "Does that apply everywhere?"

His voice is husky when he steps closer. "Careful. I like to play too."

My eyes widen at his innuendo, and a delicious shiver cascades down my spine. An image of his golden body covering mine makes me swallow. It's been too long since I indulged myself, but my attraction to two of his team members already complicates things.

He must read the answer on my face because he slowly releases my hand. "Hungry?"

The stiletto disappears into the sleeve of my robe. "Starving." Yet, I find myself unable to move away from the golden gleam in his eyes.

He leans in close and breathes in. "You smell a hell of a lot better than the wolf."

"Another reason I like The Hari," I warn him, forcing myself to step away from his mesmerizing eyes and walk over to the table. "You'd better eat before your steak gets cold." I sit down and pick up my BLT and bring it to my lips. His eyes track my every move.

Seconds later, he prowls over and takes the seat across from me. After eating a few bites, he tilts his head. "Harlequin underground. Mysterious friends. The Hari. What other secrets are you hiding?"

I chuckle. "Those aren't my secrets. I'm their client. There isn't much in this world gold can't buy."

He nods in agreement, but the air is thick with undercurrents.

We eat in silence for a few minutes.

"Look. You and your team know more about me than the rest of the world. More than I've shared in centuries, in fact," I offer, extending an olive branch.

"Which is very little," he scoffs. "Why are you so evasive?"

"Why are you so nosy?" I counter, exasperated by his questioning.

He shrugs. "You'll have to ask the Magi. It's ingrained in me. Along with a lot of other traits they deemed necessary, like the role of protector."

Hmm. Never thought about it from that angle.

"I never realized there were supernaturals here before the portals opened," I admit to him. "Are there others?"

"Magic has existed since the dawn of time. Some humans were born with it. Demigods, of course. But regular humans too. The first were called The Magi, but over time, other names cropped up. Sorceress. Wizard. Witch. Eventually, the various names combined into one—mage." He pauses, then his gaze turns speculative.

For a long second, he studies me. "In ancient times, some humans received powers as a gift or a curse." He pauses. "That's it, isn't it? Your 'gift' comes from the gods. It's why you don't smell like any other supernatural race."

I immediately hide my reaction. *Well, shit.* This took a turn I probably shouldn't have allowed. Very few believe in the gods and even fewer believe they're still around. Of course, I would get stuck in a hotel with an ancient shifter. His sharp gaze remains focused entirely on me, waiting for the answer he already knows.

Tired of the secrets and years of isolation, I cave a little. "I wasn't born with magic." It's the only way I can answer without openly admitting my powers were given to me by the gods. I snort. They weren't exactly a gift. Just a lesser punishment.

His eyes sweep the room around us as if looking for them. "I'm guessing you can't talk about it?"

I finish my sandwich and meet his gaze, a clear message in my eyes. "I should have ordered dessert."

He dips his chin. "Right." He takes a bite of potatoes, his eyes narrowed in thought.

"I called Mathias while you were in the shower. He's already presented the video to the council, but he's waiting for Jamison to finish. Apparently, they aren't happy with us." He scoffs. "I'm not too fucking happy with them either."

"How long have you worked for the council?" I ask tentatively, well aware I've evaded most of his questions.

"The Magi took the side of the supernaturals when the portals opened," he replies with a faraway look in his eyes. "My service transitioned from them to the council, and I've been with them ever since." He sighs heavily. "Maybe I'm overdue for a change."

"I know how you feel," I tell him, laying my hand on his. "Unfortunately, change isn't always an option." Even if the gods would allow me to "resign," I wouldn't. The cost is too high. I'd never find my sister.

The pity in his eyes is a bit too much for me.

"It sounds like Jamison and Mathias will be a while?"

Once he confirms, I stand and put the dishes on the cart for Sheraton to pick up. "I'm going to take a nap."

He adds his plate to the pile. "Do you mind if I grab a shower?"

"Go ahead. It won't bother me," I assure him, adjusting the robe. "Let me put on some clothes first."

As he takes the cart to the elevator, I slip into the bedroom and grab the matching lounge set off the hanging rack. Another reason I like to stay here. They always remember guest preferences. Comfy now, I return to the table.

"All done."

He's hesitates for a second, then moves toward the bedroom. "Don't open the fucking elevator door to anyone. Not even the wolf. Got it?"

My lips twitch, but when he turns to see if I'm listening, I hold up three fingers. "Scout's honor." When he continues to stare at me, I say the words he needs to hear. "I promise I won't let anyone in."

His chin dips in a curt nod, and he turns toward the bedroom, pulling off that hideous shirt along the way.

Golden skin and an ocean of muscles are the last things I see. *Damn, that man's body is perfection.*

He stops at the door, glances back, and cheekily winks.

I'm so surprised I snort at the sight. Embarrassed, I whip around and grab the bottle of wine and a glass, then plop down on the couch to pour myself a drink. I'm not a damn teenager with her first crush. A hazy image of a young man in a chiton, muscles on display, pops into my head. Relieved to know I still remember him, I sigh. Time is a warped path in my mind. Sometimes the years slip by at lightning speed; other times they drag on.

Seriously, though. When was the last time I found one male interesting, much less... two? Maybe three? A long while. At least a century. Most of the time, a night or two is enough before I'm ready to move on. Maybe it's because I haven't slept with any of them. Possible. Or perhaps it's because I'm enjoying being with them. *Temporarily, of course*, I remind myself. It's not as if this can go on forever. Even if I wish it would.

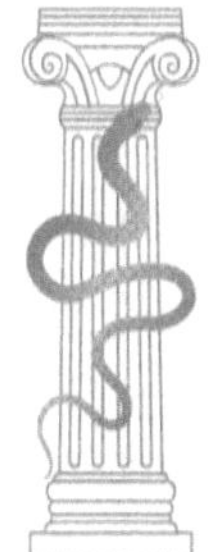

25

JAMISON

Years of my father's narcissistic tantrums have prepared me well for this job. Smooth expression on my face, I wait for the council to stop shouting at each other and come to a consensus. This is a common occurrence for them. The only thing they used to agree on is the need to take whatever steps are necessary to prevent our exposure to the humans and the return of the gods. Now, I'm not so sure.

Mathias sits beside me, his ramrod posture the only indication of his thoughts.

"They'll wrap up in a minute," I assure him.

He absolutely hates politics. When Nolan was on the council, Mathias avoided these meetings like the plague. His feelings haven't changed, although they have yet to appoint the new vampire councilmember.

Mathias showed them a video of Phaedra poisoning her victim with a ring. Proof of her lack of magic. The council was arguing over how to spin this to the supernatural society. Daegan, the dragon shifter, and Virilin, the Fae representative, feel we should be transparent and honest about her lack of magic and subsequent threat status, but my father and Osian, the Elven representative, want to continue using Phaedra as the scapegoat. Kratos, the demon representative, is playing devil's advocate right now and has yet to choose.

Unfortunately, I had to reveal Phaedra as the buyer of the key, but I added information about the attack in her apartment to prove she isn't working with the human group. Mathias' video confirmed the attack and seems to suggest a human heritage, but my father isn't buying it. He knows Letz' wouldn't have hired a human as an expert to assist him with the Nolan Westgate collection, but unfortunately for him, he can't prove it.

When he mentioned meeting her, the council asked him what race she belonged to, but he couldn't definitively answer. Her scent of jasmine and vanilla suggested Elven heritage to him, but Osian adamantly insisted she wasn't one of his. They asked me, and I truthfully told them I didn't smell a hint of magic on her.

My father came to the conclusion she was a shifter as he knows it's impossible for Daegan to know every shifter in our universe. Crafty Daegan decided to use that comment in his favor to state his protection of Phaedra until he could meet with her. From that moment on, it escalated into the current shouting match.

When my phone rings and I see it's Gatlin, I frown. He wouldn't call me when I'm at a council meeting unless it's an emergency. Picking it up, I'm surprised to hear his furious voice telling me about the attack at his house. Cold fury ices my veins. Our addresses are only known to the council. Nobody else. Relieved to know they're both safe, I hang up and glare at the council.

"Gatlin's house was just attacked," I tell them, slamming my hands on the table in front of me. Mathias flicks his gaze to me, a question in their depths, and I give him a quick nod to let him know they're okay.

The council turns to me in shock, unused to seeing me lose my cool.

"The five of you are the only ones who know our addresses. Coincidentally, you're also the only individuals who knew the number of soldiers we planned to take to the warehouse that night." I pause to let the weight of my words sink in, then drive the nail in the coffin. "Someone on this council is working with the humans."

Several chins lift in defiance, but they picked the wrong person to head security if they think I'll let this slide. "Until I know who it is, my plans will remain top secret. You'll be given updates, but I'll determine when and what. Now, if you'll excuse me, I have to check on my team."

Sharp pinpricks cascade across my back as I walk out of the room, Mathias by my side. After this is over, they'll undoubtedly ask for my resignation, but right now, they need me, and they know it. Hopefully, the thought of a traitor in their midst will make them reticent to share information with each other. To find the traitor, I need to start pinpointing who knows what.

My phone vibrates the second we're in the SUV, and I raise it to see an unknown number. "Hello."

"It's me," Gatlin says, his voice strained as if he's at his wit's end. "We took a detour."

"Are you safe?"

Amused, I listen to him rant about portals and The Hari and Phaedra's unorthodox methods.

"Where is she now?" I ask, careful not to give too much away. Our driver was vetted, but only for his loyalty to the council, not to me.

"In the shower," he retorts in a gruff voice. "Get here as soon as you can."

My lips twitch, but I manage to hold in my chuckle until after I hang up. When Mathias raises an eyebrow, I silently tell him I'll explain later.

I ask the driver to drop us off at Claiborne's, another supernatural club, but unlike Hawkes House, this one is frequented by everyone, not just the elite. From there, we slip out the back and into a portal, then hop across London a couple of times to make sure we're not followed. Hawthorne's waiting for us at the rendezvous point.

Unwilling to say anything in public, I remove my signet and conjure an invisibility cloak for the short distance to The Hari. It's not a spell I use often because it drains me, but we need to stay off the council's radar. A tough thing to do in a city wired with cameras. I should know. I've used the system enough times to catch supes.

We walk through the revolving door at The Hari and find ourselves immediately surrounded by a team of shifters.

Releasing the invisibility spell, I hold up my hands. "I'm here to see a guest."

A tall, dark-haired man steps forward. "My name is Amir, the ultimate authority here at The Hari. We have very few guests who arrive...as incognito as you. Who do you wish to visit?"

There's a menacing air about the man I don't wish to provoke. I motion him closer and murmur her name. "Phaedra Galanis."

Not a flicker crosses his face. "I'll check the registry." He motions for security to stay and walks over to an old-fashioned phone and presses a button. Listening only, he nods once and hangs up. "Follow me."

Impressed, I step in behind him, my magic ready, but he merely leads us to another wing where a solitary elevator waits with the doors wide open.

"This is Sheraton," he says, introducing me to the young man standing inside. "He'll escort you the rest of the way." With those words, he walks off, taking his security team with him.

Hawthorne whistles. "This is some setup." His green eyes scan the walls as he steps inside. "No magic in the elevator?"

His announcement brings a slight smirk to the young man's face. "Technology can hold its own magic. Don't you agree?"

Mathias steps in, and the shifter immediately moves to the other side. There's no love lost between the warm-blooded shifters and vampires. "I completely agree. Technology is a wondrous thing." He squints up at one of the corners. "Cameras. Hidden weapons." Dark eyes continue to peruse every inch. "Air vents to disperse agents. Nice set-up."

Sheraton admits nothing, only turns toward me.

"Thank you," I tell him, stepping into the elevator.

Moments later, the doors open directly into a suite. The cream and chocolate brown décor reassures me we're still in The Hari. Gatlin stands by the door, gun in hand, and he relaxes only once he sees our faces. He immediately holds a finger to his lips.

Hawthorne looks around. "Where is she?"

"Sleeping," Gatlin murmurs. "A combination of jet lag and adrenaline, I suspect."

He steps to the side, and I get my first glimpse. Curled into the corner of the couch, dark hair tumbling about her shoulders, long, equally dark lashes fanned across her sleep-flushed cheeks, she is a vision. There's a light blanket tucked around her, and I eye it speculatively.

"How was security?" he murmurs with a frown. "I haven't wanted to leave her alone to check it out."

"Impressive," Mathias answers with a low chuckle. "I'll have to upgrade the council after this visit."

I lay a hand on his shoulder. "Sorry about your home. I've sent a team over to clean up the situation and make it secure until you can return."

"Thanks," Gatlin replies in a gruff tone. "Although I'll probably have to sell it. Can't have the world knowing where I live." Gatlin motions to me. "Did you bring weapons?"

"Too many cameras, and it's still daylight," I remind him. He gives me an incredulous look. "We'll get them tonight."

He flicks a glance at her, then murmurs, "I have a theory about her." His words are barely audible as he explains the conversation he had with Phaedra earlier about the gods gifting humans with abilities. "She didn't deny it either."

Hmm. The pieces fit together in a way that makes sense. Her secrecy. Knowledge of ancient civilizations and the gods. The ability to manipulate curses and regenerate. Her unique scent.

"It makes sense."

Does it matter, though? I think about it. No. Not to me. But I don't know enough about the gods to understand the implications. Will they care if she is with us?

Three heads turn my way, expecting me to say something more, but I ignore them and walk over to her. The second I sit down, Phaedra's eyes open, and her hand whips out of the blanket, a stiletto in its grip. When she sees it's me, she tucks it away and sits up straight, then pushes her silky locks behind her shoulders.

Stretching, she peers around the room. "Sorry. This couch is heaven. How did the council meeting go?"

Her bright blue eyes find mine, and for the briefest second, I'm lost in their depths. This woman intrigues me like no other. Quietly confident. Intelligent. Mysterious.

"To be honest, not well," I admit, running my hand through my hair. "They might send out a kill order for both of us when this thing is done." I explain what happened in the meeting. "The council is on the verge of falling apart."

She nibbles her lush bottom lip as she thinks. Her tongue swipes across it, and my body automatically tightens at the unintentionally sensual movement. Silence builds between us, and I glance up to find her amused glance.

"If we have to go on the run, I know some great hiding places," she jokingly assures me, taking my hand in hers. She pauses, her gaze searching mine before she continues. "Thanks, though… for trying to deflect the council's attention. I hope it works."

There seems to be a slight note of worry in her voice, but I can't tell why. If only she would trust me with more information.

"I'm not leaving you to face this alone. I promise."

She shrugs. "The council doesn't know everything. Ask Gatlin. He found that out the hard way today." Her voice is full of amusement and a tinge of mock worry. "I might have broken him."

Gatlin huffs loudly, but surprisingly, a small half-smile appears on his face.

I chuckle. "Is that a smile? He does seem out of sorts. Mentioned something about a Harlequin? Although he didn't go into detail."

She shrugs. "It's an underground network that supplies supes with various items. For payment, of course."

Her explanation, while simple, has huge implications. As council security, I immediately want to know why we weren't aware of them, but I push those thoughts aside to focus on today's problems.

"London isn't safe for you. We need to move our visit to the bank up to tonight. Figure out where we're going next. Maybe Harlequin could get us the weapons and other tactical items we need?"

"That's their specialty," she says with a nod, looking around. "We need to put together a list first."

Mathias slides into a chair at the table, pen and paper in hand. "Ready."

Startled, she glances over at him. "Okay then. We need new encrypted phones, a way to get there without being seen, access to the vault, the key, password, and of course, weapons. Anything else?"

"Dark clothes," Hawthorne adds, motioning to his light blue button-up shirt and grey pants. "Cash. To pay for access."

Mathias picks up the burner from the table and makes a quick call to order the phones.

Gatlin walks over and sits down at the table. "I'll make a list of the weapons. I want to include a few extra items like rope, knives, a garrote…" His voice trails off as he begins to write.

I glance through my contacts to find a number, then take the burner from Mathias to make my own call. "Cian. Jamison. I need a favor. Can I get your father's number?" C. Hoare & Co is one of the oldest banks in London, and it's been in Cian's family for twelve generations. While he doesn't have anything to do with its operations, his father is an active partner and director with full access to the vault.

He's silent for half a second, then reels off the digits in a tense voice. "He's not in trouble with the council, is he?"

"No," I assure him. "I need to make a private transaction. That's all."

He heaves a relieved sigh. "Thanks. Thought I was going to have to make a choice. Anything else?"

It's obvious from the tone of his voice that the council would likely lose in that decision. It's one of the reasons I trust Cian. Family first. "No, but thank you. Your trust means a lot." He could have asked the question before he gave me the number, but he didn't. I hang up.

Phaedra motions to the hotel phone. "Hawthorne, call Sheraton and order clothes. All he needs is a description and sizes." She waves a hand at Gatlin. "As you can see, he's got good taste."

I flick a glance at Gatlin in time to see his face flush. I didn't even notice, but he's wearing a pair of dark jeans, a long-sleeve fitted shirt, and custom black leather boots from a well-known luxury designer. All of which is considerably nicer than his usual attire.

He snarls when he sees all of us staring at him. "Stop. It's jeans and a t-shirt."

Hawthorne clears his throat and picks up the hotel phone. "I'm sold."

While he's on the phone ordering clothes for us, I lean in close to Phaedra. "As soon as we have access to our funds, I'll reimburse you."

She shrugs. "Don't worry about it."

"It isn't a request," I inform her, slightly irritated at her answer.

She lifts an amused eyebrow. "If it makes you feel better, go right ahead."

Locking my jaw, I stare at her. "I pay for whatever my team needs, and that includes you." The council doesn't always give us the funds to do our jobs, but as a de Vere, I use my sizeable fortune to make sure we have everything we need. Something my father and I argue about often.

She places a hand on my arm. "Money doesn't mean much to me. I have more gold than I can spend in my lifetime, which is saying a lot. Do what you need to do."

I exhale, my irritation evaporating with her words. "Sorry. Touchy subject." Looking away from her, I pick up the burner and call Cian's father to ask him to meet us at the bank tonight at midnight.

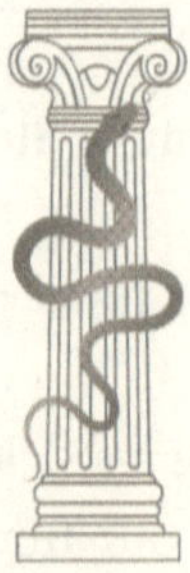

26

JAMISON

C. Hoare & Co stands in the middle of the square. Old money. After assuring him it was a completely legal transaction that requires the utmost discretion, he agreed to meet us at midnight.

It's imperative we get in and out without anyone from the council finding out we were here. Arriving early, we set up a perimeter to secure the building.

"Security guard moving on the second floor," Gatlin's low voice says over the comms. "Switching to thermal imaging."

While he assesses the building, I tap the mic. "Mathias, do you have eyes inside?"

"Affirmative," he replies a second later. "They really need to upgrade their security."

"I'll be sure to let him know," I tell him in an amused voice. "Ten minutes."

"No other heat signatures," Gatlin confirms. "Moving positions."

Hawthorne and Phaedra are waiting in the car. Courtesy of the hotel, the black sedan matches the rest of the cars on the street. Walking over to it, I open the door and extend my hand to Phaedra.

Dressed in simple but elegant tailored black pants and a matching silk turtleneck, with her hair swept up into a chignon, she exudes timeless sophistication. When she steps onto the pavement, she smiles and moves to the side for Hawthorne.

As he steps out, her eyes slide from his head to his toes in appreciation, and I want to shake my head at a look I see too often when it comes to him. Dressed all in black, his deep brown hair tamed into sophistication, he is every inch the Elvish royal the supernatural media follows so closely.

Right now, he's staring down at her with equal appreciation. Turning, he curves his body protectively around hers and places a possessive hand on her back in a statement I haven't seen him make for any other woman. His green eyes dart to me, and I see the quiet determination in their depths.

I dip my head in acknowledgement of his intentions. For a second, I forgot he was interested in her. Complicates things.

Phaedra's gaze moves from him to me and back again. "Ready?"

Slipping the gun from my waistband, I scan the buildings around us. "Gryphon. All clear?"

Gatlin confirms. "Clear."

Mathias' cool voice interjects. "Clear. Contact has arrived."

"Is that what you call the team?" she murmurs, her eyes darting around the street.

With a quick motion, I bare my arm and show her the gryphon tattoo.

She glances at my arm, then her eyes flick to my face. She frowns. "I don't understand."

My mind reels at those three words. She can't see the tattoo. The spell was designed with supernaturals in mind. Further confirmation she isn't one.

"I'll explain later," I tell her, silently conversing with Hawthorne. Gatlin's theory is right. Her gifts likely come from the gods. Hawthorne tightens his arm around her, a clear indication of his thoughts.

Within minutes, we're at the side entrance to the bank. Henry, Cian's father, is waiting with security when we enter the building. Stocky, with a full head of red-gold hair, he exudes the pride of the lion shifter that he is. Intelligent amber eyes narrow to assess whether we're a threat before he makes a subtle motion to the guard beside him.

With a flick of my wrist, I hide the gun and step forward to shake his hand. "Thank you for meeting us. I know it's unorthodox, but we need to access a safe deposit box in your vault, and we don't want anyone to be aware of it. We have the key and the required password, but we don't know the number."

Speculation crosses Henry's face, but the brief expression is gone in an instant. He nods. "Follow me." Heading to a large office in the back, he sits down at an impressive mahogany desk and turns on the computer. "Do you know the name of the owner?"

"Dr. Letz Samuels," I reply. His eyes widen at the name. As he types in the name, I turn to Phaedra. "Password?"

"SaintPeter1023," she softly replies with a small sad smile on her face as if there's something personal about it.

Henry lifts an eyebrow. "Correct. Do you have the key?"

Phaedra steps forward and uncurls her hand. "Yes."

"Definitely our key," he confirms as he examines it. "Letz didn't have a beneficiary on the box but left instructions for access to be given to whoever had the key and password. You have both. Follow me."

With long strides, he heads out of the office and down a long hallway to a staircase. We quickly make our way to the cold basement, where we're met with a locked iron gate. Once unlocked, we continue down another hallway until we reach the end, where a large vault door greets us. Dark grey with brass finishes, the old-fashioned steel door is adorned with modern biometric technology. Henry submits to an eye scan and delivers a drop of blood.

The heavy door silently swings open, revealing row after row of gold boxes of various sizes set into the wall. Henry strides over to a small box and inserts a key, then looks at Phaedra.

She moves next to him and inserts Letz' key into the other keyhole, then waits for Henry's signal. In unison, they turn the keys, and he swings the door open and extracts the long box from its secure location.

"When you're finished, press this button," he says, pointing to the discreet brass button on the wall. "I'll return." He strides out of the vault and down the hall.

Phaedra waits until he's gone before flipping open the lid on the box. Inside is a gold key and a piece of paper. She slips the key into her pocket and unfolds the paper to reveal a handwritten note.

William of Durham has the keys to the kingdom.

Hawthorne tilts his head to the side and peers down at Phaedra, whose eyes are shining with the same knowledge.

"Oxford," they say in unison, then laugh.

"William…" Hawthorne begins, but I cut him off.

"Not here," I tell him, closing the lid to the empty box. Walking over to the door, I press the button on the wall.

Phaedra taps on the paper, and Hawthorne nods, then she folds it and slides it into her pocket a second before Henry comes back around the corner.

"All done?" he asks as he walks over to the box. When we

confirm, he picks it up and slides it back into the slot. "Is there anything else I can help you with tonight?"

"No, but thank you, Henry," I assure him. "We appreciate your willingness to meet us here at such an unorthodox time and thank you for your discretion."

"We serve all our clients' needs," he replies with a smile. "No matter the request. And I assure you, we're very discreet." He ushers us out of the vault and closes the door, then escorts us out of the bank.

"Report," I order the minute we step outside.

"Clear," Gatlin confirms.

"Henry's in his office on his computer," Mathias informs us. There are several seconds of silence, then he says, "Interesting. He's erasing the video footage of your visit."

"That's unusual, but we did ask him for discretion," I reply, trying to think through all the implications of his actions.

"He's texting someone…" Mathias' voice trails off. "Damn. I can't see the message."

"Well, let's hope it's Cian and not the council," I murmur into the comms. "Everyone, meet back at the hotel." Henry doesn't strike me as the type to go back on his word. Plus, Cian's one of my most loyal agents. Let's hope that extends to his father.

Once everyone's in the car, I slip behind the wheel and place my hand on the dash. Using visual waves, I obscure the car from the cameras, allowing us to roll silently through the London streets without the cameras getting a clear picture of us or the car.

"How are you hiding us from the CCTV?" Phaedra asks.

Glancing in the rearview mirror at her in the backseat, I explain how I'm using magic to shield us. "It's a spell mages created when the cameras became a nuisance. Thankfully, we're a short distance from the hotel, so it shouldn't take much for me to power it."

She frowns. "Do all mages know that spell?"

"Yes, but not all of them can use it."

"I think the person who broke into my condo and trashed it used the same spell," she replies with a twist of her lips. "The only thing the camera could catch was his brown dress shoes."

My brows draw together. "I didn't study all the footage, so I missed it. I'll have Mathias show me when we get back."

Mathias wouldn't know that most mages can't cast a spell of this magnitude. Only the most powerful. Could it have been my father? I think about it. Doubtful. He rarely leaves London. But he has a veritable army of personal assistants sworn to secrecy that would be more than happy to cater to him. *Damn it.* That means he could be the traitor.

27

____

PHAEDRA

We arrive back at The Hari and sit down to make a plan. I show the rest of them what it says on the paper. "William of Durham founded Oxford…"

"I thought King Alfred founded it," Mathias inserts.

Surprised to hear the comment come from him, I take a moment to explain. "In the 1300s, a rumor sprang up that King Alfred had founded Oxford roughly four hundred years earlier than William, and it became widely accepted as the truth for a long time. However, it was eventually established that William is the correct founder."

His dark eyes spark with appreciation. "Thank you."

Hawthorne turns from Mathias to me, then taps the paper. "We immediately knew it was Oxford, but the second part could mean one of three places—either St. Peter's

196

College, the Church of St. Peter-le-Bailey, or St. Peter's in the East."

I beam at him. "Correct. The keys to the kingdom of heaven were given to Peter, and those are the only buildings in Oxford with his name."

Gatlin folds his arms across his large barrel chest. "We're not splitting up." His tone leaves little room for disagreement.

Jamison nods. "I agree, but the longer we spend in one place, the more likely the council will catch up with us. I don't want them to know what leads we're following. Is there any way to narrow it down?"

"Letz' group started a thousand years ago," I remind them. "St. Peter's college wasn't founded until the 1900s, so we can rule that one out. That leaves us with two. The Church of St. Peter-le-Bailey and the other church, St. Peter's in the East. Both were built in the 12th century, I think."

Hawthorne leans forward. "Actually, a church stood in the same place as St. Peter's in the East since the 10th century, but it wasn't renamed until the 12th century." He stops for a minute. "The Church of St. Peter-le-Bailey was torn down and the new church built on the site in the 16—or—1700s. I remember, because they found some earlier artifacts from my world, Langit, buried there. That timeline would make it questionable."

"I don't remember, but I'm sure you're correct," I admit with a nod. "That leaves us with St. Peter's in the East. It's been a while since I've visited Oxford, but I know I didn't visit any of the churches. I'm not sure of the layout."

"We need schematics for the building," Gatlin says as he moves around the room pulling together the weapons and gear that were delivered while we were out.

Mathias grabs his laptop off the nearby table. "I'm on it." Fingers flying, he's soon lost to the world of technology.

Hawthorne shifts restlessly beside me. "I assume we're headed there tonight?"

Jamison quickly nods. "We can't afford to wait."

With a sigh, Gatlin stops what he's doing and motions to the hotel phone. "Think your friend Sheraton will bring us some late dinner or rather..." He looks at his watch. "An early breakfast?"

I nod and start to stand, but he lays a hand on my shoulder.

"I'm quite capable of ordering us food," he assures me in his usual gruff tone. "What would you like?"

"That depends," I say, biting the inside of my lip. "How are we getting to Oxford?"

Jamison tilts his head. "It's a relatively short distance. Portal, why?"

I grimace. I'll definitely need something easy on my stomach. Turning back to Gatlin, I give him my order. "Toast, please."

He immediately shakes his head. "You need something more than a few slices of bread. We don't know how long it will take us to find this group or how long we'll be there."

"I'm not that hungry," I insist.

He narrows his gold eyes but says nothing more. "Jamison?"

"Club sandwich," Jamison orders.

"Omelet," Hawthorne adds with a look at Gatlin, who nods. "And you know what Mathias needs."

While Gatlin's on the phone, Mathias connects a gadget to his laptop. Clicking a few more buttons, he projects the schematics on the wall for all of us to see.

"Clever," I murmur.

He clears his throat and pushes his glasses up on his nose. "Thank you." Using a red laser, he circles a couple of areas. "Based on the information I found, the nave and chancel were part of the original structure along with the crypt."

Tapping on his computer brings up another image of a room made of stone with low ceilings. "This is the crypt. As you can see, it's the length of the original nave and chancel above it. There's a problem, though."

I glance at him. "What?"

"In the 1960s, they changed it from a church to a library and made it a part of St. Edmund Hall. It's open to Oxford students and faculty," he informs us. "It seems like it would be too risky for them to store relics and hold meetings there without anyone knowing. Still believe they would use it as their base?"

I think through the original logic and come to the same conclusion. "This has to be it. Crypts were designed to house relics and sacred objects. Maybe there's a priest hole or a passageway to another building or something."

Jamison studies me. "What's your level of certainty?"

I bite my lip, feeling the pressure of their eyes on me. "That's where we need to go next." I'm certain of it. "Even if it's only to get the next key or clue or whatever."

Hawthorne's green eyes lock on Jamison. "I agree."

The elevator dings, and Gatlin, who's standing guard by the elevator, immediately pulls the gun from behind his back. "Who are you?"

With those words, we all stand to confront the stranger near the elevator with a cart. Jamison and Hawthorne silently slide in front of me, and I take a step back. My body can absorb most magic, but there's been a few times when it's proved to be lethal. Thankfully, death isn't a state that's permanent for me, but it sure hurts like hell, and it takes time for me to regenerate. Time we don't have.

Tall, with brown hair and an average face, the man waves a hand toward the cart. "You ordered food, correct?"

Jamison eyes him closely, then glances at Gatlin, who shakes his head.

"What did we order?" Gatlin asks softly, moving into position behind him and raising his gun.

"I'll have to check," the guy smoothly replies, his hand reaching toward the leather folio on the cart.

"Stop," I order him, my gaze finding Gatlin. "The service is impeccable here. They would never forget the details of a simple food order."

The man whips his hand out from under the portfolio and flings a dark ball of magic toward us, then turns toward the elevator to flee, but it's too late. Gatlin drops him with one shot to his head.

Jamison stretches his arms wide, then claps them together hard, capturing the magic in a bubble of some sort. Hawthorne opens a portal beside him, and Jamison flings it into the dark void. It closes a second later.

That's certainly efficient. "Where did you send it?"

"The council has a room that nullifies magic," Jamison admits with a frown. "There's only one problem... It tracks all deposits, which means they'll be able to track it down to us here. Soon."

Gatlin stares down at the body on the floor with a furious expression on his face. "Burn it." He orders as he walks away and begins handing out weapons.

Hawthorne casually motions to the body, and it bursts into a green-blue flame. Magical fire is the only way to make sure a supernatural truly dies.

All five of us move into motion, gathering whatever we need to take with us. I pause and shoot off a text to Mercer to inform her of the breech and ask her for a clean-up crew. Once done, I exchange my heels for boots and layer on a few extra clothes, including a coat. Then, I load up on weapons.

"Ready?" Jamison asks, eyes darting from one to the other and landing on me. He holds out his hand, and I find myself reaching for it. A portal appears in front of him, making my hand tighten on his.

Gatlin strides through first, of course. Alert and ready to take on the world before we arrive. Mathias follows him, then it's our turn. As we step in, I glance back and meet Hawthorne's determined green eyes. Most of the time, they're bright and full of knowledge, but anger has made them dark and turbulent. I shiver. Glad I'm not on his bad side.

THE PORTAL TAKES us directly to High Street, and we make our way over to the former church. Now a library, the doors are locked tightly against intruders.

Gatlin takes up position between us and the street while Jamison holds his hand out toward the lock on the door. He immediately jerks his hand away and shakes it.

"There's a spell on it," he grits out. "Stings like a bloody wanker."

I dip my hand into my pocket and pull out the key from the safe deposit box. "Maybe this will work?"

He steps back, and I move in front of him. The key inserts smoothly, and within seconds, we're in the library.

"Nice of Letz to leave us a key to the front door," I murmur as we walk down the center aisle. Streetlamps from outside send light streaming through the tall windows on each side, illuminating rows of bookshelves. Lining the right and left sides of the room, they lead to the previous altar and three large stained-glass windows. The place still looks and feels like a church, with its quiet air and musty smell.

Mathias moves in front of us. "This way."

He moves quickly and quietly to the end of the room, where there's an exit door. Heading through the door, he takes the stairs down into a much darker area than above.

I stumble in the darkness, and he stops and takes my hand in his. There's strength in his cool fingers, and it reminds me of how strong he is. Vampires have unnatural speed and strength. And come to think of it, spectacular eyesight. So, why does he wear glasses? I make a mental note to ask him later.

I reach back with my other hand and grab Jamison's, creating a train for him to follow. Two flights later, we're in the crypt. The air is frigid and thick with darkness. I can't see anything. If it weren't for Mathias, I wouldn't know where to step.

"See anyone?" Jamison softly asks.

"All clear," Mathias replies in his normal low tone.

A ball of light appears above our heads. Jamison sends it around the room to peek into all the dark corners to ensure we're alone. Once it finishes, he positions it in front of us. "Where to next?"

Mathias points to the far end. "The only thing in here is the altar at the far end. I'll check it out." His hand slips from mine, and he blurs away. Moments later, he's back. "Besides a few objects on it, nothing seems to be out of the ordinary. I didn't see a door or any alcoves along the way either."

Gatlin sniffs the air. "I smell magic. Lots of it. From different races too."

Hawthorne steps up beside us. "What kind of objects?"

"A large, beaded cross, a bust, a stone box, and a mortar with a pestle," Mathias replies, his eyes darting around the space. "I'll check out the walls and see if I can find a secret room or something."

Hawthorne and I share a look, then head straight to the altar. Jamison trails slightly behind us with magic swirling, ready to defend.

Made of grey limestone and clearly old, the stone altar stands about four and a half feet tall. There's nothing spectacular about it except for the instant buzz of magic I feel when I get closer.

"Stop," Jamison orders in a low, sharp tone. His arm reaches out and pulls me away from the altar. "The objects are imbued with dark magic."

Warmth fills me, and I smile up at him. Eyes full of worry

stare back at me. My gaze drops from his eyes to his firm lips. The last time we were this close, he kissed me. He dips his head closer but stops. Breathless, I wait, but it's as if time suddenly speeds up, and he releases me.

"Don't worry," I tell him. "This is my kind of magic. The objects are cursed…"

Hawthorne lets out a guttural grunt behind me, and I whirl around to see the cross in his hand, his body arched in pain, jumbled words flying from his mouth. Tiny dots of blood appear across his arms, neck, and face, and I realize the nature of the curse. I throw an arm out toward Jamison to stop him from touching his friend.

"Don't," I order him. "I've got this." He stiffens in protest, but I shake my head. "This is what I do. Trust me. Please."

He reluctantly steps back, but the magic swirling across his hands darkens in response. I leave him and walk over to his friend.

Removing the cross, I take Hawthorne's hands in mine and stare into his tortured green eyes. It takes me but moments to snare the curse invading his body, but it feels like eternity as I watch him suffer. Like a fish on the end of the line, the curse whips and tugs, trying to escape, but this is the power given to me. Mine to command. With a final whisper of fury, it leaves Hawthorne's body and enters mine, where it's instantly absorbed.

Hawthorne heaves a huge sigh of relief and closes his eyes for a second. "There were a thousand needles pricking me all over." A white light encompasses his body as he heals, then it dims. He takes a deep breath and opens his eyes. "Where did the curse go?"

"I absorbed it," I tell him. An angry expression settles on his face, but I know what he's going to say. "It's fine. Really. Ma… curses don't work on me." Actually, most magic doesn't, but no need to give away all my secrets.

The anger in his eyes changes to a curious glint, but he simply squeezes my hands. "Thank you. That was really fucking unpleasant."

Happy he isn't delving deeper, I pull away and motion to the rest of the room. "Don't touch anything. The objects on the altar might not be the only things cursed."

Swiveling around, I hold out my hand over the bust and detect a curse. "This one is mild. It will put you to sleep."

"Wished I'd picked up that one," Hawthorne mutters.

I move on to the bowl. A reflection appears in my mind, and I know instantly what it means. "When this is full of water, a person will be compelled to stare into its depths and lose all track of time."

The mortar and pestle bring a sharp, tangy taste to my mouth, and I quickly put it to the side. "Poison curse."

The only object left is the box. Magic radiates from its surface. "Can you bring the light closer?"

Hawthorne conjures a small flame and shines it on the box.

Swirls appear in patterns on the box. The curse appears when the recipient opens the box. "Step back."

"I'm staying," he insists, his eyes moving from the box to me, and I can see the curiosity burning in him. Always seeking knowledge.

Jamison moves in closer to me and places his hand on my back.

Pressure builds inside me. Hopefully, I can contain the curse quickly. If not, he could be blinded when I open it.

My fingers slide across the swirls in a specific pattern. Every swipe changes the box from stone to lapis lazuli. Inlaid into the intense blue surface are jewels of different colors. A painted image appears on the top of the box. Portraits of two young girls dressed in white chitons. One with dark hair and the other blond.

Hands trembling, I stop and stare down at the box. A knot

grows in my throat along with white hot anger. How dare they? With one finger, I press the center of the box and lift the lid. Blue velvet embroidered with two initials—P & P. It's immediately obscured by a piercing white light that stabs directly into my heart. For a second, that terrible night in the past replays itself over and over. Captivated by the image of my sister and me, I watch every second. This is the guilt I carry in my heart and soul. And the curse attached to the box—to experience one's worst moment again and again. Tears slide down my face.

Hawthorne and Jamison curse loudly, bringing me back to the present. With little thought, I shut down the curse and remove it from the box. The light disappears, and I hear them both heave a sigh of relief. With one last look, I close the lid and slip it into my coat pocket. When I lift my head, I see Mathias in the corner, staring at me with a speculative expression on his face.

28

PHAEDRA

Stone scraping against stone echoes across the chamber as a door opens to the right of the altar, revealing a dark-haired man wearing a light grey suit. Mathias is a blur as he positions himself next to the stranger. Jamison swiftly steps in front of me, while Gatlin sprints from the back of the room to stand beside us both.

"I mean you no harm," the stranger states firmly. "We've been expecting you." There's an underlying note of excitement in his tone.

"Let's just say your intent is lost when you present visitors with a table full of harmful objects," Hawthorne interjects in a hard voice.

"None of them are designed to permanently kill a super-natural, only to dissuade them from exploring further," the man insists. "Besides, they didn't hurt her. Did they, Dr. Galanis?"

Having heard enough, I step between Jamison and Gatlin to face the man. "Who are you?"

Eyes glued to the newcomer, Mathias reveals his identity. "Rupert Evanston, vampire."

The stranger glances over at Mathias. "Dr. Rupert Evanston. Archaeologist and, yes, vampire. Although that hardly matters." Dismissing him, he turns to me. "We've waited a long time to meet you."

Rupert then motions to the passageway behind him. "If de Vere will kindly use his magic to light the way, I'll take you to meet the rest of our society."

Jamison glances at Mathias, who nods at his unspoken question, then he tosses a small ball of light at the torch near the door. Fire immediately catches, lighting the passageway with a small glow. Gatlin, our protector, stalks through the door first and grabs the lit torch. Jamison catches my hand in his and walks through with me in tow.

Looking back, I see Hawthorne enter, then Mathias. Rupert closes the door behind us all.

"Follow the passage," he tells Gatlin, who moves cautiously forward. "In about fifteen meters, there will be a small alcove on the right with a stone pedestal. In its center stands a bird. Turn it to the left."

Gatlin huffs in irritation but says nothing. It doesn't take long to reach the alcove. After following Rupert's instructions, the pedestal slides to the right, opening another dark passageway.

Jamison lights another torch, and we walk for an additional ten minutes.

"The passageway ends at a wall. It's biometric, though. Once we're there, I'll move to the front and open the last door," Rupert calls out to Gatlin.

My nose twitches in the cool dry air. They've gone to a lot of trouble to hide themselves. If I hadn't known Letz, I'm not sure

I would have trusted anyone enough to follow them through this maze. You could hide a body down here, and nobody would ever find it.

The group halts, and Hawthorne positions me in the curve of his body right before Rupert slips by us, as if he doesn't want the vampire touching me. His hand warms the curve of my hip, and I shift closer, wanting to feel his body against mine. I look up past his strong jaw and lips that beg to be kissed to find his green eyes staring down at me, and I lick my lips, wondering what his lips would feel like on mine. A spark flares between us, and the air grows heavy with tension.

Rupert shouts, "Voilà!"

Startled, I turn. The stone barrier slides open to reveal a series of steps. Reluctantly, I lift my hand from Hawthorne's chest, but he immediately captures it in his, keeping the two of us connected. *Damn, this man makes me weak in the knees.* How am I supposed to focus?

Thankfully, the stairs lead up to a circular chamber filled with wooden pews but the air remains cool and dry, like the passageway. Confused, I glance around and see plastered walls. Are we above ground or not?

"This is where we conduct our meetings," Rupert says, coming to stand in front of me. His dark eyes are alight with excitement and a glint of curiosity. "Letz and I started this journey and society together. Along with another, whom I'll introduce in a second. It's my honor to meet you, Dr. Galanis, and to introduce you to our members."

"What is the name of your society?" I ask, following the instructions Letz murmured in his last moments.

"The Keepers of the Cursed," Rupert replies with a broad smile. "Now that formalities are over, let me introduce you."

Letz said they had sixty members. Doors slide open along the walls, revealing men and women. The scent of their magic fills the air, replacing the musty smell. Walking into the chamber, they find their seats amongst the pews except for one. A familiar man, fierce-looking with a full head of hair, strides confidently down to us.

Jamison inhales sharply. "Henry?"

The man flashes a wry smile. "Hello, Jamison. I'm sorry I couldn't tell you earlier. Had to follow protocols." His gaze moves to me. "When I was younger, I dabbled in ancient history and landed a job at the Vatican along with Letz and Rupert. We started this society, and for years, I was able to indulge myself. Unfortunately, my family and the bank needed me more, but I serve whenever I'm needed. Plus, my position allows me to guard the safe deposit box. It's nice to officially meet you, Dr. Galanis."

Unnerved by all the supernaturals staring at me, I move a little closer to Hawthorne. "Phaedra, please. I'm here because of Letz. It was his dying request."

Rupert looks at Henry, and a sad expression crosses both of their faces. "This isn't how we wanted to welcome you, but we know Letz would have been thrilled to see you here."

Henry's arm sweeps out to indicate the rest of the room. "These are the members of our society. Given the circumstances, we'll forego individual introductions, but they would love to ask you a few questions, if you don't mind?"

Sixty might not seem like many, but when you thought you were the only one for thousands of years, this feels like a small army. Exposed to supernaturals in a way I never expected, I have to wonder what the gods will think of this. I didn't tell these supernaturals or lead them down this path. And technically, the work they do protects humans without exposing themselves to them. It follows the rules. Right?

Unease fills me, but at the same time, I'm curious to know about this society that claims to follow in my footsteps. "No questions about my past." When he agrees, I motion to the people surrounding us. "Okay." Hawthorne squeezes my hand, reminding me of his presence, and some of my apprehension eases.

Henry steps to the side and raises his voice. "I know we're all dying of curiosity. Dr. Galanis has graciously agreed to answer our questions. Nothing personal." His amber eyes return to me. "I'll go first. What do you do when you can't remove a curse?"

Heads swivel toward me, and I almost sigh in relief at the innocuous question. "It depends. Sometimes, I change the curse into something…milder. Other times, I take the object back to my place to study it further. In my experience, all curses can be removed, but some take longer."

Hands shoot up across the room. I motion to the young woman in the front row. Based on the faint notes of sandalwood and cinnamon, she's a mage.

"Can you give an example of changing the curse?" she asks with a tiny frown.

Nolan Westgate's collection pops into my mind. "Are you familiar with the painting of Dorian Gray?" When she nods, I continue. "I changed the curse. The painting will no longer be able to call forth the demon who created it. Instead, it will trap the individual in the painting for two weeks. Once released, the painting will go dormant again."

Excited chatter races across the room.

"Ingenious," Rupert murmurs from beside me. "Next question."

A shifter stands in the third row, gold eyes flashing. "We have a few pieces that we're stuck on. Why are some curses so difficult to unravel?"

I think about it for a minute. "Curses are made of magic, which can be as simple or complex as you want it to be. The type of magic used to create the curse is important, as well as the level of power and experience of the user."

An older man stands in the back row. "Is it true that the curses do not affect you?"

"Yes," I reply without further elaboration. The room goes silent. "Next question."

A grey-haired lady slowly stands. "Why do you do this?"

"To protect humans," I tell them, wanting them to understand the truth. This isn't about them. "Supernaturals create these objects, and humans have no defense against them. Although a great deal of my effort protects supernaturals too."

Disapproving murmurs and low tones echo across the chamber.

"Any more questions?"

Hands raise, and I call on a young man.

"Are you single?" he asks with a grin. Several people chuckle.

I open my mouth to answer, but Gatlin's gruff voice beats me to the punch. "No personal questions." I flash him a grateful smile.

Not wanting to leave them without expressing my gratitude, I turn in a circle to look at all of them. "For thousands of years, I've walked this earth, making it a safer place. This is my sole purpose and reason for existing. Not once did I question the supernaturals who created the cursed objects. Nor have I ever wished them any ill will. I simply did the job I was given."

The chamber is silent. "Honestly, I never thought anyone would notice. This entire time I've thought myself invisible to the rest of the world. When Letz told me about your society, I was shocked, but for the first time, I felt seen. I felt like the work I've done is important. That I matter in the grand scheme of this world."

"I didn't know you existed, but the fact that one supernatural would care enough to join me in this endeavor blows my mind. Sixty of you… There are no words to express my gratitude for the work you do here," I admit with a shake of my head.

"And if you'll let me, I'd like to help you with some of the more difficult cases," I offer with a tentative smile. "Between us, we'll make the world safer for both humans and supernaturals.

Thank you." I see the approval appear on their expressive faces, and I can't help but beam in return.

The room relaxes, and the questions continue for the next hour. What was the most difficult piece? Which race creates more of the objects? Can I remove a curse from a plant? That one was intriguing to me as I've never tried it. On and on they ask until I've covered most of their questions.

After they finish, Rupert raises his hand and the doors slide open, letting all the people out. Once they're gone, he turns to me. "Well done. Let us give you a tour and show you some of our more difficult pieces."

Jamison flicks a hand toward Gatlin, who again takes the lead.

Rupert leads us into another bright hallway.

"Are we above ground?" I ask, motioning to the walls.

He smiles but says nothing. I guess they don't want to share all of their secrets either. I search for clues, but there's nothing to indicate location.

We enter a room full of objects that reminds me of my vaults at home. Except they are much neater. Instead of piles of trinkets, they have carefully labeled bins.

Several individuals stand behind a table with a few pieces in front of them. Familiar magic wafts from the items. Tangy and sharp, the curses embedded in them are complex and intricate. I point to the most complex one.

"Sometimes a curse is layered." I tap the brooch in front of me. "This one was specifically designed to trap someone in their worst nightmare. That takes a tremendous amount of magic to create. Different spells layered on top of each other to sleep, to dream, to change the dreams into nightmares, to find their worst one. So you have to attack each spell one at a time."

I show them how to identify and separate the spells, then I remove the curse from the brooch. Moving on to the next piece, I have them practice while I help. As I'm bent over, a strand of hair falls into my line of sight. A hand appears. In a blur, it's gone. Startled, I look up to find Mathias' obsidian gaze staring at the man in front of me.

"Keep your hands to yourself," he orders before releasing him and tucking my hair behind my ear. He moves back to Jamison's side, but his eyes never leave the man in front of me.

"Sorry," the man smoothly inserts. "I didn't realize."

With a frown, I open my mouth, but he's already dismissing me. "Thank you. I understand how to break the curse now."

Rupert clears his throat. "Let's move on, shall we? There's something important we need to share with you."

He opens the far door, and we follow him through. Traversing the hallways, we end up at a blue door encased in magic spells and biometric scanners.

I raise an eyebrow at the level of security and flick a glance at Gatlin, who is scowling at the door.

It swings open and reveals the Temple of Hephaestus.

29

PHAEDRA

Henry is waiting for us in the temple. Or at least, their recreation of it. With magic, they've designed a completely realistic holographic image of the temple. It's startling to see the level of detail included in every aspect. Nothing has been left out. In fact, it appears they've added a few things.

Tentatively, I step into the room. It's so real I can almost smell the roses used to perfume the statues and the earthy scent of the nearby trees. I close my eyes to savor the moment. A pang of homesickness hits me, but I know what I long to see is gone and buried.

Jamison's steady blue gaze is the first thing I see when I open my eyes. Slipping through his fingers is the Greek coin he carries with him. Sharp, observant. It's easy to see why he's their leader.

Henry points to a section of the wall that's been excavated. "According to the records we dug up, a human found a panel and key in this wall in 300 BCE. It was handed down from one generation to the next for a century. After that, it was lost. How Westgate got hold of it, we're not sure, but we found them in his collection.

"They weren't magical, but they were valuable. We needed funds, so we decided to sell them. We put the panel up for sale first. When an interested group contacted us, we tried to investigate them," Rupert explains with a frown. "We have contacts all over the world but could find very little information. We thought about calling off the deal, but we were desperate, so we sold it to them."

Henry leans in. "But things took a turn after the sale. Instead of just taking the panel, they killed that young demon, Sia. Upset, we took the key off the market."

Rupert admits with a heavy sigh. "But after Letz passed, we were contacted by the group he sold the panel to, demanding we hand it over. We explained that we didn't have it. At first, they didn't believe us. Threatened us with exposure. We realized the group who broke into the museum and killed Sia wasn't the same group who bought the panel from us. We didn't know what to do except refund their money."

"Two groups," Jamison states with an incredulous look. Gatlin swears next to him. "That's why the dots wouldn't connect."

"The group who broke into my condo asked me for a panel and key. That must be the first group," I remind them. "One group has the panel. The second group has nothing. I have the key." My mind buzzes around those three facts, trying to sort through what they might mean.

"The first group knew there were two items. They purchased the panel, but you took the key off the market. So, they broke into the museum to get the key," Gatlin surmises.

Mathias runs a hand through his dark tousled hair, then looks at me. "We know the museum group and the one in your condo are the same, remember? I was able to place one man at both scenes. I've had software running for days to try to identify him. So far, no results. Maybe it's time I changed the parameters. Search the CCTVs for his location."

"Agreed," Jamison inserts before turning to Rupert and Henry. "We'll take every piece of information you've dug up. Maybe between us, we'll start to make sense of this mess."

"Absolutely," Henry answers for them both. "If you'll follow me, I'll…"

Jamison shakes his head. "If you wouldn't mind bringing the information here? This seems to be a secure place to discuss everything." His tone brooks no argument, and Henry quickly agrees and leaves to get his files.

"The group in my condo knew it was me with Letz at the abandoned warehouse, which connects them to the rooftop and his death," I remind them. "That means both groups are killers. But what is so important about this key and panel that humans are willing to kill for it?"

"Do they wield dark magic?" Hawthorne asks, his head tilted to the side as if he's trying to figure out a puzzle.

"They wield no magic," I reveal, to their astonishment.

"But the key gave you a vision," Hawthorne insists with a raised eyebrow.

How close can I get to the truth without revealing everything?

"The key was made by Hephaestus. It bears his symbol," I share with them. "The gods don't wield magic. Their power comes from a different source."

Pausing, I let them digest that info before continuing. "When I held the key, the vision showed me several blue and gold panels. Each one has images on it, but the details are hazy." I hold up my left hand. "It branded me with the Hephaestus' symbol. Although it's sort of disappeared."

All four of them crowd in to look at the smooth skin on my palm.

Hawthorne swivels around and grabs my hand. He pulls me over to the temple wall where the key and panel were excavated and squats down. "Like this one?"

Above the carefully dug hole, the Hephaestus' mark is etched into the Pentelic marble. I hold my palm up to the wall. The size fits. "Exactly like that one."

Hawthorne laces his fingers with mine and pulls me along the wall. "There are more. Carefully hidden in obscure places. I was trying to understand why the builders would place these tiny emblems everywhere." He points to several. "Here. Here. Here."

"We have the original wall. Do you want to see it?" Rupert asks, brimming with excitement. "We thought there might be more panels, so we excavated it. We didn't find anything but kept the wall. It was going to be donated to a museum when we were finished. All above board, I assure you."

Hawthorne opens his mouth but then closes it. "It's your call. We don't know what will happen... maybe nothing. Maybe something. I remember the world before the gods left, and it wasn't a good place. Supernaturals were persecuted simply for existing."

Damn. I never really thought about it from the perspective of the supernaturals. They locked me away during the first ten years of the "war." The gods fought brutally to keep the human world intact, but when it proved too much, they settled for a treaty and agreed to withdraw from the world. That's when they decided to make me an offer, which I took. I was the perfect spy. Supernatural enough to blend in if I needed to but human enough that I cared about protecting humans and this world. What if this is leading to their return? A shudder rips through me. I like the world how it is. Without them.

I bite my lip. The wheels are already in motion, and I'm not sure I can stop them. Whatever their plan is… I'm a part of it.

"Yes, let's see the wall," I hesitantly agree. "I don't think their intent is to hurt me. As Gatlin guessed, my *gifts*…came from them." I hate that word. Gifts. Maybe I shouldn't have confirmed Gatlin's theory, but if I'm right and the gods are involved, I'm going to need their help to figure this out.

The four of them share a loaded look, making me tense, but the small smile on Jamison's face tells me he's not mad about it. In fact, he seems sort of happy. Although if Mathias and Hawthorne knew the whole story, they would hate me.

Hawthorne pulls me closer. "Whatever happens, we won't let you face it alone."

I lift a shoulder, trying to be nonchalant. "I won't hold you to that if the world turns upside down."

Mahogany brows draw together, but Rupert arrives with the wall before he can say whatever he was thinking. I mean it, though. If—when they find out who I am, I know they won't stay.

Rupert sets the wall down on the stone altar. "Here you go." Hawthorne and I move closer to the marble slab.

Henry returns with a laptop and quickly disappears again. A second later, one of the members follows him in with a small table. Gatlin, Mathias, and Jamison gather around it to read through the information the society found on the group they sold the panel to so they can compare it with their intel.

I bend over and slide my hand up the cool marble. It's remarkably well-preserved for its age. As my left hand nears the symbol, it heats up, and the brand appears. Passing over Hephaestus' mark on the marble, a glow connects the two symbols but fades a second later.

"Hmm," Hawthorne murmurs. "It definitely triggered something."

"Maybe the brand is a key," Rupert interjects. "We found the symbol all over the temple. If you pass over the right one, perhaps it leads to a secret door or something."

Ancient biometrics? Hephaestus' was always creating something new. Is there something at the temple he wants me to find? In the sketch Doran did, he was one of the gods depicted on the panel. My gut churns as the tug of destiny pulls me in that direction.

Jamison comes over to stand next to us. "We made a connection between the training camp in Greece Gatlin discovered a while back and the group who originally bought the panel. Based on our surveillance, the camp is full of soldiers, though. I'll need to brief the council in order to get additional security teams assigned so we can conduct a raid."

"And that means I need to find somewhere else to go for a while," I conclude with a rueful smile. "Fortunately, I think I know where that might be." I point to the marble slab and the symbol. "The temple is full of these brands. I need to know if one of them leads to anything."

Jamison's brows draw together. "I don't like the idea of you going alone."

Hawthorne places a hand on my back. "I'm going with her. From what I know of the gods, I doubt they'll make this easy to find. Two experts are better than one. And you know I'm quite capable of keeping her safe."

Jamison gives a decisive nod. "Gatlin will hate the fact we're splitting up, but it's the right call. Take every precaution. This group is ten steps ahead of us. If anything appears remotely suspicious, find a safe place to wait it out. We'll come for you."

I glance from one determined man to the other. "If anyone wants to know what I think..." Both of them fold their arms across their chests and turn to face me, and I throw up my hands in surrender. "I agree. I agree. Besides, it will be fun having another academic nerd with me on this adventure." I slide my arm around Hawthorne's waist, and his face lights up with a broad smile.

Green eyes sparkle with anticipation, like he can barely contain his excitement over visiting an ancient temple. I see why the tabloids follow him around. Elven royalty is only a tiny part of his appeal. The passion he exudes for discovery and the world is intoxicating. He quite literally takes my breath away.

Jamison clears his throat and looks at Rupert. "Besides Henry, not a word to anyone on where she's going. For her safety, it's imperative nobody knows."

Rupert straightens and flashes his fangs in anger. "We're the last people who would ever put her in danger. Of course, we won't tell anyone."

Jamison gives a satisfied nod, then turns to me. "Can you call Maverick? You'll need a jet for all the gear. Don't tell anyone where you're going until you're on the way."

"I'll get Mercer to drop off the supplies we'll need," I tell him, my thoughts racing to make a list of everything.

He scowls. "Who the bloody hell is Mercer?"

I raise my eyebrows at his tone. "Mercer works for Harlequin."

He pulls me closer and dips his head. "Sorry. I'm a jealous wanker."

I teasingly roll my eyes, but I secretly love it.

Raising his head, he looks at Rupert. "Is there a shorter way out of here? We need to get moving."

"We have a portal," Rupert reveals with reluctance. "But you need to promise me you'll never use it to enter our society. Letz laced it with deadly spells that require certain phrases in order to enter without harm."

Jamison agrees and returns to Mathias and Gatlin to let them know we're leaving.

I smile at Rupert. Letz might have appeared as a harmless older man, but he certainly knew how to wield magic to safeguard those under his protection. "Thank you. For everything. I'd like to return if I can?"

He takes my hand in his and pats it several times. "We'd love to have you visit us. The pieces we showed you today are only a tiny portion of the artifacts we have in our possession. We could use your help. Here's my card. Call me when you're ready."

His mention of artifacts makes me think of something, and I pull Rupert into the corner. "By the way, I took the box from the altar."

There's a glint of satisfaction and knowledge in his gaze that makes me realize they know more about me than I might wish. "I thought you might like that one."

30

———

HAWTHORNE

"**N**o heroics. Get in and get out," Jamison orders. His eyes locked on Phaedra as she packs her supplies.

I place a hand on his shoulder. "I'll protect her with my life. Although I doubt she'll need it." When he turns to me with a question in his eyes, I remind him. "She's been around for thousands of years. By herself. Goddess, I can't imagine the things she's had to face on her own. I'm just happy she's starting to trust us. Let us be there for her."

"I don't like having to separate," he admits in a gruff tone. "The council. Gods. Humans. We're all caught up in something that feels beyond our control."

"We all feel that way," I assure him. "Gatlin's been pacing like a wild animal for the last half hour." We both look at where he's standing behind Phaedra with a scowl on his face. "Mathias keeps giving her updates on weather conditions, helping her

222

check off the items on her list and pack. All while he updates the temple schematics."

"He's been hard to read," Jamison lets slip. "Change is his worst enemy. The last time, it upended his life and brought him here. For a while, I wasn't sure if he'd accept her into our group, but he's slowly coming around to the idea."

I snort. "Have you not seen him watching everything around her? He's suspicious but intrigued."

Jamison's eyebrows rise in surprise. "I didn't notice."

"That's because you've been busy trying to figure out how to keep us all safe from the council and humans," I gently remind him. "Take a step back. Do what you do best. Find these bastards and the traitor. We'll have your back." I turn around. "And don't worry. I'll take out anyone who comes close to her."

The thought of someone hurting her sparks a white-hot rage in me. I might shun the royal titles I carry, but the power I hold can't be ignored. I tamp it down, knowing she needs me in a different capacity, but the thought makes me double-check the weapons I'm taking with us. Magic has its place, but I'd be a fool if I relied solely on it.

Gatlin comes over, wearing his usual scowl, and leans in close. "You know I hate this. Whatever you do, don't take your eyes off her for a second. The gods are capricious assholes. I don't know what they want with her, but I'm sure it isn't good."

My lips twitch with the need to smile at this uncharacteristic show of concern, but I don't want to discourage him from opening up in the future. "I won't."

Mathias comes over and hands me a laptop and a bag. "I uploaded the society's holographic image of the temple onto the laptop and marked every symbol they captured. It should help. You can cross them off after you've checked each one. Although they might have missed some, so don't rely solely on the data." His dark eyes slide over to her.

I hold up the bag. "And this?"

"Snacks," he tells me.

I clap them on the back. "I've got her. You two be careful and watch your backs. Jamison's too." I look over at Phaedra, who's striding this way.

Long legs encased in sleek dark pants paired with a fitted black long-sleeve shirt and tactical vest, dark hair in a tight braid, and weapons strapped to her legs and chest is a sight to behold. I take a deep breath. I've never seen anything so damn sexy in my life. And I've been around a very long time.

"Ready to go?" I ask, my voice husky despite my best efforts.

"Everything's loaded, and Charlie's filing a false flight plan," she replies in a slightly breathless voice that tells me she isn't immune to me either. "Excuse me for a second. I have to do one thing."

She strides over to Jamison. "Be careful. Don't underestimate them. Humans are clever and tenacious, especially when they believe in their cause." She tilts her head back and licks her lips. "Now, kiss me goodbye. Make it good. I need something to hold on to."

I'll kiss her. I mentally tell Jamison, who can't hear me. Next to me, Mathias freezes, and Gatlin shuffles restlessly.

Jamison darts a glance at the three of us, who are clearly watching them. He shakes his head and tries to pull her to the side.

She jerks her hand out of his. "If you can't kiss me in front of them, don't bother kissing me at all in the future." Her voice is full of uncertainty and hurt. "I don't play games, Jamison. I thought... It doesn't matter. It's clear I misread things." She looks at me. "Let's go."

Anger and determination slide across Jamison's face. He grabs her wrist and pulls her into his body. His mouth descends on hers. Passion explodes between the two of them. Her arms wrap tightly around him as she presses her body into his. His hand palms her dark curls while his other hand grips her waist.

A flare of jealousy sparks inside me. I've never seen him so free with his emotions. He's usually calm and collected. Even when his father is raging at full volume. But with her... he can't contain himself.

Neither can Mathias nor Gatlin. She affects all of us in some way. Maybe she's a siren after all, luring us in with her brains and beauty.

The kiss ends, and for a long second, the two stare at each other, chests heaving, then she pivots and returns to where I'm standing. I almost groan at the sight of her swollen pink lips. My body tightens, but I force a smile.

"After you," I say, motioning to the steps on the jet.

SHE SMILES from the seat across from me, but I can tell she's somewhere else. Her fingers glide lightly across her lips as if she can feel his lips on hers. I know I should leave her to her thoughts, but we're not alone very often, and I can't help myself.

"Have you ever been to Hephaestus' temple?" I ask, desperate to know more about this enigmatic woman. Of course, I fall back on the obvious connection between us.

Her smile deepens. "When the temple was completed, I attended the first Hephaestei festival there. Everything was so new and polished." She pauses for a second. "Returning to those sites and seeing them with crumbling stone and dust, it reminds me of how much time has passed. It's bittersweet."

"Because that was your home?" I ask, pushing her a little more. Prior to this, she had only ever admitted living there for a time. Will she let me in?

She stares at me for a minute, then a challenging glint appears in her eyes. "Tell me about Langit. Your family. Your life."

Disappointed but not surprised, I almost grimace at the turn in conversation, but I can't expect her to share if I'm not willing to do so. "Langit is a lot like this world. Full of water and plants and magic, but there are only elves in my world. It's quiet. Peaceful."

"Jamison mentioned you were royalty?" she asks, turning her whole body toward me. "What was that like?"

"My brother is king," I hesitantly admit. I hate talking about my royal status. "I was only a prince."

"Mmm. I was only a princess," she interjects with a devilish glint. "It was exceedingly boring. Always having to be proper. To scale back my emotions. To pretend I couldn't read or write or converse with the dignitaries who visited my father. Maybe it was different for you."

A princess of Ancient Greece. I heard her tell Mathias on the plane that she lost her sister. I'm tempted to grab his laptop and start searching for every king with two daughters during that time. It would take a while. Ancient Greece existed for centuries. But I curb the need to delve into her life without her knowledge. I want her to tell me.

Her words catch me by surprise, though. "I didn't mind being a prince. Although most of the time I stayed at our southern palace and did as I pleased." I think about how simple my life was in Langit. Beautiful. Easy. "My days were spent wandering through the country or working on agricultural initiatives for the crown." Time has only sharpened my memories of my homeland.

"You don't have to talk about it," she says in a gentle tone, as if she can hear the homesickness that never goes away. "I can tell you miss it."

"I want to," I insist. "When I arrived here, the fight with the gods for the right to live was my main focus. Once the dust settled and the treaty was in place, I had little to do and nothing to combat the overwhelming loneliness. I missed my family. My heart was frozen with grief. I didn't know what to do with myself. Elves from Langit wanted to establish a kingdom here, so they pushed for me to take the crown, but I didn't want it."

That's a decision I don't regret. "If you'd have asked me yesterday whether I'd like to return to Langit, I would have said yes." Her mouth turns down, and I reach across to take her hand. "It would have been an automatic response, though. I'm not the same person who came through the portal thousands of years ago. I never thought about it until this moment, but having seen this world, dived into its well of knowledge, felt the magic that fuels it, met all the races… I'm not sure I would ever permanently return."

Her blue eyes widen. "I completely understand. Life shifts and molds us along the way. If my life had followed its original path, there would have been nothing remarkable about it. I would have lived and died. And that's sad." She squeezes my hand. "I'm sorry, though. That you can't go home."

The thought of her living and passing without me ever knowing her shakes me to the core. "It would be nice to visit, but this has become my home. Over the years, I found friends and interests, but it wasn't until Jamison recruited me that I found family again. He doesn't mind having a 'nerd' on his team who's more interested in plants than saving the world."

"Nerds are sexy," she says with a sassy wink. "And technically, he has two on his team. You and Mathias."

True. "Speaking of Mathias, he sent us a schematic of the temple with all of the symbols marked on it." I flip open the laptop on the table in front of me and motion for her to take a look. "There are a lot more than I thought."

She switches to the seat beside me, and I point to the screen. Red circles indicate all of the areas in the temple that include the anvil and hammer with the same dimensions as the one on her hand. The delicious, sweet scent of her teases my senses, and when she stares up at me, all I can think about is replacing the taste and feel of Jamison with my lips. Her blue eyes widen, but I quickly look away before I do something stupid.

She turns and points to the screen. "The schematics don't include the outside. There could be more than this shows." She taps her finger on the table as she thinks. "We should start low. We can get through all the ones at my height or below pretty quickly. Then, we can think of how to get to the harder to reach ones, like those on the ceiling."

"Magic," I remind her. "I can easily use the wind to lift you up."

Her bright blue eyes twinkle against her olive skin. "Ooh, it's nice to have a partner with skills."

Remembering her speech to the society, I can't help but wonder. "In all these years, you never found someone to share this life with? To help you remove the curses of the world?"

She stiffens. "I haven't been entirely alone. There's been the occasional fling." Her voice is full of hurt and a hint of something I can't quite pinpoint. "Look. I chose this path, and I knew what it meant."

She tries to get up, and I grab her hand. "I didn't mean to offend you. Truly. I can't help but see this incredibly vibrant and intelligent woman, and I don't understand..." I stop. Any way I say it is going to sound bad, and that's not the way I intend it.

"Maybe I haven't wanted to be caught," she murmurs, moving back to the seat across from me. "Or maybe I didn't find anyone who was worth it. I'm going to take a short nap. Wake me when we get there." She pulls a blanket from the seat next to her and turns her head away from me.

Frustrated, I take a deep breath and remind myself that she shared quite a bit tonight. It takes time to break down walls. In the meantime, I'm going to put together a plan to tackle each quadrant in the temple. She's right. It's exciting to share this with someone who understands this world. I want to make sure everything goes smoothly.

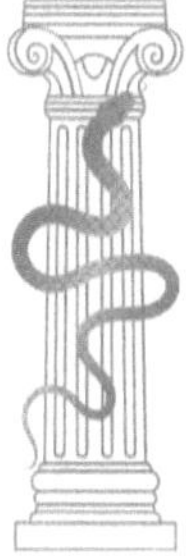 

31

PHAEDRA

Hawthorne is only curious, but it stings. It's my choice to be alone. Loving a human with their short life-span would have only brought me heartbreak, and supernaturals were a risk. Still are. Every day I spend with the four of them is exhilarating and terrifying at the same time. The gods aren't exactly forgiving, and the last thing I want is for them to end my existence. Not because I'm afraid of death. But because I would never get to apologize to my sister. Beg for her forgiveness. See her one last time. Time is the only thing that brings me closer to her. Three thousand years or three hundred thousand, I'll gladly spend those alone to get one minute with her.

The box with the initials, mine and my sister's, is tucked away in my bag. It's a miracle the society found it. I wonder if they know who I am. Rupert's expression seems to suggest

229

they've figured it out. It should worry me, but the society has kept a lot of secrets over the years, and I don't see that changing any time soon.

Charlie comes over the intercom to let us know we're landing in fifteen minutes. Opening my eyes, I find Hawthorne still sitting across from me, engrossed in the laptop. Mahogany locks fall into his face as he lifts his head, but he quickly shoves them back. Green eyes full of worry study me closely as if he's trying to figure out if I'm still upset.

"I'm sorry," I blurt out. "I'm not very good at sharing. It's not because I want to keep things from you. I… I've made decisions in my past, and right or wrong, I stand by them even if a part of me wishes for something different." And I do. These men make me want more. They fit in a way I never expected.

"I let my curiosity get ahead of my manners. I'm sorry," he assures me as he turns the computer toward me. "Take a look. I worked on a plan that I think will allow us to hit the most likely targets first. It incorporates the low to high suggestion you made earlier but rules out symbols on tiny or odd spaces."

Astonished, I examine the quadrants he's outlined on the schematics. "You worked on this the whole time I was asleep?" He put a lot of work into this plan. I cringe, feeling really bad.

"What do you think?" he asks, ignoring my question.

"It's brilliant," I reply with a rueful smile. "Thank you."

The plane dips, and Charlie comes on the intercom. "Seatbelts. We're landing."

"He does know we're immortal, right?" Hawthorne mutters with a frown.

"His aircraft, his rules," I say, mimicking Charlie's familiar response. "I like flying with him too much to rebel." Flying is much better than portals.

Minutes later, we're taxiing to the hangar.

"Thanks, Charlie," I tell him as we exit the plane. "Should I text you when we're ready to leave or catch a flight with someone else?"

"You better not," he warns me. "Jamison paid for me to be available the whole time you're here."

Shocked, I raise an eyebrow, then whistle. "That must have cost him a few gold bars."

"I'm not cheap," Charlie returns with a boyish grin. "Go. Dig. Find treasure. I'll be here." He looks around. "Somewhere with a bar. Text me when you're ready to go."

I salute him and inhale deeply, letting the smell and feel of home seep into my bones. A prickling awareness settles between my shoulder blades, and I grimace. The gods are always closest in Greece. It's why I rarely return. That and the memories.

I lift my chin in defiance and jump into the passenger seat of the Range Rover, waiting by the plane. "Let's go."

The sun is setting as we head from the Athens airport to the site. It's open to the public during the day, which means we'll likely have to return tonight, but I want to conduct a test first.

When we get there, crowds of people are meandering through the temple. "This used to have trees around it. Pomegranate, myrtle, laurel trees, and more. The smell was incredible. Vibrant. Rich." I stare at the walls, comparing them to the last time I saw them, shortly after the temple was finished. It's in remarkably good condition, given the number of years that have passed.

We use our academic credentials to slip through the line of people and head straight into the temple. Pausing for a second to orient ourselves, I use the friezes to figure out my direction. Looking up, I spot the images that depict the Fall of Troy and point them out to Hawthorne.

He nods. "West, east, north, south." Opening the laptop, he positions the schematics to mimic the same orientation. "There.

The schematics show the symbol next to the side entrance to the cella. Lower right."

We quickly move to the location and find the symbol. Hawthorne positions himself in front of me while I reach out and place my left palm in front of the anvil and hammer. Just like before, there's a small glow that quickly fades. Nothing else happens.

"It worked, but this isn't the right one," I inform him, standing to show him the quickly fading brand on my hand. "Let's grab something to eat. Once it gets dark, we'll come back. I used my Duke credentials to reserve the temple for us."

His brows crash together. "I thought the plan was to stay incognito."

"Too many guards," I tell him. "And too many symbols to check. Easier if they thought we were conducting some type of light experiment on the marble." He raises an eyebrow. "First thing I could think of when submitting the request."

"We'll need to move fast," he murmurs, eyes darting from the laptop to the room. "While we eat, I'll narrow down my plan to the most likely first. The last thing we need is for our enemies to discover us here."

I rest a hand on his arm and feel the corded muscles under his shirt. "Don't worry. I promise to protect you."

He narrows his eyes and gives me a frustrated look. "I know you see me as a nerd, but I assure you, I'm quite capable of protecting us both."

NOT WANTING to alert the entire world to our presence, we decide to limit our light to two flashlights and one lantern. The first hour goes by quickly as we eliminate seventy-seven marks. None of them results in a grand discovery.

Blowing out a breath, I look over at him. "One quadrant down. Where is the next symbol?"

Using the flashlight, he points to the wall across from us. "There."

I walk over and hold my palm up to it. "Nothing."

He crosses the spot off on the schematics and flashes his light on the next.

For the next five hours, we continue to test every quadrant until there are none left. He heaves a huge sigh and thrusts a weary hand through his hair.

"We have to be missing something," he says, squinting at the laptop.

"Take a break," I urge him. When his eyes find mine, I sit on the floor in the center of the room. "Eat some of the snacks Mathias sent. Drink some water."

"We need to keep going," he insists, but I shake my head at him.

"Frustration makes for sloppy work," I tell him. Grabbing a bag of peanut butter pretzels and a water, I munch and drink for several minutes.

He gives in and comes over and holds out his hand for the pretzels. "I know. Normally I have all the patience in the world for research and discovery, but I can hear the minutes ticking away and your safety along with it." He pops a few of the pretzels into his mouth.

"You know… there used to be two statues in here. Hephaestus' stood there." I point to a spot near the wall. "And Athena's stood across from him."

"Maybe we're approaching this all wrong," he replies as eyes follow my finger. "Tell me about the temple when it was new."

"There wasn't much more to it than it is today," I say with a shrug. "The statues. The altar. A painting in the center where we're sitting. A few more small mythological scenes painted on the pediments and the metopes that weren't sculpted."

He eyes the sides of the cella. "This is the exact center of the room. You say there was a painting right here." He pats the bare floor. "Where was the altar?"

I point to the far wall and watch as he shines the lantern on the space. "There's nothing there now. Not even a piece of rubble. Or symbols." His tone is full of disappointment.

Pain stretches across my shoulders and neck, and I reach back to rub the tense muscles. He kneels behind me and brushes my hand away. Strong fingers knead the knots as his healing powers cascade heat into my weary muscles until I'm practically a puddle of goo. The distance between us is miniscule. I'm tempted to lean against his strong chest.

Instead, I drop my head back to peer up at him. "Thank you." My voice is huskier than I would like, and the flare of heat in his eyes tells me he hears it.

His head dips, and the scent of him and his magic fills my senses. With a deep breath, I cup my hand around the back of his neck, telling him without words what I need.

Hawthorne stares down at me. "I want to do this again. With you. When there aren't any enemies chasing after us."

His lips find mine, and he claims them with a promise I'm afraid to believe in, but I let myself slide into the depths of his kiss. Unlike Jamison's fierce kisses that pull my emotions from me, Hawthorne's sensual onslaught makes me want to give him everything. One large hand slides under my neck as the other turns my body around to face his. Time slows. Filled with longing and desire, I arch into him, needing more. His hand drifts across my back and down my side, leaving a slow burn in its wake.

He groans and lifts his head, breaking the kiss, then gathers me into his arms. "I've been waiting to kiss you, and finally, here, in this temple, everything felt...right."

Damn, that's romantic. I sigh. "That kiss was worth the wait, but I don't need a perfect moment," I reply, putting my lips to his ear. "Only you. Too bad we're in the middle of an ancient Greek temple with only a stone floor."

His breath hitches. "Rain check?"

"Absolutely." I exhale and tilt my head back to study his face. "And yes, I want to do this again. With you." Tracing the rough stone beneath my fingers, I smile. "I love the feeling I get when I'm in the past. Digging for history. Sharing it with you has been amazing."

He inhales sharply beside me. "Lift your hand."

"What?" I ask, moving away from him to peer down at the stone beneath me. Light shines from beneath my palm. And it's not fading. I quickly shift to my feet and raise my hand. "It's still glowing." Excited, I stare in awe at the sight.

"Move your hand," he instructs me.

When I lift it away from the brand, the light shines brightly from the floor halfway up to the ceiling. Following it with our eyes, we continue the straight path and find a matching symbol.

He jumps up. "I'm going to lift you up to the mark on the ceiling."

Wind caresses my legs, weaving in and out as it gets stronger, until it suddenly lifts me up to the symbol. Once there, I hold my hand out and light begins to glow.

"It's working!" I exclaim excitedly. "I'm going to move my hand." The second my hand shifts to the side, the light extends fully until it meets the light from the floor, forming one continuous stream.

Hawthorne sets me down, and we step to the side to peer at the slim column of light. As the circumference widens, the light glows brighter. It increases in size until the column encompasses the center of the room, exactly where the painting used to be. Roughly six feet in diameter.

The floor beneath our feet rumbles, then stones slide to the right and left. A large hole forms, and in the center, a golden anvil with a matching blacksmith's hammer laying on its surface rises from the depths.

"Hephaestus crafted many a creation on that anvil," I say in awe at the sight before me. *Shit.* Does that mean…? I look around, suddenly fearful that the god is going to appear. Listening to the sounds of the night, I wait.

Hawthorne steps up and grips my hand. "I'm here. No matter what." Fire forms in his other hand, ready to be used at a moment's notice.

We stand together and wait. The column of light disappears, but instead of the darkness returning, the anvil begins to glow.

"What do you think is happening?" I murmur. "Can you see anything?"

Without releasing my hand, he steps forward and shines his flame on the anvil. It grows brighter. He moves his hand back, and it dims. Forward, and it glows.

He points to the words on the side of the anvil that appear when his flames skim the surface. "Our instructions?"

Releasing his hand, I step forward and read the words. "Let the flames fire the forge and the hammer reveal." Am I supposed to create something? "See anything else?"

He waves a hand at the hammer. "The symbol. It's on the handle."

I slowly reach my palm out, but no light appears. A knot forms in my throat. "I think I'm supposed to pick it up." I flash a worried look at him.

He scowls. "I don't like it."

"See any other options?" I ask, desperate to find another answer.

"No," he replies tersely. Fire erupts from his second hand. "I'll create the fire. You pick up the hammer."

The second he holds both hands out toward the anvil, fire erupts in a circle around us. Sweat immediately forms across my body as the intense heat licks at the edges. I reach out and grasp the handle, with my left palm flush against the symbol. Searing pain makes me cry out. I try to drop the hammer, but it's welded to my hand.

The flames dim, and the pain gets worse. "Don't stop!" I tell him as tears slip down my face. We must finish the quest. "Hotter. The flames must be blue."

"No!" he roars. "You'll burn up."

"I won't," I assure him. "This task was given to me. The gods leave nothing to chance. Do it." I stare into his green eyes, usually bright, now dark, a maelstrom of fear and determination in their depths.

He raises his hands. Flames pour out of his hands like a river, and the fire burns higher and hotter. Tips of white begin to appear across the flames. Muscles along his jaw tighten, and sweat pours down his face, dampening his shirt, as the magic pulls at him. His eyes remain locked on mine. He widens his stance, and the cords in his neck pop out, but he continues to feed the fire around us. The flames turn pure white. His body sways, and I bite my lip at the agony I can see in his eyes.

The hammer sears my skin, and I flinch, but not once do I let my gaze drop from his. We're in this together. Trusting the other to do our part. Pain. Heat. Doesn't matter.

He takes a deep breath, braces himself, and pushes more power into the flames. A streak of white appears in his hair, and still, he doesn't stop. My knees almost buckle at the heat around us. The flames don't burn, but the air is thick and smothering. It's getting harder to breathe. The first hints of blue appear, and at the sight, he roars and thrusts his hands out, pouring the last vestiges of his power into the flames. Pure blue flames erupt.

The second I see it, I scream, "Stop!"

He falls to the ground, eyes closed. I shift my feet to go to him, but I can't. The ritual won't let me. In frustration, I strike the hammer against the anvil. Sparks fly, and a small golden circle appears in front of me. The fucking gods and their schemes. I need to get to Hawthorne. I scream and rage as I hit it again and again. The circle widens.

A blue and gold panel appears. Small and rectangular with a golden lock on it. I reach into the circle and grab it. The second it's in my hands, the fire dies, and the floor rumbles. Dropping the hammer, I rush to Hawthorne, put the panel on his chest, and drag him to safety. The anvil and hammer disappear into the floor's dark depths.

Breathing hard, I lay my head on his chest and listen. *Thump... thump.* Slow but steady. With a trembling hand, I brush the sweat-drenched hair back from his face and place a kiss on his lips.

"Thank you."

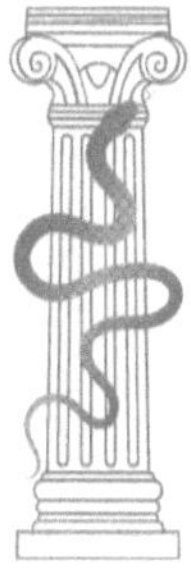

32

<u>PHAEDRA</u>

Quickly packing everything up, I stash the panel in my backpack and slip it onto my shoulders, then call Charlie. I'm stronger than a human, but I can't carry Hawthorne and all this gear from here to the distant parking lot and into the Range Rover before the sun comes up and tourists fill the area.

"Need evacuation assistance," I tell him, explaining where we're at and what's going on. "We can take the vehicle back to the airstrip."

A second later, he steps out of a portal, picks up Hawthorne, and follows me to the SUV. "Damn, he's heavy. Guess I should be thankful it's not the big guy. What is he, anyway?"

"Who? Gatlin?" I ask absentmindedly. Not once has Hawthorne moved, and I'm really starting to worry.

He nods.

"Gryphon," I murmur as we trudge down the hill. "We're

going to need a safe place to go. Somewhere he can heal." I shove a weary hand through my dark hair. "How long would it take to get to Rome?"

"If I pushed it, maybe a little over an hour," he replies with a sideways glance. "I know a healer there. Discreet. Want me to call her?"

We reach the vehicle and carefully load Hawthorne into the backseat. "Thanks, that would be great."

Not once does he stir on the way back to the plane, nor all the way to Rome.

When we arrive, the healer, a Fae named Arlie, is waiting for us. Tall, with long blond hair and mercurial silver eyes, there's a peaceful essence about her. She examines Hawthorne while I pace back and forth.

"He's in the between," she informs me in a soft tone. "It's a state elves and Fae enter into when their magic is depleted." Her gaze meets mine. "I'll give you a tonic for his physical body, but his magic needs time to regenerate."

She hesitates, then grabs my hand. "Don't let him stay in this state for too long. We can get lost in the aether. Do whatever it takes to bring him back."

I blow out a breath. Time. My friend. My enemy. "How?"

"Talk to him. Invigorate his senses. Taste. Touch. Smell. Remind him of his life. Nature helps. Take him outside," she replies, her gaze full of warmth. "Listen to your heart."

I haven't listened to that organ in a long time. "I'll do my best."

She leaves, and Charlie helps me load him into the passenger seat where I can keep an eye on him while I drive.

"I've got it from here," I assure him, not wanting anyone to know where I'm taking him. Safer that way. Hawthorne's too vulnerable in this state. "Thank you. I really appreciate your help."

Charlie's mouth compresses, and he stares at me for a long

minute. "I don't know what you're caught up in, but be careful. The council follows its own agenda. Latest chatter predicts an uprising, which won't be good for anyone. Remember, Maverick and I are a call away. Don't hesitate." He awkwardly pats me on the back and boards the plane.

The drive takes forty-five minutes to reach the villa I bought in the early 70s when modernism was on the rise. Minimalist in design and built with natural materials, the place is both airy and functional and surrounded by trees. Bonus, it's all on one level.

I pull into the driveway and take the gear into the house first. Coming back for Hawthorne, I contemplate how best to get him inside and realize the fireman's carry is my best option. Thankfully, the seat is high enough to give me leverage and hoist him onto my back.

Once inside, I maneuver to the long couch in the living room and lay him down. I'll need to move a bed into the room later, but for now, this will have to do. I return to the vehicle and lock it up.

Back inside, I lay my hand on his chest, checking it for the millionth time. His muscular chest rises and falls, and I exhale in relief. My gaze falls on the white streak in his mahogany hair, and I finger it gently. *I wonder if this is permanent.*

Jamison hasn't answered any of my calls or texts. Granted, my wording has been vague, but too much is at stake to reveal Hawthorne's condition or our location. I hope he gets back to me soon.

Rolling my shoulders, I grab a second blanket and take the other half of the L-shaped couch. Exhaustion weighs heavily on me. I can barely hold my head up. One hour. That's all I need. Then I'll figure things out. My lids close and darkness descends.

When I wake, three hours have gone by. *Shit.* I sit up and groan as the muscles in my body protest. I glance at Hawthorne, still in the same position, his chest rising and falling, which is a good sign. I glance at my phone. No messages. What the hell is going on? Should I be worried? Fear clogs my throat, but I swallow it down deep and shake my head. Can't think like that.

The backpack leaning against the couch catches my eye. Stretching forward, I snag it with my finger and pull it onto my lap, then peer inside. Blue and gold gleam against the dark canvas. I remove the panel and study it. Four inches top to bottom, and twelve inches across. Tongue and groove notches on all four sides to connect it to the other panels. The ornate lock is in the same gold patina as the key that's hidden in my vault in North Carolina. Unlike the key, the panel doesn't give me any visions. Around the lock is a circle in a bright white. Besides the delicate gold filigree, there are no other scenes or decorations on the surface.

I stand and walk over to the bookcase on the far wall. Pulling on a book about ancient tombs slides the shelves to the right, revealing a hidden vault. It takes a second to stash the panel and close everything.

Now that it's safe, it's time to help Hawthorne get more comfortable. I break down the bed in the spare bedroom down the hall and reassemble it piece by piece in the living room. Then I pull Hawthorne from the couch and carry him into the bathroom to clean some of the sweat off him from the heat of the fire.

I prop him against the wall and unbutton his shirt. When I slide my hands up his chest to tug off his shirt, his muscles contract. Startled, I glance up, but his face is expressionless. Eyes closed. *Mmm.* I do it again, and the same thing happens. *Interesting.* She did say touch. I tug off his shirt and reach for his pants.

Unbuttoning them, I let them fall to his ankles and swallow hard. Boxer briefs are one of man's best inventions. Every line is delineated. He's a work of art. Pure perfection. I reach for the washcloth on the sink and turn on the water.

"Just wash him off," I mutter to myself.

Once the water is hot, I squeeze out the excess and carefully glide it across his powerful body. Sometimes I wish I had powers. It would be nice to give him a proper shower, but I can't do it alone.

After cleaning most of his exposed skin, I drape the washcloth over my shoulder, bend down and ease one foot, then the other, out of his shoes, socks, and pants, leaving his boxers on. I wipe the sweat from my brow and carefully finish washing the rest of him. Then I stand and wrap my arm around him.

We slowly leave the bathroom and walk across the living room to the bed where I lay him down, then draw the light cotton sheet up to his waist. I stare down at him.

He didn't hesitate. When the forge called for more, he gave it everything he had...for me. The expression in his eyes told me everything. It was all there. An acknowledgement of the path he was choosing. His determination to stand with me. No walls between us. I've never experienced such selflessness. It's ironic, really. That moment forged something between us that will never be broken.

I lean forward and wrap my hands around his jaw. Lightly rubbing my thumbs across his cheeks, I kiss him. "If you wake up, we can finish what we started in the temple." That would tempt me to open my eyes.

He doesn't answer. Defeated, I tell him I'm going to take a shower. On the way, I text Gatlin. Maybe there's something wrong with Jamison's phone. Or perhaps he's chasing something down.

> Phaedra: Looking for a bright red double-decker.

That's vague enough, right?

The app shows no indication that the message was delivered or read. I bite my lip, considering the potential ramifications.

Have our phones been hacked again? Are they in danger? I'm tempted to reach out to one of my contacts, but I don't want to give away their position or ours.

Arrgh. I toss the phone onto the bed and head to the shower.

Water cascades over my sore muscles as my skin drinks up every bit of moisture the flames sucked out of me. I stare down at the symbol on my palm. Seared into the skin like a brand, I can't help but wonder why it's still there. Shouldn't it have disappeared when I finished my task?

Two panels. One key. If it's a box, there will be six panels. I think about the sketch Doran did and shake my head. Six gods. Of course it matches. The gods love their fucking quests. What does it hold though? I'm sure it's not something innocuous. Not with the elaborate measures they put in place.

Maybe only the first piece was meant to be found by humans. Certainly not the last one. My stomach clenches. Does that mean four more tasks like the one we just completed? Should I do these tasks alone? Hawthorne's locked in a comatose-like state, but what if something worse happens? What if it takes one of their lives? I could never forgive myself.

And I carry enough guilt as it is. All those years ago, I defied the gods and lost my sister because of it. Seeing Hawthorne lying so still is killing me.

Resigned, I reach out and turn off the water. A minute later, I'm padding out of the bedroom in worn sweats and an equally soft long-sleeve shirt.

"I'm back," I call out to Hawthorne. "And I'm starving. If you wake up, I'll make you the best lasagna you've had in your life." Silence is my answer. "Guess not."

Good thing he didn't answer. The fridge is bare. I'll have to get groceries delivered tomorrow. In the meantime, I reach for a box of crackers, peanut butter, and a bag of microwave popcorn. Girl dinner it is. Not wanting to eat in front of Hawthorne, I prop myself against the kitchen counter and snack while I think about how to get him to respond to me.

Touch seems to incite some reaction. I'm not sure if he hears me, but I'll keep talking to him. Even if it's inane conversation. I wish I knew for sure. Frustrated, I pick up my phone and send a text to Mathias.

> Phaedra: Could use a little help and your expertise.

Again, the app shows nothing.

The cracker in my mouth turns to dust. There's nothing I can do for them except hope they're okay. I need to focus on Hawthorne. When he comes out of this state, he can help me figure out what to do next. I grab the tonic and head back to him.

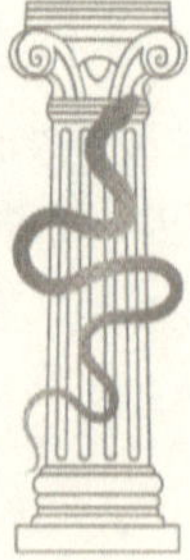

33

JAMISON

Based on the surveillance data, we realized the group was too large for us to take on by ourselves. Requesting security forces from the council without revealing the details was tricky, but it was the only way I was willing to proceed. The motion barely passed, but they were unanimous in their message—any exposure of our supernatural world would mean my immediate removal as head of security and a trial. Not that there would be much of one, since they serve as both jury and executioner.

Coordinates were given to the two planes after takeoff. Mathias went on one plane to debrief those teams, and I boarded the other to do the same. Gatlin left ahead of us to meet with the surveillance team. Once we have boots on the ground, we'll coordinate an attack based on his observations.

"We land in twenty minutes," I tell the teams, then take my seat near the front. Preliminary reports suggest at least a hundred in the enemy camp, but all of the soldiers are human. Normally, I'd take a team of forty, but with their reinforced suits and extensive resources, I decided to match them in numbers.

I glance at my phone. Hawthorne sent me a message letting me know they arrived at the temple in Athens. That was yesterday. Nothing since. I don't like it. What if they've already run into trouble? Maybe we should have gone with them. Tackled this group later. *Damn.* I hope he sends an update soon.

I trace the photo he sent of her sleeping across from him, lips swollen from our kiss at the airport. I stare at it. Every moment she challenges me. I'm not into public displays, but all the rules go out the window when I'm around her. That kiss. The world faded around us. All I wanted was her. Her lips beneath mine, her soft curves pressed into me, but mostly, her surrender. Damn if she didn't hesitate to give it to me.

The sound of landing gear interrupts the rest of my thoughts. I grimace. A good thing as I shift uncomfortably. The plane touches down and comes to a halt. I stand and circle my hand to tell them to move out.

"What have you got for me?" I ask Gatlin when he answers.

"Camp is huge. We need to come at it from all sides. As you know, there are six roads in and out. Four teams on each entrance. First wave will focus on taking out as many as possible. We'll capture any stragglers at the end. Leadership tent identified. I'll need at least ten to secure it," he tells me in a strained voice.

"What's wrong?" I ask, startled to hear something besides his usual calm voice.

"A team of eight left yesterday in two SUVs. We tracked them to Athens but lost them in the city," he informs me, his voice tight with worry.

"Do you think they know Hawthorne and Phaedra are at the temple?" I ask, my voice sharp with alarm. Hawthorne can handle himself, but a large team would be near impossible. The pit in my stomach grows.

"Probable," he replies, his voice tight. "I tried to get ahold of Hawthorne, but nothing. You hear from them?"

His use of the word *them* tells me everything I need to know. Gatlin's nature is that of a protector, and it's obvious he sees her as one of us. Something is wrong. I can feel it in my gut. *Fuck.*

"Yesterday. They arrived in Athens. Nothing today. I'll keep trying. Right now, we need to focus on this attack. Got it?" Even though it's the last fucking thing I want to do.

"Affirmative," he states reluctantly. "But I want to check on them as soon as possible." His hard tone tells me how worried he is about them.

"We'll head to Athens after we take this group down," I promise with a harsh laugh. "We're loading up. Be there in twenty. Set the timer."

Mathias, standing beside me, raises a brow.

"Let's get this over with. Be safe."

His lips compress and with a set face, he strides over to the first vehicle and gets in the passenger seat.

Gone is the nerd who stays in the background playing with computers and digging up data. This is the fighter I saw when I met him a few centuries back. He's the vampire Nolan Westgate feared the most. Mathias, the king's commander, back in his home world of Kallias.

He blames himself for having volunteered to walk through the portal. His king would have spared him, but his honor wouldn't let him. There was no way he was going to send his men alone. In doing so, he lost the one person he valued most in life—his daughter. Once the war with the gods was settled, he threw himself into searching for a way to return but could never find one.

Resigned, he drifted for a long time. Adapted to this world.

Found he had a knack for tech and making money. Became the man he portrays to the world today. Except when cornered.

It's been a long time since I've seen that expression on his face and those knives strapped to his shoulders. My smile is grim as I contemplate the surprise on his team's faces when they see the predator behind the mask.

I slide into the passenger seat and nod for us to head out. "Remember, split when we hit the next intersection." Everyone already knows which of the six roads they will follow into the compound. "Watch your backs and stay away from glowing weapons."

I pick up my phone and text Hawthorne, telling him about the team headed to Athens. He doesn't respond, which is unlike him. My gut is churning with dread, but I can't do anything about it at this moment. Our best bet is to capture the rest of this group and get some damn answers out of them.

"Intersection," I call out over comms. "Five minutes to target."

The fight begins the second each team hits the compound. Gunfire rings out across the land. Soldiers shift into animals. Some on the ground and others in the air. Vampires strike hard as they speed through the enemy ranks. The smell of magic burns the air as potions, spells, and fire spread from the outside to the center.

Coming to a stop, Gatlin strides over. With him by my side, we make our way to the leadership tent he identified earlier. "Roughly twenty to thirty inside. Fighters, every one of them. Hand to hand combat is what they want. Between the weapons that can nullify magic and their inherent combat skills, they're good enough to win. Don't let them draw you into a fight. Use your magic."

He steps away from me, transforming into his gryphon. He dips his head and immediately heads up to tear away the tent.

We follow on the ground, killing those who rush to escape his fierce talons.

Surprisingly, most of them stay to fight, blue weapons glowing in their hands. This is what Gatlin was saying. I draw a golden lasso with my magic and use it to keep them at bay. One particular soldier gets too close, and I drop it around his neck and sever his head from his shoulders.

I hear a scream to my right and see one of my mages getting stabbed with the same type of weapon that took out Letz. Furious, I whip my rope around the guy's wrist and cut off the hand with the weapon. Without missing a beat, he bends down to pick it up with his other hand but never makes it. A talon flings him into the hands of a vampire waiting nearby.

"Surrender!" I shout. "And we'll spare your men!"

A massive grey-haired man in the back laughs. "Never. We've given too much to you bastards over the years. It's time to take back this world. Make it safe for humans again." I see him raise his phone to his ear. "Now."

I hear the first detonation and see Gatlin's eagle head jerk up. Running outside, I watch in horror as explosions go off around the camp. Screams are heard from every corner. I see a shimmer to my right and turn as a portal opens. The enemy rushes into it. Another shimmer across from me. Another portal.

"Cover the portals," I yell into the comms. "Take down as many as you can before they escape." I glance up at Gatlin and turn to rush back inside, but a bomb goes off, sending me flying back from the tent in the other direction.

Darkness closes in on me.

BEEPING MACHINES. Pain everywhere. I pry my eyes open and see white walls and Mathias typing furiously on a computer beside me. Bright lights pierce my eyes, making my headache worse.

"Turn the damn lights off," I order in a gravelly voice.

Mathias turns off the lights and closes the curtains. "Better?"

"Water," I plead, my throat scratching like sandpaper. He holds a glass to my lips, and I take a few sips. "Thanks. How long have I been out?"

"A week," Mathias tersely replies.

Damn.

"Status," I demand with a grimace, knowing it's going to be bad.

"The council has placed you on medical leave until further notice," he begins. When I raise a demanding eyebrow, he shakes his head. "It's bad. The entire place was one big minefield ready to blow. Forty-seven of ours gone. Most from the explosions. They were laced with magical fire."

"And the enemy?" I ask, exhaling heavily. "They had one hell of an exit plan."

"Quite a few died but almost half escaped," he says, sitting on the bed beside me. "We don't know who opened the portals." He pauses and flashes me a look, telling me he has an idea, then he subtly nods at the window of my room where a guard is posted.

Who are they guarding? Me from the enemy? Or are they here to prevent me from leaving? Probably all of the above.

"Where is everyone?" I ask with a frown. Is Phaedra safe?

"Gatlin's on a rampage, but he's good," Mathias informs me. "We haven't heard from Hawthorne or Phaedra. Somehow, they're blocking all messages and calls between us." He curses. "I don't know how they're fucking doing it." Anger flares in the depths of his eyes. He's pissed he missed it. "I've ordered phones, but she won't have our new numbers. And the locator on the laptop is still off."

He leans down and whispers to me. "I've been in touch with Charlie. He dropped them off in Rome, but he doesn't have an address. I'm searching all the available footage but haven't located them yet."

My brows draw together. "Why did they go there?"

Mathias darts a glance at the guard and shakes his head. "Later."

"I do have good news," Mathias says with a sardonic smile. "We captured a few of the leaders. That's where Gatlin is now. He insisted on being in on the interrogation despite the council's best efforts to keep him out of it."

I push to my elbows, trying to sit up, but the world spins around me.

"Damn it, be careful. The blast nearly killed you," he spits out. "There isn't anything you can do except get better. This is getting nasty. We need you at your best."

"What did the doctor say?" I ask, easing back down on the bed.

"A week," Mathias retorts. "But I doubt you'll wait that long. Give it at least another day. Two would be better. We're working on figuring a few things out anyway."

I shake my head. "We need to search for them. In person. Now."

What if something happened to her? My mind goes to the last time I saw her. Our kiss. Gatlin's right. We never should have split up. At the time, it seemed safer for them to go to Athens, but it was a bad call.

Mathias turns his phone toward me. "If you wait, you can have first crack at this."

On the screen is a picture of a blue glowing knife. One of their weapons. I look up at him. "Who knows you have this?"

"Gatlin, me, you," he murmurs with a dangerous glint in his eye. "Apparently, it only works on those who have or use magic like shifters, mages, elves, and demons. Funny enough, it has zero effect on vampires."

34

PHAEDRA

The news is full of reports about bombs going off in Greece. Media outlets are frantic to determine the cause, but all the evidence has disappeared. Locals report a group setting up camp in the area but can recall few details.

"It has to be them," I tell Hawthorne, biting my lip. "I hope they're okay. What do you think? You know them best. Why don't you wake up and help me figure out how to contact them? Time for you to open your eyes."

His face remains blank, and his breathing even. I sit up in bed and throw off the covers. Not wanting to leave him alone, I've been sleeping beside him every night for the last week. His body responds to my nearness, muscles contracting, but that's been the extent of his awareness. Shoving a hand through my hair, I get up and start the day.

There have been no replies to any of my text messages. I

tried calling every number. No answer. The tests I ran on the phone came back clean, but I've been around too many years not to know when my tech has been compromised. How? I'm not certain, but my gut made me order a new phone. It's scheduled to arrive this morning.

After I shower, I pad into the kitchen to get a piece of toast and Hawthorne's tonic. I hold the bottle up to the light. It's almost gone. The healer said it would heal his physical body. While there wasn't a scratch on him, the depletion of magic took a huge toll, made him weak. Hopefully the tonic is working, but I won't know until he wakes and attempts to walk.

With the last bite of toast in my mouth, I walk over and drip the tonic into his open mouth, then bend down and follow it with a kiss. *Can't hurt, right?*

"It's a gorgeous day," I tell him, maneuvering his body into an upright position. "The sun is shining. There's a cool breeze. Want to join me outside?"

I quickly realized that relying on my strength to haul him around wasn't going to work long-term, so I ordered a wheelchair. Being able to wheel him from one spot to the other has been a huge help. Locking the wheels, I slide him into the seat and place his feet on the pedals.

"There," I say in a bright voice as I grab the handles. "Let's go."

The sun pierces the shade on the porch, and I wheel him directly into its rays. His burnished skin begins glowing the color of copper as if the sunshine is nourishing his body. I pick a purple flower from the nearby landscape, lavender petals darkening into a deep violet near the middle. Musky notes waft from its center. I don't know what kind it is. The plant was here when I bought the place, and it continues to bloom every year.

Holding it to his nose, I let him breathe in its scent for a few seconds. Then I brush the soft petals across his lips and over to his ear, then down his neck. Muscles contract along the way. I continue across his arms, skimming the sun-bronzed skin as the flower follows the dips and valleys of his corded muscles.

Finished with his nature therapy, I grab a chair beside him. "You know, I've never cared for anyone like this before. As a princess, I didn't really have any chores, and most of my adult life has been spent alone. Here I am, winging it. I'd love for you to wake up and tell me if I'm doing a good job."

I tilt my head and laugh. "Or do you want to complain? I'm probably touching you more than is necessary. Sorry... not sorry? You should definitely wake up and reciprocate. I mean retaliate."

Silence. "Not to mention how guilty you're making me feel for getting you into this mess. I really need you to wake up and tell me you forgive me." I lean forward and point to the corners of my eyes. "Look, I'm getting wrinkles from all the worry."

No response. I sigh and drop my head. "Seriously, though. I don't know how to reach Jamison or the rest of them. So stupid. I should have asked for an alternative. A burner. Email. Smoke signal. Anything. It never occurred to me. That's what happens when you're used to working by yourself. But that's why I need you to wake up."

Tears well, and I reach over and lace my fingers with his. I've looked at all the options but always come to the same conclusion. Moving Hawthorne is too risky. Someone could easily catch us on camera. Even if we made it to London, I don't have a secure place to take him. The Hari is compromised.

The doorbell rings, and I jump up and run to the monitors in the office. I check the security cameras and see a courier.

"Can I help you?" I ask through the intercom.

"Package here for P. G.," she says with a huff. "I need a signature."

"I'm not home. You can sign and leave it by the front door."

With a shrug, she scribbles on a slip of paper and props the box against the door, then leaves. I watch every move until she gets on her scooter and drives away.

Picking up my gun, I hurry to the front door and grab the box. The return address is a familiar one. It's my phone. That's one worry off my shoulders. I set the gun on a nearby table and stroll back outside to set it up.

"Look what came," I say, holding up the box. "Not that it will help us reach them, but at least we'll have secure communications." For the next half hour, I get the phone up and running, then place another grocery order. Two things accomplished.

"I'm going to heat up some lasagna. Want some?"

Leaning over, I place a kiss on his lips and brush his silky hair back from his face. "It's really, really good." I search his smooth expression. "I know you're in there. Listening to me. Is your magic coming back to you?"

Fear and guilt vie for first place, but I continue to shove them down deep. The present is the only thing that counts. I head to the kitchen to heat up leftovers. He missed a great lunch. I made the lasagna hoping the smell would wake him, but of course, it didn't.

One week. How long is too long? Maybe I should call Charlie and get the healer's number and ask. I think about it and decide to give it a couple more days. Time, she said. I snort. All these years I've had nothing but time, but now the clock is ticking. Loudly.

After lunch, I grab a soft sponge and a bucket with soapy water. Bathing Hawthorne outside has been the easiest. It's private, and I don't have to worry about him falling or the water splashing onto the floor.

First, I wash his hair. Spearing my fingers through his thick mahogany locks, I take the time to shampoo every strand until it's shiny and clean, massaging his head and neck. Then, I move on to his body. Over the last few days, his body has responded, muscles lightly flexing, but that's been the extent of it. My little beacon of hope. Running the sponge lightly across his chest, I can't help but devour every sun-kissed inch.

When his breath catches, it takes me a moment to understand, but the second I do, I run the sponge across his chest again. Wait. Was that…? There. His breathing, steady as a rock, picks up its pace. I inhale sharply, filling with hope.

"Hawthorne, I need you to wake up," I murmur, kissing him lightly on his lips. "Please, please, wake up. I need to see those beautiful green eyes of yours. Hear that smooth voice that sends shivers down my spine. I want to hear you say my name."

His breathing steadies again.

With a sigh, I drop my head onto his chest. A knot forms in my throat. All I want to do is cry or scream, but I swallow it down and pat his arm. "It's okay. I've got you."

I finish his bath and dry him off, then wheel him back into the living room. We usually watch a little TV in the afternoon. Lifting him into the bed, I pull the sheet up and leave him resting there.

I flip on the news and watch as the camera pans across an exploded minefield. With a gasp, I lean forward and scan the war zone. There are no bodies, but that doesn't mean much. The council would have sent in a clean-up crew before the humans got there. I hold a hand to my mouth. Did they survive?

I grab my laptop from the office and navigate to the council's website. A banner displays a message notifying users that a live press conference will be held tonight to update everyone on the developing situation.

Four hours. I set the timer on my new phone and walk over and slip into bed beside Hawthorne. Curling into him, I pray to the gods like I haven't done since I was a child, begging and pleading for their grace. Hoping they're alive. Hawthorne needs them…and so do I.

Hours later, I open the laptop and watch as Daegan, the head council leader, and Lord de Vere, Jamison's father, stand behind the podium and inform the supernatural community of the loss of forty-seven members. Shouts ring out from the crowd. They haven't lost this many in a long time. Numb, I continue to listen, but they refuse to release the list of names until all family members have been contacted.

If they're... Tears slide silently down my cheeks. I can't think about it.

The two councilmembers finish their announcement with the promise of another live press conference tomorrow.

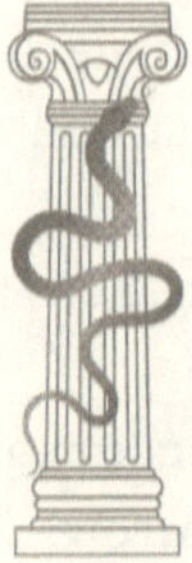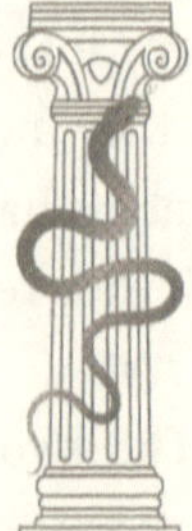

35

MATHIAS

Charlie didn't have the license plate for the SUV Phaedra was driving when it left the airport in Rome. Cameras follow the vehicle for a while, but winding roads and urban planning that evolved over thousands of years mean tracking is scattered. He tried to reach out to her for me but received no response. She must have realized the phones were hacked and ditched hers.

The laptop I gave Hawthorne has a beacon on it, but it's either turned off or the battery is dead. Still, I keep the program locator running just in case. Why didn't I add another tracker to their bags or a burner phone with our numbers? *Damn it.* I should have anticipated and planned accordingly. If I had, Phaedra and Hawthorne would be here. With us. Safe.

I take off my glasses and rub my eyes. No matter which way I turn, it's roadblock after roadblock. Jamison stirs beside me but doesn't wake up. Technically, he should be dead. At some point, I'm going to have to tell him I gave him a drop of my blood to keep him alive. We never talked about it as an option, so I don't know how he'll react.

Gatlin is supposed to return this afternoon. The interrogation isn't going well. All of the humans are willing to die for this cause, and not one has given us any leads to follow. Without evidence, we can't reveal the council's involvement, so the traitor remains in our midst, pulling our strings and accepting devastating losses.

A vampire stepped out of one of the portals to alert the human soldiers and call for their retreat. Her profile was to me, but I know I've never seen her before, and all my efforts to identify her have proven futile. She must be new to this world. We get a few every year. Most of the time, the gods are able to keep the portals closed, but on rare occasions, they open. Those who are willing to step through are searching for something—safety, a loved one, adventure—the reasons are numerous and varied. All newcomers used to register with Nolan, who would take their tithe and enter them into the official record. Nobody has picked up that task since he passed.

If the vampires are working with this human group, it would explain a lot. The weapons they use are not effective on us, only those with magic. Coincidentally, it all kicked off around the time of Nolan's death, which makes me wonder if they took him out first. An attempt to take down the council and establish a new world order, perhaps?

But who is the other group working with? They were the ones who broke into the museum and Phaedra's condo. Killed Letz. The footage at her condo suggested someone used mage magic to hide themselves from the cameras.

Vampires. Mages. Two of the strongest factions on the council. If one got an inkling the other was trying to take over, they would do everything in their power to thwart them. I frown. The only mage with enough power to fund and direct a group of humans is Jamison's father. And if he's the traitor, we're in one hell of a predicament.

The door opens, and I glance up, expecting Gatlin, but instead it's a young nurse. A shifter named Eloise, if I recall. She smiles at me, but when she does, her steps falter and her eyes widen. As if entranced, she moves closer and halts right in front of me.

Damn it. I slip my glasses back on and smoothly tell her, "Tend to Jamison."

She shakes her head and gives me a puzzled look before moving to check on her patient. "Vitals are good. I'm reducing the pain medication. He should be more alert when he wakes. If he's hungry, call us, and we'll bring him a tray."

"Thank you," I reply, watching her closely as she leaves.

To my relief, the compulsion seems to have dissipated. It's why I wear these glasses. There is a special lens in them to prevent susceptible individuals from falling under mine. While some vampires have the ability to compel, it takes concentrated effort. Unlike me. It's completely effortless and begins the moment they meet my unfiltered gaze. I've yet to encounter anyone immune to my ability.

An hour later, the door opens again, but this time, Gatlin walks through, lips compressed and brow furrowed.

"How is he?" he asks, dropping into a nearby chair.

"Should be awake soon," I assure him. "How did it go?"

A muscle tics in his jaw. "Later." He glances at the window. "I tried to get rid of the guard, but the asshole told me he only listens to the council." His eyes drift from the guard to Jamison, silently telling me we need to move him soon.

"Hmm," I reply, agreeing with him. "I haven't found them yet. I've got several programs running, but nothing has popped."

Jamison opens his eyes. "Phaedra and Hawthorne?"

His hand reaches out, and he pushes the button to raise the bed so he can sit up.

"Nothing," I tell him, watching as the guard angles his head closer to the window. "They've disappeared." I lean in close. "We need to get out of here. How are you feeling?"

He grimaces. "Like a damn bomb exploded in front of me. Everything hurts." He glances from me to Gatlin. "But you're right. What's the plan?"

Gatlin raises an eyebrow. "Can you stand?"

Jamison's face fills with determination. "Let's see, shall we?" He shoves the covers back and slowly swivels his legs off the bed until they're dangling against the side.

I reach out to help, but he pushes my hand away. Sliding his feet down to the floor, he takes a deep breath and tries to stand, but his legs crumble with the slightest weight. Thankfully, I'm there to catch him and get him back in bed.

He exhales. "Fuck. Got any other ideas?"

I exchange a glance with Gatlin. "I've got a few ideas. Stay with him. I'll be back in a minute." Leaving the room, I walk past the guard without acknowledging him. Down the hall, I ask the nurse for a wheelchair. She points to the supply closet in the hall. I grab one, remove my glasses, and head back to the room.

As I near the door, the guard stops me. "He can't leave."

I raise my head and stare into his eyes. "We're going to leave with Jamison, and you're not going to stop us. In fact, you're going to continue to see us every time you look in the room. You will not raise an alarm or call anyone. Now, tell me, when is the next guard relieving you?"

His eyes are fixed on mine. "At midnight."

Five hours. "Ten minutes before midnight, you will go to the restroom on the first floor. At twelve ten, you will return to your post. Got it."

He nods. "Yes, sir."

I pat him on the back and put my glasses back on. "Good job." Wheeling the chair into the room, I position it by the bed. "Let's go."

Gatlin gathers Jamison's things while I help him into the chair.

"I'll go first and scout for any other guards. If we get separated, my truck is on the third floor of the parking garage. Here are the keys." He opens the door and signals "all clear."

Once we leave, he strides ahead to make sure the path is clear. It takes us about fifteen minutes to get to the truck. Jamison gets in the back and lies down across the seat, clothes bunched up to cushion his head. Gatlin and I jump into the front.

"Where to?" he asks, turning on the vehicle.

"Three," I tell him.

Years ago, Jamison set up ten safe houses under shell companies. Even then, he didn't trust the council to always have our backs, and he wanted to be sure we had a few boltholes in case things went bad or we had to hide a suspect. Once we reach "three," we a portal to access "four."

Carrying Jamison into the living room, I prop him up on the couch. Sweat beads on his stark white face. The brackets around his eyes and mouth deepen with every movement.

With a deep sigh, he eases into the cushions. "Status."

"Nothing on Hawthorne or Phaedra," I begin, sitting across from him and opening my laptop. I go on to update them both on my theory about the two groups and their affiliations with the vampires and mages.

Jamison asks to see the footage of the condo, and once he sees the wavering cameras and the brown dress shoes, he agrees with my assessment. "Which means my father's involved in this mess." He rubs a hand down his face.

Gatlin leans forward. "The humans are dedicated. None of them talked. Even when we killed their fellow soldiers in front of them. They were fanatical in their defense of human rights and the need to get rid of all supernaturals."

"Which means they don't know they're working for the

vampires," I state with a frown. "Compulsion. Erased memories. Easy to do on one person. On that scale, it would take a pureblood." When they both appear confused, I explain. "As you know, most vampires are sired, and their abilities are diluted accordingly. Purebloods are born vampire and have no such restrictions."

"Like you," Gatlin says with a grim smile. "That's why you can compel so easily."

"Correct," I reply. "Although that doesn't help us. There are quite a few purebloods in this world, and most of them have the ability to compel."

"But on that scale?" Jamison asks, tilting his head. "Did Nolan keep track of everyone's abilities?"

"Probably," I reluctantly admit. "But to get access, I would have to enter the bid for his council seat. Life or death matches where winner takes all."

"That's not happening," Gatlin says firmly, looking at Jamison, who nods in agreement. "Maybe I can get back in to see the prisoners. Work the vampire angle. When is the guard change at the hospital?"

I glance at my watch. "Midnight. That gives you at least four hours."

"You going to be okay here?" he asks gruffly. "Weapons are stashed in the safe. There are some basics in the pantry for Jamison."

I wave a hand. "Go. Call me if you hear anything."

Once he's gone, I turn toward Jamison. "I need to tell you something." He turns toward me, and I take in a deep breath. "In the field, you were dying. My blood saved you."

Jamison blinks. "Will there be repercussions? Effects?"

I lift a shoulder. "I'm not sure. I've never given my blood to a mage. Only a human. Humans often heal faster and pick up slight changes like better eyesight and more strength after receiving vampire blood."

"Thank you," he replies in a serious tone. "I've got too much to live for to die."

There's a curious expression on his face I've never seen. "You're not mad? What if there are repercussions?"

"Then we'll find out together," he says with a shrug. "Got any ideas about how we can locate them?"

"Besides what I'm already doing?" I ask with a sigh. "Maybe. Something Gatlin said gave me an idea."

36

PHAEDRA

My cheeks are stiff with dried tears when I wake, and my body is completely entangled with Hawthorne's. I must have turned to him for comfort. Last night's dreams and nightmares took a harsh toll on me, the past and present colliding in a storm of memories and fears. Guilt from the past. And the present. Worry. Last time, I lost my sister. Who will I lose this time?

Stuck in limbo for the last week, the minutes and hours ticking by have driven me crazy. My mind continues to go round and round, trying to figure out what the gods could possibly want from me.

Lying in bed won't solve anything. I glance out the glass patio doors and realize the sun is rising. Time to get up. Unentangling my legs from his, I shift, preparing to move and realize his hand is on my arm. Rising to my elbow so I can stare at him,

I wait, breath held, for his eyes to open. My heart beats fast, but the seconds pass by slowly. A minute. Two.

"Hawthorne, can you hear me?" I ask, praying for the hundredth time to hear the rich timbre of his voice. "Did my tears and cries wake you?"

His smooth expression remains unchanged, and I close my eyes as my hopes are crushed. Again. I bend down and kiss him, then ease myself out of bed.

"I'm going to take a shower," I tell him, my voice breaking as the sobs build in my throat. "Then we'll head outside."

Unable to look at him, I walk away, taking refuge in the shower where I can let go and he won't hear me. At least, I think he hears me. Maybe he doesn't, but the healer told me to talk to him, so she must believe it too. Weary from worry, I lean my forehead against the cool tile and let the tears fall.

After the council's broadcasts, I reached out to some contacts to see if they could find some answers for me. I need to know if they're alive. I glance at my watch. That was eleven hours ago, and I've received no texts. A heavy sigh escapes my lips.

Determined not to drown in my own pity, I finish my shower and head to the kitchen for something to eat. I grab some toast and peanut butter. While I'm munching, my eyes drift to the empty tonic bottle on the counter. Should I call the healer and get some more? It couldn't hurt, right? Then, I could ask her how long is too long. I've given it a week.

I pick up the phone and realize it's one a.m. in North Carolina. Too early. Charlie's cranky enough without waking him. I'll wait. Besides, it's time to get Hawthorne up and outside for his "therapy."

Minutes later, I'm wheeling him into the backyard. Clouds obscure most of the sun this morning, but the cooler breeze brushing against his skin has the same effect. I leave him there and grab my laptop from the couch.

"Might as well use the time to find the most likely places for the panels," I inform him, my voice light and cheerful. "It would be nice if you were here to help me." Pausing, I bring up Horse Browser. The best academic research browser, in my opinion. "Six gods. I'm glad it's not all of them. Demeter will probably be the hardest. There were a lot of temples dedicated to her."

Diving into the results, I realize I underestimated the passage of time. "Most of the sanctuaries dedicated to Demeter and her daughter Persephone are gone." I click on the various links. "Ruins. All of them. Nothing left."

Disappointed, I keep searching. "Looks like the best one is on the island of Naxos. There are a few walls and columns left. Not much, but it's our best shot." I spin the screen around to show him. "What do you think?"

"Glad you agree," I say with a chuckle as a drop of rain falls on my forehead. Quickly placing the laptop on his lap, I wheel him around and head back inside. I grimace. I hate to put him back in that bed. "Let's do this together, shall we?"

I roll him over to the dining table and grab the seat beside him. "Perfect." Then I put the laptop where he can see it. "Next up, Apollo. Hmm. Search results show the temple in Bassae is the best preserved, but it's in the middle of a restoration. Doesn't feel right."

"Delos is a possibility," I murmur, pointing to the screen. "There are still some structures standing." Something catches my eye. "Interesting. Both Apollo and his sister Artemis were born on this island. Maybe they combined their quest. I'll dig into Artemis next."

I raise my head, and my neck protests. With a frown, I pick up my phone and notice six hours have gone by. "Damn. I'm so sorry. You're probably tired of that chair, aren't you?" Hopping up, I wheel him over to the bed and get him more comfortable, then grab my phone.

> Phaedra: Hey, it's Phaedra. Will you send me the number of the healer?

> Charlie: Glad to know you're alive. 39 343 555 5555

> Charlie: BTW. Mathias is looking for you. Said the phones were tapped. Guess you know. Is this your new number?

Inhaling sharply, I slowly let the air out at the news. Thank the goddess.

> Phaedra: Yes. Jamison?? Gatlin??

> Charlie: Mathias didn't say, and his old number isn't working. I could reach out to some contacts.

> Phaedra: I've got someone else on it.

> Charlie: OK, let me know if you need anything.

I set the phone on the table and plop down onto the sofa, blowing out a relieved breath. If one of them is alive, I'm hoping the other two made it out too. Is it a bad sign that Mathias is the one searching for me, not Jamison? I wish I knew. On one hand, I'm sure Jamison is catching hell from the council right now. But if he…

Lost in thought, it takes me a second to realize someone's in the room with us. Without thinking, I pull the gun from my back and fire. *Damn it, I missed.* I scramble closer to Hawthorne and raise the gun again.

"That was a little too close," a cool voice says from the corner of the room. "It's Mathias."

It could be a trick. I swing my gun in his direction. "Step into the light."

Tall, dark, and handsome steps forward, and I blink at the sight of him. Gone is the sophisticated nerd with glasses. A dark and deadly warrior stands in his place. Black fatigues, chest strapped with two wicked knives, and a gun in his hand. But it's not the clothing or weapons that make him appear more lethal. It's the hard look in his intense eyes and the readiness of his stance. This is a man who's seen battle.

I lower my gun and walk over to him. "Tell me you're real."

He takes the gun from my hand and lays it on the table. "I'm real." His eyes soften as his finger sweeps back the hair on my face and tucks it behind my ear. "I've been searching for you. Everywhere. This was my 'Hail Mary.'"

I swallow. He probably means Hawthorne, not me, but nobody has ever cared enough to search. His words break the dam holding me back. The overwhelming emotions I've felt this last week, worrying about Hawthorne and them, hit me like a sledgehammer. I wonder if he'll mind.

Throwing caution to the wind, I lean into his hard body and wrap my arms tightly around him. Happy he's alive and here with me. "Mathias." My voice hitches with emotion.

Strong arms circle and hold me close. I bury my face into his chest and breathe in the scent of his familiar cologne. Vampires don't have a scent associated with them. I guess it's because they don't have magic per se. Speed, incredible strength, compulsion, and rumor has it, other mind abilities, but no magic. The scent soothes me. Fills the cracks in my armor.

Needing to know, I tilt my head back. "Jamison and Gatlin?"

There's the slightest compression of his lips, and my heart sinks.

"Jamison was hurt pretty badly," he tells me. I grip his shirt tighter, and he raises a hand to cover mine. "He's slowly recovering. Gatlin was in the air when everything exploded. He's fine." His gaze darts to Hawthorne. "What happened to him? Why isn't he moving?"

Relief fills me. "Thank the goddess." I ease out of his arms and pick my gun up from the table, tuck it back into my waistband, then go on to explain what happened in the temple. "We found another panel, but Hephaestus didn't make it easy on us. Unfortunately, the trial depleted Hawthorne's magic. He's been like this ever since. I was going to call the healer again today."

Mathias shoves a hand through his silky ink-colored hair. "What healer?"

"Her name is Arlie. Friend of Charlie's," I reply, summarizing her diagnosis. "I've been doing everything she said—talking to Hawthorne, taking him outside for nature therapy, touching him." I reach out and grab Hawthorne's hand in mine. "There's been some muscle movement, but that's all."

Mathias looks at me sharply. "I see."

Uncomfortable with the expression in his eyes, I babble on. "I tried to reach all three of you numerous times. When I realized the phones must have been hacked or whatever, I didn't know what to do. In his vulnerable state, I didn't want to move him. If one of those groups caught up to us, he would be defenseless. Plus, I wasn't sure where to go. This was the closest safe house to Athens. I got a new phone and contacted a friend in London to see if you all were alive." My voice hitches at that last statement.

He reaches out and lifts my chin. "You did everything right. This is my fault. I relied on the beacon in the laptop and your phones to track you. It was stupid. I know things can go sideways in a hurry. It's my fault you didn't have another way to contact us. I'm sorry."

Astonished, I place a reassuring hand on his chest as I stare up at him. "There's nothing to be sorry for. I don't blame you."

His eyes drop to my hand, and with a blush, I remove it. Why do I feel this need to keep touching him?

"I'm not used to being responsible for someone else. It has me rattled."

"You eventually get used to it," he assures me, turning toward

Hawthorne. "I need to see if I can get into his head." He pauses. "You might want to look away."

My brow furrows. What is he planning to do? I walk around the bed to get a better angle.

Mathias bends over, turning Hawthorne's head toward me. Dark eyes stare at me with a question in their depths, but I don't know what he's asking until two fangs appear. *Oh.* I give him a slight nod and watch as he sinks his teeth into Hawthorne's neck. His eyes turn pitch black. My pulse picks up as I watch his mouth moving against Hawthorne's burnished skin. This has to be the sexiest thing I've ever seen. Makes me want to bare my neck to him.

Mathias raises his head and licks Hawthorne's neck, closing the wounds. "He's in there. Some sort of peaceful setting, from what I could see in his mind. I told him you were waiting for him. That we needed him to return. His level of awareness increased."

My gaze drops to Hawthorne. "You think it will work?"

"Only time will tell," Mathias murmurs. "Did this happen at the temple?" He lifts a strand of Hawthorne's white-streaked hair.

His words. "Yes. Can you get into anyone's mind when you drink from them?" I ask with trepidation. "Do they know you're there?"

"Yes, and yes."

Damn, that's too bad.

"Is this place yours?" he asks, looking around.

"One of my corporations owns it," I reply cautiously. "Why?"

"The council wants our heads," he reveals with a heavy sigh. "Jamison's in a safe house right now, but I don't think we should stay in London. After the fiasco in Greece, they aren't willing to let him lead our security forces. But there's no way we're giving up our investigation. We're too close."

He goes on to explain everything he's discovered about the

groups. "The group in Greece is the one that killed Sia. They're not aware they're working with vampires. Gatlin went to inform them, hoping they'll change their minds and give us some information to go on. As for the other group, we haven't seen or heard from them. They may or may not know about the mages."

"That's odd," I muse. "Vampires have no magic. How did they create portals?"

"With this," he says with a slight lift of his lips. He pulls out a stylus. "Nolan paid the mages a long time ago to develop a spell that would enable us to create a portal using simple tools. It's great because we don't suffer the same side effects as mages when we use it long distance."

I didn't realize that was an option. Not surprising for someone who hates portals. "Can anyone wield one of those?"

His eyebrow rises. "Yes." His gaze drops to my palm. "Do you have an idea about where to go next?"

"I believe so," I say, peering down at the brand on my skin. "Where are you going to take Jamison and Hawthorne?" I trace the lines of the anvil. The thought of being alone again sucks, but I can't blame him. Not with two of their team down. When he doesn't reply, I look up at him.

"Here. Where we can all be together," he states with a scowl. "There's no way in hell you're doing this alone."

I bite my lip. There's no need for them to come with me on the quests. Someone else could get hurt or worse. But I don't want them to stay in London either. Not with the council on the warpath.

"One condition." His head tilts. "How did you find me?"

"Food delivery," he says with a twitch of his lips. "You used the same credit card that you had with you when you and Gatlin escaped."

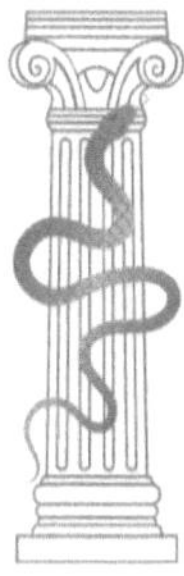

37

MATHIAS

"Found them," I inform Jamison as I stride into the living room. With a grimace, he carefully sits up. "They're alive. Has Gatlin returned?"

His brow furrows. "Not yet. I'm worried. It's not like him." He stares at me. "Something's wrong. What is it?"

Ignoring his question, I press him on Gatlin. "Think the council detained him?"

"Probably," he says, raising a hand to his head. I grab him a pain pill and some water, which he takes immediately. "I need to contact my father and find out what's going on."

He reaches for his phone and dials. When his father picks up, he puts it on speaker. "Where is Gatlin?"

His father gives a harsh laugh. "Where do you think? He's in interrogation. The council is considering a trial. Against you. They want to gather all the evidence they can before they charge you." He exhales loudly. "You've ruined our family name.

Embarrassed me. And the humans are still out there causing chaos, threatening to expose us."

"You have no right to hold him," Jamison coolly states, although I can tell he's worried about what they're going to do to him.

"We have him on camera, at the hospital, helping you escape," his father spits out. "He knew the council's orders and decided to ignore our authority."

Jamison curses loudly. "He reports to me. I ordered him to get me out of there."

"Then turn yourself in, and we'll consider letting him go," Lord de Vere promptly says. "I'm sure they'll be lenient on you. Ask for your resignation. Require you to make a public apology to those poor families who lost a loved one. Not too bad, considering."

Jamison's jaw tics. "I'll think about it." He hangs up and looks at me. "Until we have a handle on our enemies and the traitor, I want to avoid the council. We need a plan to break him out."

"I built our security systems. I'll help Gatlin, but first, I need to stash you somewhere safe," I tell him. Knowing he's going to protest, I hold up a hand and continue. "It's only until you recover. If we stay in London, they'll find us."

"Damn it," he curses. "I fucking hate this. Where are you taking me?"

"To her," I tell him. His eyes drop to conceal the spark that lights in their depths. "Do you need anything before we go?"

He shakes his head. After covering our tracks at the safe house, we step into a portal to her place.

"It's Mathias," I call out, not wanting to be shot.

She comes around the corner, gun in hand, but tucks it away the moment she sees us. Her face lights up the second her gaze lands on Jamison. Sparks fly between the two of them as they drink each other in.

I glance down at him and catch the daggers in his eyes. He's pissed that she's seeing him like this. Vulnerable. Hurt. Even though it's temporary.

I raise an eyebrow. "Couch or bed?"

"Couch," he snarls, raising a hand to his head.

I set him down gently and hand his medications to Phaedra. "I'll be back soon. I have to get Gatlin." I leave out the part where I'm going to have to break into the council to get him out. There's no reason for her to worry. "I didn't have a chance to tell Jamison about Hawthorne. Maybe you can fill him in."

Jamison opens his mouth, but I shake my head, silently telling him not to say anything. She'll only worry more. His mouth firms, and he agrees.

Phaedra sits down beside him on the couch, her fingers lightly tracing the tight lines around his face. "How bad is it?"

Leaving them here is tough. All I want to do is stand guard, ready to slay anyone who comes through that door. My fangs ache with the need to tear into our enemies. *Damn.* The old me is starting to show. *Not now.*

With a flick, I disappear into a portal and arrive at my favorite safe house in London. Firing up the computer, I watch the large monitors flicker on, one by one. Time to get to work. I flex my fingers and begin to search the council's numerous holding facilities. Over the years, I've slowly overhauled every single security system, conveniently leaving myself a back door in case we were ever hacked. Never thought I'd use it to commit treason.

Each screen shows a different facility. Images fly by too fast for the human eye to see, but vampires have the unique ability to process things at a much faster speed. Maybe because we can move so much faster than other supernaturals.

There. I stop the camera and watch six guards escort Gatlin from a holding cell into an interrogation room. Based on the large scowl he's wearing, he's pissed. I'm surprised he's cooperating.

I switch to another angle on a different screen while this one continues to run. Inside the interrogation room, Daegan walks in with a frown on his face and sits across from Gatlin. That's strange. Is he going to conduct the interrogation?

"Leave us," Daegan orders the guards. When they don't move, flames appear in his eyes. "That's an order. Unless you want to see how fast I can fry a mage?"

They scramble out the door, unwilling to incur the wrath of his dragon. *Interesting.* They were willing to defy the council leader, though. From the narrowed look on Daegan's face, I'm guessing he's aware of more than he's letting on.

Daegan glances at the mirrored wall behind Gatlin, then slides a piece of paper across to him. He folds his arms while Gatlin reads it.

I try different angles, but the rooms were designed to listen and watch, not read a piece of paper. The sheer size of the two of them obscures most of their actions as well.

Gatlin lifts his head and considers the man across from him, then nods. Daegan takes the paper and with a slight puff, burns it to ashes and stands.

"Good luck," he tells Gatlin, then strides to the door. "Put him in cell block four. I'll send additional guards to relieve you in a couple of hours."

The guard stiffly nods. He jerks Gatlin up by his cuffs, and Gatlin snarls at the guard. It's so unusual, I keep watching. Once Gatlin is in the cell, the guard picks up his cell and provides the holding cell number to someone on the phone. Traitor. Furious, I click over to the cameras in cell block four and glance at the clock. This happened two hours ago.

On screen, a portal opens in the back of the cell and Gatlin walks into it. As he passes under the camera, he flashes two fingers, then disappears.

Hurriedly closing everything down, I open a portal and step into our number two safe house. A knife across my throat greets me at the door. I strike his hand and scissor my two daggers across his neck.

"You forget who I used to be," I say with a chuckle.

His golden eyes stare back at me. "No, you forget. I'm simply reminding you. All these years you've hidden behind that bloody laptop, playing a role that defies your true nature. War is coming. Which one will you embrace when it hits?"

Stiffening, I throw him a bland smile. "You know why. Nolan would never have left me alone if I'd continued to be a threat to him. It would have endangered us all."

He scoffs. "Bullshit. You wanted to hide the monster inside."

"Maybe I did," I admit in a low voice, not wanting to admit it. "What did the paper say?"

He stares at me for a long second but finally drops the topic. "He's aware that the mages and vampires are involved. They've been quietly eliminating shifters, Fae, and elves in key positions and lobbying to replace them with their own candidates. One was a close friend of Daegan's."

"So, it is a coup," I say, thrusting a hand through my hair. "The humans are a distraction. Did you get a chance to tell the humans about the vampires?"

Gatlin shakes his head. "No." He pauses. "Daegan believes the two factions were working together until they had a falling out. Regardless, the council cut us loose. They won't support our continued investigation. Daegan asked us to continue, although he can't protect us if we're caught. I agreed."

Movement outside alerts me to the intruders the moment they enter the building. "Time to go." With a flick of the stylus, a portal opens. A moment later, we step into Phaedra's house in Rome.

"It's Mathias," I call out.

Gatlin slides a questioning glance at me.

When we step into the living room, Hawthorne is lying motionless on the bed. Jamison and Phaedra are sitting on the couch, heads close together, examining a blue and gold panel. That must be the one they found in Hephaestus' temple. She looks up and sees Gatlin. Her eyes scan him from head to toe as if she's searching for injuries, then she sighs in relief.

"Jamison told me the council locked you up," she says, flicking an irritated glance at me. "If I'd known Mathias was going after you, I would have gone with him."

Gatlin practically preens at her words. "I'd rather you stayed safe. Besides, Mathias didn't have to rescue me. Daegan set up an escape." He proceeds to share their conversation.

Jamison's jaw locks, and a tic appears. "A fucking coup. What the hell is my father thinking?"

"Who's leading the vampires? I doubt it was the woman I saw," I ask with a frown. "There's no way this was planned overnight. Everything is too coordinated. But I will say, bringing the humans in as a distraction worked. We never saw it coming."

"Maybe the humans aren't just a distraction," Phaedra says with a concerned expression on her face. "What if they're using the coup to expose themselves to the world? They almost succeeded in Greece."

Jamison shakes his head. "My father's always been opposed to exposure. I doubt he'd change his mind." He pauses. "But I never thought he'd side with humans either."

"Could be the reason for the fallout," Gatlin interjects. "Vampires want it. Mages don't?" He looks from me to Jamison. "But where do Phaedra and the key and panels come in?"

"They must think they hold some kind of power," she speculates. "We won't know until we find them, but I'm beginning to believe they're right." She picks up the panel in front of her. "This didn't come easy. It almost cost Hawthorne his life. We have to get to the other four and figure it out before our enemies find us."

Doran's drawing is in front of her. "They have this panel,

which I think is the lid. There are six gods on it. Two panels were found in Hephaestus' temple. If I'm correct, the next panel will be on Delos. The birthplace of Apollo and Artemis." She taps each of the gods in the drawing.

"I'm going with you," I state firmly.

She shakes her head.

Gatlin crosses his arms over his chest. "I'll go with her. You stay here and figure out where the next one will be."

Phaedra stands and glares at us both. "Neither of you is going with me. Look what happened the last time." She motions toward Hawthorne. "If I hadn't asked him to go, he wouldn't be in this state."

Gatlin steps closer. "If he hadn't been there, maybe you wouldn't have made it or have the panel. Ever think of that?"

She lifts her chin. "I would have found a way to start the fire." Her hands are on her hips as she stares up at Gatlin with a defiant expression on her face. "These tests are meant for me. Remember?" She holds up her left palm.

An obstinate look crosses his face, and he crosses his massive arms. "This is not a negotiation. You're not going alone. Pick. Me or Mathias."

She turns toward Hawthorne, indecision warring on her face.

Jamison tugs on her hand. "They're right. Hawthorne knew the risks. From what you've told me, he could have stopped at any time, but he didn't." His cool logic penetrates her anger.

"Fine," she capitulates and looks at me. "I want to leave at dawn."

Not liking the dark circles under her eyes, I start to question the timing, but one sharp glance from Jamison stops the words on my tongue. He's right. If I ask her to wait, she'll go without us.

38

PHAEDRA

I stare over at the bed where Jamison and Hawthorne lie. We all decided it was best to stick together in the living room, but with Jamison's injuries, there was no way he could sleep comfortably on the couch. Having gotten used to sleeping next to Hawthorne, I tossed and turned all night. Alone. My arms felt bare like they did before I met them.

The light is barely cresting the sky when I get up. Mathias walks into the living room, fresh from the shower, toweling his hair dry, chest glistening with water, silver locket around his neck, and I almost throw my hands up in surrender. Leaner than the other three, I thought he might be skinny, but apparently, it's all muscle. Abs stacked on abs. *Damn it.*

He lifts an arrogant eyebrow. "Trying to sneak out?"

I roll my eyes and stalk past him to the bathroom. "Hardly. But if we're both up, I'd rather go get it over with." My tone is snarky, but I can't help it. Every fiber of my being is dreading this quest. It takes me minutes to shower, braid my hair, and dress in appropriate clothes. Tan cargoes, a tank, a long-sleeved button-down, and hiking boots.

I stalk into the living room and stop dead. The three of them are awake and waiting for me. "What? Did something happen?" I immediately look at Hawthorne, but he hasn't moved.

Gatlin chuckles. "Easy, tiger. We're making sure you and Mathias have everything, including extra trackers." He mumbles something about an arsenal too.

Tucking my gun in my back, I check my backpack for the hundredth time. Unlike last time, we don't have schematics to guide us, but we're taking the laptop in case we need to research something. Snacks. Water. Ammo. More ammo. Matches. Climbing gear. Extra socks and a change of clothes. Ammo. I lift it up and almost groan. Seconds later, the weight is lifted off me.

"I'll take it," Mathias states firmly. When I open my mouth to protest, his dark eyes almost dare me to argue. "Vampire, remember? This weighs nothing to me."

I scan his attire and see the warrior is back. The first time I was thrilled to have Hawthorne with me, especially his brain and love of history. It felt like an adventure. This time, it feels like we're going into battle, and oddly enough, Mathias is perfect for it.

Jamison steps forward and puts his hands on my shoulders. "Don't take any chances. If the enemy shows up, promise me you'll do whatever Mathias tells you to do."

"I'll try," I reply. His gaze narrows as he waits for the answer he wants. "Fine. I promise."

His fingers lift my chin, and he plants a sensual kiss on my lips. "Come back safe."

Gatlin comes over and slips a crossbody bag over my shoulder. "There's an extra gun and ammo in there. It should be light enough for you to wear at all times." Then, he bends down and tucks an extra tracker in my right boot.

Surprisingly, the bag is a good fit. "Thank you. It's really light."

His gold eyes brighten, and he wraps me up in a bear hug. *Oomph.*

"Shoot first, ask questions later," he growls as he steps back. His eyes fix on Mathias, and a silent conversation passes between them.

I rub my damp palms down my pants, then take Mathias' hand. He pulls us into the portal, and when we step out, the Apollonian sanctuary in all its ruined glory is spread out before us. The excavation of this massive site began in 1872 and is still ongoing. There are several temples and a city, complete with residences, a market, underwater discoveries, and the infamous Terrace of the Lions.

I stride up to one of the stone replicas they added to the site and run my hand down its sleek body. Lined up like they would have been when the Sanctuary of Apollo was built, the lions are said to be the guardians of the sanctuary and Sacred Lake.

"Magnificent. The originals are in the museum over there and are made of marble."

Mathias barely glances at the statue. His head is practically on a swivel, searching for the enemy. "Where do we think we should start?"

I sigh and wonder if Hawthorne's been here. Maybe when this is all over, we can come back and help dig for the excavation. There's so much work to do here, they welcome experts from all over the world.

I look up and find Mathias staring at me, waiting for an answer. "There were three temples dedicated to Apollo and one to Artemis. There isn't much that's standing today, not even the huge statue of Apollo but enough to search. We'll start with the largest temple."

Silence reigns supreme for the first hour but Mathias' vigilance never wavers. The crowds show up, and his face tightens as he scrutinizes every person around us. The moment he thinks someone is looking in my direction, he eases his body in front of mine.

"Tell me about Kallias," I urge, tired of being left to my own thoughts. This could take hours or days.

His eyes dart to me before returning to the crowd. "Kallias is complex. There are two races—vampyrean and noble. Queens and kings come from the vampyrean race. A king was on the throne when I left."

"Why do the rulers only come from one race?" I ask, scanning a column, one of the few that are standing tall in the heat of the sun.

"Vampyreans have pure blood. We're stronger. Faster. Have superior senses," he replies, never looking in my direction.

"You're a pureblood," I realize. "That explains your ability to get into someone's mind. What else can you do?"

He flicks an amused glance at me. "Why would I tell you?"

"Because we could be here for days," I say with a smirk. "Might as well get to know one another." I try to remember all the facts about vampires. "How about compulsion?"

He stops, takes off his glasses, and stares down at me. "You will cease this line of questioning and put your hat on. You're starting to burn."

I snort. "Seriously?" He appears startled, but I shake my head and pull up my hat. "Happy? Now, where were we? That's right. Compulsion." His brow furrows, and it takes a moment, but it finally clicks. "Oh, wait. Was that your attempt to compel me?"

Squaring his shoulders and body, he steps in front of me. "Tell me where you stashed the key."

I narrow my eyes. "Not a chance."

Dark eyes burn with intense emotion, tugging at something inside me. He abruptly turns away. "Let's keep walking."

"Okaaay," I say, drawing the word out. That was weird. "So, you have a king or queen who rules the vampyreans and nobles. Don't you have any ordinary people?"

His brow furrows. "Nobles don't mean the same thing in my world. Nobles are a separate race, but they make up most of the population on Kallias. Vampyreans might rule, but nobles hold the most power. Their blood sustains us. Without them, we would die."

I grimace. "And they do this willingly?"

A pink tint crosses his cheeks. "They do. It's quite pleasurable." His dark eyes abandon the crowd and skim down the side of my neck. "Would you like a demonstration?"

I stumble on the uneven ground, and he steadies me. "Umm, no, thank you." Although my mind is screaming, *Yes, yes, I do!*

Scrambling to find another topic, I switch gears. "So, what did you do in Kallias? Do they have computers there?" To my astonishment, he starts laughing, and my jaw drops at the rich sound coming from him.

"We didn't have computers," he says. He gives me an uneasy glance. "I was a commander in the royal army."

"Ahh, that explains it," I tell him, waving a hand in his direction. "The first time I saw you in my condo, you were slitting a man's throat. But then you turned into this very capable computer nerd in sophisticated clothing. I wasn't sure which was the real you." Fierce intelligence gleams in his dark eyes. "Surprisingly, both roles suit you."

I bend down to study a mark etched into the foot of Apollo's statue, but it turns out to be a chip in the stone. When I stand, he's staring down at me with a speculative gleam in his eyes.

"You're one to talk. You were a vision in gold when I saw you at the gala. A seductress who had turned Jamison's head," he muses. "When we met, you were a fighter defending your territory. Hawthorne met a professor and teller of history. You make me wonder who we'll see next."

Unbelievable. This whole time I thought he didn't like me.

He returns his gaze to the crowd. A group of men start walking our way, and he ushers me down a side path. Then another. Three of the men break off, turn in our direction, and pick up their speed. They're definitely following us. Mathias tenses beside me.

One of them stares my way, and I freeze. Golden brown curls. A lighthearted grin. Perfectly symmetrical features. He looks like a model, but there's no mistaking those blue eyes. The same color as the sky on a bright sunny day. Apollo.

The trio continues to advance. Mathias takes my hand and pulls me toward one of the excavated residences. The gate with its padlock provides little resistance. He pushes me inside and to the corner, palming two of his knives. I draw my gun and peek around him. He mutters something and motions for me to get back. I shake my head and move to the entrance.

"They're gone," I tell him, tucking my gun away. I point to the mosaic on the floor. "This is the House of the Dolphins. There are several houses here with intact mosaics that are simply stunning." My mouth curves down. Every time I see an inlaid mosaic, I think of home. The one I lived in as a child.

Shaking off the melancholy, I turn toward the gate. "You want to hear something funny? I thought I saw Apollo a minute ago." I'd laugh but that might tempt fate. I turn back to find him staring down at the inlaid tile.

Mathias points to the mosaic, sheathing his knives. "That's the brand, isn't it?"

I squint, but I don't see what he's talking about. "Where?"

His hand grips mine, and he pulls me closer. "There."

In the center of the mosaic is an image of several triangles stacked inside each other, two lines across the point, and a circle above them. I bend down. "Damn. You have good eyesight." Inside the circle is a tiny symbol. Hephaestus' brand.

"You might want to step back," I tell him.

He moves closer. *Damn.* Nervous, I stand there for a minute, trying to figure out what's going to happen this time.

He reaches out and takes my other hand. "I'm right here."

My gaze finds his, and I tilt my head. "Why do you wear glasses? It's obvious your eyesight is perfect." Yes, I'm stalling. Sue me. I still want to know, though.

Voices echo outside the gate. "I'll tell you later."

I nod and turn back to the brand. Placing my trembling hand directly over it, I hold my breath while I wait for something to happen. A bright light appears, and I squint, trying to see past its rays. It fades, leaving a golden bow and arrow floating in the air.

Mathias moves to get it, but I pull him back.

"The gods are particular about their quests," I say softly, not wanting them to overhear me. "I wonder what they want me to shoot?"

He looks around. "That," he says, pointing into the distance. I must appear confused because he elaborates. "There's a gold serpent wrapped around an apple. It wasn't there a minute ago."

I grab the bow and arrow and follow his finger to the pedestal. Emerald eyes stare unblinking at me from the head of the snake as the body slithers around a golden apple.

Bracing myself, I pull back the arrow, but it disappears the moment I release it. "Of course it's not this easy."

"Take a few steps back," he tells me.

I step back, and the tip of the arrow returns. Continuing backward, I watch a small piece of the arrow reappear with every step until I'm standing in the mosaic with a full arrow in my hand. "Damn. They want me to shoot from here." I stare at the weapon in my hand. "And they've only given me one shot. How do I hit a target I can't see?"

My eyes find his. "Did you bring binoculars?"

Instead of answering, he tentatively reaches out and strokes the arrow. "No, but as you pointed out, I have excellent eyesight. I can help you."

I stare at him, afraid of saying yes. What if something happens to him?

He walks behind me. "Stop worrying. Take your stance."

I take a deep breath and get into position. He slides his body directly in line with mine and covers my hands with his. I silently groan as his breath whispers down my neck, making me want to turn and face him.

Not the time, I remind myself. *Concentrate on the task.*

"We're going to pull back the arrow together." Our hands grasp the nock and the string on the bow, then we draw our arms back until the bow is fully loaded.

I shift my focus to the pedestal at the far end.

"Steady," he says, adjusting our position. "We're lined up. Breathe in. Out. That's it." His voice in my ear is nothing but confident. Cool. My racing heart steadies. My breath syncs with his. Everything around us blurs. There is only this moment.

"I've got the target in my sight," he assures me. "Close your eyes."

Trust him, I tell myself. The instant my eyes close, my attention shifts entirely to him. His breaths. The muscles brushing up against me. The timbre of his voice.

"Release in 3, 2… 1," he murmurs.

Simultaneously, we release the nock, and the arrow flies from our grasp. Opening my eyes, I watch it wing its way to the column. A resounding thwang fills the air. "Did we hit it?"

He smiles and picks me up, twirling me around. "We did."

Taking my hand in his, he stalks over to the column and pulls the arrow out of the serpent—it instantly transforms into a panel. Similar in size to the one in Rome, the blue panel depicts a vase in the very same pattern as the vase in my vault. I stare at it with a mixture of horror and hope.

"Two down, three to go," I announce in a cheerful voice, hiding my shaking hands. "Let's get back. Figure out where to go next."

He studies me for a second, and I wait for him to say something, but he doesn't. He simply takes my hand in his and uses his stylus to create a portal for us to step through.

39

<u>PHAEDRA</u>

T he moment we step out of the portal, I see Arlie, the Fae healer, bending over Jamison, and I rush over. I'd given them her contact info so she could check on Hawthorne.

"Did something happen?"

She flashes a serene smile but keeps her eyes on her patient. "The tonic will work rapidly, and you'll be as good as new in a few hours."

Jamison dips his chin but doesn't return her smile. "Thank you. We appreciate your assistance." His steel-blue eyes glance past her to Gatlin, who immediately ushers her to a portal.

Mathias puts his hands on my shoulders and turns me toward the bed. "Look who's awake."

The second I see Hawthorne's sea-green eyes staring back at me, my knees buckle. Mathias immediately picks me up and places me on the bed.

In wonder, I cup Hawthorne's strong jaw and lean over to kiss him, then stop myself. What if he doesn't want me to kiss him? *Damn.* Awkward. I stare down at him, tears filling my eyes and clogging my throat. "Welcome back."

The guilt I've been carrying all week eases, but instead of feeling better, I'm on the verge of tears. "How do you feel? Are you able to walk?" Easing off the bed, I take a step back. I don't want him to see me cry.

He stands and takes my hand. "I'm fantastic. Arlie said the tonic, all the nature therapy, and our long conversations helped tremendously." He bends down and places his forehead against mine. "Thank you."

My eyes lock with his, then fall to his mouth. I bite my lip instead of doing the one thing I want. Forcing a chuckle, I step back. "I…uh…need a shower. The site was full of dirt and heat. Mathias can show you what we found."

Without looking back, I pivot and head straight to my bathroom and turn on the shower. Stripping, I barely get in and under the hot spray before the sobs spill out. Gut-wrenching and loud, my body shakes with the force of them. I press my forehead against the cool tile and let it all pour out. All week I prayed for him to open his eyes. Every day nothing happened, and my anxiety and guilt built and built until I felt as tight as an overblown balloon. What is wrong with me? I'm ecstatic, damn it. Still, the tears fall.

Lost to the world, I don't hear the shower door opening. Suddenly, he's there, pulling me into his arms and holding me tightly. I press my face against his chest and wrap my arms around him until not a sliver of light remains between us. Hot water cascades over the two of us, and the air fills with steam. I don't want to ever let him go.

"I'm here," he murmurs, stroking his hand down my back. "I heard every word you said. Your voice was soothing, reminding me of the world beyond. The need to return. To you. To see those beautiful bright blue eyes sparkle up at me. To taste the lips you kept pressing against mine."

His words break through my sobs, and I lift my head to stare up at him. "You didn't mind?"

He smiles crookedly. "I did but only because I couldn't kiss you back." His head dips, lips brushing against mine as if asking for permission.

In answer, I stretch up on my toes and capture his lips with mine. Gone are the soft, sweet kisses I gave him when he was lying so still, his eyes hidden from me, the occasional beat of his heart the only sound between us. This kiss is full of heat and need and a little bit of fear. *Please be real.*

I slide my hands up his chest and realize he's fully dressed. Breaking the kiss, I slide my hands to the first button, but again, I stop. I'm so used to undressing and dressing him. When I look up to see if it's okay, his normally bright green eyes are dark with desire and disbelief.

His hand covers mine. "Why?" His question is simple, but the answer not so much.

"I need to know you're real. All week I dreamed of you, and every morning I woke in despair. The guilt almost broke me. I need to know you're here with me, full of life and magic, not a figment of my dreams," I say, baring myself to him.

With a nod, he releases my hand. "I'm real, and I'm here with you." He chuckles. "I'm also impatient." In a flash of magic, his clothes disappear, and he hauls me into his arms. "Goddess, you feel so damn good." His lips crash down on mine, destroying every thought in my head.

I lose myself in the feel of his arms wrapped around me, his lips kissing mine, and his magic crackling around us, showing me how real he is. When I raise my head to catch a breath, his lips travel down my neck, licking and sucking to my breasts, lavishing them with attention. I moan at the feel of his hot mouth on me, his breath tickling the surface of my body. His tongue follows his lips across my body.

"I felt your sweet kisses on my lips and chest, your hands as they bathed and teased me, and I couldn't move. Couldn't reciprocate," he growls against my skin. "All I wanted was to pull you into my lap and slide my hands and mouth over every inch of you."

My hands glide across familiar dips and valleys, delighting in the sound of his ragged breaths. Wanting to know all of him, I slide my hand down and encircle him, lightly stroking the hard ridges. Strong thighs tighten in response.

"I was locked in a frozen land, unable to see or touch you, and yet, I always knew when it was night. Your silky legs would slide between mine as your arms held me tight and your mouth whispered sweet promises. Pure fucking torture. All of it."

He picks me up, and I automatically wrap my legs around him. His fingers graze the bundle of nerves at my core, then slide into the wetness below. "All I dreamed about was waking up and sliding into you."

I was ready for him the moment he stepped into the shower. "Show me."

With a wicked grin, he pushes forward, sliding into me inch by inch as if he is savoring every second. Once he's in, he stops and stares down at me with a serious expression on his face.

"I would do it all again," he tells me, his voice tight with emotion. "Just to repeat this moment."

My breath hitches at his words, and I brush his mahogany hair back from his face. Steam rises around us while my body quivers with need. "I never want to see you like that again. I couldn't bear it." The anguish in my voice reveals the truth I've been trying to hide, refusing to acknowledge.

It doesn't matter. The gleam in his eyes tells me he hears my unspoken words. His body begins to slide in and out, and the rightness of it is almost too much. I close my eyes, not wanting him to see, but he lifts my chin.

"Open your eyes, Phaedra," he orders, slowing to a stop until I comply. "That's it. Do you think you're the only one? Look at me." His green eyes blaze with emotion as they stare down at me. "I want you to see what you do to me."

His hips slowly pick up speed, and pink spreads across his cheeks. All those minutes I wished he would open his eyes. I never expected this… us… to be this…connected. Maybe he did, though. It's in the gleam of satisfaction and steadiness of his gaze. Sensations rocket through my body, and I gasp.

His fingers slip between us, and I arch my back as they glide against me, faster and faster. Already on the edge, it only takes a few strokes, then I'm lost to the waves cascading from the heart of me. I tighten my grip on his shoulders, needing something to anchor me to this world, and let myself fall.

He follows a second later, pulsing inside me, his gaze never leaving mine. Breathing rapidly with a full-blown smile, he gathers me into his arms and holds me for a long minute. "That was more incredible than I imagined." His fingers softly glide up and down my body as if he's memorizing every curve and valley.

"Mmm," I agree, content to be here with him, soaking in the scent of jasmine and musk. Unfortunately, the water cools, and reality comes crashing back. He lets my feet drop. Pulling back from him, I stare at him as I wash up, afraid that if I look away, he'll disappear.

He steps out first and grabs a towel, holding it wide. I step into it, and he wraps it around my body, then places a sweet kiss on my shoulder. Bending down, he uses a second towel to dry off every bead of water from my legs and feet.

Sea-green eyes stare up at me as if he's waiting for something.

"I…" I open my mouth, but Jamison's face stops me. What do

I say? I'm attracted to you but also to him. Hawthorne knows I've kissed him.

But honestly, who am I kidding? It's all temporary. Once they realize who I am...

His thumb smooths the line between my brows. "Savor the moment. We live long lives. Plenty of time to figure things out. Okay?"

I nod, but I'm not sure that's true anymore. This box could mean the end of it all.

DARK OBSERVANT EYES land on me the second I step into the living room, then shift from me to Hawthorne. A peculiar expression crosses his face, anger followed by sadness maybe? I'm not quite sure, but he doesn't seem happy to see Hawthorne and me. His eyes land on my fingers, nervously rubbing a hole in the hem of my shirt, and he wipes all emotion from his expression.

Gatlin sweeps in from the kitchen, holding out a spoon with red sauce on it. "Taste this." He extends it to me, and I take a tiny bite, then vigorously nod. He lifts an eyebrow. "Good, huh?" A broad smile appears. "Dinner will be ready soon. Hope you're hungry."

"Where's Jamison?" I ask, a note of hesitation in my voice.

Gatlin jerks his chin toward the back door. "Tell him ten minutes."

Nervous, I step outside and walk over to the edge of the garden. I don't know what to say to him. The minute Jamison sat down beside me at Hawkes House, I was intrigued. Pulled toward him in a way I can't explain. Same with Hawthorn the minute I literally ran into him. They appeal to different sides of me. Silence fills the space between us. I don't like it, but I need him to go first.

He pulls me in front of him, my back to his front, and wraps his arms around me. "From the moment we met, I've thought of nothing but you." He drops a kiss on my neck. "I can't say I haven't seen your attraction to Hawthorne. Or his to you. At first, I was jealous. Hated the thought of you liking him. Or having more in common with him."

I drop my head back on his chest. "I never expected either of you. Or…" Gatlin's protective nature and Mathias' intense gaze fill my mind.

Jamison shifts me around to face him. "Or the other two? Are you attracted to all of us?"

His face is hidden by the shadows of the branches above him, and I can't tell what he's thinking, but I refuse to hide what I feel. My future might be unknown and full of chaos, but I can't handle more secrets.

"Yes, I'm attracted to all of you. Although I've only acted on those feeling with you and Hawthorne," I admit with a sigh. "It's insane, really. All these years, I've been alone. Nothing more than a fling here and there. Then you four come into my life, and it's suddenly complicated. Maybe I don't deserve it, but I want to get to know all of you. Whatever that looks like—friends or lovers."

I shake my head. "But the timing of everything. This quest. The council. I'm scared that any chance we might have is fleeting. Here today. Gone tomorrow. I…"

He places a finger on my lips. "None of that matters. I don't know how Gatlin or Mathias feel. It's apparent we need to have a discussion. Regardless, I want you to know how I feel." He takes a deep breath. "I'm all in. Give me all the complications. I can handle it. Like you, I've lived a long life, avoiding entanglements, and I don't want to lose out on my first chance for something real."

Living, not existing. Forging connections. Walking the path together. It's terrifying and yet, oh so tempting. "I'm in." The words are out of my mouth before I can stop them.

He spears his hand through my hair and cups my jaw. Firm lips descend on mine, unleashing a whirlwind of sensations and need. This man kisses like he's storming the gates. As if he's been waiting his whole life to kiss me, and no obstacle is going to stand in his way.

40

JAMISON

Gatlin sets down his fork and folds his arms across his chest. "We need ammo and more supplies. Mathias needs sustenance. And we need to grab that weapon."

Phaedra looks around the table. "What weapon?"

Mathias glances up at me, and I nod. "We have one of their magical knives. Like the one that killed Letz. Unfortunately, with Jamison hurt, we only had time to stash it somewhere safe."

I'd forgotten about it. "If I can study the spell that makes it work, I might be able to reverse it." And possibly tell which mage made it. "Where is it?"

"A locker at the airport," Mathias states with a grimace.

"Heathrow?" Phaedra asks with a twist of her lips. "If we're going to London, we can pick up supplies while we're there."

She glances at Mathias. "I assume he means blood?" Her cheeks flush with pink.

Gatlin stands and picks up both his and Phaedra's empty plates. "Yes. I get it from one of my sources so we can make sure it isn't tainted."

She stands and picks up a few plates. "I'll help you with the dishes."

Mathias scans her pink face. "Does it bother you? That I drink blood."

"Why would it?" she asks, genuinely perplexed. "I asked because I wasn't sure if vampires could eat or drink anything else."

"Because you're blushing," Mathias says with a slight smirk.

Phaedra narrows her eyes at him, then bends over the table. Mathias' eyes widen as her tank top dips, revealing an expansive amount of cleavage. "You told me it was pleasurable, so I assumed you preferred to drink directly from the vein. The image of you..." She doesn't finish the sentence but instead throws him a wink and walks out of the room.

Heat fills his eyes, along with a troubled expression. "I can't compel her." His eyes dart to me and Hawthorne, knowing we'll understand what that means.

I throw up a shield to keep our words from reaching the kitchen. "You're sure?"

His jaw clenches, and he nods. "I tried twice. I'm positive. She's my mate."

Hawthorne frowns. "I'm not so sure. She absorbs magic. I know my empathic abilities didn't work on her. What if the compulsion doesn't work either?"

Mathias thinks about it. "Compulsion isn't magic. For the same reason the enemies' magical blue weapons don't work on us. Vampires don't have magic. Although it doesn't matter. Even if she wasn't..." His voice trails off, but it's apparent that he's attracted to her.

Hawthorne thrusts a hand through his hair and asks in an incredulous tone, "Damn. The three of us?"

"Does anyone know how Gatlin feels?" I ask before answering him.

"How Gatlin feels about what?" Gatlin asks in a gruff tone as he walks back into the room. Gold eyes study the three of us as he eases into one of the chairs. "What did I miss?"

"Mathias told us Phaedra is his mate," I tell him, watching his eyes widen. "You know how Hawthorne and I feel about her. What about you?"

He lifts a shoulder. "The usual. Protective. I don't know if I can feel that way about someone. The Magi didn't exactly create me with that purpose in mind."

I narrow my eyes at him. "So, you're saying you don't care for her in that way. You're neutral."

He rubs the back of his neck. "I'm saying I'll protect her the same way I'll protect the three of you. Why are we talking about this?" Irritation coats his every word.

"Because she told me she's attracted to the four of us, and this isn't something we can let develop without at least discussing it first," I reveal to them all. "I'm not thrilled that she likes all of you, but I won't deny what I feel or step to the side."

Hawthorne nods. "I agree. I'm in." He swivels toward Mathias.

Mathias' voice is terse as he comes to a decision. "I don't want anyone to tell her about the mate thing. It should be her choice to be with me and not because the fates have decreed it."

We all agree, then turn toward Gatlin, who shakes his head. "I don't know." He stands. "I won't get in anyone's way, and if something changes on my end, I'll let you know." He gathers the rest of the dishes and heads toward the kitchen.

"He's already falling and doesn't even know it," Hawthorne softly states. "When was the last time he let someone in the kitchen with him?"

We all chuckle.

I nod. "It was important to note everyone's interest, but for now, we'll continue the way we are and let things progress or not. Agreed?"

They nod right before Gatlin and Phaedra return to the dining table.

"We need to figure out how we're going to get in and out of London without being seen," I tell them. "Obviously we can portal, but to where? There are cameras everywhere."

"Not in the Harlequin," Phaedra says, sitting down beside me. "Well, except for their own. No CCTV, though. Nothing the council can tap into."

"They have weapons and ammo," Gatlin adds, picking up a pad and paper. "I'll get started on a list."

Phaedra picks up her phone. "I'll text Mercer. Let her know we have an order along with a special request. It will go over smoother if we purchase something and portal into a designated area instead of asking to use their underground network as a way station."

"How do we get to the airport locker? We have allies, but none I would trust with that weapon," I ask, mentally walking through everyone I trust. It's a fucking short list.

"I'll get it," Phaedra volunteers. When we all begin to shake our heads, she holds up a hand. "Hear me out. I'm the most logical person. The magic doesn't work on me, and by the time our enemy realizes I'm back in London, I'll already be on my way out."

Logic be damned. "No. How will you protect yourself? You can't carry a gun in the airport without setting off a million alarms."

She flashes me an amused smile. "If I don't get a gun, neither does the enemy. I can safeguard the knife with a curse. We will drive up, get our package, and drive off. Simple."

"Who's driving?" I ask her and watch her lift a nonchalant

shoulder. Knowing there is no way in hell I'm going to let her go alone, I clench my jaw and give in. "I'll drive."

Gatlin glares at me. "You know I don't like it when we split up."

He's damn good at strategy. I wait for him to sift through all the options and come to the same conclusion. "Damn it." He rests his hands on the chair in front of him. "I have to meet my contact and get Mathias' blood. We need Hawthorne and Mathias to pick up the supplies from Mercer. That leaves you and Phaedra to pick up the knife."

This was a hell of a lot easier when we weren't worried about Phaedra. We probably took too many chances, but somehow, we always made it through. Four soldiers dedicated to the job. Now, we're being hounded on all sides, and the enemy is circling, getting closer and closer.

"All the usual contingencies," I order Mathias. "But I want to take burners into the field and toss them after the mission." I tap my watch. "It's midnight in London. If we move now, there's less of a chance we'll be spotted. Plain street clothes. Handguns only."

IN FIVE-INCH HEELS and a fitted suit, Mercer eyes the five of us when we emerge from the portal. I shake her hand, surprised to see she's a Fae. Her straight pink hair and turquoise eyes suggest a fun side, but it's window dressing, likely fools people into underestimating her. The hard expression on her face is the true indication of her nature. It's odd, though. Fae typically don't sell weapons and supplies. Most of them choose to be a healer or work in a safe profession like business.

Uneasy with the number of mages in her guards, I keep my hand on the few potions in my pocket. Deadly in nature, I often carry them when using magic isn't an option. Phaedra warned me that our portal would open in a room that nullifies all magic. Dread crawls around the base of my spine. With no access to my magic, I itch to palm a gun or knife.

Mercer waves a hand toward the crates along the wall. "Everything is there. Feel free to check." Hawthorne and Mathias walk over with list in hand.

She turns to me. "A car is waiting for you outside." She chucks the keys at me, and I snatch them out of the air. "It's been spelled to evade the cameras."

Interesting. They've somehow been able to permanently apply the spell to the vehicle. "Thank you."

She raises a single eyebrow. "It's a pleasure doing business with you, de Vere."

I pause. There's a tone to her voice that I don't like. Phaedra explained Harlequin's aversion to the council, but this feels more personal. I walk over to Mathias. "Leave before the last crate is loaded."

His black eyes carefully slide past me to Mercer. "Will do." He takes a deep breath, straightening his shoulders. "Be safe."

He doesn't turn in Phaedra's direction, but I know he's dying to. "Text when you're done." I turn on my heel and stride toward Phaedra and Gatlin. We'll drop him off along the way. He'll rendezvous with Mathias and Hawthorne later.

A white Porsche Taycan Turbo idles at the curb outside, and I almost whistle. The guard beside it dips his chin when we get in, then disappears. "Harlequin certainly provides the best." Instead of taking off like I want, I carefully ease into traffic.

Gatlin pokes his head between the front seats. "Drop me off at the next corner." He turns to Phaedra. "I added a knife to your bag that can do a hell of a lot of damage. Remember, kill first."

We stop, and he maneuvers his massive body out of the car and taps the hood. The cameras will pick him up for a second, but he'll be gone by the time they realize it.

Merging back into traffic, I head toward the outskirts and Heathrow. Phaedra unzips the bag on her chest and pulls out a serrated knife. She lifts a piece of paper and slices right through it with one stroke.

"Damn. I might have to ask Gatlin for one of those."

She grins. "He definitely knows the way to my heart." Her face flushes. "I mean. Not that. He hasn't. Never mind." She grips the handle. "It's perfectly balanced too."

The airport comes into view. "Which terminal?"

"Five," she replies.

I pull up to the curb. "If you see anything suspicious, leave. We'll try again later." She waves a hand and moves to get out, but I grab her arm. "Keep your head down and hat on. Don't look up. The lockers are next to the luggage carousels. Down one floor."

Her bright blue eyes dart to me. "Stop worrying. You'll get grey hair." *Or a heart attack*, she mutters as she steps out of the car and slams the door.

The wait is interminable. Minutes tick by. The airport police come by twice to ask me to move, but I flash a badge at them. I impatiently tap my fingers against the steering wheel. Why the hell did I let her talk me into this? What if something has gone wrong? I open the car door and get out.

She comes staggering up, and I quickly get back into the driver's seat.

"Hurry," she sputters, lifting a bloody hand from her side while she stashes the wrapped item under the seat. "I need sutures. Head back to London. A friend of mine, Greta, can do them. I'll guide you once we get there." She closes her eyes.

I reach over and try to infuse a little healing into the wound, but nothing happens. "It's not healing. Damn it. Don't go to sleep on me."

She shakes her head but doesn't open her eyes.

"If you don't wake up, I'm going to pull this car into the

nearest hospital and turn us both in." *Open your beautiful eyes. That's it. Come on.*

Blue eyes, full of pain, slide toward me.

She chuckles, but it's weak. "You're not much of a nurse-maid. Good thing Hawthorne had me and not you." Her head lolls on the headrest. "Take this exit. 1122 Hartly." She slurs the last few words.

I order the voice assistant to navigate to the address using the quickest route. "Fuck, fuck, fuck." I bang my hand on the steering wheel. She doesn't move. I ignore stop signs and push the car to its limits to get to the address. Screeching to a halt, I run around and pick her up, then rush to the door of the small, attached house.

A stooped, grey-haired lady answers the door. She takes one glance at Phaedra and ushers us into her kitchen. "Lay her down on the table. I'll get my kit."

The table is pristine. I carefully set her down on it and whip off my jacket to place under her head. Brushing the smooth dark strands back from her face, I stare down at her pinched expression. Even unconscious, she is hurting.

"I'm Greta," the lady announces when she comes back into the kitchen. Setting a silver tray on the counter, she quickly cuts away Phaedra's shirt until she can see the wound. "Oooh, that's a nasty one. Not made with a regular blade. A jambiya made that cut."

My brows come together. "What?"

"A curved dagger, typically made of silver or gold," she says without looking at me. Her entire focus is on the cut. "She usually heals faster than this." She bends down and sniffs. "What do you smell?"

I bend closer to the wound and wrinkle my nose. "Licorice?"

"Very good," she replies, moving to a nearby cabinet. "I'm guessing they coated the blade with anise oil. It causes tempo-rary paralysis. Or at least, temporary for her. It can be quite lethal to others. Like us." She grabs a brown bottle from the second shelf and returns to Phaedra.

"This is going to sting," she tells me. "Hold her down."

I place my hands on Phaedra's shoulders, and the woman tips the bottle over the open wound, pouring a dime size amount into the flayed skin. Phaedra's body arches, but thankfully, she doesn't wake.

"Done," the woman states matter-of-factly. "It will take a few hours, but she'll be right as rain. That will be two thousand pounds." She thrusts her hand out, palm up.

Damn it. We only have the burners with us. "I don't suppose you take credit, do you?" She doesn't blink. "Rolex?" I point to my watch, and a spark of interest appears.

"Deal," she says, holding out her arm for me to snap the watch on it. "Magic will help her heal faster. Ok, now get out."

Startled, I realize she's not going to let us stay here. "Thank you for helping her." I pick Phaedra up and carry her out to the car. We have a safe house close to here. It will have to do.

41

PHAEDRA

S leek, sophisticated décor and a wall of glass windows are the first things I see but it's Jamison's tired face and steel-blue eyes that capture my attention.

"Your friend Greta patched you up."

I glance down and lift the light blue blanket, skipping past my black bra to the bandage on my lower right. Memories of the airport and the mage who stabbed me filter through the haze in my mind.

Parched, I swallow a few times and slide back the bandage. Red and full of pus, the wound is angry and gross. "Usually, a knife doesn't do that much damage."

"Poison," he says, holding a glass of cool water to my dry lips. "Anise oil, I think she said. It's something mages use to paralyze their enemies. Did a mage do this?" I nod, and his hand clenches. "I knew I should have gone after the weapon. Damn it."

"He made a fatal mistake," I croak. "He reached for the weapon. The tip caught him, and he jerked back, but it was too late." I lift my head. "Where is the blade?"

He waves a hand to a chair in the corner. "There. I haven't had time to look at it. I've been busy calling Gatlin and the rest to let them know we'll be late to the meeting point."

My body feels heavy, but I push myself up. "I'm awake. We should go."

He gently pushes me back down on the sofa. "You're healing, but not as fast as I'd like." He rubs a hand across the scruff on his granite jaw. "When your eyes closed, I…" He swallows. "Are you immortal?"

"Sort of," I reply. His brows draw together. "I die, but I come back. Depending on the wound, it can take a minute or a day."

He picks up my fingers and plays lightly with them. "Does it hurt?"

"It isn't pleasant," I reply with a grimace, not wanting to think about it. "Where am I? A condo?"

He nods. "It is. We use this as a safe house. Do you want something to eat?"

I shake my head and try to sit up. "I need to use the restroom." Stitches pull at my side, and I flinch.

He leans down, picks me up, and sets me down inside the restroom. "Call me when you're ready. I'm going to grab you some crackers."

When I finish, he's standing outside the door. He carries me back to the living room. "Sorry. This is the only furniture in this place. We don't stay here often." He grimaces. "Your shirt was bloody. I didn't want to leave it on."

"This is fine for now." I reach up and trace the lines of worry around his firm mouth. "As much as I love having you all to myself, I think you should help me heal this wound so we can get back to the others." When he gives me a puzzled look, I wink at him. "Magic helps me heal."

He carefully sets me on the sofa and lays the crackers on the side table. "Greta mentioned something about that, but I wasn't sure what she meant."

"Whether it's curses or spells, my body absorbs magic. Thrives on it," I reveal in a low voice, hoping the gods don't hear me. They know I can regenerate, because they gave me that ability, but not the other. "Tell me. What was the first magic you learned?"

"Fire," he says with a grin. "I was utterly fascinated by it. Had flames dancing above my cot before I could walk."

"Show me," I urge him, settling against the armrest.

He flicks a finger, and little flames appear. Dancing above me, they flicker and bend, and shine brightly. One flame turns into a tiger and pounces on a nearby lion. A giraffe eats from a tree where a monkey sits. Animals turn into soldiers marching in formation. Battleships form and sail across a sea of fire.

I laugh, delighted by his creativeness. Something I never expected from Mr. I-Need-To-Be-In-Control. "This is wonderful!" I think about how much power this must have taken as a child. "Your parents must have been freaked out by the level of magic you wielded at such a young age."

The flames die, and I'm sad to see them go.

"My mother left right after I was born, and I didn't see my father on a regular basis until I was ten years old." His voice is matter of fact, but I can hear a sliver of loneliness in his tone. An emotion I know too well.

"I'm sorry," I say, reaching for his hand. "Was your childhood lonely?"

His laugh is harsh. "Once my father saw my powers and my rebellious ways, he immediately enrolled me in military school. Power is controlled by discipline and intent, he would say. He was right. It did me good."

He never answered my question. "Although I'm not sure I like his methods, you turned out to be an incredible man," I say teasingly. "A little bossy. Broody too. Reluctantly charming." I lean closer. "Plus, you smell divine." The unique combination has driven me crazy since we met.

He chokes. "I'll own the bossy but broody?" With a roll of his eyes, he turns the tables. "What about your childhood? Were you happy?"

"It was the best," I say with a soft smile. "My sister and I were close, always playing and causing chaos. Our parents were secretly amused at their little princesses, but as royals, they rarely showed emotions."

"Hawthorne told us you were a princess."

"Unfortunately, yes," I say with a huge sigh. When he laughs, I shrug. "What can I say? It was exceedingly boring. If it weren't for P... my sister, I would have run away." Damn, that was close. I'm too comfortable around him.

Time to change the subject. I reach down and peel back the tape covering the wound. Light pink and no sign of infection. "See. It's working."

A relieved expression crosses his face. "Hmm. Does it matter what kind of magic?" He looks over at the weapon on the chair.

"Magic isn't good or bad. It just is," I remind him.

He walks over and picks up the weapon. Holding it aloft, the cloth protecting him from its deadly magic, he examines it closely. "Mage magic." His brow furrows.

"Surprisingly, not my father's. I don't know whose it is, but they're powerful. There are at least a dozen spells on it. Complex ones."

"Bring it over here."

He steps close to the bed, and the magic calls to me. I reach out a finger and slide it down the blue blade. Jerking the weapon away, he glares at me.

"What the hell are you doing?"

"Testing a theory," I say innocently. "Like with curses, I can see the spells on it. If I remove the most dangerous one, I'm curious to see if the knife will remain a threat."

"There's more than one lethal spell on this knife," he states confidently. "And you're still healing from the last encounter."

He tucks the cloth around the knife and places it back on the chair in the corner. Stalking back to me, he lightly presses his finger on my lips to stop my words. "You might be used to calling the shots, but I hated seeing you hurt. Give me a minute to recover."

"I'm healed," I protest, drawing his eyes down to my wound. "See." Not a single blemish remains. Little black suture threads lie on the smooth surface of my skin, and I brush them away, only to encounter sticky residue from Greta's medicine.

He reaches over and brushes his thumb against the wound.

A shiver runs across my body, but I'm distracted by the dried bits of blood I see. "I need a shower."

"The bathroom is fully stocked," he informs me. "I'll let everyone know you're healed, but we'll be awhile. Take your time." He pulls me up until I'm standing steady.

"Thank you for taking care of me. It's been a long time since someone cared whether I lived or died." The words emerge from somewhere down deep where I tend to shove all my emotions. Coated in gratitude and a lot of feelings I don't want to examine too closely.

His brows draw together, and he lifts my chin, steel-blue eyes locking with mine. "Scared the hell out of me, to be honest. Seeing you like that…" He clears his throat. "Go take a shower. I'll be here when you get out."

With a hard swallow, I escape into the bathroom. The shower has everything I could need, including a luxurious body wash. I sniff the masculine scent and smile. It smells like Mathias. I quickly wash up and shampoo my hair to erase the smell of medicine.

Clean, I step out into the steam-filled room and wrap a

towel around me, then comb through my wet hair. Conscious of time, I don't bother to blow dry it, but I do grab a new toothbrush and toothpaste from the drawer and brush my teeth.

Finishing up, I bend down and pick up my clothes and wrinkle my nose at the medicinal smell and flecks of blood on them. Maybe Jamison or one of the others has stocked some clothes here. Padding out of the bathroom, I find Jamison standing by the window, talking on the phone.

As if sensing me, he turns and falls silent. His gaze travels down my body, and his knuckles whiten. "I'll call when we're ready to leave." He pockets the phone.

"Do you happen to have a fully stocked closet too?" The husky tone of my voice a reflection of the thoughts running through my head.

He reaches up and begins to unbutton his shirt, and all my attention shifts to his fingers as I watch every button slip through its hole. Jamison pulls it off, revealing a white t-shirt underneath, then walks over and holds it out for me to take.

His unique scent hits me the second I take it from him and the intoxicating notes remind me of when we first met. This attraction has been simmering between us in every encounter since then, waiting for one of us to make a move, but this is the first time we've truly been alone. I lick my lips and take a deep breath, then drop his shirt along with the towel I'm wearing. Cool air drifts across my breasts, making my nipples tighten, and I lift my chin.

He inhales sharply. "I've wanted you since the first time I saw you. Sitting at the bar, the slit of your golden dress framing one deliciously long leg, one dark eyebrow raised in challenge, and an amused gleam in the depths of your bright blue eyes. If you want to walk away, do it now."

I stare up at him, remembering that night. He was mysterious. Commanding. Suspicious of my motives. There were so many layers beneath his buttoned-up demeanor. I run my hands up my body and toss my head back. A clear invitation in my eyes.

He pulls off his t-shirt in one smooth move and swoops in. Arms wrap around me as he bends down to run his nose down the side of my neck. "Mathias' body wash can't erase the smell that's uniquely yours. Jasmine and vanilla. The scent has lingered under my skin and in my mind from the beginning, driving me near mad with curiosity and need."

"Jamison," I sigh, surrendering to him.

His mouth captures mine and every tension filled moment between us is in the kiss he lays on me. Raw need eclipses his control, and it feels delicious. Powerful. I want more. Deepening the kiss, I let myself get lost in the passion between us.

Magic erupts on his hands and with a harsh exhalation, he steps back, but I immediately wrap my arms around him, holding him tightly to me.

"You don't need to control yourself." I breathlessly remind him, placing his hands on my breasts. A small current courses through me, and heat pools low. I gasp. "Take me. Show me the madness."

For a heartbeat, he hesitates, but soon his firm lips capture mine in a frenzy of desire. Magic hums between us, heightening the intense sensations bombarding us. Gone is the controlled Brit. His mouth and tongue leave my lips to skim down my body to my breasts.

I grip his shoulders, holding myself upright as he worships my aching nipples. My body arches, offering him whatever he wants, greedy for more.

He lifts his head, eyes dark with intent, and scans my face. Whatever he sees in my flushed cheeks must satisfy him, because a wicked smile appears on his face. Arms tighten as he he picks me up and lays me on the couch.

He remains motionless for a second, drinking in the sight of me. "Bloody hell, you're stunning. I want to taste every inch of you."

My lips curve, and I tug on his pants. "Not until you're naked."

My tone is demanding, but so is my need. With a couple of quick moves, he tugs them off, along with his briefs. I suck in a breath at the sight of him. Tall with broad shoulders, I follow the line of his body down to his tapered waist and muscled abs. He's not quite as muscular as Gatlin or as cut as Mathias; his sculpted muscles are sleek and lean like a thoroughbred.

I lift my hand, but he captures it and places it above my head.

"Not yet." Kneeling, his hands and mouth descend between my legs and begin an all-out assault on my senses. Nerves burn with sensation as my body quivers, begging for more. He's relentless, playing my body like an instrument.

"I need you," I beg, but he rejects my words with a shake of his head.

Fingers slide in and out of my wet heat as his thumb finds the bundle of nerves at the top. His head lifts. "I want to watch you fall apart." His voice is rough and ragged.

In response, I slide my hands up to play with my nipples.

"Fuck," he mutters, eyes lingering on my breasts. He returns his gaze to my face and quickens his movements.

My thighs tense, and my body arches. I reach out and fist the couch under me. His eyes, navy now, gleam with desire. He strokes faster, in and out of me, circling the top at the same time. Magic sparks on his fingers, and I shudder at the intensity.

Moments later, I explode in a shower of darkness and stars. The world disappears for a brief second. Heat bursts from the center of my body, filling my empty crevices, satisfying the loneliness I've carried for so long. I moan softly as he continues to stroke me. Another wave begins to build.

He removes his hand and settles his body on mine. "I need to be inside you." His voice is full of gravel as he slides into me. We both release a low moan as he begins to move. "I've wanted you for so long."

Pleasure, already building, amplifies with every hard stroke. My body rises, clenching tightly, meeting his thrusts. I slide my hand down and circle the bundle of nerves. Our breaths fill the air. I moan as I fall apart, body milking his, waves of heat rolling through me.

His mouth drops down on mine, drawing out the moment with a kiss so deep, it makes my toes curl. A second later, he lets go, finding his own release.

Head lowered, he kisses me a few more times before easing off me and gathering me in his arms. "From the moment we met, I knew it would be like this between us, but my imagination didn't do us justice." His hands glide lightly over my skin, tracing and mapping the peaks and valleys. Silence falls, and he turns toward me. "Is everything all right?"

I heave a dramatic sigh. "I'm not sure I'll be able to give you up now."

He laughs, but I know he senses the emotions and thoughts running through my brain. Hawthorne. My past. The box. For the first time in ages, I want to abandon the path I set out on three thousand years ago and find a life.

"That's too bad," he says with a satisfied smile, leaning over to give me a lingering kiss. His phone buzzes, and he curses as he reaches for his pants. "Damn. I wish we could hide here for a few days, but we need to go."

42

PHAEDRA

"You think Mercer is involved, don't you?" I ask as he parks the Porsche in the lot of the British Museum, per her instructions. "I thought it was just you being cautious when we arrived to pick up the weapons and car, but the mage at the airport arrived almost the same time I did. That can't be a coincidence."

A tic appears in his jaw. "She might be Fae, but she had a hell of a lot of mages working for her. It struck me as odd. They aren't known to associate with each other."

"Let's wait and see who shows up for the car," I tell him, dragging him behind the building. "Harlequin isn't a fan of the council, and by extension, those like you who lead their security teams, even if you're temporarily on the run. But I can't believe they would have anything to do with humans either."

A minute goes by. Then another. A shimmer appears near

the car, barely discernible in the twilight. I tap Jamison's arm, and he nods.

"What is it?" he quietly asks.

"A portal," I reply right as an elegantly clad Mercer steps out of it.

A tall, blond elf steps out behind her and grabs her arm. She shakes him off, then turns and jabs her finger into his chest. We can't hear what she's saying, but it's obviously not good. A thunderous expression crosses his face. She throws up her hands, strides over to the car and gets in, peeling out of the parking lot like a seriously pissed off woman.

"Lover's spat?" I murmur, not wanting the elf to hear us.

"I've seen him somewhere," Jamison replies, his brow furrowed. "Can't remember where, though. Maybe I'll think of it later. I wonder who created the portal. I've never seen one so transparent."

"Gatlin said the same thing. I've always avoided portals, so I didn't realize there was much difference in them," I say with a shrug.

"You're afraid of them, aren't you? We've all noticed it." His keen eyes are focused intently on me. "Why?"

Because they steal the people you love. Not wanting to lie to him, I change the subject.

"Speaking of…" I say, tapping my watch. "We should have left ten minutes ago."

His eyes narrow, but he doesn't pursue it. He takes my hand and creates his own portal in the shadows and pulls me into it. When we step out at the other end, Gatlin is waiting for us. Jamison sways for a second but quickly gains his equilibrium.

Wearing a thunderous scowl, he glares at the two of us. "That's the last time we're splitting up. I've had it. Every time we do, one of us gets injured." His keen eyes scan both of us, lingering on the button-down I'm wearing, clearly Jamison's. "Do I need to get the healer?"

"I'm good," I promise him. He lifts an eyebrow as if he doesn't believe me. "It's true." I lift the corner of my shirt and show him my smooth abdomen.

His golden gaze intensifies, but Jamison clears his throat, interrupting the moment between us. "Did you get everything on the list?"

"We have all the weapons," Gatlin informs him. "More guards arrived toward the end, but Mercer, your Fae contact, created a diversion and helped them escape."

I whistle. "Maybe that's why they were fighting."

Jamison nods and explains the scene we saw at the museum. "Possibly. What can you tell me about Harlequin?"

"Mercer is the only one I've ever dealt with," I reply with a frown. "I could ask Maverick or Charlie. They're the ones who hooked me up with Mercer. It was a long time ago, though."

Gatlin opens the car and motions for me to enter. The door shuts with a soft click.

Jamison gets into the front passenger seat and turns to me. "It couldn't hurt. I'm curious about them. The fact they've managed to stay hidden from the council is incredible. But why? What is their angle? Supernaturals don't have any laws against commerce or weapons."

Happy to have found a supplier, I never really thought of it. I pick up my phone and shoot off a text to Maverick and Charlie, asking for some insight into our mutual friends.

> Maverick: Not a door you want to open.
>
> Phaedra: Do they have anything to do with the coup?

It's a risk to ask, but I trust Maverick.

> Maverick: Maybe, maybe not. They have fingers in a lot of pies. And their reach is longer than the council's. Stay off their radar.
>
> Phaedra: Might be too late.
>
> Maverick: I hope not. Call if you need us.

I relay my conversation with Maverick to Gatlin and Jamison. "Maverick isn't one to exaggerate. We should probably limit our contact with Mercer."

Gatlin taps his fingers restlessly on the steering wheel. "We'll need another supplier. There's a gryphon in Egypt who can help us. I'll check with him."

Jamison dips his head. "The good news is we have the weapons we need to move on to the next temple." He looks back at me. "Do you know where we should go next?"

"Not yet," I reply as we come to a halt in the driveway.

Gatlin is reaching for the handle when I open the door, and he practically growls at me. "Next time, wait. Let me check the perimeter first."

I wrinkle my nose at him and turn toward *my* house as I answer Jamison. "There are three gods left. Ares, Demeter, and Athena. Ares' temple is basically rubble. I'm leaning toward either Athena or Demeter, but I'd like to get Hawthorne's opinion."

"Get Hawthorne's opinion on what?" a familiar voice asks, and I pivot to find Hawthorne propped against a wooden post near the front door.

Green eyes drink me in from head to toe, and he raises an eyebrow. I blush. It feels like there's a neon sign above my head saying I had sex with Jamison. The corner of his mouth lifts, but other than a shared look, with Jamison, he says nothing.

"Whether we should go for Athena or Demeter," I say, stopping in front of him. Seeing him standing here with his eyes open makes me breathe easier. *Fuck it.* I step forward and wrap my arms around him. Closing my eyes, I savor the warmth he exudes.

His arms close around me, and he bends down to murmur, "I let you out of my sight for a few hours, and you get stabbed? Good thing you killed the bastard." Firm lips place a kiss on my forehead as he tucks me under his arm and escorts me into the house.

"They both have two possible temples," he says, rubbing his chin. "This is your quest. What does your gut say?"

I think about the first two quests and realize the golden apple was still on the pedestal when we left. "Demeter. She's the god of agriculture and harvest and the cultivation of crops. She seems like the most likely choice."

He thinks about it for a second. "There used to be quite a few temples dedicated to her and her daughter Persephone. Most have been destroyed. From what I can recall, there are at least two dedicated to Demeter that are options. The one on Naxos and the one at Eleusis."

"It's been a while since I researched them," I admit with a wry smile. Really, with my background, I should know the Ancient Greece sites. "I..."

Mathias stops in front of me, his eyes tinged with red. "I thought you were immortal?"

Taken aback, I stare up at him. "Sort of. Why?"

"Explain," he orders with an impatient sigh. "*Sort of* isn't an answer."

"Well, you're sort of immortal. It takes a lot to kill a vampire, but you can still permanently die, right?" I explain. "I die, but I regenerate with a little bit of time. Although I haven't tested all the ways. Why?"

A muscle tics in his jaw. "Tell me what happened at the airport."

Is he upset I got stabbed? "A mage stabbed me. I killed him." He raises an arrogant eyebrow, and I lift my hands. "Umm, what?"

"Why did you need to go to a healer?"

"Because he coated it with a poison, and my body wasn't healing as quickly as usual," I reply with a bewildered glance. "Worst case, the infection would have spread, and I would have died. It's painful, and it sometimes takes time to regenerate. I'd rather avoid that scenario if I can."

The red recedes, but there's a troubled expression on his face. "Thank you for the explanation." He darts a glance at Jamison. "I'm going for a walk." In a blur, he's gone.

"Anyone care to explain?" I ask, but none of them replies. With a huff, I walk over to the table where the laptop sits and open it up. "I'm going to do some research."

Hawthorne comes over and sits down beside me. "I'll help. Bring up Naxos first."

"I don't want you to go," I murmur, not wanting the others to hear me. It's a good thing Mathias is gone. Damn vampires can hear everything.

Hawthorne swivels to face me. "If you're going, I'm going." He presses a finger to my lips to stop the protest forming on them. "Look what happened at the airport. I hate that you were hurt and I wasn't there to help you. I'm not letting you out of my sight. We're all going. End of discussion."

I study his set jaw and green eyes full of determination and realize I'm not going to change his mind. "Okay. Let's figure out which one is the more likely candidate."

We dive into the two sites over the next couple of hours, but we're no closer to determining the best one, even with all the information. They're both good candidates. I drop my head into my hands, and he rubs the muscles of my neck.

Jamison and Gatlin walk over to the table.

"We're hearing chatter about a group of humans scouring

Ancient Greece sites. It's not clear whether it's one or both groups, but we need to make a decision soon," Gatlin states firmly. "Have you two decided?"

I glance at Hawthorne. "Flip a coin?"

Jamison slides his Ancient Greece coin onto the table. "Use this."

The coin reminds me of the night we met, and I tilt my head back and smile up at him. "Thanks. Heads we go to Naxos. Tails we go to Eleusis." I flick the coin into the air, and it tumbles over and over, landing on heads.

"Naxos it is," I state with a flourish. "It's a pretty substantial site, so I want to leave early in the morning. Is that okay with everyone?"

IT's dark when we get to the site the next morning. Yawning, I stare at the temple. One of the earliest built in her honor, the beauty of the nearly white stone is hard to see in the predawn hours. Magnificent at the time, it's hard to look at it now and not see the original superimposed in my mind. All the detailed work. The statues. It was truly a ruin for a long time, but they found some of the original pieces and reconstructed it in the 1990s.

The first ray of sun breaks the horizon, and Hawthorne whistles when it lands on the temple. "You take me to all the best places." His eyes are devouring the structure in front of us. He turns to the land around it. "This location is known for its agriculture. Makes sense to build her temple here."

"You're such a plant nerd," I tease. "Feel free to look around. I'm going to search the temple."

His mouth tightens. "Not a chance. Mathias told us about

Apollo showing up at the last site. Who knows what will happen here?"

I look around and see the other three nodding. Mathias' dark eyes are sweeping the area around us, his hand on one of the knives strapped to his chest. Gatlin is setting the gear down by the temple. Jamison is calmly waiting for me to tell him what to do.

"Fine," I huff, although I'm secretly thrilled to have them all here. "Search for the symbol. Check every column and stone. If you see anything, shout."

Jamison and Hawthorne move with me toward the temple. Mathias and Gatlin start to patrol the area around us in full protective mode.

I begin with one of the large side entrances. Hawthorne picks the other, and Jamison chooses the columns. Hours go by. The sun beats down on us. Mathias comes over and hands me a water, then orders me to put my hat on. I laugh but do as he asks.

Gatlin hands out jerky, cheese, and crackers to everyone except Mathias.

I wonder if Gatlin got Mathias some blood. I forgot to ask last night.

The afternoon drags on, and we near the end of our search. "It's not here."

Hawthorne walks over. "We have a few more stones left to check, but I agree. I don't think this is the place."

Jamison finishes his section and comes over to join us. Flushed and red from the sun, he lifts a shoulder. "I don't know why you two get excited about a bunch of stones. This is extremely tedious."

My eyes meet Hawthorne's, and we both smile. "It's tedious until you find something from the past. Like a coin or a bust of a statue."

"Or a tool used to reap crops," Hawthorne chimes in.

Wait a minute. "Do you think it could be in the surrounding area? Her power lies in the seasons and the cultivation of crops." I turn toward the land. "What do you see?"

Hawthorne straightens and studies the hillside. "Potatoes." He points to a cropping of trees. "Olive trees." He walks to the other side of the temple. "Grapevines."

Jamison swivels toward me. "Spread out and check the land."

Mathias immediately moves to my side. "I'm going with Phaedra."

The other three nod and split up. Hawthorne to check the grapes and Gatlin the potatoes. Jamison heads to one side of the olive trees, so I decide to move to the other.

Tired, my feet stumble, but Mathias' quick reflexes prevent me from taking a tumble. "Thanks." I wink up at him. "Maybe you'll be my good luck charm."

The corner of his mouth curves upward, but he merely shakes his head. "I've never considered myself lucky. I worked hard for my military position. Then, I came here and lost everything, including my daughter. It took me…a long time to adjust."

There's a tang of self-loathing in his comment, and I quickly look away, so he doesn't see the guilt on my face. Continuing to circle tree after tree, I notice the light is getting dimmer.

Mathias also notices. "We'll have to come back tomorrow."

Disappointed, I nod, but as I turn to follow him, a shaft of sunlight catches something golden in my peripheral vision. Entranced, I pivot and slip between the trees. With a curse, Mathias falls into step at my side.

Ten minutes later, I stop. "It's an apple tree." I turn in a circle. "The only one in this grove of olive trees." Stepping closer to the trunk, I see the symbol etched into the bark. "This is it."

Mathias shouts for the others, and we hear footsteps running in our direction.

I hold my palm out to the tree. This time there is no light. Instead, an apple falls from the branch above me. Catching it, I carefully examine it. No serpent. The shiny red surface is the most perfect color red. Too perfect. I sniff it. Smells real.

I bring it to my lips and take a bite. Juicy and full of flavor, it's the most delicious apple I've ever tasted. Mathias glances back at me, and I smile.

Everything goes dark.

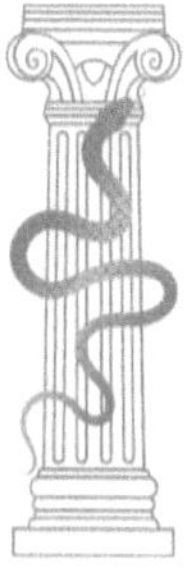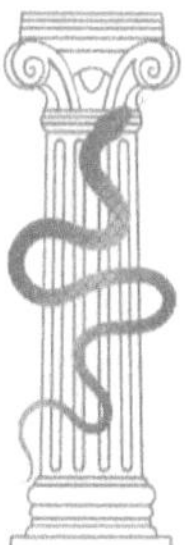

43

<u>PHAEDRA</u>

The clang of metal on metal pierces the fog around my brain, and I force my eyes open. The last thing I remember is taking a bite of the apple, then darkness took me under. I raise my hand and find a panel in my hand instead of an apple. Sitting up, I grab my phone and shine my light on it. A double-headed eagle wearing a laurel crown is depicted on the piece. The image my father used to identify our kingdom.

Dirt flies up beside me and startled, I look up and find Mathias engaged in battle with another vampire. Fangs on display, they're a blur of arms, legs, and knives. Mathias quickly dispatches him and whips around to confront another.

I jump to my feet. Shoving the panel into the back of my pants, I draw my gun. I've killed mages. A shifter too. Never a vampire. "Where do I aim?"

"Bullet to the brain," he shouts. "It won't kill them, but it'll slow them down."

"How do I kill them?" I shout back.

"Cut off their head and burn them with fire born from magic," he replies, narrowly dodging a sword. "Stay behind me. Only shoot those that get past me."

With my back against the tree, I hold the gun steady in my hand. The world around me blurs. Mathias and the vampires move too fast for me to follow. Occasionally, I get a glimpse of his fierce face, but it's gone in a blink.

Jamison appears with a golden lasso in his hand. He ropes several, then with a flick of his wrist, he decapitates them. Throwing a ball of fire on their bodies, he moves on to the next group.

"We need to get out of these trees," Jamison shouts in Mathias' direction.

More vampires pour into the area, and Mathias looks over at me. "Get her out of here. I'll cover you."

"You better be right behind us," Jamison utters in a grim voice. Mathias pauses and dips his chin in acknowledgement, then returns to the fight.

Jamison grabs my arm, but I shake him off. "We can't leave him."

"You're his biggest liability right now," Jamison says, pausing to burn a few vampires.

Several vampires circle us as we head in the direction of the temple, but Jamison wields the lasso as if it's an extension of his arm, holding them back. "Hawthorne and Gatlin are holding their own, but we need to regroup."

I look back at Mathias and see him moving in our direction. "He's coming." A vampire pops up behind us, and I fire but miss. "They're too fast."

"Save the bullets," Jamison orders as he cracks the whip, obliterating him.

We burst through the trees and into the field with Mathias about twenty feet behind us. I turn my head toward the temple and see Hawthorne twirling a staff made of fire. The second it touches a vampire, a shower of sparks bursts into the air. Gatlin stands to his right in gryphon form. Impenetrable to their teeth, the enemy is having a hard time landing a hit before his beak snaps them in two. Bodies are piled on the ground at his feet.

Jamison tosses a ball of fire at the pile and incinerates them. The three of them form a triangle with me in the center. Unable to throw any potions, I hold my gun tightly, preparing to fire at any vampires who get too close.

"Where's Mathias?" Hawthorne shouts.

"He was right behind us, but I don't see him now," I return, biting my lip. *Where the hell is he?*

A blur knocks the gun from my hand and without thinking, I use the curse that hit Hawthorne in Oxford. Dots of blood appear all over the vampire's body. He screams but can't get away from it. His red eyes lock with mine, and he flashes a bloody smile. Poof! His head is torn away by Gatlin's massive beak. Hawthorne touches him with the staff, and he's nothing but a pile of ash.

The vampires move in closer, and we back away from them. I stumble and go down; rough stone scrapes my palm. They've managed to back us halfway to the temple. Fear tries to rise, but I choke it down and get up. We can't portal out of here with them this close. We need a way to get them away from us. Just for a second.

A lone whistle pierces the air, and every single vampire stops moving.

Four vampires, three men, and one woman, stride out of the forest with Mathias hanging in their arms, and my heart plummets. He's in bad shape, blood pouring from several wounds, and he can't hold up his head.

"Give us the panel, and we'll let you live," a dark voice booms across the field.

Jamison curses, and a loud screech comes from Gatlin.

Steel-blue eyes turn to me, a question in their depths, and I nod.

"Mathias for the panel. We'll make the exchange at the temple," I shout in return.

Silence.

"Gatlin, shift back," Jamison orders. "Hawthorne, be ready to get us out of here. Not the house but close by." He turns to me. "Why the temple?"

"Because the gods favor me," I state confidently, my voice loud. Although they would never come to my rescue. Still, if the vampires are listening, this might make them pause.

"Agreed," the ominous voice rings out.

The four vampires pivot toward the temple. We move into its center and wait for them to bring Mathias to us. I glance at one of the men carrying him and realize that not all of the soldiers are vampires. That's the guy Mathias has been tracking. *Fucker.* I seethe. When they get there, they drop him at our feet. Furious, I throw the panel with all my might into the field, and all four rush to get it as if the first one to the panel will win a prize.

"Now," Jamison roars, creating a shield of fire around the temple.

Gatlin picks up Mathias. Hawthorne reaches down and grabs my hand. And the four of us enter the portal.

On the other side, Jamison takes a stance, but not one vampire comes through after us. With a jerk of his head, we hurry over a few streets and into the safety of the house. Gatlin lays Mathias down on the dining table.

"There are too many wounds," Jamison says, slipping his belt from its loops and pressing it to Mathias' mouth. "Bite on this. We'll cauterize them, then give you blood."

Hawthorne and Jamison begin to close the wounds. The scent of burning flesh fills the air, making me gag. Tears run down my cheeks while I watch Mathias strain against the pain. Gatlin returns with a blood bag in his hand, waiting for them to finish.

"Done," Hawthorne announces, wiping the sweat from his face. "Give him the blood."

Mathias rips the blood from Gatlin's hand and drinks it in three gulps. "More." His voice is guttural, not even close to the smooth cadence that usually flows from his mouth.

Gatlin takes a deep breath. "You drank the others. My contact had a limited supply. I can try to reach out to a few others."

Jamison flicks a hand, and a golden rope appears, wrapping itself tightly around Mathias. Alarmed, I reach out to pull it away, but he stops me. "If he goes into bloodlust, we won't be able to stop him." He begins to roll up his sleeve.

"You're giving him blood?"

Jamison doesn't answer, only holds his wrist up to his friend. "Take what I freely give."

Mathias turns his head, rejecting Jamison's offer. "Her."

Jamison vehemently shakes his head. "No. Mine."

"Can't," Mathias admits, sharing a silent conversation with Jamison.

"Fuck," Hawthorne curses, swiping his hand through his hair. "He can only drink directly from her."

"Why me?" I ask, staring down at Mathias.

They all turn to him, and he nods at Jamison.

Jamison takes my hands in his. "He didn't want to tell you because he didn't want you to feel forced into anything. You're his mate."

"Like *mate* mate?!" I screech, unable to believe what I'm hearing. "His forever and ever kind of mate?" Anger rises, and my eyes drop to Mathias. "Is this true?"

He gives one nod.

"I…" I close my eyes, unable to speak for a minute. *Shit. Shit. Shit.* What in the hell will the gods say about me having a mate?

Jamison takes my hand. "The mate bond means nothing unless you exchange blood. You're still free to choose. Or not."

That's reassuring. I take a deep breath and stare down at Mathias.

He coughs, and blood spills out of the corner of his mouth. "It's okay. I'll heal."

It's clear they don't want to pressure me, but with the enemy breathing down our necks, time is of the essence. I jerk my sleeve up. This is going to be bad. Really bad. But maybe it's better this way. Rip the Band-Aid off, so to speak. I'm getting too close to them anyway.

"You're going to see things. My past. Try to remember, I was fifteen when it happened. Much younger than the daughter you left behind. A stupid child who thought nothing of consequences. Not an excuse but truth," I rush to explain.

My gaze travels from Mathias to Jamison to Gatlin and finally to Hawthorne, needing to see the concern and care on their faces one last time. With a deep breath, I press my wrist against Mathias' mouth.

His tongue licks my skin, and a buzzing feeling invades my body. Fangs sink into the delicate skin, but I barely feel them. Warmth steals the words from my mouth. Heat builds along with a keen sense of pleasure. I gasp. My body becomes slick, and it takes everything I have to remain standing.

A wicked expression replaces the pain-filled one on Mathias' face. Lines smooth. Wounds heal. Dark eyes flicker with intent.

"Mathias," Jamison's quiet voice breaks the haze around us. "One minute."

Images flash in my mind. Childhood memories of days long gone. I bite my lip as time fast-forwards. Suddenly, the memory of that night pops into my head. The one I've been hiding from them all. The truth of my past. Sure, the gods don't want me to reveal myself, but this is my secret. A grey area I've avoided for far too long. The reason I was punished.

It takes everything not to rip my wrist away. I'm such a coward.

My parents went to visit a nearby kingdom. My sister and I have taken advantage of their absence to do all the things they usually forbid us to do. Swim naked in the nearby lake. Ride horses bareback. Invite our friends over for a party, so we can flirt with the nobles' sons. It's all been great fun.

My beautiful sister flashes irritated eyes at me. I've been driving her crazy all night. Blond with blue eyes, she's utterly perfect, and that's not just me thinking it. Pandora was created by the gods in their likeness. Stunningly beautiful, they gave her all their best gifts. Then they gave her to my parents to raise.

Most of the time I ignore her beauty, but tonight it gives me pause. "You truly are the most beautiful of creatures. All golden light. One day, you'll marry a king and rule as his queen."

Her irritation fades, and she laughs. "Promise?"

"Promise." I sweep by and grab her hands in mine. Swinging us around in a circle, I twirl until we're both dizzy. "I will, of course, marry the poor soul Father finds for me."

She shakes her head. "I won't let him. We'll find you a handsome prince of your own. We'll throw parties and visit each other all the time."

We flop down on the stuffed cloths piled on the floor.

"I'm bored," I say in a petulant voice.

"You're always bored," she reminds me with a laugh. "What do you want to do? Go swimming again?"

She knows I like to push the boundaries. I twiddle my fingers. "I want to go look at the vase." I turn pleading eyes on her, knowing she's going to say no.

"The gods gave it to Father and told him to hide it in the cavern. I

wish you had never seen it. There's nothing good about that vase," she refuses, her voice dismissive. "I'm hungry. Let's go eat."

During the meal, I can't stop thinking about the vase. After a bottle of wine, I stand and announce I'm going to bed. Pandora stares at me, then waves a hand good night. I sway from side to side. I'm drunk. I laugh as I leave the room.

One peek, I tell myself.

Making sure no servants are nearby, I open the painting at the far end of the hall, and step into the dark void. Thankfully, Father keeps torches near the entrance, and I light one to take with me. Down I go, into the cold darkness, my fingers trailing against the damp stone, helping me keep my balance.

When I get there, I set the torch into the wall and stand staring at the beautiful pink and gold vase with the shapes moving inside. From the first moment I saw it, I've been fascinated by it. Pandora, too, although she'll deny it. I'm convinced the gods stored something wondrous in there. It calls to me. Like it knows my name.

"I knew it!" Pandora cries from behind me.

I shrug. "I like looking at it." My hand lifts, and I trail a finger down its surface. "See, it's fine." I pick up the vase and hold it up to the light. "What could possibly be in there?"

Pandora marches over and takes the vase from me. "If the gods wanted it hidden from the world, there's a good reason." She puts it back on the shelf. "Let's go upstairs before someone catches us down here."

I grab the vase. "No, I want to look."

She yanks it from my grasp.

Mathias roars, and the memory shatters. I open my eyes and stare at him in horror.

Clothes torn, eyes red, he shoves me away from him. Blood dripping from my wrist, I reach for his hand, but he shreds the rope and slides off the table.

Gatlin steps in front of me, while Jamison and Hawthorne try to capture Mathias. He flings them away and points at me.

Vibrating with rage, he stares at me in horror. "Pandora is your sister?"

I proudly lift my chin. "Yes."

A deranged laugh escapes his lips. "Pandora. The one who opened all the portals into this world is your sister." His voice breaks. "She's the reason I lost my daughter. The reason we're all stuck here." Chest heaving, his ragged breaths fill the air. "And my mate is her sister." He thrusts a hand through his inky locks, tugging on them as if he's mad and needs the pain to convince him this is real.

The world stops, held on a knife's edge, ready to teeter one way or another. My inflection point. The moment when I can choose to do the right thing or continue to let this secret stay in the depths of the past.

But I'm not sure there is a choice. Not really. The secret is eating away at my soul. It's time to set the record straight. For three thousand years, I've pushed everyone away because I didn't want them to know what I did. My silence condemned my sister. Supernaturals blame Pandora because they can't return to their worlds and see their loved ones. No more.

Not one second of that night is lost to the haze of time. "It wasn't Pandora." The four of them turn toward me, shock on their faces. "I could tell you that in my drunken state, I felt bold. Invincible. But it would only be part of the truth. She grabbed the vase to keep it out of my hands. We fought for it. I won." I give a derisive laugh.

"In triumph or defiance, I'm not entirely sure, I opened the vase," I admit, a bitter taste flooding my mouth. All these years later, I still can't believe what I did. "A bright light burst from its depths. The earth trembled beneath our feet. She screamed for me to put the lid on, but I kept fumbling. I couldn't get it back on. She stepped forward to help and disappeared right in front of me. Into a portal."

A sob breaks free. "I'm the reason the portals opened,

allowing supernaturals to pour into this world. The reason you lost your daughter. Not Pandora. Me."

Tears roll silently down my cheeks. I look at Hawthorne. "It's my fault you were pulled into this world." My gaze moves to Mathias. "It's my fault you can't return to your daughter." I shake my head. "And it's my fault my sister is gone."

Gatlin settles a comforting hand on my shoulder.

Hawthorne looks shattered. "I…don't know what to say." He moves closer to Mathias, his green eyes full of shock and betrayal.

I look over at Jamison. "The gods were furious. In one move, I opened the doors to this world. Let all the supernaturals in. Fae, Elven, demons, vampires, and more. They immediately imprisoned me and spent the next ten years waging war with the supernaturals, trying to force them out. Although I didn't know that had happened until later."

Jamison's eyes are blank.

"For my punishment, they gave me a choice," I recall with a snort. "I could either spend an eternity serving Hades or live here and spend an eternity protecting humans. Of course, I chose the latter. I hoped that one day, if I had enough time, I'd find my sister." Not once has my hope diminished. It's in every curse I eliminate and every piece of the original vase I find.

Using the back of my hand, I swipe my tears away. "Honestly, they were happy with my decision. The gods had a treaty with the supernaturals, but they felt they needed to stack the deck. An unknown card dedicated to protecting humans."

"A spy," Jamison concludes.

I nod. "A couple of times, I slipped up. Exposed myself. They punished me. It wasn't pleasant. I got better at hiding. For three thousand years, if people got close, I pushed them away. Until you four came into my life."

Mathias scoffs.

I flinch at the sound but continue to keep my gaze on Jamison. "The walls I'd so carefully built had no defense against you. From the moment we met, I was intrigued. By all of you. I didn't want to hide the truth, but I was so afraid of how you'd look at me." *The same way you're looking at me right now.* My heart breaks.

I look at Mathias and Hawthorne. "I'm sorry. For thousands of years, I've regretted my actions. Believe me. Not a day has gone by that I haven't felt guilty. And not only because I lost the person who mattered the most to me. I've paid a million times over for this transgression, and I'll gladly keep paying until I can see my sister again."

"This is why you took the deal, isn't it?" Gatlin asks softly.

"It is," I say defensively. "Please say something."

Jamison stares at me, his eyes full of disbelief. "You knew this would destroy Mathias and Hawthorne. Yet, you continued to let them get closer and closer to you. We're a family. We put ourselves on the line for you. Hawthorne almost died. I don't know what to say."

His words are shards of glass, slashing at my heart.

I glance at Hawthorne, and he backs away. "It's a lot to process. I need time to think through all of this."

Mathias sneers when I look in his direction. "How could the fates pick you for my mate?" His voice is full of anguish and rage. "My daughter..." A startled expression crosses his face, and he immediately creates a portal. He steps through without a single goodbye and I raise a hand to call him back, but it's no use. I let it drop to my side.

Hawthorne, his green eyes full of hurt, walks into the portal behind Mathias.

Pain spears my heart. Wrapping my arms around my body, I try to keep the pain from spilling out of my chest onto the cold tile floor.

Gatlin hasn't said much. I brace myself and turn toward him.

There's a sad look in his eyes. "I don't care about Pandora or the portals. As far as I'm concerned, this world needed more magic." He tilts his head, and I sense a "but" coming. "You hurt my family. We gave you our…trust. We let you into our circle. I don't know how we're going to move beyond this."

"I get it," I murmur in a sad voice. "But honestly, I don't regret being here with all of you. Not for a second."

Jamison's blue eyes briefly close at my words, then open again. "I need time. Right now, Gatlin and I need to talk to Hawthorne and Mathias." His gaze touches on Gatlin before moving to me. He opens his mouth, then shuts it and disappears into the portal.

Gatlin grunts. "Damn it. We're not splitting up. Jamison…" Then, he too is gone.

"Too bad I won't be here," I say to the now empty room.

Tears fill my eyes, but I blink rapidly until they're gone. The last thing I want to do is destroy their family. They're right. I should never have let them get close. But I can fix it. If those panels are what I think they are… I need to finish this quest.

I rush to the safe and grab the two panels and stuff them into my backpack, then I call Charlie. "I need a portal home. Right now."

AWESOME PEOPLE

Special thanks to all these lovely people!

To my readers, friends, and fans! Thanks for all the wonderful words of encouragement, friendship, and love for my books! And for participating in my shenanigans and all the other weird things I post. You guys rock! I couldn't do it without you!!!

My awesome beta readers. They catch so many big and little things, help me with names, show me such amazing friendship, encouragement, and excitement, and they can't even share it with anyone! My books are a thousand times better because of their feedback. Thank you, Nia, Iliana, Melissa, Rachel, Sandi, and Debbie for everything!

My ARC team who gives me so much support and enthusiasm even though I drop things on them at the last minute. Ooh, look, cover reveal! Book's launching in a week! Seriously, I appreciate all of you!!

My biggest supporters—my husband and mom. I'm so lucky to have you both! Love you!

And always... a special thanks to all the wonderful authors in the writing community who support each other day in and out. Writing would be a lonely and weird world without you. It would be me and my characters sitting around chatting (drinking) while we plot the next book. Your friendship and support mean a lot to me!

ABOUT THE AUTHOR

Stella Brie lives with her husband outside of Nashville, TN. After mentioning her desire to write a book a million times to her husband, he challenged her to sit down one day and write a paragraph. Instead, she wrote her first book, *My Salvation*.

She decided to trade in her career in digital marketing, working on big brands, for this wildly creative one. Armed with a notebook crammed full of ideas, she's constantly writing about bold heroines, sexy men, and HEAs. Whether it's a paranormal book full of creatures and magic or a contemporary romance full of heat and drama, she's always thinking about how she can bring her books to life. Follow my author page on Amazon:

https://www.amazon.com/author/stellabrie

Latest News and Updates:

Facebook Group: Stella's Stalkers

Instagram: @stellabrie_author

TikTok: @stellabrie_author

YouTube! Playlists (all books): @authorstellabrie

Spotify Playlists (all books): @Stella Brie Author

Website: Stellabrie.com - Exclusive sneak peeks, cover reveals, giveaways, and more!

BOOKS BY STELLA BRIE

URBAN FANTASY WHY CHOOSE

<u>KILLIAN BLADE SERIES</u>

The Rowan (1)

The Rowan's Stone (2)

The Rowan's Destiny (3)

Wicked Savior - Lucifer's story (MF Romance) - (3.5)

The Light Falls (4) - Meri's story

The Dark Rises (5) - Meri's story

<u>GENESIS SERIES</u>

Bound by Water (1)

TBD 2026 (2)

<u>CURSES & GODS SERIES</u>

Curses & Keys (1)

Gods & Villains (2)

CONTEMPORARY WHY CHOOSE

<u>THE SAVAGES SERIES (Duet)</u>

Savage Traitor (1)

Savage Ruin (2)

Lethal Vengeance (Standalone + Spin-off)

My Salvation (Standalone)